Praise for *A Brush with Love*

"An adorable love story. *A Brush with Love* blends sweetness, breathless romance, and moments of striking vulnerability."
—Helen Hoang, *New York Times* bestselling author of *The Kiss Quotient*

"Prepare to smile, laugh, and cry your way through this witty, fast-paced rom-com debut starring a passionate heroine and a delicious cinnamon roll hero who knows how to love her just right."
—Evie Dunmore, *USA Today* bestselling author of *Bringing Down the Duke*

"*A Brush with Love* reads the way young love feels. Mazey Eddings stole my heart with this laugh-out-loud funny, almost unbearably cute debut (and she made me care about dentistry)."
—Rosie Danan, author of *The Intimacy Experiment*

"I'm obsessed with this book, and I fully intend to never stop yelling about it. With a shimmering voice and razor-sharp wit, Mazey Eddings has crafted a contemporary romance masterpiece that made me want to hug my dentist. There is an extraordinary amount of empathy in these pages: Harper and Dan are so lovably flawed, and Harper's mental health journey landed right in the center of my heart. The most intoxicating slow burn I've read in ages."
—Rachel Lynn Solomon, author of *The Ex Talk*

"Harper and Dan have my whole heart. I love everything about this book, from their adorable meet-cute to their unconventional first date, to the two of them working through their very real—and therefore not always pretty—issues. Dan is a soft, swoony hero, Harper is a relatable heroine who struggles with anxiety, and every page of the way I was rooting so hard for them to find their happily ever after. *A Brush with Love* is funny and cute while also exploring serious topics, powerfully underscoring the truth that relationships require work, and that happy endings are for everyone."   —Sarah Hogle, author of *Twice Shy*

"Tenderly written and oh-so-sexy, *A Brush with Love* brims with emotional depth, whip-smart banter, and sizzling chemistry. This romantic comedy completely stole my heart."
        —Chloe Liese, author of *Only When It's Us*

MAZEY EDDINGS

ST. MARTIN'S GRIFFIN
NEW YORK

First published in the United States by St. Martin's Griffin, an imprint of St. Martin's Publishing Group

A BRUSH WITH LOVE. Copyright © 2022 by Madison Eddings. All rights reserved. Printed in the United States of America. For information, address St. Martin's Publishing Group, 120 Broadway, New York, NY 10271.

www.stmartins.com

Designed by Devan Norman

Library of Congress Cataloging-in-Publication Data

Names: Eddings, Mazey, author.
Title: A brush with love / Mazey Eddings.
Description: First edition. | New York : St. Martin's Griffin, 2022.
Identifiers: LCCN 2021043964 | ISBN 9781250805980 (trade paperback) | ISBN 9781250805997 (ebook)
Subjects: LCSH: Dental students—Fiction. | Anxiety disorders—Patients—Fiction. | LCGFT: Medical fiction. | Romance fiction. | Humorous fiction. | Novels.
Classification: LCC PS3605.D35 B77 2022 | DDC 813/.6—dc23
LC record available at https://lccn.loc.gov/2021043964

Our books may be purchased in bulk for promotional, educational, or business use. Please contact your local bookseller or the Macmillan Corporate and Premium Sales Department at 1-800-221-7945, extension 5442, or by email at MacmillanSpecialMarkets@macmillan.com.

First Edition: 2022

10 9 8 7 6 5 4 3 2

For all my anxious angels and worry warriors.
Don't let the monsters get you down.

And for Hamda, the woman I admire beyond measure and
the best friend I could have ever imagined. We did it!

AUTHOR'S NOTE

Dear Reader,

While this story is a romance that will (hopefully) make you laugh and smile, please note that there are sensitive topics, including loss of a loved one and the complexities of living with a general anxiety disorder. There are also moments with potentially triggering content, including an on-page panic attack, discussions of grief, sexism, and ableist language.

These last two are vehemently condemned by the narrative, the characters, and myself.

I hope I have handled these topics with the utmost respect. Please take care of yourself while reading.

Love,
Mazey

CHAPTER 1

HARPER

"Shiiiiiiiit."

Harper's curse was lost to the wind as she whipped her foot out of an icy puddle and gave it an aggressive shake. Nothing screamed "perfect start to a Monday" like drenched scrub pants and freezing rain pelting down from every angle.

A dull, December gray hovered over Philadelphia, making coffee the city's last source of warmth and happiness. Chugging down the final drops of her own lukewarm cup, Harper wondered why she left bed before April.

With the empty thermos tucked back into her bag and soaking bangs poking her in the eyes, she ducked her face to the wind and trudged the final, miserable blocks to Callowhill University's School of Dental Medicine.

She swiped her ID badge against the security reader and rushed into the school's warm lobby, her face instantly starting to thaw. Mild chaos already swamped the check-in desks, while soaked patients waited in stiff pleather chairs for their names to be called, looking the standard degree of annoyed and apprehensive that was an occupational hazard for dentists.

Harper absorbed the early morning energy as she ripped off her gloves with her teeth and shoved them into her coat pockets. She went to work on her wet mess of bobbed black hair—scrunching and finger-combing in vain against the knots already starting to form.

A group of residents strode through the swinging doors of the Oral Surgery and Trauma Clinic next to where she stood. Her fingers stalled halfway through a rat's nest of tangles to observe them like a wild-life documentary. Right on cue, anxiety made its regularly scheduled morning appearance and beat a tiny hammer against her chest.

That would be her someday soon.

Hopefully.

While most dental students focused on drilling and filling their way to retirement, Harper dreamed of facial reconstructions and corrective jaw surgeries, each day orbiting around the singular purpose of becoming an oral surgeon.

But with residency match day a little more than a month away, Harper was stuck in a unique version of a worry-ridden hell. Having spent the past four years working her ass off for flawless grades, incredible hand skills, and publishable research, there was nothing more she could do than idly wait while random program directors and admissions departments determined her future. All her dedication and drive reduced to test scores, her GPA, and a trite personal statement.

The stress had her averaging a solid three hours of sleep a night, the rest of the time spent staring at her ceiling while what-ifs and worst cases swirled through her brain and down her throat, settling sickeningly in her stomach as worry cuddled close to her chest.

Before her mind spiraled into a total panic, a tap on the shoulder broke her trance. She turned and was assaulted by the blinding smile of her best friend, Thu.

"Caught ya lusting again," Thu said with a wink.

Harper rolled her eyes. "Hardly. Less than a month ago I had to stage an intervention to get you to stop cyberstalking UCLA's provost for admission news."

Having matched into UC's orthodontics residency in late November, two months earlier than surgery, Thu hadn't missed an opportunity to torment Harper on her unknown future.

"You were like a feral animal when I made a grab for your phone," Harper added. She still had rug burns from Thu tackling her to get it back.

"What's some mild manhandling between friends," Thu said with a wink. She pulled back her hood, raven hair tumbling down in immaculate fishtail braids and makeup so perfectly applied that somewhere a YouTube beauty vlogger shed a single tear at its glory.

Harper scowled.

"Wow. Isn't it a little early on a Monday to be the physical embodiment of perfection? I mean, you actually have the nerve to show up to school looking like it's not pouring rain and seasonal depression isn't in full swing?"

"Aww, I love it when you sweet-talk me." Thu linked her arm through Harper's, leading her toward the morning's histopathology lecture.

"How'd the date go last night?" Harper asked as they weaved through the school. Thu had been excited at the prospect of a free meal with a quarter-way decent-looking guy, holding out hope that he had a great, compensatory personality. A free meal was a free meal, and Thu would never pass up a chance at love or food.

"Oh, you mean with the only guy on Tinder who hasn't sent me an unsolicited dick pic?"

Harper nodded, trying to look sympathetic through her grin. While random dude nudes plagued the majority of women on Tinder, Thu attracted unwanted cock shots at an alarming rate.

"To start"—Thu shot Harper a sidelong glance that told her to buckle up for a wild ride—"he kept calling me 'thuh.' I get it, my name isn't phonetic—whatever—I'm used to it. But, when I tried to make it easy on him and told him to pronounce it 'two' like the number, I shit you not, he stared at me for a solid minute before laughing and saying he liked funny girls."

Harper snorted.

"Then, he took me to a shitty Chinese restaurant because he thought I'd 'enjoy ordering in my native tongue,' and 'it would make me feel more at home,'" Thu said, using dramatic air quotes for emphasis.

"Stop it."

"I swear. I first tried to explain that Vietnam is not China, but that seemed too advanced a geographical concept. Then I told him it didn't even matter because I'm second-gen from Jersey, but this also must be a hard idea to grasp."

"Who wouldn't be confused?"

Thu shot Harper a look before continuing. "I suffered through mind-numbing conversation about his intramural Frisbee team, and the time he grew out his back hair for a year because he lost a bet. I didn't even throw up. Aren't you proud of me?"

"Was it the Frisbee or the back hair that made you want to vomit?"

"Frisbee. And when he drove me home, he asked me if, *as a dental student*, I had an automatic oral fixation."

Harper slapped a hand over her mouth as she tried to stifle a laugh. "Shut the fuck up. What did you say?"

"I said, 'Sadly, no. But if I did, you *and* Freud could suck my dick,' then went inside and sewed my vagina shut."

Harper cackled so hard, tears pricked at her eyes. "I'm sorry, it's not funny. I shouldn't laugh." She choked on the words and tried fanning her face to gain some composure as they descended the few flights of stairs to the basement lecture halls.

"No, you shouldn't. Because it gets worse."

"Thu, it's impossible for that to get any worse."

Thu shook her head in defeat. "To put a cherry on top of the world's most microaggressive first date, he sent me a full-frontal an hour later and asked me if Chinese girls liked sausage."

"What! Let me see."

Thu scrolled through her phone and handed it to Harper.

"Huh. Awful lighting," Harper said, squinting at the world's most unimpressive dick pic with a mixture of horror and delight. "What did you say back?"

Thu let out a long sigh as she took back her phone. "I told him the truth, that it looked like a crunchy Cheeto with the powder licked off. Harper, have you ever had the overwhelming urge to rip out your reproductive tract and use the fallopian tubes to choke the stupidity out of men? Because that's where I'm at."

Thu's disdain made Harper laugh even harder.

"I'm glad you think my misery is so funny," Thu snapped, working to suppress a smile.

Harper was about to ask if this gem could be The One, when her foot slid through a puddle on the linoleum floor, and the world fell from beneath her.

Adrenaline prickled through every corner of Harper's body as she fell down the final flight of stairs. She clawed for the railing, grasping at nothing but air. Her breath slammed into a knot in her throat as her butt and back rebounded against the last few steps.

The last thing she saw before squeezing her eyes shut and smacking onto the tile floor was a long pair of legs crumpling as she crashed into them.

Her head rocked back, hitting the ground with a muffled thud, as something landed on her chest, knocking any remaining air from her lungs.

She lay still for a moment, not trusting the world to stop spinning, as she did a quick mental scan for injuries. She realized she was mostly fine, besides a throbbing head and bruised ass. Her biggest concern was trying to breathe as a heaviness weighed down her sternum and her heart pounded against it.

Never one to miss an opportunity for minor hysterics, Thu shrieked through Harper's fog as she rushed down the stairs, adding to Harper's already pounding headache. "Ohmygod, ohmygod, Harper!!"

But, as Thu's voice hovered directly above Harper, it morphed from a dramatic shriek to a mischievous drawl. "Wow. Oh my God, *Harper.*"

Harper squinted her eyes open to look up at her friend, who was staring with a shocked grin at Harper's chest.

Harper looked cross-eyed down her body in confusion. Short waves of chocolate brown hair fanned across her chest. Her eyes traced over a golden profile, down the graceful slope of a strong nose, to a cheek pressed firmly against her breastbone. A tan powder dusted the face and clung to long, dark eyelashes.

Head still spinning, she reached out, dusting the powder off the lovely nose. With a startling flash, the eyes shot open, and the head moved slightly to look up at her. The intense and uncomfortable feeling of falling swamped her all over again as forest-green eyes rimmed with honey locked onto hers.

"Are you okay?"

It took Harper a minute to realize where the voice was coming from. It wasn't the words or the movement of the finely formed mouth that made her aware of it—not even the rumbling of the question reverberating against her chest—but the tip of a tongue darting out, wetting a delicious pair of lips and removing the coating of powder, that made Harper return to her senses . . . and fully acknowledge that a random man's face was pressed extremely close to her boobs.

With that, Harper came back to earth, and her torso shot up from the floor. The man let out a soft groan as his head jolted from her chest and landed awkwardly in her lap. She scrambled to sit up on her knees as he disentangled himself from her. At the same time, Thu crouched down, pretending to drape a comforting arm across Harper's shoulders as she whispered, "Holy shit, he's hot."

Harper whipped her head to look at her friend, eliciting another wave of throbbing pain through her skull. Massaging her temple with one hand, she pushed Thu away with the other.

"Are you okay?" the man repeated, looking at her with genuine concern. Seeing him head-on made Harper feel like her heart was throwing confetti around her chest.

Okay. Wow. He's absolutely gorgeous. Cool.

She squeezed her eyes shut and took a steadying breath. No one actually looked that good; she must be hallucinating.

But, opening her eyes, it was confirmed with a red alert of embarrassment that no, she wasn't seeing things, and yes, the man she'd body-slammed was, in fact, as good-looking as he'd first appeared.

His hair had that perfectly mussed look that begged her fingers to run themselves through it. His jaw and cheekbones could cut glass, and the tiniest hint of stubble dusted his skin. Where she expected to see an equally chiseled nose was one that was a touch big, the tip forming an adorable, rounded bulb. It was a nose that could easily look goofy on a softer face, but it worked to ease the sharpness of his other features just enough to create an endearing and approachable quality.

Harper continued to stare at him, now unable to look away. She must have really hurt her head.

"I . . . I fell down the stairs," she explained, surveying the scene around her. Thu let out a snort that she disguised as a distressed sob.

The stranger cocked a lopsided grin at Harper, a small dimple peeking out of one cheek. The urge to touch him struck her again.

"I saw. It was hard to miss if I'm being honest," he said with the slightest hint of teasing. "But seriously, are you all right?"

Harper opened her mouth but wasn't sure of the right words to explain that she'd never felt this disoriented in her entire life, dazed and tongue-tied by his face, of all things.

He studied her carefully, and her cheeks flushed to the point of discomfort. Harper pushed herself to standing and dusted off the weird powder from her scrubs. Glancing around for its source, her stomach dropped as she realized what she'd done. Not two feet away, a shattered stone model of a patient's dentition littered the ground.

One of the trickiest parts of dentistry was taking a good impression of a patient's upper and lower teeth. A dentist had to work quickly to mix alginate powder to the perfect rubbery consistency, then jam it into the patient's open mouth and mold it around their teeth, often causing them to gag and dry heave in the process—throw up was not a rarity in the whole ordeal.

It was pure torture for everyone involved, and a task that often took many tries for students to master before they had a workable mold, much to the dismay of the patient. The mold would then be taken to the wet lab for setting into stone, which was a bitch of a process itself. All in all, models were an absolute pain in the ass to make and something you guarded with your life if done well.

Harper's eyes widened in horror, and her gaze snapped to the man she'd crashed into. He was similarly dusting himself off, as he looked with absolute misery at the massacre of his project. She realized with an even stronger pang of guilt that, based on the graduation year embroidered above the breast pocket of his scrubs, he was a first-year student. She'd destroyed something that took even seasoned seniors countless tries to get right, let alone someone newly learning the technique.

"I'm so sorry!" she blurted out, scurrying over to the fragments to see if anything was salvageable. Thu moved with her, picking up the pieces farther down the hall.

"I slipped and—and everything is soaking wet, and—and—rain! So much rain! Oh my God, I can't believe I broke this. I feel—I mean—I'm so sorry. I—" She turned to look at him, lost for words on how to remedy this.

"It's okay. Don't . . . worry about it," he said, dragging a hand down his face and squeezing his chin as he continued to stare at the mess with a pained expression. After a moment, he composed his features and offered her a sad half smile.

"I really am so sorry," she repeated, her fingers practically itching to reach out and touch him. He was so damn pretty, her breathing hitched a bit.

"Accidents happen. Please, don't worry about it." He bent to scoop up the pieces, his scrub top pulled taut across his broad shoulders as he gingerly collected the fragments. Guilt drowned Harper's stomach. Guilt and something that felt a tiny bit like lust.

"At least let me help you fix it," she blurted out, surprised at how urgently she wanted him to say yes. He looked over his shoulder at her and lifted an eyebrow.

"You don't have to do that."

"I want to. Please. It's the least I can do."

"Harper's a lab goddess. She'll help you make a new one in no time," Thu quipped, moving back to Harper's side and handing over the pieces she'd collected.

He stood, and Harper was forced to take a step back and tilt her head to meet his gaze. At five foot two (and a half) she stood about eye level with his nipples. It wasn't an awful view. His lopsided grin and dimple were back as he gave her an appraising glance.

"Okay, lab goddess, you've got a deal. But it's due tomorrow, so I understand if you're too busy."

"That's fine," she mumbled, wanting to melt into the floor at her new nickname.

"I'm Dan, by the way," he said, reaching out a hand to shake hers. She returned the gesture, and Dan's touch plucked at the already frayed threads of her composure, causing her pulse to flutter and her skin to prickle as his long fingers wrapped around hers.

This was all very . . . weird. While she had a handful of failed dates and unimpressive hookups under her belt, Harper usually observed guys with detached objectivity. She wasn't blind and could appreciate that, yeah, some guys were cute, some were funny, some were even undeniably hot. But a man had never triggered anything inside her that made them worth her time or energy.

But something in the way Dan looked at her had her heart acting like quite the little drama queen.

It was probably that shameless fucking dimple.

Harper's eyes flicked to the embroidered name over his breast pocket that came standard on all school-issued scrubs. *Daniel Craige*.

"Do you have a license to drill?" she blurted out.

Dan's eyebrows lifted, and he blinked at her, making Harper cringe so hard, she almost snapped a neck muscle.

"Sorry, license for what?"

Harper cleared her throat. "To drill. Like, um, with a handpiece. Or like . . . license to kill . . . you know, Daniel Craig . . . James Bond . . ." She flapped her hand toward his chest, letting out a nervous giggle that ended with a mortifying snort.

At this point, Harper was confident she was concussed. Or hallucinating. Anything for this not to be real life.

Dan looked down to his chest, then back to Harper. A funny smile quirked his lips, and he opened and closed his mouth a few times before finally finding words.

"I don't," he said slowly, fully grinning now. "But whatever helps you remember me." Then the bastard actually *winked* at her.

If any more blood rushed to Harper's face, she was fairly certain she'd suffer from a subdural hematoma. And hopefully die.

"So, tonight?" he asked after a moment.

"What?"

"The model? Want to work on it tonight? I can meet you in the lab at five, after classes."

"Oh, um, yeah. Right. Perfect." She noticed she was still holding his hand and dropped it like he'd burned her. He let out a soft laugh.

"It was nice to meet you, Harper." He stared at her for another beat before moving down the hall, tossing the stone pieces into the trash as he went.

Harper watched him retreat, then flushed again when he glanced back over his shoulder and caught her staring. At his butt.

"I remember the first time I ever talked to a boy," Thu said at Harper's shoulder. Harper whipped her gaze to her.

"Excuse me?"

"No, I mean it's cool that I got to see what was clearly your first interaction with a man. Ever. Very smooth, Harps. I had no idea you were such a James Bond junkie." Thu didn't even try to hide her smug smile as she walked past Harper and to the auditorium.

CHAPTER 2

HARPER

"Harper met a guy today," Thu told their friends Lizzie and Indira during lunch. Per their usual routine, the four of them convened at Big Joe's Coffee where Lizzie worked, the shop located directly between the dental school and Callowhill's medical school, which Indira attended.

"What guy?" Lizzie and Indira said in unison.

"Thu, shut up," Harper groaned. Thu hadn't dropped the topic all morning.

"A gorgeous man literally fell into her lap," Thu said, taking a big bite of the warm cranberry scone Lizzie plopped in front of her.

While technically a barista, Lizzie had a muffin-shaped heart that beat only for baked goods, and she spent more time preparing treats for the pastry case than actually helping customers. Much to the dismay of Big Joe.

"What guy?" Lizzie hissed, leaning so far over the coffee counter, she was close to rolling over it.

"You all would dismally fail the Bechdel test right now. How very unfeminist of you. I hope you're ashamed," Harper mumbled, digging into her own scone.

Thu rolled her eyes. "Oh yes, Harper, how *dare* I get excited at your first interaction with a hot guy in the four years I've known you. I should be very ashamed, indeed."

"I interact with guys!"

"You haven't been with a guy since, what, undergrad?" Indira asked, sipping her coffee. "Mercury went into retrograde yesterday, so I knew shit was about to get wild, but I definitely didn't see something like this happening."

"If someone doesn't give me details about this guy in two seconds, I swear I'll start screaming at the top of my lungs," Lizzie said, a glutton for drama.

"Lizzie, you *work* here."

"What's your point?" Lizzie said, fixing her with a look of genuine confusion.

Harper buried her head in her hands as Thu relayed the embarrassing scene in such graphic detail that Harper wondered where she could get some bamboo shoots to shove up her fingernails instead of this torture.

"He's definitely into her," Thu concluded with a satisfied nod.

"Such a good call with the fall, Harps. Very rom-com meet-cute. Works every time," Lizzie said.

Harper stared at her. "I didn't throw myself down the stairs on purpose, you troll. I slipped on a puddle."

Lizzie rolled her eyes and tossed her long, red hair over her shoulder. "All I'm saying is that if you *did* fall on purpose to catch his eye, I wouldn't judge. Not like I haven't done worse."

"Like the time you joined that marathon training club because you saw that cute guy signing up?" Indira offered. "Or when you decorated that croissant to look like a vulva, hoping the hot customer would get the oh-so-subtle hint?"

"Or that time she completed the five-pound burger challenge at Puddy's because she wanted the guy in the corner to be impressed? That one was amazing," Thu added.

Lizzie nodded sagely. "You can't say I'm not dedicated to my art."

"But back to Harper's new boyfriend. What's he like?" Indira never let things go.

Harper groaned. "I don't have a boyfriend. I broke his stone model, and I'm helping him make a new one. Purely academic. And I'm fine, by the way, if anyone was wondering. Only bashed my head on the floor. No big deal, try to rein in the worry."

Her friends groaned in unison. "Oh, okay. She's reverting to the academic excuse again. How original," Indira said to Thu, ignoring Harper's scowl.

"Saw this coming. 'My future is too important. No distractions. Blah blah blah.'"

"My future *is* too important," Harper said defensively, swiping crumbs off the counter.

"You'll avoid dating forever with that one," Thu said. "Maybe—and this is absolutely batshit ludicrous, so bear with me—but maybe you try dating to *include* someone in your future. Wild, I know."

Harper rolled her eyes.

Thu's gaze narrowed, and her teasing took on a more serious note. "You kind of have the future thing figured out, though. You're graduating in a few months, and we all know you'll get into residency and move to a new city, so why not have a little fun before you go? Because you know after that is private practice and shucking wisdom teeth for the next thirty years, resulting in a cushy retirement. Seems like the only future you haven't planned is one where you have someone to share that with. Kind of a sad way to go through life if you ask me."

Harper opened her mouth to defend herself, but Thu held up a hand to silence her.

"And no matter how much you're going to argue and say surgery isn't a *job*, it's a *passion*, you're smart enough to recognize the burnout that's attached. With no one around to share that with, it seems a surefire way to end up not only alone but extremely lonely . . . But what do I know?" Thu said with a shrug, giving Harper a meaningful look before digging back into her pastry.

Harper stood in stunned silence, unable to meet any of her friends' eyes. As it always did, her nervous body picked up the tension shift immediately, overreacting to the energy a thousand-fold. Her heart started thrumming, blood painfully pulsing to the very tips of her fingers and toes as anxiety swirled around her chest.

"I'll see you guys later," Harper said, hoisting her backpack onto her shoulder and turning to leave.

"Oh, come on, Harps, she was just teasing," Indira said, reaching out and squeezing Harper's arm.

"I know," Harper said, plastering on a fake smile as embarrassment pricked at her eyes. "I really have to go study, though." She bolted for the door and headed back to the dental school, working to compress that growing anxiety into a tiny box in the pit of her stomach.

Her friends didn't get it. Harper doubted anyone ever would.

It wasn't like she wanted to be like this. She *was* lonely—but it was a loneliness so bone-deep, it wasn't something a simple boyfriend could take away. Her constant flood of panic wasn't an emotional hurdle she needed to jump, it was her second skin, a pulsing physical barrier that kept her separated from everyone.

How was she supposed to date when even the simplest things threatened to disrupt her emotional equilibrium? How was she supposed to regularly and willfully plunge herself into the heart palpitations and a churning stomach that came with opening herself up to someone? And how was she supposed to expect another person to see her chaotic ugliness and still want to be with her?

There was no point in setting herself up for failure.

CHAPTER 3

DAN

Dan couldn't suppress his grin when class let out. He'd spent most of the day zoning out of lectures, Harper's warm brown eyes and nervous smile popping into his mind and sending a jolt of excitement to his fingers.

"Dude, you okay?"

Dan snapped back to reality to find his friend Alex eyeing him.

"Yeah, why?"

"I've never seen you smile at school before."

Dan opened his mouth to argue, but realized Alex had a point. Dental school had been a choice not entirely Dan's own, and as his first year clipped along at a brutal pace, the stress of the program and competitive attitude of his classmates did little to assure him he'd chosen wisely.

"I think I met a girl," he muttered. He didn't really want to talk to Alex about it, but couldn't resist the urge to bring up Harper. Alex's eyebrows disappeared behind his floppy black hair as he fixed Dan with a sly smile.

"What girl?"

"Her name is Harper. She's a fourth-year, I think."

Alex's smile turned to wide-eyed shock. "Harper Horowitz?"

Dan shrugged, studying Alex's reaction. "I didn't get her last name. Why? Do you know her?"

"Um, yeah, I know her. She's like some sort of genius gunner or something."

"Gunner?"

Alex rolled his eyes. "You know—the over-the-top intense people who will do anything to get into residency. Studying all night, straight As, perfect board scores. She's OMFS, so that's super gunner status. She basically has her choice of specialty program."

"OMFS?" Sometimes it felt like he and Alex spoke different languages that were vaguely similar, but the most essential points were lost in translation.

"Seriously? Are you even in dental school? Oral and maxillofacial surgery. It's the most competitive specialty to get into. Those kids are ridiculously cutthroat—nothing but studying and practicing. I'm pretty sure Harper's top of her class too, so I imagine she's pretty intense."

Dan focused on stuffing his laptop into his backpack, avoiding Alex's questioning looks. Alex's description didn't match up to the endearing girl Dan had thought about all day. She'd seemed a bit on edge, sure, but far from cutthroat—and she was clearly kind, or she wouldn't have offered to help him.

While Harper didn't seem particularly intimidating, he couldn't deny that she held a certain intensity about her.

She was also cute as hell.

"Dude, are you blushing?"

Dan ducked his head and zipped up his bag. "Of course not. It's warm in here." He tugged at his collar for effect.

"So, are you taking her out?"

"No. Not yet, at least. She broke my stone model and is helping me redo it tonight," Dan said, standing and slinging his backpack over his shoulder.

Alex's eyes went wide with horror as he followed Dan into the hall.

"She broke your model? From the impression *I* did for you? Didn't you already have to redo it, like, four times before that? I thought you were going in early this morning to finish it."

Dan shrugged. Yes, he'd gone through a truckload of impression powder before giving up and begging Alex to take the impression for him. And, yes, he'd begrudgingly gone in at six a.m. to finish it that morning. But all of that seemed rather insignificant now.

Alex continued to complain about his wasted time and effort as Dan's phone buzzed in his pocket. He frowned down at the screen before hitting the Decline button.

A text pinged through a few seconds later:

> Please call me, habibi. I'm having issues with the practice's patient retention and need your help. Like I told you, this is really going to affect our finances, and I can't do all of this on my own.

Dan deleted the message.

"What kind of asshole declines a call from his mom?" Alex asked, staring at Dan's phone.

Guilt slammed into him, but he corralled it into a dark corner of his chest and locked the door. Since his mom had gained full control of the family practice, there was always a new emergency. A new threat to her livelihood. Another burden Dan had to carry to ensure she was okay. Dan had never thought of his mom as a helpless woman, but she seemed to be crumbling without someone to tell her exactly what to do and when to do it.

"I'm . . . busy," Dan said, waving his hand down the hall.

"You're always 'busy' when she calls, huh?"

Dan shot him a look as he pocketed his phone. "It's really none of your business, is it?"

Alex held up his hands in surrender. "Whatever. I'm just saying, she's offering you a job on a silver platter as soon as you graduate. It wouldn't kill you to answer her calls sometimes."

"It might," Dan mumbled, ending the conversation. Alex didn't know the half of it. He didn't understand the overwhelming swell of guilt and bitterness that came as side dishes to that silver platter.

They rounded the corner to the lab, and Dan's eyes landed on Harper.

She sat on the large wooden bench in front of the lab, her feet tucked beneath her and a hefty textbook perched in her lap. She twisted one of her soft curls around her finger while she squinted at the page in concentration as her friend from earlier chatted away next to her, oblivious to Harper's focus.

As if feeling his gaze, Harper's head lifted, and her eyes traveled to Dan. A slow, honeyed smile lifted the corners of her mouth, and Dan felt his own mimic the look. She clapped her textbook shut and raised her hand in a small wave. The gesture was sweet and almost vulnerable in its sincerity, and it made Dan's heart ping-pong against his chest.

"Whoa, who's her friend?"

Dan had forgotten Alex's existence, and it took him a minute to follow his friend's gaze to the girl next to Harper.

"I don't actually know. She was there this morning."

"You have to introduce me," Alex said, running a hand through his hair.

"Did you just . . . primp?"

"No! I didn't *primp*. I . . . had an itch," Alex shot back.

Dan bit back a grin and nodded at his friend's reddening face.

Harper stood as Dan walked toward her, shoving her textbook into her backpack.

"Hi," she said, shifting her weight from foot to foot.

"Hi."

Dan's eyes were locked on hers for a long, beautiful moment before a loud throat-clearing drew his attention away.

"Sorry to interrupt this, uh, eye contact, but I'm Thu." Harper's friend stuck her hand out toward Dan, but Alex grabbed at it with such speed that everyone flinched.

"Sorry. Hi, I'm Alex—Alex Huang. Dan's roommate . . . Alex Huang."

"Smooth, *Alex*," Dan mumbled, and Alex shot him a dirty look.

"Aaron, was it?" Thu asked with a furrowed brow, continuing to shake his hand. Alex's face fell in confusion, but Thu broke into a grin before continuing, "I'm just fucking with you, Alex Huang. It's nice to meet you."

"And I'm Dan," he said, offering Thu a small wave before turning his attention back to Harper with an uncontrollable smile. "Ready to do this?" He gestured toward the lab, and she nodded.

They shot quick goodbyes to their friends then moved through the doors.

"I'm sorry again about this morning. I promise we can power through this and I won't break anything else." She gave him a sheepish grin.

"Don't apologize. Accidents happen. I'm excited to work on it." He followed her down the aisles to her workstation. She glanced over her shoulder at him.

"You're excited to redo something you already finished?"

"Well, no. I'm never really thrilled to do anything in here, but word on the street is you're quite the oral superstar."

Harper stopped in her tracks, and Dan almost plowed into her. Her eyebrows shot up behind her bangs, making her eyes comically wide while her mouth opened slightly in a small O of surprise. Dan cringed, waving both hands in front of himself.

"No! No. *No.* I mean professional oral superstar—holy shit—No. Stop. Oral medicine—superstar. Dental prodigy. I'm trying to say I'm excited to learn you—From!—From you. That came out weird. This is weird. I'm . . . weird." Dan clamped his mouth shut so hard, his teeth rattled, and he looked around the room for a window to throw himself out of. Anything to end the misery.

Harper's lips pursed as she tried not to laugh, her cheeks rosy with embarrassment.

"You *are* weird," she said at last, her grin winning out.

Dan ran a hand through his hair and let out a shaky sigh. This wasn't off to the best start. Harper recovered her composure and sat down at her station, indicating for Dan to pull up a chair. He rolled one up next to her and watched her grab the different instruments and materials without a trace of hesitation in how the pieces would work together.

Dan was captivated by her hands. They moved with such grace and determination, like a concert pianist's fingers dancing along a length of keys. Dan couldn't help but compare them to the bruteness of his father's from the few occasions Dan had actually paid attention to his work. His dad's hands had always moved with impatience, as if every step was an inconvenience to his end goal as he barked out orders to Dan or one of the dental assistants. But Harper's were soft. Intentional. Fascinating.

"So, we'll do a few alginate impressions on the mannequin first. You've used alginate before, right?" she asked, her voice taking on a businesslike tone.

"The powder that you mix into a sort of putty for impressions? Yeah, I think that's what they used last time during the demonstration."

Harper nodded then stood to lower the fold-out mannequin. It sat between them, its eerie, vacant eyes staring blindly at the ceiling and a gaping mouth filled with fake practice teeth poised in a silent scream. Dan grimaced.

"All right, let's see what you've got."

Dan's eyes shot to Harper. She gestured at the counter now covered in various dental tools and mixing instruments. Insecurity rippled down the back of his neck to the tips of his fingers at her expectant look.

Lab work was not one of his strengths—he had yet to actually discover *any* strengths in dental school—but he didn't want to make a fool of himself in front of her.

"Do you have any advice?" he asked, reaching for the alginate packet and squinting at the directions.

Dan's attention shifted as Harper nibbled on the corner of her full bottom lip while she thought.

"It's cliché, but the best thing you can do is practice and practice and practice, until it's the easiest thing in the world. And then practice it a couple more times." She gave him an encouraging smile. "It's also important you dive right in. Don't overthink it, just do it." She leaned her hip against the counter and waved her hand over the supplies. Dan took a deep breath and nodded.

He measured out the alginate into the mixing bowl and added the water. He stirred it vigorously like he'd watched Alex do, trying to look like any of it felt natural. He slowly and carefully scooped the goo into the impression tray, making sure to fill it edge to edge.

Positioning himself behind the mannequin, he paused to carefully align the tray then pushed the putty against the upper teeth.

And nothing happened.

Pathetic. His father's voice snapped like a whip across his psyche.

Dan closed his eyes and blew out a breath. He'd done it wrong.

Again. What should have been an oozy mixture was a solid block in the tray, not budging against the plastic teeth. He'd moved too slowly, the alginate setting before he even had a chance to use it.

It was a rerun of every other lab experience. He would sit and watch his classmates pick up techniques and perfect procedures while he fumbled his way through the lab manual, botching every assignment in an endless parade of frustration and failure with just enough embarrassment for it to physically hurt. But suffocating guilt and familial duty always stopped him from quitting.

"Try again."

Dan opened his eyes. Harper was looking at him, her deep brown eyes warm and crinkled at the corners with a gentle smile. She touched his wrist, making the hair on his arm stand up straight. He felt the warmth of her fingers through her gloves, and the sensation coursed up his arm in a golden buzz.

He nodded, flicking the rubbery material out of the tray, and started again.

CHAPTER 4

HARPER

Harper held her breath as she watched Dan mix the alginate for the sixth—no, seventh—time.

Brow furrowed in concentration, he scooped it out and filled the impression tray, moving with a new, fragile confidence that made a balloon of pride float into her chest. He stood behind the dummy and slid the tray into place. His eyes met hers, and she felt almost as desperate as he looked for this try to work.

The defeat bruising his face after that first attempt had fissured through her heart so deeply, she actively resisted the urge to push his hands away and do it for him while simultaneously cradling his troubled, gorgeous face against her chest and whispering that it would all be okay.

She'd settled on gentle encouragement, thinking face cradling was slightly in the realm of inappropriate lab behavior. She ducked her head to look into the mannequin's mouth, taking careful note of the angle of his hands holding it in place. She nodded at him and smiled.

"I have a good feeling about this one."

His eyes lifted to hers for an anxious moment before returning to bore into the dummy as though glaring at it hard enough would force it to cooperate. She took a moment to observe the tight clench of Dan's chiseled jaw, the tension in his broad shoulders as he held his fingers against the tray in the dummy's mouth, small knots of muscle rising gently along his forearms in focus and frustration.

"Here, just . . ." She pressed against Dan's side, sliding one arm along his and moving the other beneath his chest to meet his long fingers on the other side. She gently moved to relax the angle and pressure of his fingers, twining theirs together in a way that felt far too familiar while they waited for the alginate to settle.

The proximity slapped her senses, every nerve ending bubbling up in a golden pop of excitement where her body pressed against his side. Harper could feel Dan's eyes on her, but she kept her gaze fixed on the dummy. Dan shifted on his feet, and her heart pounded against the side of his broad chest. Her palms were clammy in the latex gloves, and she felt her fingers buzzing and humming where they twisted with Dan's.

She heard him swallow and couldn't help but glance up. His eyes were hot and bright as they roamed her face.

It was overwhelming and intense—far too intimate while not being intimate enough. It didn't feel possible to look away.

"This is probably set," she whispered.

"Okay." He didn't move.

They stared at each other for another moment before Harper sucked in a deep breath and dropped her arms, stepping away. She felt the immediate loss of the closeness and wanted it back. Dan looked at her for a second longer before straightening up and rolling his shoulders.

Harper tugged at her hair, the delicate pull working to center her ceaselessly frazzled nerves. She watched as Dan pried the tray out of the dummy's mouth. He stared at it for a moment, tilting it at various angles before thrusting it at Harper.

The look he gave her was so vulnerable, it made her heart

stutter. She took the finished product and held it under the station's fluorescent light. Her eyes traveled over the canyons punctuating the mold, small peaks and deep valleys dancing across in the familiar pattern of anatomy. No air bubbles. No voids. Her heart swelled then exploded in tooth-shaped confetti.

"It's perfect." She beamed at him.

"Really?"

Relief flooded Dan's features, and a lopsided smile broke across his face. He closed the distance between them and enveloped Harper in a hug. She gave a squeak of surprise as his arms wrapped around her. He pulled back to grin even broader down at her. She stared at her hand and wondered how it had made its way to his cheek, framing that ridiculous dimple. Harper couldn't seem to move it. Dan didn't seem to mind.

"I'm really proud of you." She was surprised by how genuinely she meant it.

"Couldn't have done it without your help." Their gazes held for a second too long. At the same moment, they felt the familiarity of their closeness collide with the sharp reality of being near-strangers to each other.

Harper cleared her throat, and Dan dropped his hands from around her body. She attempted a casual eye-roll and gave his cheek a gentle, old-lady pat before moving back to her seat, Dan following.

"I would say you've officially joined the ranks of the lab goddesses."

He laughed. "My mom will be so proud. What's next?"

"We go into the wet lab to pour in the liquid stone, and then let it set. After that, we'll be good to go."

"Cool. That sounds like something I can only mess up two or three times instead of twenty." He swept a hand over the mess they'd created. Harper had the not-so-subtle sense that Dan gained no enjoyment from the process.

"Hush. You're learning," Harper scolded before giving him a smile. She turned to organize the chaos at her station and grab the next tools they would need.

"Have you used a high-speed vibrator before?" she asked.

Dan's head snapped up, and he looked at her skeptically, eyes narrowed.

"That question sounds like a trap . . ."

Harper blushed at his meaning and gave an involuntary snort of laughter. She rolled her eyes, trying to save face.

"Oh my God, are you twelve? The tabletop vibrator." She waved her hand toward the adjoining wet lab, her words becoming flustered as his wicked smile grew. "The heavy-duty dental vibrators."

At this point, he was downright snickering at her. She clapped a hand over her face and made a blind punch for his shoulder in a weird attempt at self-preservation.

"I'm sorry, Harper, are these names supposed to indicate that what popped into my head is somehow wrong?"

Her face flushed a deep crimson, and she peeked at him through her fingers. Dan's smile grew wider, that gorgeous dimple making another guest appearance. He was so cute it was almost obscene.

"I officially hate you. It gets air bubbles out of stone pourings." She gave his wheeled lab chair a hefty push with her foot and he started to roll away, laughing. Harper broke out in helpless giggles.

"I'm sorry—I'm sorry! You would think they would come up with names a little less . . . primed for innuendos," he said, wheeling back toward her.

"I think to be an innuendo, it has to be subtle. That was anything but." She turned back to their work, but the smile refused to leave her heated cheeks. "I guess they assume the future doctors of America are a little more mature than that."

"Guess I'm not cut out for the job." Something sadder and darker flitted to the surface of his gleaming eyes, but it was gone before Harper could define it—his goofy smile firmly back in place.

They spent the next half hour in the connected wet lab. Harper showed Dan how to mix and set the powdered stone, the finished product coming out nearly perfect with minimal issues along the way. They both shared a moment of delicate pride at what they'd created together. As they were cleaning up, Dan broke the peaceful silence that had fallen between them.

"Do you want to grab some food?"

Harper's eyes darted up to his. Working together in the lab was one thing. The lab was her domain, her safety net of skill, and a place she rarely felt awkward or nervous. Interacting with Dan in the real world felt infinitely more terrifying.

"T-together?"

"Preferably. I mean, we can sit at different tables if you want? I hate to think I'm that terrible of company."

"No! No. That's not what I mean. I—I mean—we don't really—know each other . . . Do we?" She searched his face for confirmation.

Dan let out a soft laugh. "No, we don't," he confirmed, ducking his head and running a palm across his neck. "Which is kind of why I asked."

Her eyes bounced around the room, unable to rest on one thing, as the familiar pulse of anxiety started in her stomach and radiated outward to her limbs.

It wasn't that she didn't *want* to eat with him, it was more that she didn't know if she physically *could*. The whole exercise had been a teaching one, a situation that provided her confidence and a constant flow of conversation. Helping him had automatically afforded her value and didn't require her to slide real pieces of herself across a table in an exchange of emotional currency.

Sharing a meal tilted the dynamic in a way she didn't think she was capable of functioning in, not when he made her nerves feel like they'd been plunged into a socket with a metal fork.

"I have to study," she blurted out. This was the truth. Glancing at the clock on the wall, she felt panic tickle at her rib cage.

"Who doesn't?" He shrugged. "But you also need to eat. Fuel that big ole brain." He tapped his finger lightly on her temple, and Harper felt like she was going to pass out.

All she could do was stare at him, paralyzed by the equally strong forces of want and fear. It wasn't a new sensation; she was constantly immobilized by warring impulses until anxiety eventually won out and she retreated from the tempting distraction.

But as Dan smiled at her—a look that was warm and soft and encouraging—want gained the upper hand.

"Come on," he finally said, grabbing both of their bags and slinging them over one shoulder. He took her hand and led her toward the exit.

"Where are we going?" she asked nervously, but she didn't try to take her hand away.

CHAPTER 5

DAN

Stepping out of school was like stepping out of a bubble. No one was fully human under the fluorescent lights of the clinic. Emotions and personalities were largely unzipped and hung up outside the school doors, allowing only the callused skin of *intellectuals* to enter. Leaving at the end of the day left you feeling naked and exposed, blinking at the world around you and trying to remember how to be a person.

Dan lifted the collar of his coat against the wind and jammed his frozen fingers into his pockets. Glancing at Harper, he felt the delicate thread of their newfound closeness fraying. He wasn't sure how to navigate the awkward reality of being strangers in the real world.

Her eyes danced around the street, unwilling to land near him for too long. Dan was glad to know he wasn't alone in his cluelessness about what came next. He was struck by the overwhelming impulse to do something ridiculous, like lick the tip of her nose or say something stupid just to make her laugh. He wanted to watch the nervous energy drain from her face and see it bloom with humor.

Harper cleared her throat, and he realized how long he'd been staring at her. *Super chill, Dan. Really killing it.*

"Do you like Jewish delis?" he asked. "Like hoagies and stuff? I've heard of this great place on Eighth and Sansom I've wanted to try."

Because, obviously, big greasy sandwiches were the epitome of romance and seduction.

Harper's eyes creased with a smile. "Dan, my last name is *Horowitz*. I don't think it gets any more Ashkenazi than that. Of course I like Jewish delis. Are you talking about Martin's?"

"You've been?"

She laughed. "Only a few times a week for the past four years. Martin, the owner, knows my rabbi back home."

"That's a small world."

Harper shrugged. "Jewish geography is alive and well. Let's go. I'm freezing."

They walked the few blocks in companionable silence, the sharp bite of December wind offset by Harper's warm energy.

Harper beat him to the door and held it open for him. Dan smiled and stepped inside, the blast of heat in the shop making him strip off his coat while the smell of pickles and fresh bread had his mouth watering. A surly man whom Dan assumed to be Martin was hunched over the counter.

Martin shot Dan a dirty look as he walked in, but straightened and offered a toothy grin when Harper followed behind. Dan wouldn't be surprised if she had that effect on every man.

"Harpa, my princess!" The man's Brooklyn accent boomed through the deli. He shuffled between the counters and moved toward them, wrapping Harper in a hug. "How ya doin', sweetie?"

Before giving her pause to answer, he turned to size up Dan.

"Who's the goy?" he asked sharply. The mood took a sharp left turn and landed somewhere between meet-the-father and overly-protective-uncle territory. Dan was glad there weren't any shotguns mounted on the walls as Martin continued to stare at him.

"Martin, this is my . . ." Harper paused and gave Dan a searching glance. ". . . friend. My friend Dan. We go to school together."

"Nice to meet you," Dan said, stretching out his hand. Martin shot him a skeptical look before returning the shake, squeezing harder than was necessary. Dan squeezed back.

Dan glanced over at Harper and caught her staring, slightly slack-jawed, at his forearm. He flexed—inadvertently of course—and felt a primitive thrill when her eyes widened. Interesting.

As if sensing him looking at her, Harper's gaze shot to Dan's face. Busted and guilty, Dan dropped Martin's hand and pretended to study the menu.

"The usual, dollface?" Martin asked, moving back behind the counter.

"Yes, please. With extra Russian dressing."

Martin winked at Harper and turned an expectant stare to Dan, who was only one column through the ridiculously extensive menu.

"I'll do the Slammer," Dan said, choosing the first thing his eyes landed on. Martin nodded and slapped the giant sandwiches together with surprising speed. Dan pulled out his wallet as Martin set their meals on the counter, but the man stopped him with a raised hand.

"Harpa eats free. So do her . . . friends," Martin said, giving Dan another skeptical sweep up and down.

"I insist." Dan handed over his credit card.

Martin gave him a thoughtful look then nodded, taking the card and ringing him up.

"You didn't need to do that," Harper said, turning to Dan.

He shrugged. "Want and need rarely line up," he said with a wink. Color exploded on her cheeks, and she swallowed.

"Well, thank you."

Harper stared at him a moment longer before awkwardly reaching up and patting his shoulder. He fought back a grin as she cringed and jerked her hand away. She snatched up the sandwiches and darted to a table in the back while Dan finished with the receipt.

When he looked up, Martin was glaring at him. They stared at each other for a moment, a healthy dose of fear trickling down Dan's spine.

"Don't try anything smart," Martin said at last, his eyes flicking to Harper for a second before he turned and lumbered off, leaving Dan nodding foolishly in his wake.

CHAPTER 6

HARPER

Harper wondered which was the best way to request they eat at different tables. It was either that or rub her face against the deli slicer to put an end to the torture. Those were the only two solutions she could think of that would save her heart from the lethal dose of adrenaline and estrogen that pumped through her every time Dan said something. Or looked at her. Or blinked, for fuck's sake.

She went into rationalization mode: So she had a crush. A huge, throbbing, gut-punch crush. Big deal. Crushes were fine. Crushes could be *crushed down* with enough willpower and mental stamina. She had those two things in spades. For example, she'd shown an exorbitant amount of willpower when she hadn't run her teeth over Dan's forearm like a feral animal while he shook Martin's hand.

As Dan sauntered toward the table with drinks—of course he sauntered, heaven forbid he walk like a normal human instead of each step being adjacent to soft-core porn—Harper readied her nerves. She could do this. She could sit and have a normal conversation with him. She had years of pretending like everything was fine while anxiety melted her insides to pieces.

He sat, and she handed over his sandwich.

"Are you a religious man, Dan?" Harper asked, before releasing her grip on the food.

"Not particularly," he replied with a wary look. "Why?"

"Because that first bite is going to be a spiritual experience."

"Yeah?" He started unwrapping the sandwich.

"Just your typical soul ascension. Heavens parting. Angels singing. Nothing too dramatic. I don't want to oversell it."

Dan laughed, and she smiled back at him. A comfortable rhythm was settling between them, and her heartbeat was returning to an almost human level. Even her lusty sweats were drying. She could *so* do this. Her chances of surviving the night without a heart attack were increasing every second.

And then he took a bite of the sandwich.

And moaned.

A gritty, masculine, overtly sexual moan of pleasure.

Her underwear lit itself on fire, and her palms vibrated against the table. Harper was, once again, anything but comfortable.

"This is the best sandwich I've ever had," Dan said through a mouthful of pastrami, totally oblivious to Harper's physical crisis. "You drastically undersold it. This place is incredible."

He took another bite, closing his eyes in enjoyment. She wanted to lick a stray crumb off his lip.

"One of my favorites," she said, unwrapping her own sandwich with shaky hands. "Martin's a little coarse, but besides that, the place is perfect."

Dan stopped mid-chew to stare at her. "A little coarse? Harper, he's like sandpaper."

Harper laughed around a bite of food, and a charming shower of crumbs landed on the table. *Godfuckingdammit.*

Dan's smile was huge as he handed her a napkin.

"He seems to really adore you, *princess*," he teased, and Harper rolled her eyes. "You said he knows your rabbi. Do you go to temple with him or anything like that?"

Harper shook her head, swallowing the bite of food and covering her mouth with an attempt at a dainty hand. "Martin and his wife have me over for dinner sometimes, but I don't go to temple that often—the High Holidays mainly. I should be better about it but . . ." She shrugged. She only had so many hours in a day, and 90 percent of them were dedicated to school. Or being anxious about school. "It's something I feel connected to without having to go every week. My friends and I try to go to Shabbat at the Jewish Student Center as often as we can, though."

"What's Shabbat?"

"The Jewish Sabbath. It's from sundown Friday to sundown Saturday. It's a time for rest and reflection—no work, no chores, no technology. It's common to have a big dinner on Friday nights with certain rituals to remind us of the covenant. That's what I go to."

Harper took a sip of her soda. "The one at school is pretty low-key. My friends aren't even Jewish, but I think they like having the time to step back and reflect . . . and the wine and free meal don't hurt. But I like to be as plugged in to the community as I can, with what little free time school offers. It helps me, I think."

Dan watched her thoughtfully, and Harper pressed her lips together. A small knot formed at the back of her throat, and she tried to swallow past it. She usually guarded personal artifacts like that, and her center felt jolted at how easily it slipped out. She looked down at her food.

"Do you mind if I ask you to elaborate on that?" Dan asked.

She chewed on her lip. This was feeling a little too real. A little too personal. Harper's friends teased her about being guarded, but she viewed it as self-preservation. Walls were good. Walls were safe. Walls offered protection when her anxiety made it feel like the world was falling apart and her body was quickly dying.

She looked back at Dan. His green eyes were filled with soft encouragement. She thought of the vulnerable way he'd trusted her in lab, and felt herself remove one brick from her wall, just wide enough to stick her hand through.

"I don't know. It's complicated, I guess," she said with a nervous laugh. "There was a long period while I was growing up where I questioned and doubted a lot of the faith aspects, but even through all that, I felt a part of the community. Judaism has all these layers outside of faith that makes it really incredible—the food, culture, history—it always made me feel like I had a home to turn to. A safety net of people that would welcome me in." She emphasized this by gesturing toward Martin, who was now bickering with a new customer, and she and Dan shared an amused look.

"As I came to terms with my own roadblocks with faith," she continued, "being Jewish became an important part of my identity, I think. I mean, obviously, no group of people is perfect, but I'm privileged enough to feel I belong to something greater than myself."

Dan looked at her as though he saw something more than just Harper sitting in front of him, and it created a shaky feeling in her stomach. She shifted in her seat.

"What about you? Are you religious?" she asked, breaking the silence.

The intensity of his stare broke, and he laughed.

"This got pretty existential, huh? I'll take the blame for that. Not your normal get-to-know-you talk."

"No, it's not." She laughed back, feeling some tension drop from her shoulders. "But sharing is caring, so it's your turn." She wasn't going to let him get a piece without giving one in return.

He chewed on a bite of food, a faraway look in his eyes. "Not really. It wasn't something my family ever talked about. My dad was Irish Catholic, and my mom is Muslim, though she learned pretty early on after immigrating here how uncomfortable it made people to hear that. She doesn't talk about her experiences much with me, and I don't know that she was ever particularly devout, but I do think she may have slowly lost part of her connection to it."

"I'm sorry," Harper said. "That probably sounds like the world's greatest platitude, but I am. No one should have to lose a piece of themselves to make others comfortable."

Dan gave her a soft smile. "Thank you. I agree." He took a sip of his drink. "But yeah, my dad was adamant about church at Christmas and Easter, but all religion was pretty much ignored the rest of the year."

He wiped his hands on a napkin. "I got the sense growing up that they couldn't agree on how to show me both, so they settled on showing me neither. Or, more likely, my dad decided that's how it would be," he said with a small frown down at the table. "He dictated a lot like that."

After a moment, he turned those gorgeous green eyes to her, sweet and unguarded. "To answer your question in the most roundabout way possible: No, I'm not religious. But I like to think I believe in something. I just don't know what that is yet."

They stared at each other for a few heavy moments. He was an open book, and Harper wanted to devour every page. She'd never felt this overwhelming need to learn someone like she wanted to learn Dan.

"So, what do you like to do for fun?" Dan asked, breaking the silence and returning to his food.

She stared at him in disbelief. "Really? *That* question? That has to be the worst question of all time."

He tilted his head with a confused look. "Why? It's a bit more neutral than religion, don't you think?"

"It makes me forget every time I've had fun. Ever. It's like asking someone their favorite movie. The second that's asked, it's like you've never seen a movie in your life."

He gave her a bemused glance. "My favorite movie is *Die Hard*."

She rolled her eyes. "You and every other dude."

He let out a loud laugh, and it warmed something in Harper's chest.

"Am I not original enough for you, Horowitz? What's yours? It better be super obscure and artsy."

"I. Don't. Know," she growled. "Questions like that make my brain dissolve."

"What about a favorite TV show?"

She stared at him blankly. "This is emotional guerrilla warfare."

"Color? You have to have a favorite color." He was enjoying this.

Harper glared at him for a long moment before answering. "Purple."

"Okay, we're getting somewhere. It's like I really know you now."

"Yup, all my secrets."

"Maybe not all of them, but I'm getting close."

Their eyes met as they smiled. Dan looked at her with a light tenderness that set off alarm bells in her mind. This was feeling like a date. Which it absolutely wasn't.

"Okay, am I allowed to ask where you're from? Is that a less touchy subject?" He still held a teasing glint in his eye, having no idea how touchy it actually was for Harper.

She thought about her answer, chewing on the inside of her cheek. It had been so long since she'd done this. Since someone asked questions to get to know her, requiring her to actively think of how much of herself to give away. Enough to satiate a person's curiosity without explaining too much of her past to make everyone uncomfortable.

Where was she supposed to start? How do you casually explain that you never had a dad and no longer have a mom? How do you tell someone you don't feel *from* anywhere because any sense of home was lost in a night?

You don't.

Not over hoagies, at least.

Harper didn't want to see that awkward flash of pity cross his face, have it hanging, heavy and pathetic, between this fragile bond of friendship they were forming. More than anything, she didn't want to pick at the scab she worked so hard to keep covered.

"I guess home is here. I grew up in Maryland until I was twelve and then went to live with my aunt and uncle on Long Island after that." She started tearing little pieces off her napkin, focusing on the frayed edges. "I moved here for undergrad and never left. I felt sort of settled." She squeezed her eyes shut for a second, pushing the floating memories out of her mind. "What about you? Where are you from?"

"Haverford. It's a boring suburb about forty-five minutes from here," he said with a disinterested shrug.

"At least you get to spend your early twenties in a fun city like Philly. Enjoy being young and spry while you can, you'll feel old in no time." She cringed. She sounded like a middle-aged mom.

"How old are you?" he asked with a laugh.

"You aren't supposed to ask a lady her age." Especially when the lady was definitely older than the hot guy asking. Dan carried himself with a youthful openness that made it seem like the years had yet to wear down his energy. "I'm twenty-six," she conceded. "Old and decrepit to you, I'm sure."

He shot her a quizzical smile. "Why's that?

"I don't know. I remember being in my first year, and at twenty-two, anything over twenty-five seemed old and disturbingly adult-ish. It felt like my midtwenties were centuries away, and it was some big milestone of maturity." Harper crinkled her nose. "And then you blink, and all your friends from undergrad are getting married or having kids or buying a house. You feel this bizarre mix of desperately old and desperately young, and you aren't re-ally sure how someone your age acts because you realize that past twenty-five, you aren't actually an adult—you're just good at pretending to be one on social media."

Dan chewed on another bite, watching her. "That's pretty spot-on."

"I probably sound dumb and preachy, but I swear you'll get what I'm saying in a few years," Harper said, taking another bite.

He paused, eyeing her. "How old do you think I am?"

She chewed, looking at him closely, something she hadn't allowed herself to do all evening at the risk of spontaneous combustion. The sharp angles of his jaw and cheekbones were a far cry from the softness of a boy's face, and the gentle lines that bracketed his mouth were a testament to how often he seemed to grin. But his eyes still held a reckless spark. He seemed to show his emotions easily—humor, vulnerability, kindness—all surfaced in an unguarded way that made him youthful and energetic.

"Twenty-one, twenty-two-ish?" she guessed.

His eyebrows shot up, and a smirk tugged at the corners of his mouth.

"I'm twenty-six too. A 'nontraditional' as the school likes to call me." He brushed some crumbs from the table, his smile dimming.

"Really?" Harper said, barely masking her disbelief. Something about assuming he was younger had given her a false sense of confidence, a safety net of "older womanhood" that now felt disastrously immature. Thinking she was drastically older—as drastic as four years can feel in your twenties—allowed her to feel safe, as though any flirtation was a harmless indulgence.

Knowing that he was the same age, going through a similar quarter-life identity crisis, created a different sense of level ground that felt ridiculous and overwhelming.

"What made you start so . . ."

"So late?" Dan finished with a laugh. "Believe it or not, I was actually all registered and ready to start four years ago—so with your class, I guess—but I backed out at the last minute. Much to the dismay of my family." Another laugh, with much less humor, escaped him. "It's weird to be starting now. I feel too old to be undertaking something so huge, but too young to already have every step of my life planned out in this weird linear fashion."

"Why'd you back out?" Harper asked. The idea was so foreign to her. Having a plan, a clearly defined path, and deviating from it was the most reckless and dangerous thing a person could do. It made her pulse hammer in her chest and wrists just thinking about it.

His demeanor changed, his relaxed, playful posture transforming into a stiff spine leaning back and away, a dullness filling his features.

"I felt pulled toward something different," he said. "Finance," he added.

"Finance?" Harper couldn't hide the distaste that covered the word, her head jerking back. "That sounds incredibly boring."

"*Boring?* Numbers are the most interesting thing out there."

Harper shook her head, crinkling her nose. The idea of numbers and spreadsheets and math being interesting was inconceivable. "You're deranged. It doesn't get more boring than *finance.*"

"More boring than scraping crap off nasty teeth?"

Harper's head shot back in genuine shock. She loved the satisfying rush of scaling plaque off teeth.

"You don't like doing prophies? There's nothing more exhilarating than getting that hard-to-reach calculus off. It's like watching someone pop a really gross pimple, satisfying and mesmerizing."

Dan stared at her like she had three heads. "You and I have very different definitions of satisfying. Satisfying is finding the natural patterns and trends in numbers. Manipulating them and moving things around, working until you finally solve this incredible puzzle. *That* is satisfaction." He gave her a smug grin.

She couldn't do anything but shake her head, stunned. How could anyone think there was a career more satisfying than dentistry?

"And here I was, thinking you were perfect . . ." she said softly. She clamped her jaws shut at the realization that she'd said the thought out loud. Dan's eyes went wide with a dangerous glint that flooded her with embarrassment and panic.

"So this was fun," she rushed out, standing up and nearly knocking her chair over. "I better get home."

She moved to reach for her coat, and her hands shook as she turned it around and around, trying to find the armholes that seemed to have sewn themselves shut during dinner.

She was about to drop the damn thing and make a run for it, but Dan's hand closed around the neck of her jacket. His other hand gently grasped hers, and he spun her away from him. She heard the coat ruffle behind her, then felt him slipping it over her shoulders. Her throat felt dry, and her skin tingled at the fabric's drag over her arms.

"It's getting late. I'll walk you home," Dan said in a gravelly whisper, dangerously close to her ear.

Her thighs turned liquid-y.

"That's okay," she said, taking a big step away from him. "It's cold, and you should go home."

He stared at her with a bemused smile. She shifted from foot to foot. "And I have a quick stride. It's not far. Plenty of . . . lights . . . around."

He continued to stare at her with mock interest as she rambled. He slipped on his own coat.

"So many lights," she said weakly.

"So you said. Lead the way."

CHAPTER 7

DAN

"So, what did you do in . . . *finance?*" Harper asked as they walked to her apartment, the word coming out like it tasted sour. Dan couldn't help but laugh.

"I worked as a junior portfolio manager at a firm up in New York."

Harper glanced at him in surprise. "That sounds important."

Dan shrugged. If he talked about his old life too much, he'd miss it.

"Why'd you leave?" she asked.

There weren't enough drawers in the world to unpack that emotional baggage, so he tried to wave off the question.

"You'd probably find the reason as boring as the profession."

"Maybe . . . but I doubt it."

Dan let out a deep breath, not wanting to go there. "It's a long story. My dad got sick, and I came back to help my mom during the transition. They . . . She's a dentist. She worked part-time at his practice, but now she's the only one running it, and she's overwhelmed. She seems to think she's incapable of handling it on her own and she'll lose the whole thing. She . . . *suggested* I make a career change and go into the family business." He was quiet for a moment before adding, "Persuasive woman."

"Did your dad . . . Is he okay?"

"He passed away," Dan said without emotion. Because he didn't feel any.

But the sadness that filled Harper's eyes made him want to take the words back.

"Hey, it's okay," he said, tucking an arm around her shoulders and squeezing. "We weren't close. It wasn't a big deal." Only changed the trajectory of his life and saddled him with an overwhelming sense of duty to his mom. No big deal at all.

"Oh," she said softly, pushing her hair behind her ears. They continued walking in a loaded silence before she spoke again. "I . . . I lost my mom when I was twelve. If you ever want to talk about your dad . . ."

"I don't," he said, the words sharper than he'd intended. Harper flinched, blinking up at him.

They looked at each other, the heavy, shared burden simultaneously bonding them together and wedging them apart. Dan didn't say anything more, and they both bent their heads, staring at the ground as they walked.

"This is me," Harper said, gesturing at an old, converted brownstone on the corner, holiday lights strung around the railing at the front steps.

Dan followed her up the stoop, and Harper turned to look at him. They lingered outside her door for a beat too long, alternating between stolen glances and staring at their feet.

Dan knew this marked the definitive end to any real reason for them to spend time together, and a sharp pang of dread punched at his ribs.

Harper fiddled with her keys but didn't move to go inside, and Dan clung to the hope that maybe she didn't want the night to end either.

He pushed the hair off his forehead and let out a deep breath, watching the puff of mist it created.

"So, what are you studying for tonight?" he asked.

"Advanced pathology," she answered automatically. "You?"

"This week is immunology . . . I think. It's hard to keep track," he said, dragging a hand across the back of his neck. "Pretty overwhelming."

"It's like drinking from a fire hose."

Dan chuckled, but his heart sank. He felt the conversation ebbing, and he scrambled for the best way to ask to see her again.

"Do you want to come upstairs?" Harper practically shouted the words at him, and he blinked at her in surprise.

"To study," she added quickly. "I can make . . . coffee. Or something." She looked up at the sky like she was begging for help.

"Coffee would be great," he said, trying to control the spark of happiness that ignited in his chest.

Harper's eyes flicked to his face, and she nodded. She jammed her key into the lock, and Dan noticed the shakiness of her hands. Her whole body seemed to be vibrating.

She opened the door, and they walked across the foyer to the elevator. They waited for it in tense silence, Harper tracing random patterns on the floor with the toe of her shoe.

The energy between them shifted dramatically, and Dan worked to keep his own body still. He refused to walk into her apartment with any assumptions. Even if this turned out to be the world's most platonic late-night coffee, it still meant more time with Harper. But he couldn't completely ignore the hope that it would be something . . . more.

The elevator *ding*ed and the doors slid open. Harper stepped aside, letting him go in first.

"It's a bit small," she said, following him in.

That was an understatement. The elevator was ancient and almost comical in its tininess, so narrow they couldn't stand next to each other. Harper stood in front of him, and his body became hyperaware of hers. Each of his cells strained to touch her.

She pushed the button for the fourth floor and let out a shaky breath. Harper's warm scent filled the space, making him want to breathe in every inch of her. She felt like an energy, a force that invaded his senses.

"It's, um, slow," she said, staring up at the old dial showing the elevator's rise. Dan looked at the graceful curve of her neck and decided he wouldn't care if the elevator stopped altogether.

"I don't mind," he murmured, tilting his head to say the words closer to her ear. He watched her swallow and saw the pulse fluttering at the base of her throat. Her breathing picked up, and Dan's blood heated as he imagined how the little puffs of breath would feel against his skin.

The air stilled, and everything paused. Harper closed her eyes, and the tension in her muscles hinted at the battle raging in her mind. Dan felt a decision pressing against them, filling the space between their bodies.

Harper let out a breath and leaned, almost imperceptibly, into him. A featherlight touch of her back to his chest.

Electricity shot down his spine, and he stiffened at the thought of touching her. Pressing himself to her. Pushing her up against the wall and dragging his lips down her neck, feeling the short waves of her black hair between his fingers.

The elevator *ding*ed again, and the sound made them both jump. Harper bolted out and down the hall as soon as the doors opened.

Dan scrubbed his hands over his face and through his hair, feeling like his brain had short-circuited, making it impossible to move. Being half-hard didn't help his situation, and he willed his dick to stand down as he followed her.

Dan's lust-muddled nerves knotted into apprehension, and he considered coming up with an excuse to leave. Not because he didn't want to spend more time with Harper, but because he couldn't get a clear read on her, and the last thing he wanted was her feeling uncomfortable.

She stopped at a door near the end of the hall and flipped through her keys before unlocking it.

With her hand on the knob, she turned to look at him, squinting one eye and scrunching up the rest of her face.

"So, I'll be honest, I have no idea what state my apartment is in, and I apologize in advance if it's a train wreck."

Dan laughed, hoping it helped to dissolve some of the tension. "Being roommates with Alex has pretty much exposed me to the most hazardous living conditions a person could experience. The city's housing department is petitioning to condemn him. He's a threat to tenants everywhere."

"Thank God for heroes like you, absorbing his toxic waste."

He shrugged in mock humility. "I do what I can for the people. A lab is bringing me in for genetic testing. I may or may not be joining the X-Men in the coming months."

Harper laughed, pushing the door open and stepping inside, flipping on the hallway light as she went. Dan followed and they both slipped off their shoes.

"You'd be okay with wearing the spandex?"

"I'd need a few months to get bodysuit ready, but if the objectification of my ass can save the world, I'm willing to make the sacrifice."

"So selfless."

His heart swelled a size at her teasing. Talking to her pushed energy through his limbs and down to his fingers, like he'd been a man starved for human connection.

They stood inside her apartment, grinning at each other. Her eyes were warm and rich, reminding him of a cup of coffee he'd gladly drown in. Dan's hand lifted on its own accord and brushed her short hair behind her ear.

Harper opened her mouth to speak, but something out of the

corner of his eye caught his full attention and pricked every survival instinct in his body.

A huge, animalistic mass barreled down the hall at full charge. Dan couldn't make sense of what he was seeing, but his hair stood on end as he heard its low growl. His heartbeat matched the rapid pounding of its paws on the wood floors.

Adrenaline took over, Harper's safety his top priority. Dan registered a door to his left and ripped it open, pulling Harper in with him and slamming the door shut behind her before she could speak. His body took on a protective posture, caging her against the wall.

"What the hell are you doing?" Harper's voice was panicked. Dan moved to cup her face between his hands.

"Okay, Harper, don't freak out but there is an animal in your apartment," Dan said, his voice coming out in frantic bursts. "It's some sort of giant raccoon maybe? Or a bobcat? Do they have bobcats in Philadelphia? It was angry and charging. I need you to remain calm," he begged, feeling anything but. "I'm going to investigate, but please, stay in here, so I know you're safe."

"Dan, I—"

"Shh, please, I need you to stay calm." His own fear escalated as he heard the soft thump of a paw clawing at the door. "Maybe you should find animal control's number while I figure out what it is. It looks about twenty or thirty pounds, I'm not sure."

"Listen, it's—" He placed a finger over her lips to silence her, not wanting her panic to flame his any further.

"I'll be okay," he said gently, brushing a hand across her cheek. "Please, don't worry about me. But stay in here. I don't want whatever it is to attack you."

His panic mixed with a throbbing sense of heroic pride as he saw the glint in her eyes. He moved her away from the door and steadied his hand on the knob. With a deep breath, he counted to three then whipped the door open, blocking the entrance so the animal couldn't get to Harper.

His eyes darted around, ready to fight off an attack. They landed on a huge pile of long, gray fur sitting right outside the door. His mind couldn't process the weird, now docile, creature stretched out before him.

It gave a tiny mewl and rolled to show a white belly. What the fuck was it?

Dan heard sobs coming from behind him, and he turned to comfort Harper, ready to tell her whatever it was, it seemed calm, and she was safe. Instead, she was doubled over, gasping for air through laughter. He stood there, dumbfounded by her strange coping method for fear.

"Are you okay?" he asked, putting a hand on her shoulder.

"I'm sorry," she said, wiping tears from her eyes as she stood. "I don't mean to laugh. You were so chivalrous and ready to fight." With that, she snorted and laughed even harder.

"Are you really not concerned that there's a wild animal in your apartment?" He still couldn't control the edge of panic in his voice.

She took a steadying breath. "It's my cat, Dan! It's Judy. Judy, the cat."

Dan turned his head in disbelief to look at it. It was stretched out, close to four feet long, tufts of long gray and black fur draped around it on the floor. He guessed it weighed close to thirty pounds, maybe more. Its large amber eyes stared at him as it rolled back and forth in search of attention.

"That's a . . . cat?" He turned back to Harper, eyes wide with confusion.

"Yes." She giggled and placed a hand on his shoulder. "She's a Maine coon. They're kind of big."

He whipped his head back to the creature. "*Kind of?*" His voice broke. "I thought it was a predator! That's not 'kind of' big. That's a huge, ginormous, absurdly large cat."

"Don't listen to the mean man, Judy," Harper cooed in a singsong voice as she pushed past him and hefted the mammoth fur ball into her tiny arms where it—Judy—hung like a ragdoll. The juxtaposition of this pocket-size woman holding the world's largest cat made hysterical laughter bubble out of Dan's throat.

"You named your cat Judy?" Of the long list of questions he had about her "pet," the name seemed the best place to start.

"Yes. Big Booty Judy." She nuzzled her face into the fur. Judy started purring at a volume close to a motorboat.

"But why that name? Isn't that a little bit . . . old lady for a cat?"

"It's dignified," Harper said, giving him an expression that said this fact should be obvious.

Dan took a cautious step closer and stretched out a finger for Judy to sniff. He generally enjoyed cats, but he still wasn't entirely convinced that's what this creature was. Judy's amber eyes lazily surveyed the finger before she dramatically turned up her head and exposed her giant neck for scratches. Dan obliged, and it was like her purring was hooked up to a music amp as it vibrated around the tiny hallway.

"Aw, she likes you! She's usually picky with people."

Harper beamed, a smile that crinkled the corners of her wide eyes and made Dan's heart melt into his stomach. He'd permanently strap that giant cat in a Baby Bjorn and wear her on his chest, scratching Judy's chin for the rest of her life, if it meant Harper would continue to reward him with that smile.

After a few moments, Harper gingerly laid the giant down and turned to Dan.

"Come on, I'll make us that coffee."

CHAPTER 8

HARPER

Any tension that had dissolved with Judy's unceremonious appearance resurfaced as Harper finished prepping the coffee. She couldn't control her fidgeting. Her skin felt stretched and tight, buzzing with heat like a fever about to break. She wanted to unzip from it, find relief from the oversensitization.

She looked around for a distraction and decided that music would help break up the silence that was slowly eating her alive. She chose a playlist at random and a song began thrumming from her nearby speaker.

"I like your kitchen," Dan said, leaning against the counter and looking around.

Surveying her space, Harper knew that was a bold-faced lie—it was a hot mess. The narrow galley style meant that the cabinets banged into the opposite side when she opened them, annoying her so much that most things were housed on the limited counter space in controlled chaos.

Dan's body curved to fit into the tiny room, his long legs reaching across to the other side while he ducked his head slightly for the low ceiling.

"You barely fit," she said with a smile.

"It does seem a bit more Harper-size," he said, laying a palm against the ceiling without having to stretch. "I'm not convinced you can reach the top shelves, though."

He gave her body a pointed inspection, and she felt herself flush. Again.

"Why do you think I bought such a long cat? I hoist Judy up *Lion King* style, and she gets all the hard-to-reach items for me."

He laughed and the sound made her bones feel like they were melting.

"You're so funny. I love that," he said, dimple and all.

Heat flooded her body. A giddy rush made her want to run into her room and fling herself on the bed so she could scream into her pillow like an infatuated teenager.

Instead, she turned to pour them coffee and hide her ridiculous grin.

She passed him a mug, and they sipped their drinks in comfortable silence. Judy joined them in the kitchen and stretched out to fill the majority of floor. Harper and Dan took turns rubbing her exposed belly with their feet, warmth and contentment slipping around them like a blanket.

Dan fit into her tiny sanctuary like a puzzle piece she hadn't realized she'd been missing. The reality of that thought clanged around in her mind, but she filed it away to be overanalyzed later, choosing instead to enjoy the comfortable moment.

But, because the goddess of hormones decided she hadn't suffered enough that evening, "Crash Into Me" by Dave Matthews Band started blaring through her speakers. She jerked so hard, coffee sloshed from her mug, and she dug a toe into Judy's side, making the cat flee dramatically. Perfect timing for the world's swooniest song.

Everything felt instantly more intimate and claustrophobic with the sultry music. Harper would go to battle arguing it was one of the most romantic songs ever written, and she often whined to her friends that her biggest regret in life was not losing her virginity to it, but now was not the moment for any additional sensuality.

She glanced at Dan, hoping he hadn't noticed the song or her reaction, but he gave her an amused smile.

"Do you listen to this un-ironically?"

Her brows snapped together. "What?"

"This song. Isn't it a little . . . cliché? Like every cheesy, late nineties sex scene has this playing in the background."

Her jaw dropped. "This is an amazing song!" She was borderline yelling.

He bit back a smile. "Isn't it about stalking?"

"That was a silly interpretation of it," she said, waving him off.

"You think Dave Matthews misinterpreted his own song?"

"Yes! Well . . . no. I don't know. It doesn't really matter what he says it's about. You can't listen to it and not get all . . . melty." She trailed off, not able to meet his eyes.

"Melty," he repeated, that dimple taunting her.

She nodded. Glancing at him, she saw heat in his eyes. The soft acoustic melody continued around them, and Harper desperately tried to get more air into her empty lungs. She took another sip of coffee, glancing around the cramped kitchen.

"Well, come here," he said, taking her mug and setting it on the counter, then turning back to hold her hands in his.

"W-what?"

He took a step closer, lacing their fingers on one hand and wrapping his other arm loosely behind her.

"You can't listen to a melty song and not dance to it, can you?" he said, swaying them gently.

Harper couldn't think of a response and decided that wide-eyed shock was better than trusting her voice. She wasn't sure her spine could feel any stiffer. Every nerve in her body had rerouted itself to the point where his hand rested on her lower back.

"Is my dancing that bad?" he asked after a moment, destroying her with a boyish grin.

"What?"

"You look very afraid."

Harper let out a too-loud laugh and tried to force her shoulders to relax.

Harper and Dan weren't pressed against each other, a few inches still separated their bodies, but that somehow made it worse. She felt the proximity of his chest, the strength of his arm around her, the heat of his skin, and it was like a battle of energy waged between their dangerously close limbs.

Her muscles strained with every sway and rock of their bodies, wanting more than just this taste of his nearness. Her heart pounded against her chest like it wanted to break free of her and lodge itself firmly next to his.

Dan started humming the melody, making Harper want to lay her ear at the base of his throat and feel the vibrations.

"Who's cliché now?" she said, the words almost a whisper. She looked up at him and he narrowed his eyes in response.

"The song may have some merit," he said with a shrug. "Tell me what you like about it."

Harper shrugged back. "It feels kind of raw," she said after a moment, nibbling on her bottom lip. "It's strange and haunting but also . . . fun? It makes me want to want someone that badly. It *feels* like romance."

Having no firsthand experience at actual romance, just awkward dates and lackluster sex, this was a guess. But, if it was anything like whatever the hell was unfolding in her kitchen, romance felt like drowning.

Dan's gaze flashed with hunger, but it disappeared quickly. He moved them toward the kitchen doorway, maneuvering the tight space with smooth steps. She felt his chest rise and fall with each inhale, almost meeting hers.

Shaky and overwhelmed, Harper squeezed her eyes shut. Anxiety screamed for it to end, while another fragment of her mind begged for more.

Dan's body gravitated closer.

Closer.

So close that if either of them breathed, they would touch.

His hand skimmed from the base of her spine to lightly grip at the side of her hip, and heat followed the path, settling low in her belly.

For a single moment, he squeezed her tightly against him, his fingers pressing fire into her hip.

Then his hand dropped.

And he shifted away.

"I see what you're trying to do, Horowitz, but I'm sorry to say, I'm impenetrable to your tricks of seduction."

Harper's head jerked back, and she stepped away from him, banging into the countertop behind her. His dark and playful eyes skimmed over her.

"What?— No. Stop it. I'm changing the song." She groped blindly for her phone, but he dropped his hand on top of hers.

"I'm sorry, Harper. I'm just not that kind of guy." He traced a gentle circle across the back of her hand.

"Wait, what?"

His wicked eyes bore into hers for a second longer before he moved out of the kitchen and into the hall, tugging her behind him.

"It's a personal rule, really," he said over his shoulder.

"What is?"

Reaching her front door, he turned to face her. His lips were pressed into a crooked line, halfway between a laugh and a sad frown.

"I don't put out on the first date. Need to know you'll still respect me in the morning." He tapped her on the nose with his index finger. "We'll reevaluate on our third date, but I have a good feeling," he said with a wink. Her mouth went slack.

"Are you high?" she managed to splutter out.

"Now I'll get out of here before we both do something we'll regret. I can't imagine it's easy to keep your hands off me," he said, offering a sympathetic shrug. His wicked mouth twitched with a grin.

She gaped at him. "What the hell are you talking about?" she managed to ask.

His face softened. "I'm teasing you," he said, using the pad of his thumb to smooth the furrows between her brows. "Thank you for the best night I've had since starting school."

His voice was sincere and the words reverberated through Harper's chest. He stepped back and Harper blinked at him.

"See you around, Harper," he said in a husky voice.

He bent and brushed his lips over her cheek. The light touch released a fire hose of adrenaline and lust, drowning every nerve ending in her body. He opened the door and stepped out, giving her one more glimpse of his elated grin, before closing it behind him.

She stood there for several minutes, replaying the scene over and over in her head. She slumped forward and dropped her forehead to the door, a small smile breaking across her lips as a new thought played on loop.

He'd called it a date.

CHAPTER 9

DAN

"The average was eighty-four percent. That's rather embarrassing for your class," the professor said, shooting a glance around the room. "Callowhill holds you to a certain standard, and this type of performance does not meet it."

Dan had trouble processing how anyone viewed an 84 as a bad grade, but Callowhill was on a different level of over-the-top.

"There are members of this class who seem far too comfortable with inadequacy," the professor continued, his gaze flicking toward Dan. "And I feel the need to remind you, school policy defines anything below a seventy percent as failing. Such grades will result in mandatory remediation and a potential need to repeat the year."

He swept another hostile glance across the auditorium. "I do not look forward to inevitably seeing some of you in remediation this summer."

The professor stared straight at Dan, too long for it to be a coincidence, before giving the class a flippant wave of dismissal.

The hum of conversation filled the room as people packed up their belongings.

Dan stared numbly at his school-issued tablet. It was official.

He was failing immunopathology. And close to failing neuroanatomy. Might as well tack osteology onto the list.

He wasn't failing for lack of trying. Dan put in the hours, all-nighters, flash cards, online videos, trying anything and everything to make the information stick. His brain actively rioted against retaining any of it.

Disappointment. The sharp snap of his father's voice bounced around in his skull. Dan pushed it away before it gained purchase in his thoughts.

"Woof. Rough time there, Danny-boy?"

Travis Giles, topping the charts as one of Dan's least favorite people, leaned over the auditorium seats to wedge himself between Dan and Alex, his hot breath hitting Dan's cheek.

He smelled like milk. He looked like milk too.

"Daddy's legacy can get you into school but can't get you the grades you need to graduate? How sad," Travis said, clucking his tongue. "Good thing your mom is standing by with a practice ready so you don't actually have to work for it."

Travis was a prick.

But he also wasn't wrong.

At the start of the year, Dan walked into orientation assuming most of his classmates would be there out of a similar sense of crippling guilt and familial obligation.

He'd quickly realized that while plenty of his peers were similar legacies with a practice waiting for them after graduation, he was alone on his island of misguided purpose, without anyone to commiserate over things they'd rather be doing with their lives than what was expected by their parents.

"Oh, fuck off, Travis, no one gives a shit," Alex said, not even bothering to look at him. Dan felt a pang of gratitude toward his one friend.

"What? Am I saying something untrue?" Travis shot Alex a challenging look.

Travis had painted a target on Dan's back from day one, looking to carry on the Craige versus Giles family dental feud, which was every bit as boring as it sounded.

Their dads were different sides of the same coin, Dan's father gaining his fame and glory from his innovations in cavity prevention, Travis's father accumulating his wealth and power through boutique dental mills that drilled and filled at an alarming rate. Both men were dicks as far as Dan could tell.

"You think your legacy admission to this school is any better than mine?" Dan shot back.

"No, I think my ability to pass classes while being here makes me better than you," Travis said. He pushed away from the seats, leaving before Dan had a chance to think of a reply. There wasn't really anything to say to the truth, though.

As if Dan didn't already feel enough like a piece of shit, he received a text from his mom.

> I'm having dinner in the city this
> week with Dr. Cochran. Will you
> join us?

Absolutely not. While Dan's parents had run a thriving practice, his father had also worked with Dr. Cochran to pioneer a new system of cavity detection and prevention that brought cost-effective relief to underdeveloped countries. The breakthrough elevated both intolerable men to celebrity status in the dental community, casting a halo of altruistic perfection around the Craige family practice. A halo Dan knew he had no chance of keeping intact.

Before he could think of the politest way to say *Fuck no*, another text buzzed through:

> I wish you would call me. I miss
> you.

Guilt almost spurred him into agreeing to dinner, and he realized how naïve he'd been to think anyone in this place could ever relate to the river of bad blood and unavoidable sense of duty Dan was drowning in, his mother's well-being officially his responsibility.

But he also knew what dinner would entail: endless praise for his dad's memory, mind-numbing discussion about the practice, his mom's heartbreakingly subtle hints at how much she was struggling to manage everything, how scared she was of losing her livelihood, losing the thing her husband had valued above all else.

The weight of it would likely snap his spine. Dan ignored the text.

"Don't listen to him," Alex said, zipping up his backpack and pulling Dan out of the sharp memory. "That exam was killer. They should start handing out lube before tests if they're going to fuck us like that. Travis is probably just jealous."

Dan snorted. "Jealous? Of what?"

"I don't know, your good looks and radiant optimism?" Alex said.

"Har har."

"Listen, I can't tell you why it makes him feel better to put you down, but it does. Their whole family is like that. Don't give him the power."

"Thank you, Oprah. That was beautiful."

"What do you have next?" Alex asked, breaking the awkward tension.

"Specialty rotation. I'm in oral surgery this week. What about you?"

"I have a free block this afternoon, so I'm heading back to the apartment. Gonna stop at the grocery store first. Anything you can think of that we need?"

"Probably coffee."

Alex rolled his eyes. "Yeah, no shit. You think I would let us go without coffee? We would die."

"You're a domestic angel. Not sure what I did to deserve you," Dan teased. Alex gave a grunt of dismissal, refusing to take the bait.

"See you at home, dipshit," he said, striding out of the auditorium.

"Love you too," Dan yelled over his shoulder, laughing at Alex's embarrassed flinch and proffered middle finger.

Dan made his way across the building, dragging his feet and dreading the next hour spent "assisting," which translated to him sitting there while an upperclassman struggled through a procedure and inevitably called in a resident or attending to clean up the mess.

What. A. Rush.

He signed in at the surgical clinic front desk and went to sit in the student break room, waiting for his assigned upperclassman. He scrolled through his phone, his thoughts quickly and inevitably returning to Harper.

Like a normal person, he'd gone home last night and scoured the internet for her. To his disappointment, she had all her social media locked down with an infuriating level of privacy. He spent the rest of the night with her laugh playing on loop in his mind, his hands buzzing with the feel of her as they'd danced.

It had taken all his self-control not to move closer or let his hands slide over her. He'd wanted to grab Harper by the hips and push her up onto the messy countertop. Kiss her. Touch her. Learn the body that held such an impressive mind.

Instead, he'd thought about cold showers and baseball, made a hasty exit, and spent the long walk home coming up with different scenarios of what could have happened if he'd stayed.

Despite his dick's outrage, he was glad of his choice. Dan preferred the long game over short-lived flings. He wanted Harper to trust him. So, he'd wait. Blue balls and all.

Dan heard footsteps moving down the hall, slowing as they approached the break room, and he absently wondered if it was his upperclassman coming to collect him. When the person turned into the room, he couldn't help but laugh at his incredible luck.

Harper stopped in her tracks, eyes wide.

Then she smiled.

CHAPTER 10

DAN

Dan could almost see the thought bubble forming over Harper's head, and he knew the line she was about to deliver. As she opened her mouth to speak, he cut her off.

"Are you stalking me?" he asked. Harper's head drew back as he stole the words from her. An incredulous look glinted in her eyes.

"Just here for a lock of hair and then I'll leave you alone," she said, looking like she still wasn't sure what to make of him.

"I'm not really willing to part with any of it, but I'd be happy to sneeze into a tissue if that's okay with you." He ran a hand through his hair and cringed as he realized how much he flexed his bicep.

Meathead.

Excessive masculine pride replaced his embarrassment as her eyes lingered on his arm a beat too long before flicking back to his face. A blush crept up her throat.

"I appreciate you being such an easy target," she murmured, eyes moving around the room, "but what are you doing here?"

"I'm scheduled to be your shadow, I think. I'm on a specialty rotation today."

She nodded coolly but picked at her nails. Her eyes bounced up to his, and he saw the nervousness there.

"Is that okay?" As excited as he was, he didn't want to annoy her.

"Of course." She waved him off, moving to action. "We have a difficult first patient, so don't engage too much. You might give him more to complain about."

He touched a hand to his chest in mock offense. "Me? I'm sure my winning personality will make his day all the brighter."

"I'm sure," she said, looking skeptical.

Harper handed him a yellow isolation gown to wear over his scrubs and pulled on her own. She moved into the hall and Dan followed.

She weaved through the clinic with the same confidence he'd witnessed in the lab. Each step was purposeful and determined, her hands knotting the tie of the isolation gown around her waist with agile fingers.

"We're extracting the retained root tips of number thirty-one. The radiograph indicates the roots might be close to the IAN, so we'll need to be careful. Number thirty has serious decay and gingival overgrowth, so it could be tricky to extract in one piece, but I have a new technique I'm excited to try. The patient has high blood pressure and is a prolific smoker. His history of tobacco use could result in wound-healing complications and leave him susceptible to infection, but that's not anything you have to worry about today," she said, glancing at him over her shoulder.

Dan blinked at her, trying to translate the terms he vaguely recognized while also counting his teeth with his tongue. Harper gave him a gentle smile, pausing outside their assigned operatory.

"His bottom-right second molar only has roots left in there, and the tooth in front of it has serious decay," she said, tapping on her right cheek. "It's causing him a lot of pain. The root tips might be near the nerve that runs along the jaw bone, so we need to be very cautious in our extraction," she explained, a smile tugging at her lips, "but I've been reading up on an approach that's had great recent success, and I'm excited to try it." An eager glow emanated from her smile. "Smoking has been shown to affect wound healing in multiple ways. Decreased proliferation of red blood cells and macrophages, increased chance of micro-clots, decreased oxygen to wound sites that can lead to necrosis— these are all things you'll learn later in pathology. You're lucky, this is a fun case to see your first year."

Her smile was infectious.

"You really like this, don't you?" he asked.

"Well, duh," she said, shooting him a goofy grin. "Relieving people's pain, getting to work on the complexities of the body, all within the confines of a millimeter or two? What's not to love?" She tucked her chin to her chest and fumbled, trying to tie the smaller strings for the neck closure behind her. "You clearly hate lab work, but don't you at least like this part of it?"

Dan didn't want to dampen her enthusiasm with a definitive "hell no," so he shrugged and reached out a hand. "Here, let me." He turned her gently, brushing her hands away. His fingertips grazed against the nape of her neck, and she sucked in a breath. He hummed to himself as he tied the knot, fighting a smile at her reaction.

"All done." He felt her take a deep breath, her shoulders ris-ing, before she turned. When she faced him, she was composed and serious.

"Thank you," she said evenly. "Like I said before, his chart notes indicate he's a tough patient, so try to not let him bother you. I'll need you to be ready with certain tools, but the most im-portant thing you can do is keep the suction steady so blood and debris don't pool during the extraction."

He nodded, ready to work, wanting to impress her. She turned and headed into the room.

"Hello, Mr. Owen. I'm Dr. Horowitz, and I will be your student dentist for today's procedure. How are you?"

A surly-looking man in his midfifties sat in the dental chair, arms crossed against his chest and a firm grimace on his face.

"I've been waiting for fifteen goddamn minutes for you to show up. So, not great, sweetheart," he said, looking Harper up and down.

"It's Dr. Horowitz," she said, and Dan pressed his lips in a firm line to hide his smile. "I'm sorry to hear about your wait. We'll get started right away." Harper washed her hands at the small sink in the corner.

Mr. Owen scoffed, then turned appraising eyes on Dan. He gave Dan a once-over before offering a stiff nod of approval. Dan had a sense of where this was headed, and he didn't like it.

"All right, let's get started," Harper said, snapping on gloves. "Do you understand what I'll be doing today? We have plan—"

"Why don't you let the doctor speak, sweetheart," Mr. Owen said, cutting her off and waving an impatient hand at Dan. "Let the man do his job."

The air whooshed from the room. Dan's eyes snapped to Harper's but, to his surprise, she looked unfazed. Despite her calm, he was swarmed with the need to defend her, protect her.

"As I said before, I'm Dr. Horowitz, your student doctor. This is Dan and he will be my assistant."

Mr. Owen turned to Dan with an incredulous scowl. Dan stared back in silence, arms crossed over his chest. Mr. Owen apparently took Dan's disdain as a nonverbal declaration of allegiance, directing his next words only to him.

"I don't know what this—this . . ." He flapped his hand toward Harper. ". . . *girl* thinks she's doing, but I'll have you take the tooth out. It'll need muscle. A small thing like her won't do it right."

Dan's anger burned, and he opened his mouth to tell the dick exactly what he was going to use his muscles for, but Harper cut him off.

"Mr. Owen, I'm highly prepared for your case. I've done extensive treatment planning with the surgical clinic's attending, and your general dentist. Dan is a first-year student on a rotation to observe and assist. Now, let's begin. I would hate for you to be even further off schedule, since timing is so important to you."

She said this with kind indifference and turned to lower the patient's chair. Dan balked at her level-headedness when all he wanted to do was rip this asshole's tooth out with his bare hands.

"No! I'm not having some stupid little girl working on my mouth! Get me a male doctor. Now."

Dan took a step toward the man. "Okay, ass—"

Harper cut him off.

"Dan." She said his name with a snap, and he shut his mouth at the angry flash in her eyes. She fixed him with a stern look for a moment before turning to Mr. Owen.

"Why don't you tell me exactly what concerns you."

Her spine was stiff and her stare hard as she said this, but Dan still wanted to step in and defend her. He didn't want this man's toxic words to touch her. Dan knew how easily another person's doubt could seep below the skin like a poisonous cloud, settling into bones and chipping away like a cancer. He wouldn't let anyone do that to Harper.

Mr. Owen's face twisted. "Little slow, honey? Let me repeat myself. I don't want a woman botching up my goddamn tooth. Why sit here and have you strain your little arms for an hour just to have you go and get a man to come and fix your mistakes? The tooth is in there deep and good, the other doctor told me so. It's *retained*." The man gave a cocky smile like he was some sort of Einstein instead of a rotten-mouthed dipshit. "You don't have what it takes."

He folded his arms over his chest and shot a smug look between

Harper and Dan, as though his logic was foolproof. Dan's heart sank when he saw Harper nodding. Nope, not while he was around.

"Listen up, dic—"

"Dan." Harper's voice cut through the room.

He met her heated stare. Why was she getting mad at him? Why wouldn't she let him handle this guy for her?

Harper cleared her throat and moved to the computer. She clicked through a few screens before pulling up an X-ray of Mr. Owens's lower jaw. The remaining teeth in the man's mouth glowed white on the image, jutting at unnatural angles and littered with dark shadows that even Dan's untrained eyes knew meant decay. Two twisted roots were buried partially below the bone near the back, the tooth next to it almost completely black and tilted at an odd angle.

"So, here is your panoramic. As you can see"—she pointed to the small line of jaw bone the teeth rested in—"your lack of oral hygiene and neglect of your gums has left you with severe alveolar bone loss. This means that your periodontal ligament is almost completely worn away from the root of your teeth, including these retained roots and molar geared for removal today. This bone loss means your teeth are so *weakly* held in your mouth, they don't need a lot of force for me to remove them." She shot Mr. Owen a tense smile.

"Believe me," Harper continued, "I've removed much sturdier teeth from men with drastically stronger, thicker bone. In fact, an excess of force—the force you seem to expect from a male practitioner—would likely shatter your *delicate*, rotten tooth and bone, leading to excess trauma." She leaned against the sink counter.

"Any excessive trauma could result in the piercing of your inferior alveolar nerve, causing paresthesia, or the molar fracturing in the socket and the need for a surgeon to lay a flap, causing greater wounds. Your years of smoking mean you have disrupted wound healing and would put you at risk for infections and possible necrosis. I don't believe in laying unnecessary flaps and prefer to do the least invasive methods of removal to also prevent alveolar fracturing during the procedure—a common complication seen when *big, strong* men whip impacted teeth out with too much force."

Harper wore an expressionless mask. Dan couldn't look away. He wished he had popcorn. She was *good*.

"So, Mr. Owen, my *womanly* hands are the best to handle the fragility of your neglected tooth. It will likely pop right out." She made a loud popping noise that made both men jump.

"You see, you aren't special, Mr. Owen. You're one of the least exciting cases I have, compared to something like an orthognathic surgery or trauma intervention."

She paused again and gave him a beaming smile. Both Dan and Mr. Owen gaped at her.

"But," she continued, unfazed by the shock bouncing between the men, "as this was supposed to be a fast procedure, I have another patient scheduled in half an hour. Since we have wasted so much time arguing, I'm going to have to dismiss you as a noncompliant patient. I hope you have a great day."

Harper pushed away from the counter and moved toward the door.

Mr. Owen's mouth flapped open and closed like a dying fish. "Get me your supervisor!" he croaked.

Dan bit back a laugh at the crack in Mr. Owen's voice.

"Gladly," Harper said, barely turning her head over her shoulder. "I'll send Dr. Ren in to speak with you. Dan, could I have a word in the hall?"

Dan followed her out, wanting to prop her up on his shoulder and carry her around the clinic for a victory lap. But as soon as the door clicked behind them, Harper turned on him.

Slight cracks showed in her calm composure. Anger heated her cheeks and her dark eyes were sharp and alert. He felt his own temper rise at the fact that the idiot had hurt her, and he prepared to apologize on the man's behalf.

"Harp—"

"What do you think you're doing?" Her voice was harsher than he expected.

"W-what?"

"What was all that about? You were two seconds from exploding in there and the last thing I needed was another hotheaded man to deal with."

Dan's head jerked back. "What?" he repeated, totally lost. "That guy is an asshole! And I wanted to tell him. He can't talk to you like that. Especially because you're a woman."

Harper closed her eyes slowly, as though counting to ten, and let out a deep breath. Her coffee-black eyes flashed open and locked onto his.

"Dan, I appreciate you wanting to defend me, I really do. But you swooping in to save the day only works to discredit me further."

"What? How?"

She licked her lips and sucked the bottom one between her teeth. "Men like him are a losing battle. They're set in this archaic mindset that no amount of yelling or brute force can reason with. He looks at me and sees a small girl playing make-believe as a doctor. Men like him"—she pointed at the door—"decide from the moment women like me walk into the room, that we're a threat to their outdated thinking and need to be put in our place. If I raged and yelled, it would solidify in his mind that women are too emotional to be taken seriously. Having someone like you fight my battles? It's almost worse. It's showing that I can't handle myself. It's like I'm a damsel in distress, and you're the gorgeous hero who waltzes in to save the day and pull out the stupid tooth. It invalidates me even further in his eyes."

"So you just pick and choose your battles? Even though that guy is completely off base and has no right to treat you like that?"

"It isn't picking and choosing battles. It's knowing how to fight them."

"Has stuff like this happened before?" His brows furrowed even further. Harper looked at him like he was an innocent kitten.

"This happens all the time. Many men don't trust women to work on them. They don't believe we're capable of skilled clinical work. Hell, many male *faculty* members have the same belief."

"But that's . . . stupid," he said.

A warm smile crinkled the corners of her eyes. "I agree, but you going ham on some crotchety man won't change centuries of chauvinism."

She raised her hand, moving it like she was about to stroke his cheek, causing his skin to buzz in anticipation as it hovered between them. He saw the moment she became aware of the gesture and dropped it heavily to her side.

"You wait here," she said. "I need to get Dr. Ren." Dan nodded and watched her retreat down the hall.

He leaned against the wall, letting his head drop back with a *thud.* He dug the heels of his hands into his eyes and groaned quietly. *Dammit, feelings are exhausting.*

After a few minutes, Harper reappeared at the end of the hall, a tall, wiry woman walking with her.

"Dan, this is Dr. Ren, chair of the OMFS clinic," Harper said when the women stopped at the door.

Dan shook the intimidating woman's hand, her height allowing her to look down her angular nose at him. Her clothes were clean and tailored under the crisp lines of her white doctor's coat. Everything about her was sharp.

Without a word, Dr. Ren rapped on the door, then entered.

Mr. Owen stewed in the chair, his face purple. Seeing that

Harper's direct supervisor was a woman, he shook his head and let out a grunt.

"Great," he growled. "Another one. Is there a gentleman I can speak to?"

Dr. Ren's eyes narrowed. "No. And hello to you as well. I've heard you are noncompliant with the surgery, yet unwilling to leave." Her voice chilled the room. Even Mr. Owen cowed a bit.

But the bastard didn't know when to stop. "Listen, lady, I just want a man to come in here and pull my goddamn tooth. I don't understand why that's so hard for everyone to get. Take one look at this girl and tell me she can handle it," he said with a challenge.

All eyes turned to Harper, but she continued to stare at Mr. Owen, looking bored. Dan couldn't help but smile.

Dr. Ren let out an exasperated breath. "I do not know why you think you're entitled to disrupt my entire department with this inane request, but since you have removed me from issues that actually matter, let me make myself clear: Dr. Horowitz is a gifted student and her talents are wasted on this conversation. If you want to pick your surgeons based on prejudice, go to a private practice. Do not come to a teaching clinic and insult our students, and, in turn, insult me and my ability to mold incredible doctors regardless of their gender or any other qualifier you may possess. We have the right to refuse treatment to any patient who is insubordinate to the care of our clinicians. A security guard is waiting for you in the hall to escort you out. I'm sure you'll be pleased to know it's a man."

Dan felt like starting a slow clap.

Dr. Ren turned and left the room, Dan and Harper rushing out after her.

"Thank you, Dr. Ren," Harper said. Her admiration for the woman was obvious.

"Of course," Dr. Ren said with a curt nod. "Let me know if you need anything else."

Dan and Harper made their way back to the student break room, a giddy energy growing between them.

"I'm sorry you didn't get to practice your technique . . . thing," he told her. She smiled at him and shrugged.

"There will always be more teeth to pull. I still have one more patient this afternoon. It's just a consultation, but it's for corrective jaw surgery and a really interesting case."

Her passion was intoxicating, and he almost envied her for it. It was rare to see someone so in love with what they did. He doubted he could ever muster up that kind of excitement for dentistry, but the way Harper's enthusiasm radiated off her made anything seem possible.

When their eyes met in the lounge, the energy heated.

He wanted to hug her, touch her, give her a kiss that expressed how amazing he found her.

They stared for half a second longer, but when he took a slow step toward her, she broke eye contact, gaze darting around the room like she was searching for a life vest on a sinking boat.

Fidgeting, she reached into her scrub pocket and pulled out a pen, clicking it repeatedly. She glanced at the clock.

"I better finish out his chart before my next patient," she said, clicking the pen so rapidly, her thumb blurred.

"I better go too. I have another class starting soon."

Harper nodded, pursing her lips and bobbing her head in rhythm with the clicking. She still didn't look directly at him.

Dan moved to her and plucked the pen from her hand. Harper gaped at him. Before he could lose his nerve, he grabbed one of the napkins sitting on the table and scribbled down his phone number.

Harper's hand was still poised in the air, and he pressed the pen into her palm, using his hand to close her fingers around it. He lifted her other one and put the napkin in it.

Harper's head whipped back and forth between Dan's face and the paper. After several seconds, she cleared her throat.

"Wow, did I just score your digits or something?" she said with an obvious effort at sarcasm.

"Yes." He tilted his head to meet her gaze, and his heart somersaulted when her eyes locked onto his. "I hope you use them," he said, and left the room.

CHAPTER 11

HARPER

Harper did *not* use his phone number.

She spent Tuesday night an absolute mess, picking up and throwing down her phone every seven seconds, typing in his number then deleting it at warp speed. At one point she tried stuffing her phone under her bed to get some space, but ended up on her belly, dusting the floor as she fished it out minutes later. Harper resigned herself to staring at the screen and willing the perfect words to type themselves.

On Wednesday, Harper left her phone at home, deciding it was best not to text him at all. What would be the point? She wasn't looking to start anything up with Dan, and the way he made her heart riot in her chest and her blood boil in her veins could not be healthy. This new decision didn't stop her from pulling his number out of her pocket between patients, folding and unfolding the flimsy napkin until it threatened to tear. It wouldn't matter if it did; she had the numbers memorized already.

By Thursday afternoon, she'd drafted so many mental text messages to him that the random string of words stopped making sense. Harper found herself looking for him at every turn, and it became painfully obvious how off her A-game she was during a treatment planning seminar with her academic nemesis, Jeffery Giles.

Dr. Giles, Jeffery's father and an associate clinical faculty member, was leading the seminar; the school had ignored his blatant knack for putting profits over patients when he'd been given the position.

Harper and Jeff had been paired to treatment plan for a medically compromised patient needing substantial prosthetic work. Harper had taken the lead on the case, outlining the gold-standard treatment to help prevent future issues for the patient down the line. Jeff had been relatively useless, knowing he was guaranteed an A because his dad led the course and telling Harper that, since all she did was study anyway, it'd make more sense for her to take the lead. He'd offered Harper something close to genuine praise when she'd sent him the proposal, though.

"Using implant-retained dentures after the alveoloplasty would cut down on the chance of future bone loss and the patient needing greater rehabilitation in a few years," Jeff said, finishing the presentation with a smug grin on his face. Their plan was far more extensive than any other group's, and Jeff loved any chance to flex his intellect, despite it being Harper's idea.

Dr. Giles was silent, staring at the pair. "Really?" he said at last, steepling his fingers on the glossy wood table. "This is your plan, Jeffery? Providing a Medicaid patient Cadillac-level treatment? How do you propose they'd pay for it?"

"I was hoping to talk with financial services about discounting the patient's fees," Harper cut in. She'd anticipated this question. "They've come here for over ten years, and because some of their past treatment has led to the state they're in now, we should rectify that. Plus, taking extra steps with this reconstruction would end up saving money on future treatments they may need if we went with lower-caliber options."

Dr. Giles scoffed.

Jeff darted a look at Harper, his confidence gone, calculating how to win back Daddy's approval.

"That makes no business sense, Miss Horowitz," Dr. Giles said.

"But it makes clinical sense," Harper countered.

Dr. Giles sighed. "No practice would be sustainable if they waived fees for top-of-the-line treatments left and right."

"That may be true," Harper interrupted, "but this is a teaching clinic funded on student's tuition, grants, and insurance reimbursements. Our high-risk, low-income patient population needs this type of care."

Dr. Giles scowled at her. "The practicality isn't there, and I'm not going to argue the point. I'm shocked you put your name on this, Jeffery."

Jeff stuttered. "I—she—"

Dr. Giles continued to stare at his son.

"I thought it could be a teachable moment," Jeff said at last, his features snapping into a condescending smile at Harper. A few students in the seminar snickered. "Being book smart doesn't always equate to clinical intelligence."

"Yes, because back-alley dentistry for a patient with chronic issues epitomizes clinical intelligence. I really need to get my nose out of the books," Harper snapped back.

Jeff rolled his eyes, opening his mouth to fight when Dr. Giles interrupted him.

"We'll continue on with presentations next week," he said, waving the small group away in dismissal.

"What the hell was that?" Harper hissed, turning on Jeff. "We could have cited some research and clinical cases instead of rolling over like that. The patient needs this type of treatment and you know it. Their past low-caliber care got them to this point."

"There's no need to get hysterical," Jeffery said, packing up his laptop. "It was a bad idea, end of story. How predictable of a woman to let her emotions lead her into a poor business decision."

Harper's blood boiled. "Thank God you embrace toxic masculinity with such gusto. The world would be in pieces if it weren't for your total lack of compassion," Harper said, storming out of the room and into the hall.

She was annoyed and frustrated and couldn't help but think that if she'd been more focused this week, not losing her damn mind over a boy, of all things, she could have been quicker to argue her case. She needed to focus the fuck up.

She avoided lunch with her friends, stationing herself in the rarely used school cafeteria to cram in some studying. The anxious voice banging against her skull drowned out the one preoccupied with her silly crush. It frantically reminded her of every single thing she needed to get done, and every single possible consequence if she didn't, causing her nerves to swell with the familiar overflow of worry, that painful energy stampeding through her veins.

Sometimes she wondered what it would look like inside if she could open a little door to her chest. There'd be her heart, of course, thrumming like a hummingbird's wings with the force of a hammer. But she also imagined sticky, tangled swirls of indefinable colors—some dark and frightening, others soft and welcoming, most fluorescent and sharp. There'd be barbs of chaos poking into peaceful corners, shards of memories sealed away in locked boxes. Small little worker bees zipping and humming through her chest, resting between her rib bones, trying to clean up the mess, but ultimately making it worse in their flurry of energy.

In short, pure mayhem.

Hunkering down to study, she buried her phone in the bottom of her backpack and pulled out her textbooks, starting to read. With each paragraph, her pulse slowed until she found her normal rhythm, scribbling notes as she read, and slipping into that secure realm of control and order she needed to survive.

"You didn't call."

Harper's head snapped up so sharply, she winced at the pinched muscles. Dan stood across the table, fixing her with puppy-dog eyes while a smile tugged at his lips. She swallowed hard, trying to think of something to say.

"Hi," she finally managed.

"Hi," he said, pulling out the chair and sitting. "Not even a text. You're breaking my heart here."

Harper's mouth opened and closed like a gaping fish.

"I'm not sure I can play coy any longer," he continued, folding his hands in front of him and giving her a frank stare.

"This is you playing coy?"

Dan grinned. "You have reduced me to the least chill guy in the world. Do you have any idea how many times I've checked my phone in the past two days? I swear I keep hearing it vibrate, but then I look—nothing. I'm pathetic. I don't even care."

Harper shook her head like she was trying to dislodge water from her ears. He couldn't be for real.

"So, it's time to be direct," he said. "I want to take you on a date. Tomorrow night. Do you have any food allergies or aversions I should be aware of?"

Harper looked around the room, thinking this must be a joke. Things like this didn't happen. "Are you messing with me?" she asked.

"No. Does seven work?"

"What?"

"Is eight better?"

"I can't go out with you," she said, laughing in spite of herself. "I have plans Friday night."

"Saturday then."

"How do you know I'm not busy on Saturday?"

"I don't. I'm just desperate."

Harper stared at him, searching for the joke, but he was serious. "Well, you're very subtle about it at least," she said, chewing on her lip to hide the grin that was trying to break free. His eyes lingered on the spot as he smiled back.

"What are you doing on Saturday?" he asked, his voice deep and slow, the words humming straight through her chest.

Harper floundered for something, anything, to use as an excuse. "Errands." She tried to look smug and disinterested, but they both knew she wanted to see how far he'd take this.

"What kind of errands?"

"Grocery shopping."

"Great. I love grocery shopping."

"You're messing with me." It was no longer a question.

"I'm really not. What time do you go? Morning? Afternoon?"

She shook her head. "On a Saturday? I don't like crowds. I go later."

"Later like . . . ?"

"Late." Harper would gladly shop at one a.m. if it meant she could avoid crowds and spare herself the overwhelming, pulsing energy of busy stores that tripped off her anxiety like a live wire in her chest. Even the idea of it sent a burning wave of hot panic crashing through her gut. She hated having to regulate even the most mundane aspects of her life this way, but she could either keep everything on the tightest leash possible, or lose control of her feelings altogether.

Dan gave her a calm, expectant smile, letting the silence build. Harper let out a sigh.

"I go around dinner time. Like sixish."

"Perfect. I'll pick you up at six on Saturday."

"What?"

"I'll see you then." He paused, a spark dancing in his features as he studied her. "I'm really excited," he said, reaching across the table to give her hand a gentle squeeze. The touch hummed up her arm like music.

Dan pushed up from the table and moved toward the hall. He glanced over his shoulder and caught her looking at him. She felt herself blush, but she didn't look away. She let the electric grin spread across her face before dropping her focus back to her textbook.

~

Harper hadn't been lying about having plans Friday night, plans that didn't even involve studying . . . for the most part.

Harper and her friends made their way across Callowhill's campus to the Jewish Student Center for the weekly Shabbat dinner, a time for them to reflect on the good in their lives and enjoy themselves without the distractions of phones.

After the candles were lit, wine poured, and blessings said, Thu, Indira, and Lizzie turned to Harper with expectant glares on their faces.

Shit. How do they know?

Ignoring their inevitable interrogation and the flurry of nerves in her chest, Harper gave her wine some individualized attention, guzzling it down before they pounced.

"Harper?" Indira's copper eyes bore into Harper's, eliciting a fear only a best friend could create. "Is there something you wish to tell us?"

Harper squirmed in her chair.

The answer to that was a hard *NO*.

Harper had purposefully avoided telling her friends details about Dan, mainly because she didn't know where to start. It wasn't that she didn't trust them, but Harper had always struggled to define and process her feelings, needing time and some semblance of mental order before facing their questions.

Her friends were talk-things-out types of people, conveying

every detail of a situation and wanting input from the group to navigate their emotions. Harper loved listening and helping them; she liked to think she was a relatively levelheaded counterbalance to some of their more (extreme) emotional responses, but when it came to her own feelings, it was overwhelming to be asked questions and given advice on something she hadn't even processed for herself.

They were still staring, and Harper let out a long sigh. Not meeting any of their eyes, she poured herself another large glass of wine and gulped down a good portion of it.

"How did you find out?" she asked, trying to be cool. *Don't let them smell your fear.*

"Dan told Alex, and Alex told Thu, and Thu, like a *real* friend, texted us. Immediately," Lizzie said, shooting Harper a hurt glance. "Why wouldn't you tell us he asked you on a date?"

"Why are you talking to Alex?" Harper asked, turning her attention to Thu. This was new. And interesting.

"Nope. We're not talking about me. We want details," Thu said. Indira and Lizzie nodded in solidarity.

"There isn't anything to tell. It's hardly a date. We're going grocery shopping." They all stared at her.

"Grocery shopping? Is that code?" Lizzie asked, her face pinched in confusion.

"What could that possibly be code for?" Harper responded.

Lizzie gave Harper a mischievous smile and waggled her eyebrows. "Something along the lines of 'tossing your salad'?"

"Should I even ask what that is?" When it came to Lizzie, the less details the better.

Lizzie gave the table an evil grin as she leaned in with a stage whisper. "It's where, as a rigorous, sultry lover, you spread the butt cheeks of your partner nice and wide and give it a good, hard—"

Thu slapped a hand over Lizzie's mouth as Rabbi Merow

picked the worst possible moment to walk past their table. He tried to control his shock, and Harper offered a weak wave as he shook his head and continued past.

Harper pinched the bridge of her nose. "Tell me, Elizabeth—because I'm dying to know—which parts of my personality have *ever* given you the impression that, on a first date, I would be engaging in ass play."

Indira gave a snort and buried her face in her hands while Lizzie shrugged. "It's trendy with the kids these days."

"That's true," Indira said through her giggles, cocking her thumb at Lizzie.

"And this"—Harper pointed her finger around the table at her friends—"is why I didn't tell you. You're all ridiculous. And not helpful."

Her three friends cupped their hands around their mouths and booed, then dissolved into more laughter. When their giggles died down, Indira turned to Harper, her expression shifting to something more serious.

"Now here's the actual reason you didn't tell us: You don't want to admit you like this guy," Indira said. "Telling us about it would make it real, and you'd rather die than admit you're human and have a crush on a hot guy and now can't dedicate every single thought you have to school like the little cyborg you are."

Harper flinched. "Wow, Indira."

Her friends regularly teased her about her intensity over school, and it was rare for their poking to hit a nerve, but that had done the trick. Annoyance bubbled under Harper's skin. While they knew Harper better than anyone, they didn't have the right to act like they knew everything about this too. If Harper didn't know what this was, how could they?

"Maybe I didn't tell you because what would be the point? It's not like it's going anywhere. I'm moving in a few months—I don't even know where yet, for fuck's sake—so there is literally no sense in starting something. At. All. Or, maybe I didn't tell any of you because you're all annoying and meddling, and I knew you would involve yourselves and make a mess of it. I mean, heaven forbid I act like a big girl and do anything without consulting you three on every detail." She shot them a dirty look.

"But you're right, Indira, I'm the one with issues, even though none of you have had a relationship last more than three months. So please, tell me exactly how to handle this. You're all experts."

Harper sat back in her chair, not looking at her friends, her hands shaking as she folded her arms across her chest. Her heart thumped against her rib cage, the confrontation leaving an uncomfortable prickle along her skin. And she hated that. She hated that she couldn't even indulge in righteous indignation without that pulsing sense of anxiety hovering right below the surface; anything upsetting her carefully controlled balance threatened to push her into full-blown panic.

Her friends gave her shocked looks. They all took a sip of their wine and stared down at their plates. A few tense minutes passed before Indira broke the silence.

"I'm sorry," Indira said, giving Harper an even look. "We're just excited because . . . well, he's really hot."

"So hot," Lizzie agreed. "Like, no-hole-is-sacred level of hot." All three of them gave Lizzie a double take. "Tell me I'm wrong," she said.

Laughter dissolved the tension.

"Are we still going out after this?" Thu asked, taking a bite of food.

Lizzie squealed. "Let's go to that new club on Chestnut and Nineteenth. I feel like dancing," she said, shimmying her chest.

"Harper doesn't do clubs," Thu said, pretending to honk Lizzie's tits.

"Harper doesn't have to go," Harper chimed in. She would so

much rather go home and study than try to navigate a club, especially one that she hadn't confirmed met her Going-Out Rules.

Rules were her life preserver in the choppy storm of anxiety and she clung to them with white knuckles.

- Bars and restaurants needed tall ceilings and lots of windows.
- Going out meant going early to avoid late-night crowds.
- Claim a table on the outskirts, and always bring a friend willing to push through crowds to get to the bar.
- Never leave home without the rules lest you wind up in a bathroom stall, panic pulsing at your temples and tears streaming down your face as you try to remember how to breathe, simultaneously praying someone finds you and saves you from the impending feeling of death, and praying no one ever witnesses your shameful and mortifying lack of control over your own emotions.

"Harper promised us one night out a week for senior year since she'll be abandoning us for some out-of-town residency," Indira said, pinching Harper's cheek.

"Let's go to Fat Louie's Brewery," Thu said, finishing off her wine.

Harper eyed her friend. "You hate the beer there. We could do Sunny Point Pub."

"Nah, Fat Louie's is great," Thu responded, avoiding everyone's eyes as she gathered her things. "Let's go."

CHAPTER 12

DAN

"I'm sure they'll show soon," Alex said, checking his phone again.

Dan nodded and took a swig of his beer, eyes fixed on the door. When Alex first mentioned Thu's invite to "bump into them" at the bar, Dan had jumped at the idea. But as each second ticked by, Dan's choice to surprise Harper felt a little less sweet, and a lot more stalkery.

Dan stood, deciding to sneak out while he could still save face, and turned to tell Alex he'd see him at home. Thu's voice cut him off.

"Well, isn't this a small world," she said, leading her group of friends, all but one dressed in scrubs, toward the table.

Dan's eyes flew to Harper to gauge her reaction.

She stopped in her tracks, eyes going wide, and gripped Thu's shoulder. Dan watched her lips twitch as she hissed something into her friend's ear. Thu turned to look at her and offered an innocent shrug. Harper's cheeks reddened.

"What are the chances?" Thu said loudly. Harper shot her an angry glare before closing her eyes and taking a few deep breaths. When she opened them, she looked a bit more composed and gave Dan a soft smile.

"Mind if we join you?" Thu said to Dan and Alex as the women hopped up on the bar stools around the long table. Dan felt an over-the-top rush of excitement when Harper took the seat next to him.

"I guess you weren't wrong when you called us meddling," one of the friends whispered to Harper before reaching out a hand to Dan. "Hi, I'm Indira. I've Facebook stalked you thoroughly."

Dan's eyes widened, and he glanced at Harper, who buried her head in her hands. He busted out laughing.

"Dan. Nice to meet you."

"And I'm Lizzie. I focused more on your Instagram," the red-headed friend not wearing scrubs said, giving him a wave.

Dan felt his face heat, and he gave them both a smile. "That was probably extremely boring research."

"I think we were disappointed with how little there was to see," Lizzie said.

"Yeah, I don't post that often."

"Well, yeah, but more so, we were hoping you were really into something like swimming or underwear modeling. Just something that showed a bit . . . more," Lizzie said, her eyes flicking over him.

Dan's mouth hung open before he burst out laughing again. He looked over at Harper, who stared up at the ceiling with a pleading look in her eyes. Lizzie and Indira turned their attention to Alex, who only had eyes for Thu.

Dan risked a friendly pat to Harper's shoulder. She looked at him, her face so miserable, he couldn't decide if he wanted to laugh or hug her to his chest. Probably both.

Instead, he slid his half-full beer in front of her. She offered a weak smile before grabbing the bottle and taking a huge gulp.

Dan stood. "Do you want something different to drink?" he asked.

"You might as well bring me another one of these," Harper said, giving the beer a tiny shake before taking another swig.

"You got it."

Harper reached for her purse, but he stopped her. "On me."

She opened her mouth to protest, but he turned to the others at the table. "Ladies, can I get you something to drink?"

"I'll take a lager," Indira said.

"Same," Lizzie added.

Dan turned to Thu, but she was too engrossed in her conversation with Alex to notice his question.

"Get her a cider or something sweet," Indira said, nodding at Thu.

Dan rapped his knuckles on the table and nodded, then walked to the bar.

Waiting on the drinks, he turned to look at the group. Thu and Alex were leaning toward each other, talking and smiling, while Lizzie and Indira were locked in an animated conversation, saying something that made them both laugh. Dan couldn't see Harper's face, but he could tell by the tilt of her head that she was bouncing between the conversations and other noises in the room, never focusing on one thing for too long. Her body always seemed to hum with energy, her mind pulled in a hundred different directions. Dan wondered what it'd feel like to be the sole focus of her attention, what the magnitude of that energy would do to a person.

Drinks in hand, he moved back to the group and set the bottles on the table. He took his seat and Harper smiled at him, her shoulders less tense with an empty bottle in front of her. Dan hooked his foot at the base of her barstool and turned her seat gently so their knees touched. The contact felt like an electric current.

"This place is cool," he said. "I've never been here before."

"It's Harper's favorite," Lizzie chimed in. "She always makes us come here instead of any of the thousands of *fun* bars in Philly."

"I didn't pick it tonight." Harper shot a look at Thu, who gave her a guilty smile.

"Why this bar?" Dan asked. "Their beer?"

Harper shrugged, taking a sip of her drink. "The beer is good, but it's mainly the space. Other places get so crowded and noisy and just too . . . bleh," she said, sticking out her tongue. "Fat Louie's is huge, and you can always get a table, and it feels like I can breathe. Plus"—she turned to her friends—"at those other *fun* bars, I'd never be able to hear all the nonsense you like to spew."

Lizzie and Indira clinked their bottles together before taking a drink.

The conversation started flowing smoothly through the group. They ordered another round as Lizzie entertained them with stories of being a high school wild child, and Alex had everyone doubled over with laughter at stories of his mother.

"I swear, the second I turned eighteen, my mom made me a profile on a dating site. She said she didn't trust me to find a wife, so I should focus on school while she handles the other 'stuff.'"

"Isn't that a bit invasive?" Harper asked, wiping at her eyes as she giggled. Dan loved seeing her laugh. He wanted to take a picture of the way her eyes creased and her nose crinkled. Capture the rosy stain of her cheeks—his new favorite color.

"Alex talks to his mom, like, fifty times a day. Doctors say they've never seen an umbilical cord stay attached this long," Dan chimed in, making the girls giggle harder.

Alex rolled his eyes. "What kind of dick doesn't answer the phone when his mom calls?" Alex shot back, giving Dan a pointed look.

"Cheers to that," Harper said with a sad smile, clinking her bottle with Alex's. Guilt flooded Dan as a mental stream of missed calls and unanswered texts from his mom filtered through his mind. He shook himself, not wanting to go there. Not tonight. Not anytime soon. He'd completely rerouted his life for his mom, for fuck's sake. He should get a hall pass on a few missed calls.

"You guys want to play pool? A spot just opened up," Alex said, nodding toward the billiards tables in the corner.

"I'm in," Thu said, getting up from her seat. Lizzie and Indira followed her lead.

Dan glanced at Harper. She stared at the densely packed corner, chewing on the inside of her cheek.

"I'm good," Dan said, and he noticed her shoulders soften. Alex shrugged and the group left to play.

An awkward silence hovered between Dan and Harper, both looking around in opposite directions.

"I'll be right back," he said, leaving the table.

He walked to shelves in the corner, scanning and pushing through discarded boxes and pieces until he found what he was looking for. He walked back to the table with what he hoped would be a decent icebreaker.

"Jenga?" Harper asked, arching an eyebrow as he stacked up the wooden tower.

"Get-to-Know-You Jenga," Dan said. "Every successful piece removed means you get to ask the other person a question."

Harper eyed him for a moment before nodding and taking a sip of her beer.

"Ladies first."

She slid out a block near the top and tapped it on the table, staring at Dan. His heart hammered against his chest.

"Do you have any siblings?" she asked.

"No, I'm an only child. Do you?"

"You have to take a block before I answer a question," she said, smiling at him.

He pulled a brick out a few rows below hers. "How old were you when you had your first kiss?"

Surprise flashed across her face. She shot him an embarrassed grin. "Eighteen. I was late to the game."

"Were you not allowed to date in high school?"

"I was," she said, running the Jenga piece through her fingers. "I just never thought about it. And then I turned eighteen and was like 'oh wait, this is probably something I should do before going off to college,' or whatever. It's stupid."

Dan didn't think anything about her was stupid; he wanted to learn every arbitrary detail she kept so close to her chest.

"And you asked me two, so I get a bonus." She pulled out another piece. "What do you do to work out?"

Dan's head pulled back with a smile. "Who says I work out?"

Harper's eyes traveled down his body before returning to his face and giving him a skeptical look. His blood heated and he ducked his head with a laugh. He liked seeing her inch out of her shell.

"I really don't do that much," he said, running a hand across the back of his neck. "I like to run, and I lift weights once or twice a week."

"Running?" she said with a wince, giving a dramatic shudder before grinning at him. Dan laughed.

"What's your bonus question?"

"Umm . . ." She studied him for a minute. "First scar and how you got it."

Dan lifted his chin and pointed at the thin sliver running beneath it. "Street hockey when I was eight."

Harper leaned forward for a better look, and Dan felt the heat of her breath on his throat. She reached up and traced it, the pad of her finger barely touching his skin and leaving a scorched path in its wake. He swallowed.

"If you squint hard enough, it kind of looks like a shark fin," she said, dropping her hand. He immediately missed her touch.

"Fits my dangerous personality and bad-boy charm."

"Ha! Yeah right," she said, pressing her thumb once more against the spot with a laugh. "You're as soft as they come."

Dan sputtered at her in mock outrage. Harper dropped her head to her hand and giggled at his indignation.

"It's your turn," she said after she caught her breath, gesturing at the game. Dan plucked out a block.

"How do you like your coffee?"

"With my oxygen," Harper responded, already pulling out the next piece. "Favorite flavor of ice cream?"

"Peanut butter chocolate chip. Yours?" He pulled out a piece and watched the tower sway for a second.

"Strawberry."

"Wow, you actually have an answer for a favorite things question?"

"I try not to mess around when it comes to food."

"I'd like to take you out for ice cream sometime," Dan said, his eyes wandering to her lips as he imagined the cool taste of strawberries on them.

Harper looked down, tucked her hair behind her ears, and let out a giggle. "It wasn't your turn to ask another question."

"It was more of a statement."

Dan reached out, gently placing his hand over hers where it rested on the table. She glanced up at him through her lashes, her big brown eyes warming him, making him feel like he'd stepped into the sunshine after months of clouds, every cell hungry for more light and heat.

"Should we get one more drink?" Harper asked, breaking the tension and looking at their empty bottles.

Dan eyed her.

"Are you sure that's a good idea?"

Harper turned to him, playfulness in her eyes. She clapped her hands down on his shoulders and tried to give him a serious look, but her lips twitched with a smile. "It's a great idea."

"Hmm, I'm gonna go ahead and say you're a lightweight." He tapped her nose with his index finger, letting it rest there.

Harper stared cross-eyed at it for a moment before moving her head and making a show of baring her teeth. She surprised them both when she opened her mouth and nipped at the tip of his finger with gentle pressure.

He hissed out a breath at the feel of her teeth around him, his blood pounding through his body. They stared at each other for a long moment.

"Let's have one more drink," she said, her teeth still lightly clamped around him, causing her words to distort. Dan gave a soft laugh and withdrew his finger, running his knuckles lightly against her cheek.

"One more drink," he said slowly, and she rewarded him with a smile that would make the sun jealous. "But a Harper-sized drink. A beer in a shot glass–sized drink," he added, before getting up and pushing through the growing crowd to the bar.

He glanced toward the pool tables on his way, and saw their friends bickering over a shot, a small pile of dollar bills stacked on the corner of the table. Despite the newness of the people, Dan couldn't ignore the growing sense of belonging.

He got the drinks and moved back toward the table, a giddy buzz of excitement in each step.

"Thank you," Harper said, as he set the drink in front of her. "You even gave me a big-girl glass. How generous." She tapped his shin with her toe, making him smile.

"I aim to please," he said, shooting her a wink and loving the blush blooming on her cheeks. "Is it my turn?"

Harper clucked her tongue and wagged a finger at him. "Nope. It's mine," she said, her smile turning lazy from the mixture of laughter and drinks.

She pulled out a piece and the tower swayed dangerously. It didn't fall.

"How old were you when you lost your virginity?"

Dan choked on a sip of beer. When he caught his breath, he gaped at her wicked grin for a moment before laughing.

"Liquid courage, huh?" he teased, tilting his head toward her drink.

Harper shrugged.

"I was sixteen," he said, pulling at the collar of his shirt. The bar was about fifty degrees warmer than it had been a minute ago.

"How was it?" she asked, her eyes exploring his face. Dan felt his whole body come alive under her gaze.

"Isn't it my turn?"

Harper arched an eyebrow and plucked out another piece. "How was it?"

"Okay . . . that's cheating, but whatever." Dan ran a hand through his hair, unable to hide his embarrassed grin. He knew he was blushing. "I was a horny teenage boy. It was awesome. I was awesome. Rave reviews. Best twenty-eight seconds ever."

Harper laughed so hard she snorted, then slapped her hands over her face. Dan couldn't resist joining in.

"Okay, your turn. Age. Rating. All the good stuff." Dan pulled out two more pieces.

Harper tried to steady her face, but giggles kept slipping out. "I was eighteen. Big year for me."

"Clearly. So? How was it?"

Harper took a breath and blew it out, still smiling at him. She reached out, grasping his hand in both of hers. He didn't know what she was doing, but he couldn't stop staring at the points where their skin met.

She lifted his hand, looking at it closely. Then, without warning, she jerked it forward, toppling the remaining pieces of the Jenga tower. She laughed even harder.

Dan's jaw hit the floor. He was about to give her hell for

cheating, when a bulky frat guy stumbled into her back, jolting her forward.

"Watch where you're going, man," Dan said, placing a hand on her arm. The guy gave a drunken laugh and turned back to his group.

The brewery was filling up with a rowdier late-night crowd. Dan saw the moment Harper became aware of the swarms of bodies surrounding them. A spark of panic ignited in her eyes as her gaze darted around the room. Her smile dropped and her cheeks lost their rosiness, a light sheen of sweat replacing it almost instantly. He watched as she sucked in a gulp of air that seemed to get stuck in her throat. She tugged at the collar of her scrub top then turned to the table, trying to fix the game with shaky hands. Dan placed his palm on her back.

"Do you want to go outside? Maybe get some air?"

Harper's gaze shot to his and she nodded, panic flooding her features. "Yeah, that sounds good."

They grabbed their coats and Dan maneuvered them through the bar, never taking his hand from Harper's back. He didn't understand why a small tremor hummed through her, or where the panic came from, but he wanted to help relieve it.

When they got outside, Harper stepped away from his touch and leaned against the brick building. She sucked in a huge breath, then another, before closing her eyes against the wind.

Dan stared at her. The tension in her body slowly uncoiled, muscle by muscle, the worried creases between her eyebrows relaxed, and the tight line of her lips eventually softened.

"You okay?" He took a step toward her and her eyes flashed open, landing on him. She gave him a soft smile, slow and sweet like honey. The movement of those full lips captivated him completely.

Something caught her attention, and she pulled her eyes away from him. Looking up, she let out a soft coo of excitement. "It's snowing," she said in hushed awe.

With her head tilted back, she moved away from the wall and turned slowly, watching the flakes fall around them.

Dan's heart gave an uncomfortable squeeze. He felt too much at once. It shouldn't make sense that the sight of her spinning in the snow made him feel like he'd been hit by a truck. It shouldn't feel good to be dizzy with thoughts of her.

But somehow it did—like all the weird turns his life had made were to lead him to this spot on the sidewalk so he could watch Harper drop her guard and enjoy the snow.

He moved toward her and she spun into him, gripping onto his coat for balance. "I love the snow," she said with a serene smile.

"Really? I hadn't noticed."

Dan took her fingers from his coat and chafed them between his palms, trying to warm them. He brought his mouth to their clasped hands and blew hot air against them, enjoying the familiarity of the gesture, the closeness it made him feel to her. He glanced at Harper's face and noticed her parted lips, the reckless glint in her eyes.

"What is it?" he asked into their hands.

"You're dangerous," she said simply.

He cocked his head. "How so?"

She looked at him, her eyes traveling over his face, then slid one of her hands from his grasp and brought her fingertips to his temple. She stared at the spot where she touched him. Harper dragged her fingers down along the angle of his chin, causing his breath to catch.

"You distract me. It's like everything else dissolves away with you," she said, her index finger tracing the shape of his lips. "It's different."

His heart hammered in his chest, threatening to burst out and lay itself at her feet. He wanted to nibble her finger, take it in his mouth and kiss it. Claim it.

"Good different?" He couldn't hide the self-conscious tone of his question, but he darted out his tongue, giving her finger a playful lick. She giggled and wrapped both of her arms around his neck, swaying them from side to side in a rhythmless dance.

"Hmmm, I don't know," she teased, a tipsy smile dancing across her lips.

Dan dropped his forehead to hers. He could smell the beer on her breath and the snow on her skin, all mixing with that sweet, floral musk that was uniquely Harper.

He brought his mouth a whisper from hers, every nerve in his lips hyperaware of the unbearable closeness. "Can I help you figure it out?"

He moved his lips even closer, so close it seemed impossible to hold the distance, the heat between their skin turning to fire. But he wouldn't kiss her on the lips—not yet; he was saving that.

But he'd be damned if he wasn't going to get a taste. He moved his lips to the corner of her smile and pressed them against her, dragging them along the beautiful line of her jaw. His mouth traced the curve of her throat, and he touched his tongue to the spot where her pulse pounded. Harper's breathing hitched and Dan smiled against her.

"Any clarity?" he asked, his lips never leaving her skin.

She swallowed heavily before giving a quick shake of her head.

"No? Let's see."

He repeated the path up the opposite side of her neck, his lips dragging delicately against the softness of her skin. Dan felt Harper arch into him, and when he reached her ear, he gave the small lobe a playful nibble.

"Any closer to figuring it out?" he whispered, placing his hands on her hips and pulling her closer, the pressure of her body driving him wild. She shivered.

"N-no," she said hoarsely. Her chest rose and fell with jagged breaths.

Dan smiled at her effort. He breathed her in once more, then pulled his head away sharply.

"That's a shame," he said, working to hide his smile at the small guttural noise she let out. He moved to disentangle himself from her arms, but Harper clutched at him, stuttering in protest.

Before she could get any words out, a voice cut through their haze.

"There you are," Indira said, stepping out of the brewery. "We called a ride. Are you—" She stopped in her tracks when she saw them, causing Lizzie to run into her. "Oh, sorry. Let's . . . we'll . . ." Indira whipped around blindly and crashed back into Lizzie, who was blatantly staring.

"You go, Dental Dan," Lizzie said in awe as Thu and Alex joined the pack.

Harper dropped her arms and stepped away. Dan fought the instinct to pull her back and tell everyone to fuck off. He liked Harper's friends, he really did, but they were some of his least favorite people in that moment.

Thu eyed them closely. "Fun night?" she asked, the corner of her lip twitching.

"Yep," Harper responded, looking at the ground. "You said you called a ride?"

"Yeah, it's pulling up now," Indira said, eyes bouncing between Harper and Dan.

Harper nodded and moved toward her friends. Dan caught her hand.

"Hey," he said, ducking to meet her eyes. "Thank you."

She blinked up at him, her brow furrowed. "For what? I should thank you. You're the one who bought the drinks."

"For talking to me," he responded, giving her arm a light squeeze. "I'll see you tomorrow."

CHAPTER 13

HARPER

Harper stared at her closet. What the hell did people wear on dates? To a *grocery store*? As Harper flicked her way through her pitiful wardrobe for the sixty-seventh time, she decided she needed to stop messing around and call in a pro. She reached for her phone and FaceTimed Thu. After a few rings, her friend picked up.

"Hey, dude."

"Hey. I may or may not be in panic mode," Harper said, digging through her drawers as she clutched a towel around herself.

"What's wrong?" Thu asked, rifling through her nail polish bottles, only half listening.

"I have no idea what to wear. What does anyone wear when their closet is ninety percent scrubs? Where do people our age even shop for clothes?"

"Dark web mainly." Thu propped her phone against the wall, her attention now fully absorbed in painting her toenails.

"I'm serious! Help meeeee," Harper whined.

"Want to borrow my titty tassels?" Thu asked, not even bothering to look up.

Harper sighed. "You're useless. Bye."

"Sorry, sorry." Thu looked at the camera. "Let's decide on a vibe. Tell me what you're going for."

Harper chewed on her bottom lip. "I don't know. Is dental-student chic a vibe?"

"No. That's an oxymoron."

Harper started slowly banging her head against her closet door. She felt nervous and queasy and was about three minutes away from canceling the whole thing.

Last night had been . . . a lot. She didn't know how she was expected to see Dan two days in a row and survive it. Plus, she'd been so keyed up by the time she got home that she hadn't made a dent in her reading for class . . . Maybe canceling would be for the best.

That chronic nervousness hummed just below her skin, always tempting her to stay home, bury herself in work, maintain impenetrable control of her small world. For Harper, control was always the winning choice over the unknown.

"Harps, you're making this way too hard. What would you wear to brunch? Or out to dinner with us?"

"I don't know. Leggings?" Harper couldn't remember the last time she'd put conscious thought into an outfit. Wearing scrubs every day to school made it easy to forget that actual cute human clothes were a thing.

"Great. Wear leggings." Thu's attention returned to painting.

"All my leggings are dirty or have a hole in the crotch."

Thu snorted. "Even better. Easy access for Dental Dan."

Harper chose to ignore that one, feeling like they were making progress. Maybe she could do this. "I could wear black underwear to blend over the hole? I'd have panty lines but—"

Thu's eyes whipped to the phone screen with an appalled look.

"Harper Hannah Horowitz, you are not this clueless. You're a big girl who knows better than to wear leggings with holes, never mind *panty lines*"—she shuddered—"on a first date. Use your giant genius brain and wear a normal outfit," she said, pointing at the camera.

"Squeeze that hot piece of ass into a pair of skinny jeans, put on a bra that pushes your titties up to your neck, find a T-shirt—preferably a dark one because you get sweaty when you're nervous—and finish it with that biker jacket you stole from me. Then go and take about six shots of whatever alcohol you have and calm the fuck down," Thu said, glaring at Harper for a solid minute before returning to her toes.

Harper glanced at the time and realized she only had fifteen minutes to finish getting ready. Her stomach squeezed and fluttered. Butterflies didn't do it justice; it was more like a giant hawk flapping around in there.

"Thanks, Thu-Thu, you're the best. I'll call you later."

"Wear a condom. Make good choices. Don't be afraid to live tweet this."

Harper ended the call and hoisted a dark pair of jeans over her clammy thighs, then opted for a slightly more sensible bra than Thu suggested. She finished pulling on her shoes when the intercom buzzed. She answered it in about 0.004 seconds.

So chill.

"Hello?"

"Hey, it's Dan. Ready Freddy?"

Harper let out a fangirl-like sigh and rested her forehead on the door. He was so *cool.*

"Be right down," she said into the intercom, praying her voice crack wouldn't be noticeable on his end. Every inch of her skin tickled, and her fingers felt jumpy with nerves. She tried gulping in a few deep breaths and ended up doubling over, violently choking on air and spit.

Judy made a soft mewling sound at Harper's feet, and Harper gave the cat's chin a scratch.

"Hi, sweet-precious-angel-baby. This might be goodbye, because mommy is likely going to die of a heart attack tonight due to a boy with one dimple who makes her brain sludgy."

Judy tilted her head.

"And the scariest part is," Harper continued, "I kind of like it. I'm so screwed."

Judy gave a graceless flop to her side to expose her giant belly.

Harper sighed. "Good talk, Judy."

She took one more deep breath and headed out the door.

There was no hiding the smile that pushed itself across her cheeks when she saw Dan leaning on the railing outside of her front door. The sharpness of her nerves morphed into a fuzzy sort of excitement.

As she stepped outside, he smiled too. A huge, unabashed grin pointed directly at her in a way that made warmth flood her chest.

"Hi," she said, and raised her hand in an awkward flappy wave.

"Hi," he said back, mimicking the gesture. She watched his eyes travel the length of her body. "You're wearing clothes." He sounded surprised.

Harper's eyes shot down herself. This was . . . true? She gave him a questioning look. "It's a little cold to go without . . ." A gust of wind whipped at her hair as if to prove her point.

"Yes—sorry—that was a weird way of saying it. I realized I've only ever seen you in scrubs."

She let out a too-loud laugh and tugged at her hair. "Should I change?"

"No! Sorry." Dan rubbed a hand over his eyes and groaned. "Wow. I'm bad at this. This is me trying to tell you that you look really nice." He shot her a goofy grin that squeezed her heart.

He leaned in close to her ear and said, in a stage whisper, "Next, I'll show you how I can fit *both* of my feet into my mouth . . . at the same time."

Harper let out a burst of laughter. The fact that she wasn't alone in her obnoxious twist of nerves helped settle her churning stomach. Kind of.

They started walking.

"So where do you grocery shop?" he asked.

"It's a toss-up between the overpriced co-op and the world's jankiest Fresh Grocer." She waggled her eyebrows at him. "Take your pick."

"As much as I'd like to spoil you with expensive produce, an extra-janky Fresh Grocer sounds way more fun."

Harper stopped and put a hand on his arm, stopping him in his tracks. "I hope you're not implying you're buying my groceries."

He smiled down at her. "I'm not implying anything. I'm stating a fact," he said, and continued walking.

"Um, no." She did an awkward little half jog to catch up with his long stride.

He shrugged. "We'll see."

"Yeah, we will," she said sternly.

He shot her a wink and her knees turned watery.

"What did you do today?" Dan asked, placing a guiding hand on her back as they crossed the street. The soft gesture made happiness purr through her, reminding her lonely body of the incomparable comfort of simple human touch, and how long she'd been deprived of it.

"Let's see," she said, missing his hand when he pulled it away, "I went to the gym for a quick two-hour workout, then got breakfast with an old friend. Afterward, we went to the art museum and discussed the merits of impressionism, then finished off with ice-skating at City Hall. I had just pulled out some homemade cookies before you picked me up."

Dan shot her a look. "Really?"

"No. I stayed in my pajamas and studied all day." Harper was rewarded with the richness of his laugh, like hot chocolate warming her insides.

"Ah, so you live up to your nonstop studying reputation?"

Harper shrugged. "I do other stuff too."

"Like what?"

"Like getting tricked into seeing a guy at a bar, or being talked into dates at grocery stores." She shot him a teasing smile.

Dan fumbled for words, and Harper decided she liked watching him squirm.

"The thing last night was not my idea," he said, a blush forming on his cheeks. "Thu orchestrated that, telling Alex what a good idea it was. By the time she was done working her magic, he and I both thought it was the best plan we'd ever heard." He jammed his hands into his pockets and Harper wanted to reach in and thread her fingers through his. "I'm sorry. I hope . . . I don't know, I hope I didn't cross a line with that."

"Hey," she said, tilting her head to meet his eyes, "don't ever tell Thu this, but I'm glad she's so sneaky."

"Yeah?"

"Yeah. Otherwise, I might never have known how good I am at Jenga."

Dan laughed again and reached an arm around her shoulder, giving her a light squeeze that flooded Harper with warmth and want.

He unhooked his arm as they entered the grocery store, and they searched through the carts for two that had all four wheels attached. The store was undeniably grimy, but the food was cheap, and when every dollar in your bank account technically belonged to the government via student loans, there was little room to complain.

"So, what's first on your list?" Dan asked as they moved through the store.

"I'm a big fan of snacks," Harper said, gesturing toward the bright boxes of processed foods filling the first aisle they turned down. "I try to let the junk food speak to me, not the other way around." She tossed a box of crackers into her cart.

"And what does the junk food say?"

She picked up a package of Oreos and held them in front of her mouth. "It says, 'Pick me, Harper. I'll make you feel so good. You'll love the way I taste.'"

Dan's eyes flew open and Harper cringed. She'd meant for it to sound goofy. It objectively did *not*.

"Do all of your snacks talk dirty to you?" Amusement danced across his stupid gorgeous face.

Oh God, not the dimple.

"Just the Oreos," she said, turning away from that lopsided smile before she licked it off him. "They're the sluts of the cupboard. It's a well-known fact."

Dan laughed, and they continued to weave through the aisles. The universal awkward silence of two nervous people swelled between them, and Harper scrambled for a topic.

"So . . . how was school this week?" *Wow. Scintillating.*

Dan gave a noncommittal shrug. "This week was better than most, I'd say."

"Yeah? Why's that?"

Dan didn't say anything. His eyes locked with hers for a long, meaningful pause before sweeping down her body, and back to her face. He raised his eyebrows, the light in his eyes doing strange things to her heart.

Time paused with his look. Her mouth went dry, her limbs heavy with the need to move closer to him. In that space between seconds, she wanted to run her fingers through his hair and press her hands against his chest while dragging her lips along his jaw. She'd never had such a desperate physical reaction to someone in her life. It was terrifying to feel so out of control. But in that moment, Harper kind of loved it.

Before she could give in and bridge the distance between them, a woman pushed a screaming child into the aisle, talking into her cell phone over the wailing. Time began ticking again.

Harper pushed her cart into the next aisle without waiting, working to remove the cotton from her head and regain normal function in her hands and feet. She tried to suck in a few steadying breaths. It didn't help.

"I heard something about you the other day," Dan said, rolling his cart next to hers.

She squinted one eye at him. "Uh-oh. What was it?"

"I heard a rumor you're top of your class."

Harper let out an internal sigh of relief. Good. Back to school. School was easy. School was a safe topic of conversation that didn't make Harper want to rip Dan's shirt from his body.

She gave a mock gasp and slapped a hand to her chest. "How scandalous. People and their gossip these days. I hope you don't think less of me."

"No, now it's just confirmed that you're a genius," Dan responded, grabbing a packet of napkins and throwing them into his cart.

Harper turned to him, rolling her eyes. "I'm not a genius, I'm hardworking. There's a difference," she said, picking up some cheap paper towels. "And I'm not sure I'm top. I'm kind of battling it out right now."

"Yeah?" he asked. "Who's the poor soul?"

"Have you heard of the Giles family? I think there's one in your class. But the oldest one, *Jeffery*—never Jeff—and I are pretty neck and neck. He's gunning for oral surgery too."

Dan came to a halt and whipped around to face her.

"Harper." His eyes locked on hers as he gripped her by the shoulders. "I *hate* those guys," he said, giving her shoulders a squeeze that traveled down her whole body.

Touch. Touch. Touch.

"Hate isn't even a strong enough word," Dan continued. "They're the *worst*."

Harper's eyes almost rolled back in her head. Was anything hotter and more validating than hating the same people?

A quick glance at his forearms on either side of her pushed mutual hate to a close second. She considered warning him to rein in the sex appeal, because he was one dimple-flash away from Harper pushing him up against the paper towel stacks and climbing him like a tree.

"They suck," Harper said. "They're legacies too, which makes them even worse. They flaunt it like some badge of honor—I mean, at least have a little class and *pretend* to be humble. They act like it's their right to be a doctor and not a privilege. I could write my entire dissertation on the corruption of that family. The dean even takes them all *golfing*. Does it get any more patriarchal dick-rubbing than that? All the legacies are privileged pieces of shit."

"Yeah, that's . . . wild," Dan said, dropping his hands and looking away, a weird tension snaking across his shoulders.

"Do you think you'll beat him?" he asked after a moment. His eyes returned to her and lingered on her mouth. She instinctively licked her lips.

"I hope so. It would bring him down a notch. At the end of the day, matching into residency is obviously more important than where I rank, but it would feel so good to beat him. And when I get in my uber-competitive mode, it kind of fuels that fire."

"What does uber-competitive Harper look like?"

"Scary," she said with a smile. She liked it when he teased her. "If competitiveness was a competition, I'd have a competitive advantage."

He let out a gravelly laugh that pebbled her skin.

"Is it just with school?"

"Ha. No. It's with everything. My friends banned me from watching the Olympics last year because I kept challenging them to different events. It's a very real problem."

Dan absentmindedly pushed and pulled his cart with his foot while he watched her, and the flex of his lean muscles beneath his jeans made her want to bite his thigh.

"So if I asked you to race, would you do it?"

Her head jerked back. "Like, around a track?" She looked again at his long legs and pictured them flexing and stretching in a run. She imagined them, toned and lean, in a pair of athletic shorts (maybe even a nice dusting of leg hair?), the loose fabric of the shorts allowing everything to bounce and—

He asked you a question, pig.

Harper cleared her throat. "I have to take about eight steps to match one of yours. I'm competitive, not stupid."

"No." He shot her a challenging smile. "Here. With the carts."

"What? In the grocery store?" She snorted out a laugh, and a boyish grin stretched across his face.

"Why not? The aisle is wide enough for both of us and completely empty. We haven't seen anyone for at least five minutes." He leaned in with a wolfish smile. "First one to the end?"

She stared at him, her smile falling when she realized he was serious. "We can't. We'll get in trouble." Despite her words, the impulse to accept the challenge burned through her.

"Scared of being banished from this beautiful Fresh Grocer?" Dan said, looking at a spot near Harper's feet where a tangle of knotted hairnets, mixed with chunks of grocery store debris, sat like a disturbing tumbleweed.

"I wouldn't call that a tragedy . . ." she mumbled, trying to kick away the pile and getting it caught on her shoe. "What's the prize?

"If you win, I'll let you take me on a second date."

She barked out a laugh. "And if I lose?"

"You let me buy your groceries. Without," he cut her off as she opened her mouth to protest, "putting up a fight."

"Shut up. I can't let you do that."

"So you know I'll win?"

Dan was the worst kind of evil. The adorable kind.

"Wow. This is quite the trap." She tapped a finger on her chin, eyeing him closely.

He shrugged, holding that maddening smile. She looked at the carts and down the aisle, playing out different scenarios and weighing her chances. She had an idea.

"You're on."

Dan's mouth opened in a surprised grin.

"But here are the rules," she said. "You only get three strides to push off and then you have to hop on and keep control of the cart. If you hit the shelves, you lose."

"Deal," he said, reaching out a hand. They shook on it.

They grabbed their carts and backed up a few paces to the start of the aisle, locking eyes. Sharp energy crackled between them, and her palms started to sweat.

As he narrowed his eyes and sized her up, the ridiculousness of it filled her with a bubblegum-pink joy that she hadn't felt in years.

"I'll even let you count us down," Dan said with a wicked grin.

"And who says chivalry is dead?"

She took a deep, steadying breath. "On your marks." She planted her right foot behind her and grounded it against the linoleum for grip.

"Get set." She adjusted her hands on her cart.

"Go!" She pushed off with all her strength, stretching her short legs to their maximum stride for three pushes before hopping onto the cart. As she'd anticipated, Dan's longer legs had given him an advantage.

The nose of his cart was a few inches ahead of hers, as she'd predicted, putting him in the perfect position for her to move in for the kill. She shifted her weight to one side, making the front of her cart veer toward his. Dan's head shot to look at her the moment before impact, and she saw the fear. She could almost smell it.

BAM.

Her cart jammed into the side of his, causing its wheels to jut off course, and he rammed into the shelf with a bang.

The crash threw Dan's equilibrium off-kilter, and he flew into a pyramid of paper towels displayed off the shelves.

Harper, on the other hand, quickly righted her weight and centered herself in the lane, gliding gracefully across the finish line. A ridiculous amount of pride swelled in her chest.

She hopped off the edge of her cart with a flourish and bounced on her toes. Dan was still laying in the rubble of the paper towel heap, and she waited for him to get up.

"I won," she preened.

Dan didn't move.

"You were a fierce competitor though," she called down the aisle.

Still nothing.

With a pang of panic, she hurried to the site of the collision, hovering over his still body, her palms clenching and unclenching as she waited for him to move. His eyes were closed and his legs were bent at odd angles beneath him.

"Dan?" Harper's voice was an octave too high. "You okay?"

She reached out to press a finger to his pulse, wanting to avoid moving him too much if he was hurt. Harper almost made contact with his skin when his eyes flashed open.

He grabbed her outstretched hand and pulled her down on top of him. She let out a shriek of surprise as she collapsed against his chest and the cushy paper towels.

"You play so dirty!" he said, tickling her sides. She squealed, trying to squirm out of his strong grip.

"No I don't!" She pushed against him. "There was nothing in the bylaws about physical contact! I won fair and square."

"And risked my life and limb to do so," Dan said with a noise somewhere between a laugh and a growl that sent an effervescent burst through Harper's body. "You could have killed me. I could be *dead*, Harper."

Harper let out a gasp as his tickling doubled in effort. "I think you're being a bit ridiculous," she choked out.

She nuzzled her face closer to the crook between his arm and chest.

To protect her chin from tickles. Obviously.

"*I'm* ridiculous?" He jolted them both up to sitting with ease, holding her in his lap, his arms wrapped loosely around her. "You just Tonya Harding–ed me in a shopping cart race, but *I'm* ridiculous?"

They both shook with laughter, and their eyes locked in a moment of sharp intimacy. He flashed a devastating smile, and Harper had to remind herself how to breathe. It felt like her heart was expanding in her chest, wanting to pop free from her rib cage and knock at his, hoping for company.

Dan's fingers traced up her arm, leaving scorched nerves along their path. He settled his palm at the angle of her jaw and let it linger. Waiting.

The moment felt like a beginning or an end, and it was up to Harper to decide. She felt poised on the brink of a huge precipice that she could either fling herself off or retreat from to the safety of solid ground.

It would be so easy, so natural, to lean forward and press her mouth to Dan's, morphing the unspoken possibilities into reality. It would feel so undeniably *good* to give up overthinking fear and embrace pure want instead.

But the rational part of her brain—the louder, stronger, anxious part—scolded her emotions into submission. This wasn't the way you stayed safe and whole. She didn't even know where she'd be living in a few months, but she knew it wouldn't be here. It could be on the other side of the country, for all she knew. Her time with Dan had an expiration date before it even started, and the pleasure of recklessness wouldn't soothe the hurt of an inevitable broken heart. Harper had long ago made the executive decision that she'd dealt with enough pain in her childhood and wouldn't willingly subject herself to any more.

"We should clean this up," she whispered hoarsely, pulling her head back a fraction. She didn't miss the disappointment that flickered in Dan's eyes, but he quickly replaced it with a smile.

"You want *me* to help you clean up *your* crime scene?" He slid her off his lap and she tamped down the urge to cling to him like a needy toddler.

They restored the display pyramid to the best of their abilities and finished shopping with awkward small talk and long silences.

At the checkout counter, Dan pulled out his wallet at the same time Harper reached for hers.

"Nuh-uh, no way," she said, waving at his hand. "A deal is a deal. You lost." She fumbled to pull her credit card out of its pocket, and he gave her a bemused smile.

"Don't worry, Harper, I'll still honor your rights to a second date," he said with a wink, sliding his card out smoothly and moving to put it in the chip reader.

"Stop it," Harper said, giving up on her wallet and wrapping both of her hands around his wrist, tugging at it sharply. His arm jerked into a stack of coupons sitting on the counter and sent them flying. The checkout clerk let out a dull sigh.

Harper shot the woman an apologetic smile, which turned into a gape when Dan easily pulled against Harper's grip, lifting her clutched arms up as he inserted the card.

"I can buy my own groceries. I'm . . . I'm a feminist," she said weakly, watching the receipt print out. "Independent."

"I know you are," he said with a smile. "But—also as a feminist—I can buy your groceries too. Now let's go, you're making a scene." He grabbed the grocery bags in one hand and laced his fingers through Harper's with the other, leading them out of the store.

CHAPTER 14

DAN

"Do you have anything particularly perishable?" Dan asked as they walked along the darkening streets. "If not, maybe we could get coffee?" He pointed his chin toward a café a few stores down, still holding Harper's hand. He had no intention of letting it go.

She looked up at him with a sweet smile. "Coffee sounds good." Harper studied him and Dan saw a new openness in the way her eyes met his.

As if noticing it for herself, she looked away and dropped his hand, running her fingers through her hair and giving it a gentle tug before tucking a lock behind her ear.

Dan tamped down the pang of disappointment. He could be patient. He'd wait however long it took for her to let him in, brick by brick.

They stepped into the warm café. Mismatched furniture filled the space, art lining every inch of the walls. Shelves and cabinets sat in the corners, overflowing with books and board games, discarded pieces littering the tables throughout the shop.

After ordering their coffees, they chose a table near the front window and sat in happy quietness, sipping their drinks and watching people pass in the December chill.

A pile of checkers and poker chips were stacked on the table, and Dan watched Harper's hands as she fiddled with the pieces, running her nail over their edges and turning them between each finger. He wanted to map the strong tendons and blue veins that stood out against her skin, trace her angular knuckles, and entwine her long, nimble fingers with his own.

Her hands were always moving, taking every opportunity to flex and stretch. It was like she discovered the world around her by using her hands, every touch allowing her to find the nuances of her environment, flitting along with a delicate grace as she explored hidden patterns she seemed to sense before she saw.

He loved watching her hands.

She wrapped them around her coffee cup and brought it to her lips.

"What are you staring at?" she asked over the rim.

Dan's attention snapped to Harper's face.

"Your hands," he admitted with a sheepish grin.

Her eyebrows lifted behind her bangs. "My hands?"

"I like watching them explore. They're fascinating."

She gave him an incredulous frown that made him laugh.

"They are! Your hands are beautiful. I mean . . . all of you is beautiful," Dan's heart beat up into his throat as the words spilled out. "But I'm admiring your hands in particular tonight." He ducked his head, worried that he'd said too much.

But holding back that simple truth would be like denying the sky was blue or grass was green. She was beautiful and she should know it.

Harper let out an embarrassed snort of laughter and clapped a hand over her eyes. Adorable dimples wrinkled her chin as she tried to suppress a smile, and Dan tried and failed to hold back a laugh.

"I. Hate. You," she said, her hand still covering half her face as the smile won out.

"Why's that?" he asked, tugging at her wrist. She kept it firmly in place.

"Because you're a terror. An absolute terror."

"What? How?"

With a long, defeated sigh, Harper propped her elbow on the table, careful to keep her eyes shielded. "You make me so nervous, and I don't know how to deal with it. Not looking at you helps," she said, gesturing at herself with her free hand. "I let myself relax for one tiny second and think that any of this can actually feel normal, then you do something absurd like smile or call me beautiful and it's like . . ." She pressed her lips together like she was about to reveal something too honest.

"Like what?" he asked, his hand circling her wrist and running a coaxing thumb over the back of her hand.

She let him pull her hand away and fixed him with her gaze, searching his face. Harper opened her mouth to speak, but closed it and shook her head with a smile.

"Nervous," she finally said, letting him know he wouldn't get anything further. "You make me nervous."

Dan wanted to pull the unspoken words from her—wanted confirmation that he wasn't the only one drowning in this tidal wave of feeling.

But instead he sat there and sipped his coffee, letting her lead them.

Her hands returned to play with the checker pieces and Dan watched her body relax a fraction.

"Talk to me about school," Dan said, handing her a few stray checkers to add to the tower she was building. Harper looked at the pieces and smiled.

"What do you want to know?"

"What are your plans after graduation? You want to do surgery, right?"

Her eyes sparked with excitement, and tenderness flooded his chest. He was so undeniably fucked.

"Surgery all the way," she said, relaxing back into her seat and smiling as she looked back out the window. "I applied to a bunch of residency programs—New York, California, Texas—and I'm waiting to hear if I matched into any of them. If I don't get accepted, I'll do a surgical internship or something like that. I'll know one way or another in a few weeks."

Those places were . . . not exactly close.

"Do you have a top choice?"

She nodded, their eyes meeting in the reflection of the window. "Dwyer's Hospital in New York."

"Why there?"

"It's a level-one trauma center with complex cases, and I'd work holistically with other surgery specialists on bigger ones. With oral surgery, it's so much more than pulling teeth. Reconstructions, cancer treatments, transplants, it's endless." She turned away from the window to look directly at him, her eyes holding an excited wildness that Dan wanted to drown in.

Her passion was intoxicating. He almost envied her for it. Dan had felt something close to it, but when he'd shared his ambitions with his parents, telling them he was backing out of his original Callowhill acceptance and taking the position in New York, his father had all but backhanded him, cutting him with a slew of belittlements over what a stain he was to all that they'd worked for until Dan wanted to drown in his overwhelming shame. His mom had stared quietly down at the floor.

"When I talked to the current residents at the interview, they told me about the incredible cases they saw right from the start," Harper continued. "One guy said he scrubbed in on a facial reconstruction for a gunshot wound his first night on call. It's extraordinary to have opportunities like that."

"So you're a fan of the gore?" Dan asked. He'd never seen someone smile so radiantly over a bullet to the face.

"Love it. The more the better," she said over the rim of her coffee cup before taking another sip. "I feel like it's how I'll know

I'm really helping someone. Doing something that can save their life or change it so drastically . . . it's an amazing privilege."

"Why oral surgery?" Dan asked.

Harper's mouth twisted. "I just told you."

"No, I mean why *oral* surgery? Why not neurosurgery or cardiology or any other type of surgery?"

The change was instant. Dan watched the blinds close over her eyes and her arms cross over her chest. She gave him a stiff smile.

"I guess I just really love teeth," she said, not meeting his gaze.

Dan gave a noncommittal hum as he sipped at his coffee. He wanted to press her for more. He wanted to dig, find the source of the sudden change and ask her about it, get every detail from it. Knowing that wasn't an option, he studied her, tracing her features for anything they could reveal.

After a moment, Harper brought herself to look at him, peeking through the blinds and deciding how much he could be trusted to know. Something softened in her expression as she landed on some piece she could offer.

"I guess more than anything, trauma to the head and neck can change so much of a person's life. Whether it's pain from an impacted tooth, or trauma from a car accident, or even physical abuse—these patients will wear their experience on their faces forever," she said, her eyes going somewhere far away again. "I won't be able to take away the pain of their experience, but I can put care and compassion into every suture, work to minimize every scar, allow people to get back to feeling normal."

Harper stared out the window for so long, Dan assumed she wouldn't say anything more. But, in a whisper more for herself than for him, she added, "I want to make a difference."

It was in that moment Dan knew he'd never deserve her, but he wanted to spend every day telling her how much of a difference her existence made.

Silence curled around them and Dan let it linger. He liked their ability to be quiet together. Everything about his reaction to Harper was new and disarming. Like being punched in the gut and grabbed by the throat, forced to stare into something beautiful and terrifying.

Harper gave him a self-conscious look, and he wanted to wrap her in his arms and protect that passionate flame that burned so brightly inside of her. He couldn't help but reach across the table and place his hand over hers.

Harper looked at their hands and smiled—a beautiful, happy grin that made it hard for him to swallow. Their eyes met for an effervescent second and then her brow furrowed. She gently pulled her hand from his and glanced at her watch.

"I'm sorry, I'm blabbing on and on," she said, not looking at him. "I should probably get going, though. I still have to study tonight."

Dan deflated at the looming goodbye, but nodded in agreement, knowing he had to try to cram in some pointless late-night studying too.

"I'll walk you home," he said as they stood, and he helped her into her coat.

∽

The walk to her apartment was freezing, the wind whipping their faces and leaving a bone-deep chill.

Harper brought her fingers up to her lips and blew into them a few times for warmth before giving up and shoving them into her coat pockets. Holding the grocery bags in one hand, Dan reached out the other arm and circled it around her shoulders, tucking her into his side.

When they got to her place, Harper untangled herself from his arm and ran up her stoop, jamming her key into the lock with record speed. She ushered Dan inside, and they crashed into the foyer, gulping down warmer air.

Her hair was a wild mass of waves from the wind, cheeks bright red from the cold, and Dan resisted the urge to lean forward and kiss the tip of her pink nose.

Tension pumped around them as they defrosted, and questions whirled through Dan's mind. Would she invite him up? Would they make plans to see each other again? Would he finally be able to kiss her delicious red lips and bring a physical form to the connection he felt for her?

Harper looked at him and audibly swallowed. Her eyes were filled with fear and fire that set his heart hammering.

"Well," she said, bouncing on her toes. "This was fun."

Dan chuckled. This was the best day he'd had in months.

"Yeah, fun," he said, taking a step toward her.

"And thank you, again, for the groceries." She wouldn't meet his eyes.

"My pleasure," he murmured, taking one more step and coming toe-to-toe with her. He set the bags on either side of her feet.

All coldness had left the small space. There was nothing but heat radiating between their bodies, fueled by their rapid, humid breaths. Their chests were rising and falling sharply, creating the whisper of a touch with each inhale.

Dan wanted to close the distance, broach the centimeters that separated their bodies. Touch and grab and hold every inch of her.

The urge was so far beyond lust.

It was the simple, primitive need to feel connected.

Something deep within him recognized a matching piece in Harper. He knew the moment his lips touched hers, that piece would pivot from searching to found.

He lifted his hand and cupped her jaw, rubbing his thumb across her soft skin. He felt her tense for a moment before relaxing and pressing lightly against his palm. He let his fingers trail down her throat and rest on her shoulder as he looked into the bottomless depths of her near-black eyes before closing his. He pushed forward.

Where his lips should have felt the soft lusciousness of hers, there was . . . nothing.

He blinked open his eyes.

She'd pulled her head back.

Holyfuck. Holyfuck. Holyfuck.

He had misread this.

Holy. Fuck.

He had no idea what to do. His neck snapped back, and his spine went ramrod straight as he took a giant step away from her.

"I'm so sorry," he said, embarrassment pounding through him.

He'd been so sure she felt the connection too.

Harper reached out and grabbed his coat collar, panic in her own eyes. As she registered what she was doing, she dropped her grip like she'd been burned. She buried her head in her hands and let out a long groan.

"It's not you," she said, the words muffled by her hands. "Please, please, *please* don't be sorry. I-I wanted you to kiss me . . ."

Dan stared at her, waiting for more of an explanation.

"*But?*" he finally prompted.

She sighed and looked at the ceiling, knotting her hands in her hair, as her words tumbled out in a rush. "But I know that if you kiss me, I'll want more than that, and I can't do more than a kiss. I can't do any of this right now."

There was a heavy, silent pause.

Dan opened his mouth, choosing his words carefully. "Harper, I'm not expecting you to have sex with me, if that's what you think any of this means. I hope you know I would never assume that of you."

She snapped her gaze to his, and her face flushed crimson.

"No! No. I know that's not what you mean by any of . . . this. That's not what I'm trying—I mean, if only it were as simple as us just having sex."

Dan's eyebrows flew up.

"Fuck! I'm messing this up," she said, tugging at her hair. "What I'm trying to say—I guess I mean." She took a deep breath and closed her eyes. "I'm trying to say that I like you. And if you kiss me, I'll want more. I'll want more dates and more kisses and more time with you and I can't do that right now . . . Not at this point in my life."

He stared at her. He'd be more than happy to give her all those wants ten times over. "Why?"

Her face was pained as she chewed on her lip. "Because none of the programs I applied to are in Philly, which means I'll be leaving in May. And maybe that seems far off to you, but I can't have these distractions, and neglect everything I've been working toward, for this to end in a goodbye in five months."

Dan felt her words sink into his skin. It wasn't the idea of Harper moving or the distance that would separate them that scared him. She could tell him she was moving to China and he would walk, run, or swim to see her as often as he could. Miles were a minor barrier to be with a person like her. It was the fact that she assumed five months would end in goodbye.

"I can't lose sight of what I've been doing all this for. I just can't," she continued. "You've been jumbling my mind and taking up all my thoughts and now, more than ever, I need to keep a clear head and my eyes on the prize." Harper looked at him, eyes tinged with sadness. "I have to follow this path I've created for myself—it's not something I expect most people to get, but it's something I have to do. And avoiding distractions is the only way to do it."

A distraction.

Dan would admit that the title stung. He didn't want to be

a distraction. He wanted to be a cheerleader. A stress reliever. A laugh. A kiss . . . He wanted to support her.

Harper took a shaky breath but met his eyes with resolve. "I think we should just be . . . friends."

And there it was.

"Friends." Dan repeated the word slowly and with a grimace. It left a bad taste in his mouth, and he wanted to remove the word from their vocabulary.

But Dan could still reach into some small, logical corner of his brain that wasn't plastered floor to ceiling with thoughts of Harper and reason how difficult the situation must be for her, that she needed to do what she thought was right. Her walls were steel-enforced, and her resolve just as strong. Dan could either walk away or stand at the perimeter, as close as she would let him.

Any Harper was better than no Harper.

"Of course we can be friends. I would love to be your friend," he said.

She looked at him warily before offering a sad smile. "Really?" she asked, picking up her foot and giving his shin an awkward nudge. Dan returned the gesture with his own foot.

"Really," he said. And he meant it. "But is there any chance you are referring to the type of friends that also make out occasionally?"

She let out a bark of a laugh. "No. I don't kiss my . . ." She waved a searching hand.

"Friends?" he added smoothly. Harper bobbed her head nervously, lips pressed into a thin line.

"Harper?" he said after a moment.

"Hmmm?" she hummed, her eyes dancing around him. He took a step toward her.

"I'm going to be the best *friend* you've ever had." He gently pinched her chin and brought her eyes to meet his. They were filled with hunger and conflict.

"Thu might have something to say about that," she said in a breathy whisper.

Dan let out a soft laugh. "No doubt, but I'm up for the challenge."

They stared at each other for a long moment, both on the verge of giving in to what they craved.

But Dan wouldn't push her.

He wanted whatever parts of Harper she was willing to give him, and he wouldn't be greedy and demand more.

But the urge to lay his mouth on hers, even for a moment, was too strong to deny. He had to give in, just this once.

He moved in slowly and pressed his lips against her forehead in a featherlight touch. The simple press of her soft skin against his lips sighed through his body. It soothed the ache in his chest. Calmed the fire in his veins. He lingered, for only a second, before whispering, "Good night . . . friend," then pulled away from her and reached for the door.

"Is that how you say goodbye to all your friends?" Harper called after him, her voice slightly hoarse.

He shot her a cocky grin over his shoulder but pushed the door open and kept walking. "It is now," he said back.

CHAPTER 15

HARPER

About a week later, Harper and Dan sat on her couch while a movie played on the TV.

Because that's what friends did.

They sat stiffly on a couch.

Pretending to watch a movie.

While making sure to keep a solid six inches of friend-zone space between their bodies.

Meanwhile, Sexual Tension had invited herself over and squeezed in between them, laying an inappropriate hand on Harper's thigh and giving it periodic squeezes that sent butterflies much lower than her stomach. It was the sickest form of torture.

Want coursed through Harper, drying her throat and making her skin buzz. She ground her teeth together and squirmed on the couch, trying to ease the aching tension that was building through her. She looked at Dan from the corner of her eye, and wondered how the hell he looked so cool, so *calm*, when her body was about to implode in a lusty rampage.

She hated him for it.

A raw wildness was working its way to the surface of her skin, and she was helpless to do anything but give in to the torment, feeling like it had the power to break her bones.

While Dan sat there.

Staring blankly at the TV.

She let her head drop onto the back of the couch and worked to keep her breathing under control. As Harper walked herself through a mental cold shower (even in the coldest shower, Dan's body was there to distract her), she saw his hand twitch. She wanted to cry out in relief. It was the first sign of life in what felt like hours. Harper held her breath.

His fingers twitched again.

Facing straight ahead, pretending to be engrossed with whatever was happening on the screen, every cell in her body pivoted its attention to the spot where his hand lay between them.

In the subtlest of movements, one that Harper couldn't even trust to be real it was so small, his hand seemed to move closer to hers.

Her body reacted as though he'd raked his teeth over her inner thighs. Liquid heat flooded through her, pooling low in her belly, pangs of anticipation unfurling across her body. She felt fevered and overwhelmed; the drumbeat of her pulse threatened to crack open her chest.

His hand continued to slide closer, moving at a glacial pace. Harper wanted to claw at his hand. Place it on her body. She wanted to destroy any space that still sat between them.

But she couldn't do anything but sit.

And watch.

And wait.

Every minuscule extension of his arm promising to soothe the fire licking at her skin, calm the pleasure-pain that was radiating through her.

His hand was so close, she could feel the heat of it rolling off his skin and crashing against hers, causing her nerves to riot violently for more. Her body hummed with frantic anticipation.

If he'd do it—if he'd touch her—maybe she would be okay.

Maybe she wouldn't lose her mind and crack her body from the need that held every muscle locked in place.

Her face wasn't directed at the TV anymore. All her attention, every ounce of focus, was locked on that hand. Her heart was squeezing so tightly she worried what would happen if he withheld his touch any longer.

Slowly, so slowly she thought she might scream, she watched as Dan extended one long, beautiful finger. No movement had ever seemed so important as watching the tip of it hover right above her outstretched palm, greedy and waiting. He pressed the pad of it to her and dragged it across her palm.

Harper.

Lost.

Control.

His touch hadn't healed her aches like she'd desperately needed it to; it had only made them worse.

She flung her body at him, any gentleness lost in the all-consuming need for more. She was drowning in it, and she needed the feel of him to keep her afloat. Her legs wrapped around him and she pressed herself into his lap, grinding every inch of her body against his. She needed pressure.

And contact.

And more.

More.

She knotted her fingers in his hair, the soft locks like flames licking her hands. She wanted to burn.

Dan's chest was heaving against hers in violent, racking breaths.

"What are you doing?" he whispered hoarsely, before dragging his teeth down the column of her throat. She groaned.

"I don't want to be your friend. I don't want to be your friend." The words came out strangled and broken as she repeated them over and over. Every admission brought her exquisite pleasure, releasing her body from a cage of her own making. They were a blur of torn clothes and gripped flesh, the feel of skin on skin making them both sigh in relief. Through it all, she repeated the words until they were nothing but unintelligible gasps.

Finally receiving the connection she was rabid for, her eyes locked on Dan's. For one breathless moment, there was no hurt or angst or worry.

Only them.

He opened his mouth to speak. "Harper, I—"

BEEP. BEEP. BEEP.

Harper's eyes snapped open and she jolted up in bed.

She was panting, sweaty, and confused as her bedroom came into focus. Her carefully organized desk in one corner, Judy perched on the windowsill in another. Her bed and the mocking light of dawn surrounded her as the dream went fuzzy at the edges.

As her pulse settled back to sustainable, reality dropped coldly around her. Not only did Dan fill her every waking thought, he also infiltrated her dreams on a regular basis and set her off like a horny prisoner at a conjugal visit.

She hurled her body back against the bed and turned to her pillow, letting out a raspy groan of frustration. Her alarm still blared on her nightstand, and she fumbled blindly to turn it off, groggy from her too-few hours of sleep.

She'd stayed up way too late—again—texting Dan into the dark hours of the night, where the things said didn't feel real or permanent, little messages in a bottle sent out to sea. Every buzz of her phone sent an echoing ping of excitement through her body, making her fingers fly over the screen until she was giddy and shaky with enjoyment at the silly exchange.

By three a.m., they weren't even using words, just an exchange of GIFs and memes in a secret language of intimacy and humor they were both working to decode.

Grabbing her phone now, she unlocked it and automatically opened her texts with him, picking up right where they'd left off, as was her new morning ritual since deciding to be annoyingly responsible and asking for friendship.

Being friends with Dan sucked ass.

Not because he wasn't a great buddy to hang out with—much to Thu's dismay, he was quickly climbing the list of Harper's all-time favorite people—but because he made it so damn hard to not think of how much more she wanted from him.

Over a week had passed since she'd friend-zoned their growing connection, and each day reached a new level of frustration—sexual and otherwise.

They both made an unspoken pact to spend all their limited free time together: Looking for each other in the morning with an extra cup of coffee. Lunches walking around campus. Evenings in study rooms, where little actual studying was done, and a lot of stolen glances and shy eye contact were made instead.

When she was around Dan, Harper indulged parts of herself that anxiety had drowned away—she was goofy, carefree, addicted to the feelings he pulled from her. But none of that changed how she still had to white-knuckle her way through a normal day, panic constantly screaming at her that the world was about to crash to bits. Where in that mess was she supposed to build a foundation with another person, when everything felt dangerously out of her control? Like one step off course would send her entire world hurtling out of orbit.

At this major juncture in her life, she needed to concentrate on the things she *could* control—school, grades, career—and unwaveringly focus on her end goal. Because, regardless of what either of them felt now, she'd be leaving in four short months.

Leaving. Leaving. LEAVING. She slapped the heel of her hand against her forehead with each reminder.

She already cared for Dan so much that the idea of saying goodbye even as friends made her chest ache. Setting her silly little heart up for even more trouble would be devastating. And

Harper wasn't naïve enough to buy into the ridiculous fantasy that a relationship could survive years of physical distance, especially when she'd also be working seventy hours a week at the hospital. Impractical didn't even come close to describing it.

Harper stared at her ceiling, feeling the crushing weight of emotions she didn't have names for. It was in moments like this that she wished so desperately for her mom. She wasn't sure if her mom would've been helpful—every day it was a little bit harder to imagine what her mom would do or say—but Harper believed her mom would help her strike a balance between the two seemingly opposite things she wanted. If nothing else, her mom would be able to give her a hug, something Harper had wanted for so long it was physically painful.

But Harper didn't have her mom.

Instead, she had confusion and anxiety and loneliness and a threatening degree of horniness.

Harper's friends were all but useless—telling her to stop being an idiot and jump into bed with Dan as soon as humanly possible, having little empathy for her reluctance to involve her heart at this point in her life when her mind had always been her guide.

Giving her pillow one last groan, and with a few very adultish punches and kicks into her mattress, she rolled out of bed and got ready for school.

∾

During lunch, Harper and Thu met up with Indira and Lizzie in the atrium and camped out on a long couch stationed across from the Orthodontic Society's ticketing table for the upcoming dental prom, "Filling Groovy," being hosted that weekend.

Although Indira attended Callowhill's medical school, the dance was open to all professional programs, and Indira successfully smuggled Lizzie in as her date every year.

Indira, Lizzie, and Thu were buzzing with excitement, huddled together on the couch and keeping up a constant stream of gossip and predictions for the drunken escapades of their classmates as people stepped up to the table to buy tickets.

Harper didn't understand why any mid-twenty-year-old would be quite this excited for a school dance, but the yearly ticket sellouts and ridiculously swanky venues proved that no group of people was ready to bump and grind harder than sexually frustrated dental nerds.

Not sharing her friends' enthusiasm, Harper stayed on the couch as they all got in line to buy their tickets. She tucked her knees to her chest, resting her forehead against them as she gave in to her exhaustion.

"Sleepy?"

Harper's lips curled against her knees in automatic pleasure at that voice.

Dan's words were Pavlov's bell and she was his giddy puppy, salivating for the treat of his attention. She lifted her head, not even trying to hide her smile; it didn't feel right to try to dim this type of excitement.

Dan stood above her with two coffees, his crooked grin focused fully on her.

"I'm exhausted and one hundred percent blame you," she said.

"Yeah, sure. All my fault." He rolled his eyes. "I figured you were probably as tired as I am and in need of a caffeine boost," he added, handing her a cup.

"Saint Dan, patron of caffeinated beverages and tired girls," she said, taking the coffee and patting the spot next to her.

He sat close, their thighs touching, and even that contact had her heart feeling like it was jumping up and down on a trampoline.

"Still on for studying tonight?" Dan asked.

Harper nodded, swallowing down a gulp of coffee. "Yeah. My place?"

"Sounds good. I'll pick up dinner. What do you want?"

"You don't have to do that. I can make . . . something," she said, gesturing her hand vaguely.

Dan shot her a teasing smile. "Really? *Can* you? Because I've seen your cupboards, Horowitz, and there's a startling amount of Technicolor-wrapped foods in them."

"Oh, my apologies to the health nut, I didn't realize boxed mac and cheese is *soooo* much worse for me than Daleng's greasy pad thai."

"So you want Thai again?" Dan asked, taking another sip of coffee.

Harper gave him a sheepish smile. "Yes please."

"That'll be the third time in a week."

Harper shrugged. "When it's that good, why fight it?"

"I don't know," Dan said, drawing out the words. "I think Ekta's Indian buffet we went to last Wednesday may be better. We should go back soon."

Harper nodded, thinking back to the night.

They'd gorged themselves on curry and laughter, eventually rolling back to Harper's apartment and deciding they were too stuffed to study. They'd put on a random movie, sprawling out on the couch and promising to hit the books as soon as their stomachs didn't feel like they were going to explode, but they'd fallen asleep after the opening scene.

Harper had woken up hours later to the slow, steady rhythm of his heart against her cheek. Dan had held her cuddled against his chest, his body stretched across the couch and arms wrapped snugly around her, sending a punch of overwhelming affection through her. Her throat had constricted, and unexpected tears had pricked at her eyes, all the feelings she held so closely in check bubbling to the surface in that vulnerable hour of night—painful and wonderful all at once.

She had closed her eyes again, allowing his comforting scent to make her dizzy and happy as she nuzzled her cheek closer against him. She'd squeezed her arm across his stomach and latched on as tightly as she could.

Harper had wanted to take the feeling of protection and peace she'd found with him and keep it in her pocket—a reminder of how the moment glowed just for them, warming parts of her heart she had long left cold.

But the feeling wasn't something she'd planned and therefore couldn't be trusted.

It was the way life went. When you loved something, it left you, and the pieces you had to pick up after were sharp and sliced you open again and again.

Harper had opened her eyes, the gentle glow of the TV creating distorted shadows across the room. Her gaze had stopped at the pile of abandoned textbooks on the floor, her stomach clenching, the sudden, and all too familiar, shock of adrenaline bringing her body to attention.

That was also the problem.

There was no balance with Dan—her feelings bolting out of her like they were all or nothing—every other responsibility cast aside. Something about him encouraged her to shed her anxiety like a coat and bask in the lightness of a warm day.

And that was terrifying.

Anxiety was Harper's guide, her constant companion. If she wasn't anxious, there was no way she could still be on course. She'd traveled with anxiety for so long, it had morphed into a sick energy source she used on her career path. She didn't know if she had the ability to succeed without it.

A few tears had overflowed from her eyes as she'd mourned the moments like this that she couldn't have again. Moments she couldn't want.

She had crammed her heart behind its walls, then pressed a soft kiss to Dan's chest, allowing her lips to linger for a moment.

She'd pushed herself up and moved off the couch, draping a blanket over Dan before retreating to her room.

He hadn't been there when she'd woken up the next morning.

Coming back to the real world and the buzzing chatter of the atrium, Harper realized Dan had been talking to her, his head tilted and a sly smile on his lips.

"Sorry, what?" she asked, shaking off the memories.

"I said, 'I'm winning.'"

"Winning what, exactly?" Harper set her coffee down and turned to face him with narrowed eyes.

The corners of Dan's lips quirked. "At texting. You fall asleep first *way* more than I do."

She gaped at him incredulously. "That's not a thing."

"You know it is, and you know I'm winning. You're mad because you hate to lose."

"Okay first of all," she snapped, poking his chest, "I'm not losing. I can't lose at a game I don't know I'm playing. Secondly, that doesn't make you better at texting. If anything, it means you're the more boring texter and you put me to sleep. Thirdly, that isn't a thing."

Dan opened his mouth to argue, but Harper cut him off. "And fourthly, I don't trust you to keep score. Ever."

Dan let out a barking laugh. "Such vicious words from someone who doesn't know the most basic game in millennial social interactions."

It was Harper's turn to try to argue, but he silenced her with a finger pressed to her lips.

"And I figured you would accuse me of fudging the numbers, so I kept track," he said with a smug smile, thrusting his phone at her.

Harper snatched it and started scrolling. He had screenshotted countless late-night conversations.

"You screenshotted all of this? You're such a dork!" she said, trying to hide her dismay that she did seem to fall asleep first.

"I'm the dork? Harper, the other night you had a one-woman debate about the merits of amalgam versus composite fillings. I even stayed awake for *that*. But you couldn't stay up when I was telling you about how *Die Hard* is one of the best modern sociological commentaries on collectivism in our society? Admit it, I'm a texting hero."

She stared at him for a moment before dropping his phone on the couch and grabbing both of his ears.

"I don't know what the hell you're talking about at this point, but you're so infuriating, you make me want to shake you," she said and gave his head a mild rattle.

He laughed at her, activating his dimple. Harper wanted to kiss that damn dimple off his smug face.

"I'm sorry I'm such a better friend than you," he said, still laughing. "I could tutor you if you want. Give you a textbook and you'd be an expert in no time." He reached out and tickled her sides, forcing her to drop her grip and squeal like a child.

"Stop it," she screeched, grabbing at his wrists.

Her hand shot out and squeezed right above Dan's knee, a spot she'd discovered was extra ticklish, and he made a high-pitched squeak then sandwiched her grip between his large hand and the warmth of his thigh.

These were the moments she adored most—their talking and teasing made her giddy with an abandon she hadn't felt since childhood. In these moments, they had the potential to be anything. Everything.

It would be so easy to say she changed her mind, tell him she wanted more. He wouldn't ask for clarification or reasoning. He'd simply go from holding her hand as her friend to holding it as someone more.

The intimacy was broken as Dan's eyes slid over Harper's shoulder, his face going blank. He moved his hands off her and cleared his throat, angling himself away. Dan picked up his coffee and gave it his full attention. Harper's head swiveled to see what had distracted him.

All three of her friends were back from the ticketing table and were staring.

Hard.

Indira's jaw hung in an open-mouthed grin, while Thu sported a knowing smirk. Lizzie's eyes were wide with wonder, and she lifted her hands, jabbing her index finger through her circled thumb and forefinger in the universal sign of banging.

STOP IT, Harper mouthed with all the silent force she could muster. They started giggling. They really were the absolute worst.

Harper turned away from them, and their laughter quieted as they moved to a different couch across the atrium, probably a better vantage point for their incessant spying on her and Dan.

Harper continued to stare straight ahead as the awkward silence grew. After a moment, Dan ducked his head to catch her eye, the tension dissolving as they both started to giggle.

Dan leaned forward, resting his forearms on his knees, large hands cradling his coffee cup.

"Are you going to that?" he asked after they got their laughter under control, pointing his chin toward the ticketing table.

Harper scrunched up her nose. "Me? No."

"Why not?"

Harper shrugged. "I didn't even consider it. I'm not great in crowds."

Which was an understatement.

Dances were not for her. All obligatory experiences in middle and high school had left her such a mess of fried nerves and depleted energy, it wasn't something she was dying to give another try. Even the idea of being surrounded by a sea of bodies and noise brought sweat prickling across her skin and a queasy pulse of adrenaline surging through her veins while anxiety trickled like acid from her chest to the pit of her stomach.

He gave her an appraising look up and down. "Scared your shortness creates a high trample risk?"

"Har har," she deadpanned, giving his shoulder a push and working to downplay how accurate he was. Crowds left her with nothing but fear, like she'd never be able to take a proper breath again, crushed under the weight of a hundred bodies.

"We should go," he said after a moment.

"To the dance?" she asked in horror.

"Yeah."

"Together?" she blurted out, panic ballooning in her chest.

"Wow, Harper . . . that's so forward of you." He gave her a cheeky shrug. "I do owe you that second date. Fair is fair."

The bastard had the audacity to wink.

She landed a sharp punch to his shoulder. "Why do you love torturing me?"

"Harper! Stop begging! You're looking seriously desperate right now. I'll take you to prom."

Harper was about to argue when he stood up from the couch, stretching his arms sleepily over his head. The movement pulled his scrub top up, exposing a sliver of taut skin and the dark band of his underwear. Harper's mouth watered as she took in the ridges of his hip bones and the dusting of dark hair in the center of that ridiculously hot V thing guys have.

As the tiny, non-lust-crazed part of her brain registered how long she'd been ogling, her eyes shot from his body to his face.

A knowing smirk tugged at his lips and he ran a hand through his hair. He turned and walked to the ticketing table while Harper gawked after him.

CHAPTER 16

HARPER

As Harper lay bottomless on a massage table, the soles of her feet pressed together in butterfly position while a stranger held a wax strip above her pubes, she wondered which life choice had been the wrong one.

It was probably naïvely assuming that when Lizzie had asked her to get their hair done before the dance, she'd meant their heads.

Or maybe it was Thu giving her an evil smile when she'd said she had a buy-three-get-one-free deal on "spa treatments" that was Harper's for the taking.

It could also have been allowing Indira to peer pressure her into her first wax as they'd argued outside The Waxed Peach: Your Body, Your Brazilian.

No matter what it was, Harper regretted every choice that led her to this physically vulnerable position while Becca, her wax-ette, geared up to rip out her pubic hair.

"You doing okay?" Becca asked, hovering over her.

Harper choked on nervous giggles. "I'm . . . s-so . . . s-sorry," she said, tears gathering at the corners of her eyes. "I don't know why I'm laughing. I'm just so naked and it's all s-so ridiculous."

Her knees started bouncing from the giggles, making her laugh even harder at the absurdity of it.

"Totally normal," Becca reassured. "I'm going to do the first application now."

All humor was lost as Becca patted the strip down the right side of Harper's bikini line, the sharp tugs of the movement making tears prickle in her eyes. Before Harper could suck in a deep breath, Becca ripped off the strip, and it felt like someone slapped Harper with a million giant, tense rubber bands. She gasped at the pain and her knees instinctively slapped shut, locking Becca's hand between her thighs.

"Nope!" Harper bolted up, gracelessly sliding off the table and exposing her whole ass to Becca. "No, sorry. I can't do this." She tried hopping into her leggings, her feet getting tangled in the fabric.

"But I only did one spot," Becca said with horror. "You—you can't walk around with only one strip done."

"I promise you, I don't mind," Harper said, trying to untwist the stretchy fabric from around her thighs, all dignity gone.

"But—but—"

"Becca, you seem great. I'm sure you're wonderful at your job. This is a me thing, not a you thing. I will pay you to let me leave this room so I can start to forget that pain."

Harper rifled through her wallet and pulled out a fat tip for Becca. She all but threw the money at her as she rushed out of the room and onto the street.

Fifteen minutes later, her friends emerged from their own torture appointments, shooting her knowing smiles.

"Sooooo," Lizzie drawled, looping an arm around Harper. "Do you love it? Do you feel sexy?"

"I couldn't let her finish," Harper said, staring at her friends. "How could you set me up for that? That hurt so fucking bad."

"What do you mean you didn't let her finish?" Indira said, looking scandalized.

"She ripped off one strip and I swear my life passed before my eyes, it hurt that badly. I made her stop."

They all stared at her in silence before Thu cut in. "Okay, two things. One: You want to pull out people's teeth for a living. You don't have room to talk. Two: Are you telling me you're sporting a half bush right now?"

Harper opened her mouth to say something, but sighed and gave a defeated shrug, nodding.

"Oh my God, can I see?" Lizzie shrieked with glee.

"What? No!"

"Well . . . that will certainly, uh, be a surprise for Dental Dan," Indira said, trying and failing to hold back giggles.

"I can *promise* you, Dan won't be seeing it." Harper turned, and they all started moving down the street.

"You ready for tonight?" Indira asked.

"Now that I can't walk? Yeah, I feel super ready for the dance," Harper said, trying to ignore the anxiety lazily pulsing through her stomach. She'd been doing her best to push away thoughts about the dance and crowds of bodies pressing around her, but the harder she tried *not* to think about it, the more her anxious brain latched on to the idea, twirling it over and over in her mind in a panic-inducing swirl.

"Dan's gonna choke when he sees you in that dress," Thu said, thumbing through her phone.

As soon as they'd heard Dan was taking Harper to Filling Groovy, Harper's friends shoved her on the next trolley to Center City for a dress.

"Yeah? What's Alex gonna do when he sees you in yours?" Harper asked.

"We get it, you both have automatic dong opportunities tonight. Spare us, please," Indira teased.

"You guys are still coming to the pregame at our place, right?" Lizzie asked, draping an arm around Indira.

"Yeah. Is it just us, or did you invite anyone else?" Harper asked.

"Just us? Oh sweetie," Indira said, touching a hand to her heart. "Our pregame is legendary. Open invite."

Harper swallowed. "Isn't your place kind of . . . small?"

"We make it work," Indira said with a shrug. "Why? What's wrong? You're all sweaty."

Harper waved Indira off, pretending to read something on her phone, while adrenaline pumped through her heart in vicious squirts, trickling like acid from her chest all the way down to her fingers and toes.

The conversation turned to how they would do their (head) hair and what shoes they were going to wear, but Harper didn't hear anything over the blood pounding in her ears and the ragged sounds of her breaths.

Open invite meant crowds. A small apartment meant nowhere to escape. Harper had never told her friends about her claustrophobia. It was one more thing that made her feel separated from everyone, and pretending it wasn't real was easier than having to explain the panic that instantly gripped at her joints and made her want to bolt on the spot.

Excuses swirled through her mind—anything to avoid the night ahead. It had to be good. Convincing.

Harper was deciding between a stomach bug and period cramps when Indira said her name. Harper's head snapped to her friend.

"Sorry, what did you say?"

"I said, 'We're really, *really* excited you're coming tonight.' It means a lot to us that we finally get to do this with you."

The earnestness in her friends' smiles punched the air from her already deprived lungs. She didn't want to let them down, ruin their fun. She didn't want to be chained to her apartment by the iron restraints of anxiety. She wanted to feel like a normal fucking woman doing a normal fucking thing. Not this shameful, unstable bundle of nerves that controlled her every step.

So she'd go.

But Harper was scared.

CHAPTER 17

DAN

Dan was excited.

Like, stupid excited. For something *school*-related. He didn't even recognize himself.

He spent most of the day pacing aimlessly around his apartment, doing dishes, scrubbing floors, double-checking all the clocks with his phone because it seemed impossible for time to actually move *that* slowly.

All the while, Alex trailed him like a nervous puppy, asking an endless slew of questions.

"You sure it's chill if I come along with your group?"

"So . . . Thu's gonna be there, right?"

"Should I wear the silver tie or the yellow tie?"

"You said you think Thu will be there?"

"Hey, do you know if Thu has a boyfriend?"

Dan had responded curtly with "Yes. Yes. Silver. Yes," and "How the hell would I know?" before getting so annoyed that he subjected himself to a long run in the freezing winter day.

By the time he returned home, he'd burned off enough restless energy and wasted enough time that he could start getting ready. He hopped into the shower, letting the hot water ease the tension in his shoulders as his thoughts inevitably drifted to

Harper, and the ultimate fantasy of having her in there with him, her slick body beneath his hands. Too soon the water started to cool, and he stepped out, wrapping a towel around his hips.

He moved to the sink and wiped condensation from the mirror before lathering shaving cream over his stubble. He dragged the razor down his cheek, letting himself get lost in the rhythm of the movements as his mind continued to feast on fantasies of Harper. Her lips. Her touch. Her hands.

He was absorbed in a daydream of what it would feel like to press his shaved cheeks between her thighs when Alex pounded on the door.

"Dude, you almost done? I have to shit."

Poof.

His fantasy (and erection) disappeared without a trace.

Before Dan even answered, Alex threw open the door.

"Sorry, man, but I can't wait. I got that gas station sushi again for lunch," he said, frantically shuffling for the toilet.

Dan closed his eyes and did a quick calculation on how many weeks until his lease was up. Alex was a great friend but a disgusting person to live with.

"Was last time not lesson enough?" Dan asked, setting his razor down and moving into the hall as Alex found noisy relief. Maybe finding a sublease wouldn't be that bad?

"I know but it's so cheap. And it tastes good going down," Alex said, the sentiment emphasized by an exceptionally loud fart.

Sleeping on the streets might even be something to consider. He was glad the door was closed, but noise still traveled.

"So, you excited for tonight?" Alex asked.

"No, don't worry, make yourself comfortable. Let's chitchat while you destroy our bathroom. Not like I was doing anything in there. I wanted a half-shaved look anyway."

Alex wasn't perturbed. "Think you'll finally get lucky tonight with Harper?"

"We're just friends," Dan said, sounding unconvincing even to himself. He wasn't about to tell Alex how desperately he hoped tonight changed things.

"Sure, dude," Alex responded dryly. "Seriously, how long are you going to wait it out with her? You need to get laid. Bad."

Dan sighed. "I'm sorry, Alex, but it bothers me that I'm the only one uncomfortable with us having this conversation while you're bottomless. Can you hurry up?"

With a flush and brief handwashing, Alex emerged, looking relieved and a little sweaty. "All I'm saying is, there are plenty of hot girls out there. You can't wait on one woman forever."

Dan shrugged as he went back into the bathroom. For Harper, he could.

After he finished shaving, he went to his room, flicking through his closet. He pushed to the back, retrieving his nice suits and dress shirts.

He used to dress up every day for his job, and he missed the way the suits always made him feel purposeful and put together. He pulled out his favorite black suit—a classic cut, tailored to sleek perfection.

It used to be his lucky suit. He'd wear it to important meetings or lunches with big clients. Pulling that jacket on in the mornings in his shoebox-sized apartment gave him a sense of purpose, like he was suiting up for a battle he was guaranteed to win.

The version of Dan who'd worn that suit had felt alive, fulfilled—every day a chance to do what he loved: talk to people, manipulate numbers, make decisions, put together all the moving pieces.

Dan hadn't felt like that man in a long time.

His phone buzzed with a text, and he jumped on it, expecting it to be Harper. He frowned down as he saw his mom's name on the screen. He slid open the message.

I can't believe you didn't call me
today.

Dan's blood froze in his veins as he looked at the date then
reread the message.

December 20th.

Fuck.

Dan dropped the suit as memories from the last time he'd
worn it, one year and two weeks to the day, flooded through him.

He'd been heading into the office early, a cocky grin plastered
on his face at his perfect call on an alternative scenario outcome
for the passing of a tax cut bill that many senior managers had
overlooked. It was a risky move for a junior manager to contradict
those above him, but Dan had advocated for a change in the
company's stop prices, and his plan ended up saving the company, and its clients, ridiculous sums of money—making Dan the
office hero and inflating his usually minor ego to supersized pro-
portions.

He'd worn his nicest suit in preparation to present a debrief-
ing, explaining what the past forty-eight hours had meant for the
company, and offering suggestions on where to go. He'd been a
few blocks from the building when he'd gotten the call from his
mom.

Now, with numb fingers, he dialed her number.

It rang twice, then went silent, his mom's breathing coming
across the line as she waited for him to say something.

"Hi, Mom," he finally managed to push out.

"Hello, habibi," his mom, Farrah, said, her voice steady, trying to hide the pain that crackled right below the surface.

"I'm sorry I didn't call sooner. I didn't realize what day it was."

"It's been a year, Daniyal," she shot out, using the Arabic pro-
nunciation of his name. "Not ten. How could you not remember?"

Dan did remember. He remembered his mom's crying on the phone as she told him his father had been rushed to the hospital. The way he'd taken the first train to Philadelphia. He remembered holding her in the hospital waiting room as she cried into his shoulder, pressing the words 'cancer' and 'a few weeks' into his nicest suit.

He remembered feeling both numb and shattered. Angry and relieved. Confused by how something like cancer could take down Dr. James Craige, pioneer of the dental field, savior of teeth, frigid father, emotional tyrant. But most of all, he felt worried for his mom and how this would rock her world.

"I . . . I haven't been paying attention to dates lately," Dan said. "It was a mistake."

Farrah sniffed. "Do you not mourn for him? He was your father."

"No, he was an asshole."

"Daniyal," his mom snapped.

"No," he cut in. "You know he was. Just because he's dead doesn't mean we have to pretend he was some sort of saint. Being dead doesn't make you a good person, Mom."

"He *was* a good person. He helped countless people. His foundations, his practice, his charity work—"

"Yeah, but what about his family?" Dan shot back, his voice rising, bitterness and anger swelling up inside him in a sudden tidal wave of hurt. "What about how small he made you become to accommodate his vision? Everything you had to give up? Or the fact that the practice was always *his*, despite the work you did together? His name, his business, his legacy, and fuck us for wanting any individuality in that, right? And now we're supposed to pretend he was some hero?"

His mom was silent on the other end, and Dan decided to go for broke. "It won't make you a bad wife to admit your husband was a piece of shit."

"I'm not going to listen to this," Farrah said, before hanging up on him.

Dan clenched his phone in his fist, hitting the corner of it against his forehead a few times before chucking it on his bed. The seal had been broken, the memories of that day bursting in from the shadows of his psyche.

He saw the tubes twisting in and out of his father's body, machines beeping and humming as they stood guard over him, the acrid smell of hospital disinfectant burning through the room.

James Craige had always been large. Imposing. But under the harsh lights and thin blankets, he looked small. Fragile.

Dan sat in the chair next to the bed and took his father's hand. After a moment, he stirred from his sleep and blinked up at the ceiling. James slowly noticed Dan's presence and eventually turned his head to his son.

A sour grimace covered his face as he looked Dan up and down. He pulled his hand from Dan's grip.

"Nice suit," James said with a scowl.

"Hi, Dad."

A long, heavy silence stretched between them. Dan sat back in his chair, scrubbing at his face, exhaustion settling in his bones.

"Tired? Being a desk jockey wearing you out?" his dad said acidly. "Surprised you could find time to grace us with your presence."

"Dad." Dan reached for his father's hand again, but the man moved it out of the way. "Of course I'm here. When Mom called me I-I . . . she just told me. I'm sorry I—"

Harsh laughter cut off Dan's words.

"Don't pretend like you care, Daniel. We've never had to pretend before. Why start now?"

Dan's heart sank. Even in the face of death, his father was going to play this game? Perpetuate their battle to his last breath?

"Dad, no matter what differences we've had, I want you to know, I'll make sure Mom is okay. Always."

His father stared at him for a drawn-out moment before letting out another cold laugh, spittle landing on his thin blue lips. The suffocating weight of his father's disdain reduced Dan to the cowering boy he once was.

"Daniel, do you have any idea what it's like to lay here dying and hear you tell me that? That you think you'll care for that woman, when you've never once met a single expectation? With your fancy suit and pretty-boy haircut, you expect that to bring me peace? You were too spineless to become a doctor, too spoiled to do the one thing you were supposed to do, and yet I'm supposed to believe you're suddenly going to step up and be something other than a stain on the family?"

A muscle in Dan's jaw ticked. A swell of rage threatened to consume him.

It always returned to this point. No matter what paths their lives took, they always ended up right here: son against father, wants against expectations.

Dan resorted to his oldest defense.

Sarcasm.

"Glad you think I'm so pretty, Dad."

James sneered. "You're such a disappointment. Do you know that?"

"Gee, Pops, I had no idea. Wish you would have told me sooner."

Dan pushed up from his chair, moving to the door. His hand was on the knob when his father spoke again.

"You act like it's only me. She's disappointed in you too, you know."

Dan stopped, his back still to his father.

"You've let your poor mother down. She'll lose the practice

now. Did you ever think about that? I'm here dying, and that poor woman will be directionless because you couldn't do what needed to be done three years ago for your family. But you come here, in your hotshot suit with your promises to save the day while you hold your mother's hand. Don't pretend to be the hero, Dan."

Dan tried to control the anger that shook him. He wanted to take those words from the air and shove them down the man's throat until he choked. He wanted to ask why. Why did it matter so fucking much what he did for a career as long as he did something? Why did a family legacy matter to his father so much more than the family itself? And Dan wanted to ask himself why he couldn't have done it. Why he couldn't have kept the peace, gone to school, gone into practice, done what he'd been told to do. Guilt wrestled with rage as Dan looked at his mom through the small window in the door, her back hunched in sorrow, her face turned down.

Dan didn't have a perfect relationship with his mom—she nagged, he didn't call enough, they bickered and poked at each other—but he loved her. And, regardless of how irrelevant his father's opinion was, the idea of being a disappointment to her wrecked him.

There wasn't one thing Dan could have said that would cut his father as deeply as those words cut him. So, he did the only thing he could. He walked out of the room to go check on his mom.

Now, as he stood in his closet, holding that same suit, he felt a stab of loss over everything that had changed.

He was no longer that guy who loved his job. No longer climbing the corporate ladder. No longer talking to his mom.

He was a twenty-six-year-old, dissatisfied student, failing a program he wouldn't graduate from until he's thirty, with concrete plans to take over a practice he didn't want at his grief-stricken mother's demand. He was a passive bystander in his own life, the wants of others dictating his future.

He shoved the suit deep into the back of his closet and locked those bitter memories back in their box.

~

"I'm going to pick up Harper," Dan yelled to Alex an hour later, pocketing his keys and wallet. "I'll meet you at Lizzie and Indira's. You have the address, right?"

Dan grabbed the wine bottle he'd bought, hoping to share a drink with Harper before the night officially started.

"You're sure I should wear the silver tie?" Alex asked, walking into the kitchen in his dress shirt and underwear, a rainbow of silk ties clutched in both fists.

Dan shrugged, eyeing his friend. "You okay? You seem to be putting a lot of thought into this."

Alex nodded absentmindedly, still analyzing his options. "I'm trying to make a good impression."

"A good impression for *Thu?*" Dan drew out the name with a hint of teasing, desperately grabbing at any lightness and humor he could to keep the earlier memories at bay.

"Yes," Alex answered plainly, and Dan was surprised at the sincere anxiousness in his friend's eyes.

"Don't sweat the tie, Alex. You two will continue to hit it off. But if you don't like the silver, go with the black with stripes. That's a cool look."

"Yeah?" Alex's face lit up as if Dan had told him he was the prettiest girl at the ball.

Dan couldn't hold back a laugh as he moved to the door. "Yeah. Text me if you have trouble finding the place," he said over his shoulder, leaving the apartment.

Even the harsh wind on the street couldn't dampen Dan's mood as he made his way to Harper's apartment.

Tonight felt pivotal. Important.

He wanted it to be perfect. He wanted Harper to have fun, to feel beautiful, cared for. He wanted her to see how right it was for them to take the leap.

Getting to her place, he punched the buzzer and bounced up and down on his toes, trying to warm up his frozen legs.

"Hello?" Harper's voice crackled over the intercom.

"Hey! It's me." Right away, the buzzer sounded and the door clicked open.

Dan opted for the stairs, bolting up them two at a time to burn off the excited pulse of energy through his body. Reaching her unit, he took a moment to catch his breath, leaning his forehead against her door and giving his smile free rein.

With a deep breath, he knocked lightly and adjusted his tie. Dan heard heels clicking on the other side of the door, and Harper swung it open.

The air rushed from his lungs and his heart squeezed.

She was devastating.

The soft waves of her hair framed her lovely face, her lips painted a deep red that taunted Dan to bite and suck at them until they were parted and panting.

Emerald silk glided down her body, her skin glowing against it, tempting Dan to reach out and touch her. Straps of fabric wrapped around her neck, forming a deep V down her front. He followed its path, memorizing the swell of her breasts, the subtle points of her nipples hinted at through the liquidy fabric. Dan stiffened as he imagined undoing the bow at the back of her neck, watching the silk slide down her shoulders and fall to her waist. He dragged his knuckles across his mouth as he imagined the cool silk against his heated skin, pulling at the fabric hugging her hips, seeing the dress in a green pool on the floor.

"Hi," she said hesitantly, and Dan's gaze snapped back to her face, focusing on the chocolate depths of her eyes.

"Why are you staring?" she asked, her eyebrows puckered as she smoothed a shaky hand down her belly. "Is something wrong?"

Dan shook his head, trying to clear it. "No, sorry," he said through a dry throat. "It's just . . . You look incredible."

A pale pink blush spread across her cheeks and she opened her mouth to say something, but closed it, stepping aside to let him in her apartment.

"This is for you," Dan said, handing her the bottle of wine. "I thought we could have a drink before we head out?"

"God, yes," Harper said, turning for the kitchen.

Harper dug around in a drawer for a wine opener before uncorking the bottle and pouring them both huge servings.

"Cheers," Dan said.

Harper's glass was already halfway to her lips, but she clinked it with his before chugging it down like a shot and pouring herself another.

Dan noticed the tremble in her hands as she brought the glass to her lips for another long gulp, the tension in her shoulders as she set it down. Her eyes bounced around the room while she fisted her hands in the skirt of her dress, then smoothed them over the fabric repeatedly. Dan grabbed one of her hands, catching her gaze as he gave her fingers a squeeze.

"What's wrong?"

She looked up at him, and her eyes were swamped with a vulnerable fear.

"I . . ." She pursed her lips, searching his face. She blinked multiple times and tamped down whatever emotion had been peeking through.

With a deep breath, she plastered on a smile and let her gaze travel over him.

"You look really handsome," she said, her sincerity ballooning Dan's pride. "You should wear a suit every day."

"Your wish is my command," he said with a wink.

A more genuine smile tugged at her lips, and he watched her shoulders relax a fraction. Dan didn't want to flirt or tease right now; he wanted to find out what was bothering Harper so he could fix it.

"We should probably go," Harper said, glancing at the clock on her stove. Dan hesitated, prying questions on the tip of his tongue, but he nodded, and they finished the wine in their glasses.

The walk to Lizzie and Indira's apartment was tense and quiet. Dan sensed Harper was somewhere far away, somewhere he couldn't reach.

Walking through the small courtyard outside of the apartment building, they found Thu and Alex sitting on a bench talking. Harper offered them both a terse hello and stood stiffly as Thu hugged her.

They made their way into the building to join the party and Thu shot Dan a questioning look and a nod toward Harper. He responded with a desperate, confused shrug.

Laughter and shouts punctuated the thudding music as they approached the unit.

"Seems like we might have some catching up to do," Thu said with a daring look to Alex. She opened the door, and they took in the scene of crowded bodies in the space.

Clusters of people in suits and dresses lit up the room. A beer pong table sat in the center, rowdy dudes cheering with each toss while others swarmed the booze table set up against the wall.

Energy pulsed through the crowd, and Dan couldn't help but smile as something like enjoyment filled him, encouraging him to let loose and have a good time.

He reached for Harper and pulled the coat off her shoulders, draping it with his on the growing pile to their right.

Turning back to her, he traced his fingers along her exposed back. He was surprised to feel a thin film of cold sweat covering her skin.

Glancing at her, he took in the clench of her jaw and tight press of her lips. The color was drained from her face, and he was about to ask her if she needed to step outside for a minute when a loud shriek caught his attention.

Lizzie and Indira barreled through the crowd toward them, giant glasses of wine sloshing as they went. Dan barely had time to brace for impact before Lizzie launched herself into a violent group hug with all of them.

"It's about time!" Lizzie squealed, letting them go.

"Dan! Thank you for finally getting our Harper to one of these!" Indira said, grabbing him by the hand and tugging him farther into the apartment. "Let's give you a tour."

Lizzie moved next to them, sweeping a hand across the room. "This, my friend, is the Bone Zone. Please, make yourself at home."

"Bone Zone?" Dan repeated with a laugh.

Lizzie nodded. "The zone in which we bone. Kitchen is that way," she said, pointing to the back right corner where a wall cutout showed more people lingering by the fridge.

"Bathrooms are down the hall," Indira added, doing a game show hostess gesture to a hallway on their left. "Shall you be in need of a bedroom, please use Lizzie's, not mine."

Dan shot Lizzie a disbelieving look, but she nodded seriously. "I lost a bet," she offered as an explanation.

He let out a deep laugh and turned to look for Harper.

Thu and Alex leaned against the wall near the door, eyes only for each other, no Harper in sight.

He scanned across the room, no trace of her glossy black hair or the green of her dress.

His heart kicked into gear.

She was gone. And something in his gut told him she wasn't okay.

CHAPTER 18

HARPER

Dying.

I'm dying.

The thought repeated itself on loop through Harper's mind.

Bees stung through her veins while fire ants bit along her screaming skin. She wanted to run, but her legs were cemented to the floor. The panic was going to kill her.

Somehow, she managed to put one foot in front of the other and moved down the hall, trying to escape it.

Black crept in at the edges as she collapsed against the bathroom door. She pressed the burning skin of her cheek into the cool wood, trying to focus her swimming vision on the doorknob. Her sweaty palm slipped off it over and over again.

Harper squeezed her eyes shut, trying to think past the high-pitched ringing in her ears. With a raw, shaking breath, she opened her eyes, forcing her trembling fingers to the knob with what little control she had left. She latched onto it and turned, using the last of her strength to push it open.

She fell to her knees as the door swung open, and she knew she'd never get up again. Her fingers unclamped from the knob and she slumped against the back of the door, shutting it in the process.

Harper tried to gulp in air through her closing throat and dragged shaking hands through her hair, tugging at the roots, trying to come back from the edge of anxiety. It was useless. The monster had already pushed her off the cliff and was now cutting her open with a scalpel. It laughed at the chaos in her body, dumping adrenaline on her fragile nerves.

Cold sweat turned the silk of her dress into a heavy rope that clung around her body, suffocating her. A wave of nausea lurched her forward onto her hands and knees, and she dry heaved over the floor.

She dragged herself to the bathtub, twisting to rest her back against it. Her head lolled forward between her knees while blood pumped viciously through her body. The monster draped a heavy, pulsing blanket over her senses, and she felt herself begin to fade.

Somewhere, far away, there was a knock on a door. "Harper?" a muffled voice called, the sound traveling to her underwater.

The monster dragged its long, jagged nails down her spine, making her teeth rattle.

"Harper, I'm coming in."

She tried to lift her head, but the monster gripped the back of her skull, pushing it down.

"Shit. Harper, look at me."

Strong, familiar hands shooed the monster's claws away. A touch she'd come to recognize gripped her shoulders. *Dan.*

"Look at me. Please."

Warm hands cupped her cheeks, moving her face to look up at him. His green eyes bore into her. Steady. Unblinking. An anchor.

"You have to breathe."

Harper obeyed, sucking in a deep breath that got stuck at the top of her throat, the pressure issuing another wave of panic.

"Breathe, Harper."

Slowly, the oxygen crawled through her limbs, tickled in her fingers. She tilted her head back further and gulped at the air ferociously.

She was breathing again.

It was raspy and exhausting, but air was flowing in, and air was flowing out. Her lips felt swollen and tingly, and her skin hummed.

"That's good. Deep breaths. I'm here."

From somewhere outside of her body, she felt her jellied arms reach out blindly for him, clutching at his suit jacket. She focused on the texture of the material, trying to ground herself like therapists had taught her as a child.

It feels thick. It feels cool. I can feel the different threads weaved together.

The *whoosh*ing of blood in her ears was dialed down to a muffled thrum. The monster still lurked behind her, but it wouldn't dare touch her now that Dan was there.

Dan shifted to pull away and Harper cried out, clinging to him, clawing at him.

He wrapped his arms around her with just enough weight to make her feel safe. Harper closed her eyes.

"I'm not leaving. Here, give me your hand." Dan traced down her arms and entwined his fingers with hers. The feeling of skin against skin sent a soothing wave of calm up her arm. He shifted away again, but he didn't let go.

Harper heard the opening of a few drawers and the running of water before he knelt back in front of her.

"I think this will help," Dan said, letting go of her hand and pushing the bangs off her forehead.

Harper let out a whimper of relief as he pressed a cool washcloth against her skin, trailing it down her temple and across her cheek. He started whispering sweet words. Love words. He told her she was brave. That she was strong. That he had her, and he wasn't letting go.

With each stroke of the wet cloth, the monster faded away. Weak relief bloomed slowly in her chest.

After a while, Dan set the cloth down and ran his hands through her hair, massaging her scalp in a way that made her sigh in relief. Harper didn't know how long they sat like that, but eventually she felt her body's ownership return to her—exhausted and overused, but hers.

She finally opened her eyes and looked at Dan.

He was crouched in front of her, his body tense. His hands left her hair, traveling down her arms to rest on her thighs. Worry tightened the skin of his face, and his jaw sharpened with the clench of his teeth as his eyes scoured across her face. She brought a shaky hand to rest on his cheek and smoothed the wrinkles between his eyebrows with her thumb.

"I'm sorry," she whispered hoarsely. "I'm embarrassed you saw me like that . . ."

Emotion flashed in his eyes and his grip tightened on her thighs.

"Don't you dare apologize. All I care about is if you're okay." His voice was gravelly and strong, and Harper wanted to melt into its sound. She nodded weakly.

"I'm okay. This happens sometimes."

"How often?" he asked, still studying her face.

"It hasn't been this bad in a long time. I'm usually good at hiding it. I'm always hiding it," she said weakly, her eyes fluttering closed. "It's crowds. They . . . overwhelm me . . . a bit." She tried to give him a sad smile.

He groaned and dropped his forehead to her knees.

"Harper, I'm so sorry. I didn't listen when you tried to tell me. I had no idea it'd be like this." He let out a rattling breath.

Harper's fingers threaded into his hair, enjoying the way the chocolate waves slipped between them.

"How could you know something I didn't tell you," she said,

twirling a lock around her pinky. "I thought I could manage—I thought maybe I could pretend that it happens to someone else, not me . . ." she trailed off, knowing it would always be her.

Living with that chronic panic in her chest, that constant thrum of anxiety, sometimes made her forget how much worse it could be. But this would always, *always* be her. A mortifying, uncontrolled mess.

Her hands moved to his jaw, pressing his chin up so he'd look at her. She wanted Dan to see her. He obliged, his green eyes locking on her, his large hands tracing soothing circles up and down her thighs.

Every wall she'd ever built lay in a crumbled heap around them, and Harper was too exhausted to start rebuilding tonight. For once, she didn't want to guard her words and pluck them carefully from her mind. Harper wanted Dan to know.

"It started when I was twelve," she told him, cupping his cheeks. "The claustrophobia, I mean. My anxiousness . . . well, that's always been there. But I was in a car accident. My mom was driving."

Harper stared at him, scared that if she looked away, she'd be back in the passenger seat, looking at her mom.

"It was November. I remember it being so dark. I think it was icy—isn't that always the case? No one's ever told me it was icy, but my mind has always locked on to that idea . . . made it the unequivocal truth." Harper cleared her throat.

"My mom was my whole world—whose mom isn't at that age?" she continued, her voice coming out in a hoarse whisper. "But what I had with her always felt special . . . even when I had her, I knew what we had was special. I'm glad I'll always know that." Harper's throat started to burn, and she blinked through the tears pricking at her eyes.

"She raised me herself. I never knew my dad, and I never really cared. Things weren't perfect—she was a single mom, I was an anxious kid, it never felt like there was enough money, enough security—but things were . . . happy." A hot tear slid from the corner of her eye as her mother's radiant smile beamed in her memory.

"The night we got into the accident . . . I've always thought it was strange, but all I remember are the lights. I don't remember the sound or the feeling of the impact, just these blinding lights, spinning and circling. The car flipped, I guess. I didn't realize that at the time. All I knew was that I was suddenly so . . . so trapped. I couldn't move my arms, my legs. Everything was dark and I was stuck and I thought I would never be free again. I started to freak out and panic and just—I couldn't even scream. It was like I couldn't get any air into my lungs. It was so quiet, so still. I thought maybe I was dead. Dead and alone."

Dan stared at her, tense and still. She picked up one of his hands that was resting on her thighs and held it in both of hers, tracing his long fingers.

"But then the silence broke. It was the most overwhelming chaos you could imagine. People were shouting and screaming and there were these bright lights that felt like they were burning me. Then these hands started grabbing and pulling at me. It felt like all those hands would rip me apart."

She took a deep breath, trying to remember it without feeling it. Why did she always have to keep feeling it?

"All I wanted was my mom, but instead I got this huge crush of people. In reality, it was probably only a few medics, but at the time it was so much.

"They put me in an ambulance, and even that felt too small and suffocating. All I wanted was my mom. I didn't know where she was or where I was or what was happening. But I needed her so badly. I screamed and thrashed to the point that they eventually strapped me down. It was—" Harper shuddered, swallowing down painful sobs that wanted to rip from her chest.

"I found out later they'd taken her to the hospital in a different ambulance. Then she—" The words caught in her throat. There were some things that she'd probably never be able to say, never be able to tell him. She'd said enough. "She passed away that night."

Harper closed her eyes. She wore her vulnerability now, uncomfortable and tight, and the last thing she wanted to do was look Dan in the eye while it was visible—but she knew she needed to.

She opened her eyes and looked at him.

And he looked back.

She wasn't still trapped in that car. She wasn't still screaming and alone.

She was anchored in that tiny bathroom, secured by the strength of his eyes and the weight of his hand on her thigh. She was saying words that felt sharp enough to kill her.

But they didn't.

His eyes didn't drown her in pity or ask her more questions, they held her in heartbreaking tenderness—softness for all her jagged, broken edges.

Keeping his eyes locked onto hers, he lifted their joined hands and placed a soft kiss to her knuckles, that single touch thanking her for her words, cherishing her pain.

"Let me take you home," he whispered against her skin. "You've had a long night."

Something desperate and sharp pierced through her, and she squeezed his hand. "I don't want to be alone right now. If I'm alone I'll just lie in bed and think about everything and feel worse and embarrassed and—and—" She threw her arms around his neck, clinging to him.

"Please," she breathed into his neck. "I feel like I kind of need you right now." The words were raw and exposed, but she didn't care.

Dan's arms wrapped around her waist, fingers dancing up the notches of her spine, his touch stitching her pieces back together. Dan pushed his face into her neck and inhaled deeply.

"Whatever you want. Let's go."

CHAPTER 19

HARPER

Harper felt lighter. Freer.

Dan now held a piece of her, and instead of feeling tethered and crushed, she felt something like joy at the release of the burden.

He led her from the bathroom, guiding her along the outskirts of the party toward the door. His warm hand splayed across her back anchored her focus, keeping her calm. The night was a disaster, but maybe it could be salvaged.

As they maneuvered around the last clumps of bodies, a blond head bobbed in front of them, blocking their escape.

Or the night could get a million times worse.

Jeffery Giles leaned against the wall, a smirk curling at his lizard-thin lips.

"Harper, what a surprise to see you in the real world. I almost didn't recognize you without a textbook glued to your nose," he said, eyes flicking up and down her body, "What dragged you out of your hole?"

"Oh, I get it," Harper said, slapping a hand to her forehead. As exhausted as she felt, she dug into her energy reserves to muster up some sarcasm. "You're making fun of me for studying so much. How disarmingly original. I'm shocked it came from you."

"Harper, sweetheart, I would never make fun of you. I think it's adorable how hard you try to keep pace and come in second. I guess learning just doesn't come as naturally to some."

Dan tensed behind her. "You can't talk to her like that," he said, his voice filled with warning. He slid an arm across Harper's collarbones, holding her close against his chest. "Why don't you step aside. We're trying to leave."

"And who are *you*?" Jeff said.

"That's Dan Craige," Travis chimed in, squeezing through a circle of people to clap a hand on his brother's shoulder. They shared a weighted look, and a slimy sense of understanding crossed Jeff's features, making Harper's stomach curdle. She didn't know what knowledge passed between them, but anything that gave Jeff such gross satisfaction couldn't be good.

Harper looked around, trying to figure out the best way to push through the interested crowd eyeing them.

"Dan," Jeff said, drawing out the name. "I've been waiting to meet Callowhill's biggest letdown. So sorry about your dad, by the way. Always sad to lose a modern-day hero." He turned his greasy grin back to Harper. "What hypocritical company you keep, Harper. I thought you got off trashing legacies like us."

Uneasiness trickled down Harper's spine and she looked at Dan for understanding. He wouldn't meet her eyes.

"What's that supposed to mean?" she shot at the brothers, trying to keep her tone even.

"Come on, Harper, let's get out of here." Dan laced his hand through hers and tugged her toward the door.

"Oh, how hilarious, she didn't know. Guess I gave the whiny bitch something else to complain about." Jeff's voice was lowered and directed to Travis, but it caught right in that rare pause between songs and conversation, where a single noise becomes a room's focus.

Harper's body tensed as Jeff's words slapped her skin.

Bitch.

It ricocheted across the room, splattering against the walls and dripping into puddles on the floor. It made her feel so small, like her body was folding in on itself.

A tense silence descended, fracturing through the party like a spider web of cracked glass.

And that silence, that pretense of surprise, hurt Harper even further. It wasn't like the sentiment behind Jeff's comment was shocking or new, it was just more direct than the constant stream of sexism that flowed through medicine.

It was present in the way advisors looked surprised when she said she wanted to do surgery, asked her when she'd find time to have a family. Evident in the way men spoke over her, ignored her. Grossly obvious in the way older attendings told her being cute helped with interviews, winking like it was some sort of inside joke, eclipsing her hard work with the fact that she was a woman. All of it thrown around so casually and subtly, it left her wondering if she even had a right to be offended, or if she was just being "too sensitive," as women were also frequently accused of. She turned slowly, hating how her stomach swooped and skin prickled with embarrassment—silent, evil questions of her worth trying to snake into her brain—hating the tears pricking at her eyes as she forced hers to meet Jeff's.

"I imagine it must be difficult to have masculinity so fragile you feel the need to take cheap shots at me whenever you can. Does it keep you up at night?"

Jeff let out a nervous laugh, looking around at the room. "Oh, come on, it was a joke! Obviously, it was a joke. Everyone's so sensitive anymore."

"I don't hear anyone laughing," Harper said, locking eyes with Jeff's, refusing to let him look away.

Harper stared at the human trash can for a moment longer, watching him squirm, before she turned back to Dan. Tension radiated from his body, his narrowed, violent gaze focused on Jeff. Harper tugged at Dan's hand, taking a step toward the door. He slipped his hand from her grasp.

With sharp strides, he moved to stand in front of Jeff, looking down on the smaller man. The room was frozen, all eyes locked on the confrontation. Jeff shrank under Dan's gaze, beads of sweat forming on his upper lip. A muscle ticked in Dan's jaw, but he was otherwise still. Harper realized she was holding her breath, once again unable to get air into her lungs.

Jeff swallowed audibly. "Listen, I didn't mean any—"

Dan's hands shot out, fisting in Jeff's suit jacket and smashing his back against the wall.

"No, you listen, you piece of rat shit. If it makes you and your brother's dick hard to make fun of me, be my guest. I don't give a shit." Dan's voice was filled with controlled hate, and Travis slinked a few steps back, disappearing into the crowd.

"But you better keep Harper's name out of your filthy fucking mouth or I will personally come to your house and feed your blond head up your asshole and make you tell me how it tastes. Does that sound fun to you?"

Jeff stared at him in trembling silence. Dan gave him a rough shake and Jeff's head bounced against the wall.

"I asked you a question. Or are you too stupid to answer me?"

"N-no," Jeff stuttered out.

"No, what?" Dan moved his face a centimeter from Jeff's.

"No, that doesn't sound fun." Jeff's voice cracked.

Dan stared at Jeff a moment longer, the chords of his neck taut and thick. Harper couldn't think, couldn't act. All she could do was watch.

"Leave. Her. Alone. Clear?"

Jeff nodded and Dan dropped him. Jeff crumpled, but Dan caught him by the neck of his coat and pulled him to standing, brushing at Jeff's shoulders and straightening his wrinkled jacket.

Jeff relaxed a fraction as hushed murmurs filled the room. Harper sucked in a breath and looked down at her shaking hands. She hadn't realized she'd been holding them in tight fists, red crescents marking her palms where her nails had dug into her flesh.

"Now, I would suggest that you flex your stomach," Dan said calmly. Harper's gaze shot back to them.

"What?"

Dan sighed and looked at Jeff as if he was the stupidest person he'd ever met. "Flex your stomach because I don't want to be accused of sucker punching you."

Jeff gaped in confusion, but Dan didn't offer a third warning.

His arm moved in a blur, arcing back gracefully before giving a sharp thrust forward, driving firmly into Jeff's stomach. Jeff let out a choked squeal and keeled over, gripping his torso.

Dan turned from the crumpled mess and stalked back toward Harper, adjusting his cuffs with sharp jerks. Without a word, he snatched up their coats and placed a hand on Harper's back, guiding her to the door.

CHAPTER 20

DAN

There was too much space between them. Dan wanted to tuck Harper into his chest, kiss away the worried creases around her eyes, take her home and hold her all night.

Instead, he stayed rooted to the spot on the sidewalk, watching her retreat further and further into herself, back hunched and arms wrapped around her body as she looked at him.

"Are you okay?" he managed to ask.

She nodded and continued to stare.

"I'm sorry if I upset you," he said, raking his hands through his hair.

"Upset me?" She blinked at him, eyes owlish and vulnerable.

"Upset you by hitting that guy. By stepping in. I-I'm not usually . . ." He loosened his tie, searching for the words. "I'm not like this."

She gave him a blank look. "Like what?"

Dan groaned in frustration, throwing his arms out. "Like this! I don't hit guys at parties or yell at old men visiting the dentist. I don't show up uninvited to bars or dance in kitchens to awful nineties songs. I don't do possessiveness. But when it comes to you . . ." He gestured at her and started pacing.

"When it comes to you, I'm an idiot. I say something stupid or do the wrong thing. I have this caveman urge to strangle every guy who looks at you the wrong way. I want to walk three steps ahead of you to protect you from the world, because you're nobody's punching bag." He glanced at her, his voice softening. "I constantly want to touch you. Hold you. Smother you with kisses. I dream about you. Think about you—it's just you. Twenty-four seven. Only you."

He stopped, scrubbing his hands over his face before arching his neck and looking up at the sky.

"And the thing is, I know you don't need me. I know you don't need me to protect you or shield you or play some hero at the party, but I can't sit back and let you go it alone." He huffed out a breath, turning to look at her.

"I don't know what I'm doing when it comes to you. I don't know if I'm a meathead idiot or the friend you asked for, or something in between. I'm wrecked. I'm turned inside out and—"

Harper stepped forward, placing a finger to his lips, shutting him up.

He was frozen, trying to read the emotions flicking through her eyes. They stood still for several seconds, just staring.

Slowly, her hand slipped to the nape of his neck, tugging him down, hugging him to her.

His heart felt like it might crack from the gesture.

Dan wrapped his arms around her waist, enjoying the simple pleasure of being held and holding her back. He breathed into her neck, absorbing her heat and the sweetness of her skin. He wanted to stay there forever.

"What did they mean about your dad?" she whispered against his throat after a pause.

His spine stiffened. He didn't want this moment to be tainted, for the closeness to end. Harper strengthened her grip around him, kneading her fingers into his neck to release the tension.

"Don't pull away," she said, her breath warming his skin. "You don't have to tell me, but please don't pull away."

He'd lay his soul bare if it meant he could continue to hold her. Allowing himself one more second in that perfect moment, he pressed a kiss to the crown of her head, memorizing the feel of her hair against his skin.

With a sigh, he pulled back just enough to look at her.

"Have you heard of the Craige-Cochran Caries Detection and Prevention System," he asked, his tone going flat.

She gave him a wry smile. "Duh, it's one of the greatest advancements in cavity prevention since water fluoridation."

Dan nodded. "So you've heard of Dr. James Craige."

"Of course. He and Dr. Cochran are the fathers of contemporary restorative dentistry. What's your point?"

He gave her a pointed stare.

Dan could see the wheels turning in her mind and her face snapping into wide-eyed fascination when it finally clicked into place.

"You're related to Dr. Craige?" Disbelief and something close to awe covered her features.

"He was my father."

Her mouth gaped for a moment before her face fell and sadness filled her eyes. "I'm sorry, Dan. You must miss him so much."

Dan stepped back, the cold replacing Harper's warmth. He didn't want her apologies, and his father's memory didn't deserve her sincerity.

"Why didn't you tell me?" she murmured, searching his face.

"I was going to tell you—I really was—but then you started talking about all of the assholes riding on their parent's coattails, and I didn't want to be placed in that category, even though it's true, his reputation is the only reason I'm here."

Harper opened her mouth to speak, but Dan couldn't stop the words pouring out. "And how do I tell someone like you that he's not someone I'm proud to know? One of the most famous practitioners in modern dentistry, and I hated his guts—I didn't know what you would think of me. And then if you equated me to someone like Travis or Jeffery because of my dad, it would drive me out of my mind, and I didn't want you to think that my last name is all that I am because I don't think that's true and—"

Harper stepped forward and pressed her soft lips against his, cutting through his words and stealing the air from his lungs. Time started and stopped where their lips met.

The taste of her. The feel. All he could do was wrap his hands around her waist and bring her closer against him, returning the kiss in all its gentle chaos.

In every imagining, Dan had pictured their first kiss to be wild, frenzied. He'd assumed that when he finally pressed his lips to hers, it would be nothing but uncontrolled hunger and passion. A clashing of teeth and bruising of lips as they finally came together in the moment they'd been circling endlessly.

But it wasn't.

It was soft.

And tender.

And raw with vulnerability.

It was the air he didn't know he needed.

Harper sighed and melted further into him. Dan lost himself in the sensation of his hands splaying across her body, his legs tangling between hers. Her tongue slid over his and the feeling hummed into his bones. She was the most delicious thing he'd ever tasted, and he knew he'd never get enough.

Dan pulled her closer still, his whole body straining to touch hers. Their lips molded together in a conversation that words had failed. In that kiss, their weary souls reached out for tentative touches, soft strokes, offering nothing more than recognition and acceptance.

Their kisses slowed to languid brushes, desire building in their chests. She pressed one final touch to the corner of his mouth and pulled away, meeting his eyes.

"I don't have this innate hate for people born into a family name and class that affords them certain privileges—that's life," she whispered against his skin. Dan nodded and moved to kiss her again, their lips pressing against each other in small smiles.

"What I do hate," she continued, looking up at him, "are the people who act like they're *entitled* to those privileges because of their name." She moved her hand to the nape of his neck, running her fingers through his hair. "That isn't you. That could never be you."

Dan pressed his forehead to hers and closed his eyes, enjoying the gentle stroke of her hands. She didn't judge him. She didn't press him for more. With Harper, he wasn't a student, he wasn't a letdown, he wasn't someone's son. He wasn't anything more than himself.

She was Harper and he was Dan. And that was enough.

"Do you want to start tonight over?" Harper asked. "We can order a pizza and sit on my couch and drink and talk and pretend none of this happened?"

Dan's eyes shot open, locking on her. "I'm not going to pretend that kiss didn't happen . . . I'm not going to let *you* pretend that didn't happen."

She huffed out a laugh and rubbed the tip of her nose against his. "We can remember that happened, but everything else was just a really bad dream." She stepped back from him, a mischievous smile tugging at her lips. "Regardless, you look like you could use a *friend* tonight."

Dan grimaced and Harper burst into laughter. A growl bubbled from his throat and he pulled her in for another tight hug. She wrapped her arms around his waist and sighed.

"You really are my best friend," she whispered against his chest.

He smiled as his heart beat into his throat. "All part of the plan, Horowitz. Now let's get that pizza."

CHAPTER 21

DAN

Dan lay propped up on his elbow across from Harper on her living room floor, a ravaged pizza box and two empty wine bottles littered between them. Harper used his discarded suit jacket as a pillow while she leaned back against the base of the couch, the skirt of her dress pooling in an emerald sea around her. Judy used the layers of fabric to duck and hide while Dan teased her with his undone tie, making Harper giggle when the cat pounced so hard against him, she knocked him off balance.

"Listen," Dan said, chucking the tie out of the room and causing Judy to chase after it. "Tobey Maguire is the best Spider-Man casting in franchise history. I'm not gonna fight you on this one."

Harper let out a choked shriek, her eyes sparkling from the combination of drinks and conservation.

"You're so wrong. Andrew Garfield was the best Spider-Man we've had and ever will. There is no argument," she said, leaning unsteadily across the pizza box to poke him in the chest.

Dan leaned in too, capturing her hand. "Are you *kidding* me, Horowitz? Garfield? Pssht. I could at least understand you following the masses and obsessing over Tom Holland, but *Garfield*? Tobey Maguire is the only Spider-Man I'll acknowledge. Those tears? Iconic. It's a cinematic masterpiece and you'll never convince me otherwise."

Harper gave a slow, drunken shake of her head. "You're so blind. It's like saying Chris Evans isn't *actually* Steve Rogers and *Captain America* was poorly cast."

Dan paused, his wineglass halfway to his lips, and thought for a moment. "They could have done better."

Harper's jaw crashed to the floor. She blinked at him for a long moment before giving her head another shake and reaching for the wine bottle, muttering about flagrant disrespect, in her home of all places. She turned the bottle upside down and gave it an impatient shake as two drops fell into her glass. Her lips pressed into a pout as she looked to Dan.

"Empty? Why's it empty?"

Dan laughed. "That's what happens when two people try to drink Philadelphia County dry."

Harper's brows furrowed as she looked around. "I think I have a bottle of Manischewitz from last Seder. I'll go get it," she slurred, propping herself onto her hands and knees and pushing up to standing. She swayed for a moment before plunking onto the couch behind her with a soft *oof*.

She blinked and looked at the couch, then to Dan. "I'm supposed to be getting the wine," she drawled. "Why'm I sitting?"

Dan shook with laughter. Harper stared at him for a moment before her face broke into a wide grin, hiccupping giggles bursting out.

Dan pushed himself up and shuffled to kneel in front of her.

"How drunk are you?" he asked, eyeing her carefully.

She giggled again and pinched her thumb and forefinger close together, squinting through the tiny space. He smiled at her and she met his eyes, moving her hand to brush at his cheek. Dan sighed and planted a kiss on her palm.

"Come on lovely one, time for bed," he said, patting her thigh. He stood and reached out his hands to help her up.

She beamed up at him with a smile like the sun, her eyes bright and filled with tenderness, making Dan's skin warm.

"*Lovvvvely?*" she crooned, clamping one hand over an eye to focus on him. "Do you *lovvvve* me?"

Dan's breath caught in his throat. He looked at her shining eyes and rosy cheeks, then around at the empty bottles littering the floor. He took a deep breath.

"Yeah, I do. I love you. I love you very much." He'd be damned if he answered her question with a lie. She deserved to know she was loved, regardless of if she remembered it or not. And based on how much she'd drank, he was very confident she wouldn't.

Harper stared at him for a moment, her features melting into wonder. She dropped her head back against the couch cushions and blinked.

"He loves me," she whispered to the ceiling, a smile breaking across her cheeks. She let out a muffled squeal, and Dan watched her toes curl and uncurl against the floor in excited waves.

He loved her. It was simple.

She was. He loved.

Her head rolled forward to look at him. "You probably think I'll forget this tomorrow," she slurred, her eyes narrowing in suspicion.

"I'd put money on it." He laughed.

"No!" She shot off the couch and jumped on him, knocking him onto his butt and pushing him to the floor as she lay over him. Dan let out a winded groan as Harper sat up to straddle his chest. She hovered above him, going a bit wild-eyed as she raked her gaze over his face and chest.

"What are you doing?" He chuckled at her serious expression.

"Studying you so I don't forget. You're my textbook right now."

"I'm your—"

She pressed a finger to his lips, cutting him off. "Sshhh, I'm learning. You can quiz me tomorrow."

Harper's eyes traveled over him as if she were desperately trying to commit every inch to memory.

He let her look him over for another moment before sitting them both up.

"All right, lightweight, you need sleep."

"What? No! I have to tell you something," she said, entwining herself around him.

"What's that?"

"I *want* you," she whispered, then pressed a sloppy kiss against his mouth. Dan grinned and gave her one gentle kiss back before pulling away.

"I want you too," he said, tucking her hair behind her ear. "And I'll have you." Her eyes turned smoky and she leaned in, but he pulled farther back. "But not drunk."

With a swift movement, he stood, slinging Harper over his shoulder. She let out a squeal of delight and began pounding on his back.

"I'm not tired!" she whined.

He gave her butt a playful pat, making her squeal even more as he carried her to the bedroom. Once there, he tossed her lightly on the mattress and she laughed.

Harper scrambled to her knees and reached out her hand. "Come here."

When he didn't take it, she humphed out a breath, and reached behind her neck, undoing the tie of her dress. With shocking speed, she wriggled out of it and crawled toward him on her hands and knees. She hadn't been wearing a bra, and her movement pushed her breasts up and together between her arms. Dan's throat went dry and his eyes shot to the floor—there was no use torturing himself.

Bending down, he picked up discarded pajamas and turned back to Harper. She sat back on her heels, a hungry look in her eyes. Her lips parted as she stared at him. She ran her hands down her body, over her chest, stomach, lower still.

"I ache for you," she whispered, her fingers playing with the band of her underwear. "I need you."

Dan's cock twitched, but he shook his head, deftly tugging the T-shirt over her head and caging her arms to her sides. She let out a muffled whine and gave him a hurt look when her face popped through the neck hole.

"What are you doing?" Her bottom lip quivered. "Don't you want me?"

Dan groaned and dragged his hands over his face.

He managed a weak smile. "I want you more than you know. But I need to know you want me back"—he held up a finger at her sound of protest—"when you're sober. I can wait till then and you can too."

He kissed her forehead and gently pushed her back onto the pillows. Dan tugged the pajama bottoms up her squirming legs.

"Will you at least lie with me?" she asked, her eyes vulnerable.

Like he could ever deny her that. Dan moved his hand to her cheek.

"Scoot over."

Harper beamed as Dan flicked off the lights and moved beside her, lying on his back and cradling her head to his chest—enjoying the overwhelming pleasure of holding her to him. She traced her finger over his shirt in small patterns for a quiet moment before stilling, her breathing growing deeper. He thought she'd drifted to sleep when she spoke.

"Can I tell you a secret?" she whispered.

Dan swallowed. "You can tell me anything."

"I think I might love you back."

CHAPTER 22

HARPER

Harper woke to the feeling of being stabbed in the brain with a pickaxe. She squinted one eye open and let out a deep groan at the sunlight streaming happily through her window. Burying her head back into her pillow, she vowed never to drink again.

She groped around at her side for Judy, her trusty cuddle bug, wanting to nuzzle her aching skull into that delicious, tubby belly. A mix of cuddles, coffee, and carbs was the only way she was going to survive this hangover. She continued to reach for her cat, who could always be counted on to be *right there*, but when no fur met her fingers, she sensed something was amiss besides her splitting headache and rolling stomach.

She pushed up to sitting, squeezing her eyes shut against a wave of nausea, and swung her legs off the side of the bed. Her toes tangled in the cool silk of her dress on the floor. She stared down at it, searching her alcohol-soaked brain for memories of the night, but most of it was black.

There was the awfulness at Indira and Lizzie's place. Pizza and wine—way too much wine—at her's. Dan's infectious smile making her feel safe and free to indulge.

And the Kiss.

She definitely remembered the Kiss. There wasn't enough

wine in the world to make her forget it. Her lips buzzed with the memory of his. Strong. Wanting. Perfect.

She let out a groan, pressing the heels of her hands into her sockets. It wouldn't do her any good to keep reliving it. She had no idea what time Dan had ended up leaving or how she'd managed to drag her drunk ass to bed, but she knew she'd have to talk to him at some point about the Kiss.

It shouldn't have happened. It thrilled her and electrified her and made her feel terrifyingly alive. She'd been too vulnerable, too open. Harper needed to restore boundaries and get some space, because the taste of him made her desperate for more. She needed to stick to the goddamn plan that was supposed to carry her to graduation and wherever came after.

She wasn't the girl who kept her mind on a guy and fingers glued to her phone, allowing a stupid crush to tip the scales and detract from her goals—so she needed to stop acting like it. With a final heavy sigh, she heaved her body off the bed in search of her cat and an IV drip of coffee.

She padded down the hallway toward her kitchen and nearly jumped out of her skin at the sight of a body on her couch. She put a shaky hand over her heart, trying to calm its berserk rhythm, as she took in the scene.

Dan was asleep on the couch in an upright position, Judy's giant body stretched bonelessly across his shoulders, jutting his neck forward at a severe angle. He still wore his suit pants and button-down, looking incredible even through a rumpled night, and Harper felt a twinge of regret and shame that such a nice suit hadn't been put to use at the dance.

Looking at Dan, she was overcome with indescribable tenderness. No one had ever witnessed her panic at that level, her instincts always telling her to shield it from others, that voice in her head telling her it was a shameful thing that needed to be kept hidden, that there was nothing anyone could do for her anyway.

But Dan had seemed to know what to do. How to bring her back from that dark and isolated place. Harper had never felt so protected.

But she also had questions that trumped letting him continue to sleep. Shuffling closer, Harper stretched out her leg and poked his knee a few times with her big toe. He started, eyes flying open and head trying to push upright against Judy's girth. The cat meowed and slinked off his shoulders while Dan rubbed his neck. His gaze traveled around the room, landing on Harper, a shy smile spreading across his face.

"Morning, sunshine," he said through a yawn, standing to stretch his arms above his head.

"H-hi," she stammered out. Even after their time spent together, his beauty still managed to catch her off guard.

Finishing his stretch, he dropped his hands to her shoulders, then ran the backs of his knuckles up and down her arms, sending a shiver of pleasure down her spine and leaving goose bumps across her skin. She ducked her head and became hyperaware of her state of dress.

Harper crossed her arms over her chest and took a step back, turning away slightly. She wasn't wearing a bra and her T-shirt did nothing to hide her obnoxious nipples peeking through to say good morning. She was relieved to feel the elastic of her underwear firmly in place.

Her stomach flip-flopped. With no memories to go on, there was a very real possibility that Dan had dressed her. Which meant he might have *un*dressed her. And seen her boobs. She flushed crimson at the idea. It wasn't that she *didn't* want Dan to see her naked, just that she'd want to remember it if he had.

Dan opened his mouth to speak, but Harper cut him off, feeling overwhelmed.

"Coffee?" she asked, whipping around and heading for the kitchen, her voice three octaves too high.

She banged around in the cupboards and drawers, the coffee-pot clanging against the counter as she moved, trying to calm her racing thoughts.

"Harper?"

The closeness of his voice startled her. She turned to see him leaning against the doorway, eyeing her closely, his arms crossed over his chest.

"Hmm?" she hummed, turning back to scoop the grounds into the filter.

"Are you feeling okay?"

"Fine. Fine. How are you? Fine?" She stood on her tiptoes to grab a mug from the top shelf, but it dropped from her shaking fingers, landing in the sink with a clang. She reached for it and Dan's hand closed over hers, turning her to look at him.

"Can you put a pause on the coffee for a second and talk to me?" he said gently, tilting his head to meet her gaze. "You seem to be freaking out just a tiny bit."

She let out a nervous laugh but met his eyes.

"It's just . . . this has never happened to me, but I don't really remember what happened last night after we got here and it has me kind of . . . yeah, freaked."

Dan's free hand reached up slowly, tucking a strand of hair behind her ear.

"I think one or two extra *bottles* of wine might be responsible for that," he said, letting his fingers linger on the side of her throat. "We left Lizzie's apartment and came back here with pizza and drinks. I stayed to make sure you were okay and didn't get sick during the night or anything."

"I guess . . ." She sawed on her bottom lip with her teeth. "I guess what I don't remember is if we—um, if we . . ." she waved her hand, searching for words. Dan stared at her blankly.

"Did we hook up?" she blurted out.

Dan's brows shot up so high, they almost disappeared into his hairline. After a moment, a small, gentle smile tugged at the corners of his lips.

"Of course not. We'd both had way too much to drink. I would never do something like that."

As if to prove his point, he took a step back from her. She instinctively reached for him but dropped her hands. Space was good. Space was right.

"Oh, thank God," she sighed out, a bubble of relief filling her chest. Harper didn't miss the flash of insecurity that crossed Dan's face, but it was gone in an instant.

"I mean—not that I think hooking up with you would be bad. I'm sure you'd be great—*ohmygod* no, that's not what I—I just meant . . . I would want to, um, remember it . . ."

Heat flashed in Dan's eyes and Harper clutched the hem of her shirt, needing something to hold on to. That was not the right thing to say. That was not part of the Just Friends Contract. Her throat locked up and she began coughing spastically.

Dammit, why am I so bad at this? Harper screamed at herself. Dan so willingly teetered on the gentle edge of vulnerability while Harper sprinted in the opposite direction, screaming the wrong thing all the while. She felt the impulse to keep talking, not wanting to leave enough time for her previous words to gain purchase and stand awkwardly between them.

"So, um, did you change my clothes?" she asked, twisting the edges of her T-shirt. Might as well belly smack into the embarrassing details.

Dan's eyes flashed to her pajamas, lingering just a beat at her chest. Harper assumed it was more likely because he could see her heart body-slamming itself through her shirt than a fascination with her itty-bitty titties, but her nipples were still standing tall, so anything was possible. Regardless of the reason, she felt a pleasant flush of heat at the attention. His gaze shot to the floor and he rubbed a hand over the back of his neck.

"Well, I got you to your room and uh"—he cleared his throat—"you took your dress off . . ."

Harper's entire body flushed with embarrassment, and she brushed a hand over her face.

"I didn't see anything," he added hastily. His eyes landed on her chest again and she knew he was lying. Her mortification swelled in her stomach.

"I grabbed your T-shirt from the floor and threw it on you. Same with the bottoms. I tucked you in and stayed with you for a bit, but eventually moved to the couch so I wouldn't scare you when you woke up." A violent blush erupted on Dan's cheeks, making her heart inflate. The coffeemaker was the only sound in the room as they both tactfully looked at the floor.

Dan lifted his gaze and met her eyes with a new seriousness.

"But you should know that we kissed last night. When we left the party. You weren't drunk then, but just in case you forgot . . . I figured you should know everything that happened between us."

Harper wanted to open a small window in her chest and release the thousands of butterflies that were fluttering through her body. He was good and kind, and in that moment, her heart beat only for him.

Not willing to fight the instinct, she reached out her hand and cupped his cheek.

"Thank you for taking care of me," she whispered, looking into his blazing green eyes, waves of tenderness and excitement unfurling deep in her belly. "And I do remember the kiss."

Heat and affection radiated off Dan, tempting Harper to give in, to get closer—plans and control and focus be damned. But even if she did hand over her mind and body and told her anxiety to go to hell (as if), a clock would still be ticking down to her departure. There was no reconciling her few months left when Dan still had three years ahead of him—an obstacle that easily crushed any vulnerable infatuation.

"Care to repeat it?" he asked, interrupting her thoughts.

Dan stepped closer, moving his hands to her waist. Every muscle wanted to move toward him. Instead, she leaned back, putting a hand between them. He looked at the roadblock, then at her eyes, his own filled with questions.

"I haven't brushed my teeth," she said feebly.

Dan huffed out a laugh. "I appreciate you being the conscientious dentist, but at this point, I don't care." He cocked his head to the side and inched closer.

"And we're still just friends." The necessary words squeaked out of her mouth and she wanted to cram them back down her throat.

He stared at her incredulously before dropping his arms. He opened his mouth and Harper thought he was going to argue. Instead, he turned away from her, dragging his hands over his face and letting out a groan.

"*Really?*" he finally said, turning back around to look at her.

No. "Yes. Nothing's changed."

"Nothing," Dan repeated.

"I'm still moving this summer."

Dan blew out a heavy breath through his nose. After a pause, he fixed her with a smile that didn't quite meet his eyes. But as he continued to stare at her, looking her up and down, the smile turned almost wolfish.

"That's fine," he said at last.

"Really?"

"Yes." He stepped closer, erasing the space between them as his eyes bore down on her. "Of course it's fine. Because when we do finally get together, you won't have blacked out the night before. I won't have slept with a fifty-pound cat on my neck. And you won't wake up wondering if we did anything. Because you'll know. And you'll want more. So take your time, Harper, I've got nowhere else to be."

Dan grazed his knuckles along her jaw, making her shiver. He dropped his hand and stepped back.

They stared at each other, the moment heating to the point of combustion. Harper could feel the fire of his touch all over her body, even while his hands were balled into fists at his sides.

A loud knock on her door made them both jump.

"I didn't hear your intercom buzz," Dan said, turning narrowed eyes in the direction of the front door.

She glanced at the clock and groaned. "That'll be my friends. We study on Sundays and Lizzie brings us baked goods. They have my spare key."

With her hangover just gaining momentum, the last thing she wanted to deal with was their line of questioning at Dan leaving still in his suit.

"I'll get out of here then," Dan said, rubbing a hand over his forehead.

Harper stepped around him, and he followed her to the door. She took a deep breath before opening it.

Thu, Indira, and Lizzie stood clustered in the doorway, plastic bags of food in their hands. In the span of the world's longest second, all three of their jaws dropped as they noticed Dan standing behind her.

"Bye, Harps. I'll see you tomorrow." Dan leaned in and kissed her forehead. "Ladies." He greeted them with a nod, maneuvering past their frozen bodies to escape down the hall.

The four women stood there staring at each other, before Indira broke the silence.

"Told you he'd see that half bush."

CHAPTER 23

HARPER

Harper's hungover stomach lurched as she stared at the cinnamon rolls Lizzie had brought over. She pushed her plate away and rubbed her temples before risking a glance at her friends. Lizzie looked the worst, green and slack-jawed, a cloud of alcohol fumes almost visible around her as she sprawled out on the couch. Thu looked only marginally better, wearing oversize sunglasses and taking tentative sips from her coffee.

Indira was a shiny contrast to the group, her eyes fresh, luscious curls pinned back on one side. Her straight spine and clasped hands made it obvious that an interrogation would happen before any studying took place. Harper slow-blinked at her perky smile.

"How are you not hungover?" she asked in utter disbelief. Indira's olive skin was literally glowing. It wasn't right.

Indira made a show of flipping her hair. "Well, it's this amazing new energy drink called self-control. You just make sure you have a tiny bit before you start drinking and *poof*"—she clapped her hands together, making them all jump and groan—"you wake up hangover-free. Patent pending."

Harper rolled her eyes and turned to her laptop. "Does it have any negative interactions with your preachy pills? I know you'd be devastated if those stopped working."

She scrolled through her clinic schedule for the upcoming week, anxiety leaking into her stomach and her pulse thrumming in her fingertips as she thought of all the things she needed to get done, all the things she'd been neglecting.

Indira cleared her throat and steepled her fingers on the table. "So first things first. Are you okay?"

Harper felt the weight of their eyes pressing on her. Memories from last night scratched at her throat, but she pushed them away. She didn't want to talk about it. She wanted to pretend it never happened.

"I'm fine. I just don't like crowds." Thu scoffed at Harper's understatement.

"The Jeff thing was super fucked up, though. I'm sorry he was even there. Invite has always just been word of mouth," Indira said.

"Yeah, well, he showed his whole ass last night, didn't he?" Harper said, pursing her lips at the memory. Unfortunately, her friends knew all too well the unique and visceral pain that came with being called a bitch.

"And then Dan was there to hand it to him," Indira added with a smile.

"Yeah, and if he didn't get the message from that, I think I'll just have to let Dr. Ren know what a sexist little asshole Callow-hill has applying to OS residencies. She's pretty tapped in to the admissions community and might have a thing or two to say to program directors," Harper told them casually.

"You devious little genius," Thu said, before taking another swig of coffee. "I fucking love that."

Harper pursed her lips to try to hide her smile.

"So, you're sure you're okay?" Indira pressed, eyeing her.

"Fine. I promise," Harper mumbled, looking over a clinical competency criterion that was due next week. Her palms itched as her to-do list grew.

"Good. On to the important things then." Indira cleared her throat once more, working to keep a straight face. "Did y'all hump?"

Lizzie gave a weak snort of amusement from the couch, but Harper kept her eyes trained on her laptop.

"Like bunnies," she deadpanned, scrolling through a class web page.

"Dammit, Harper!" Indira slapped her palms on the table, making Lizzie grab her head with a whimper.

"The evidence is overwhelming but you're gonna play nonchalant? In all the time we've known you there's been no dick. Now there's dick and you *dare* withhold details on said dick? Nuh-uh, not gonna happen."

Thu even found the strength to whip off her sunglasses and glare at Harper in solidarity of Indira's moving speech.

"First of all, there was no . . . dick," Harper said, pointing at them. "And you want details? After having a full-on freak out in the bathroom, he brought me home, I ate a shit ton of pizza and blacked out from wine. Really classy night for me. How was yours?"

"Where'd you get the pizza from?" Lizzie asked, eyeing the box on the floor.

"Does it matter?" Harper said with a sigh.

Lizzie held up her hands in defense. "I was just wondering if there's any left. I need a level of grease that a cinnamon roll won't provide."

"Not now, Lizzie," Indira snapped, before turning back to Harper with a crestfallen look. "So that's really it? No dick?"

"That's it." Harper turned back to her laptop in an attempt to end the line of questioning. "How was last night for you all?"

"It was fun. We danced, and drank, and missed you. Thu got freaky on that Alex kid."

"Alex, huh?" Harper said, turning to Thu.

"Not a thing," Thu said, waving her off when Harper opened her mouth to push for more. "But nothing else happened with

Dan? Nothing at all? Because I have a hard time believing that."

Harper let out a sigh, blowing a puff of air that lifted her bangs off her forehead. They knew Harper was withholding and weren't above beating it out of her if necessary.

"We may have had a moment," she said quietly, guzzling down water to put off answering Indira's imminent questions.

"Well, shit, Harper, try not to be so graphic," Thu said, making Lizzie laugh while she scavenged through the abandoned pizza box on hands and knees. Harper shot them both the finger.

"What kind of moment?" Indira asked, a manic thrill animating her features. She'd found a thread and she was holding on for dear life.

Harper rolled her eyes, trying to downplay the swell of excitement she felt thinking about Dan.

"An intense kind of moment, okay? A kiss-in-the-rain, movie-level, electrocute-your-senses, rip-your-panties-off kind of moment. We kissed after we left the apartment, and it was amazing, and he opened up to me about stuff with his dad and . . . I don't know. It was special. And then we got pizza and he ended up staying the night. On the couch," Harper added quickly, raising a hand to Indira's silent screech.

"I seriously can't believe you guys didn't bone," Thu said, joining Lizzie at the pizza and sniffing a cup of garlic sauce.

"I'd certainly bone him," Indira said. "He has that type of hair that looks like he just had the best sex of his life, then rolled out of bed to get you brunch."

"I've thought about it a lot, and I've decided he could make a hole," Lizzie added, chewing on discarded pizza crust.

"He's so pretty, I bet he doesn't even 'make love,'" Thu said with finger quotes. "He makes art." She gave a hip thrust to emphasize her point. Lizzie and Indira nodded in agreement, all with a faraway look in their eyes that lasted longer than it should.

Harper cleared her throat and they snapped out of their fantasies.

"So, you had a 'moment,'" Indira said, adopting Thu's finger quotes. "What does this mean? Are you guys dating? Are you opening up that door?"

"I don't know," Harper mumbled, running her thumb along the edge of her textbook. *Wrong answer.* "I mean, I do know, and the answer is no. We're *not* dating and I'm *not* opening that door," she said more firmly, pressing the pad of her thumb into the sharp corner of the textbook's cover. "I'm moving as soon as school's done anyway."

"Why does moving automatically mean it will end?"

Harper shot Indira an incredulous look. "Why does no one seem to get how serious that is? I'm not stupid enough to think that a five month . . . whatever . . . would be strong enough to survive long distance. It's impossible to make something that new survive. And, more importantly, I don't have time to give a relationship with him what it would need."

"What would it need?" Lizzie asked.

Harper took a deep breath. "When I'm with him, I don't feel balanced. Nothing else matters except him and I, and that's not right. That's not something I can do right now and that's not the woman I am. I've come this far, and it'd be ridiculous for me to throw everything away for some guy."

Her friends shared a look before Indira spoke. "Focusing only on grades and school isn't balance, sweets. It's actually extremely unbalanced. You're smitten and that's normal! Who wouldn't be totally wrapped up in a hot guy who adores them?"

Indira reached across the table and squeezed Harper's hand. "He brings something out in you. You're . . . playful when you're with him. Your smile's brighter, you laugh harder . . . Having a life *and* career is possible. People do it all the time." Indira's eyes were soft as she spoke, but Harper turned away.

Indira was talking about a life that Harper didn't feel could be her own.

If she couldn't feel in control of the one she was living now, how could she ever manage welcoming another person into the chaotic storm?

"We better start studying," Harper said, waking up her computer.

Another glance passed between her friends, but Harper ignored it. They settled into their natural rhythm, typing away notes and asking the occasional question to the group, Lizzie playing on her phone and periodically calling them nerds. Harper was preparing for a particularly tricky root canal case scheduled for Wednesday when Harper and Thu's computers pinged in unison.

"Practical grades are up," Thu said as she scanned the email. "Took the attendings long enough."

Practicals were graded based on live performance and didn't offer the same instant score reports their electronic exams did. Harper felt the drowning sensation start. The practical had not gone well for her and she knew she didn't want to see her score.

She'd gone in groggy and unprepared for the treatment planning assessment, having stayed up way too late talking with Dan, per her new routine. She'd also spent the morning lingering at the coffee shop next to school, laughing with him when she'd intended to go in early for some last-minute prepping.

"I passed!" Thu cheered. "Thank fuck for that."

"Well, aren't you just the little superstar," Indira said, pinching Thu's cheek as she leaned over her friend's shoulder to look at the notes.

No point in delaying it. Harper logged in to check her score, fingers jittery as she typed. It felt like acid was dripping into her chest.

B-.

Fuck.

Harper pushed back from the table, tears stinging at her eyes, embarrassment and shame telling her to run.

She knew her friends wouldn't get it—hell, most of the time *she* didn't even understand her obsession with grades. Those little letters could seem trivial and inconsequential in the grand scheme of life, but they choked her. They wrapped their arms around her throat and squeezed all the air out of her. She felt childish and stupid for caring so much, but she had no control over the circling obsession. Being able to rationalize their overall insignificance and still have the overwhelming compulsion to excel made it all the worse.

"What's wrong, Harpy?" Thu asked, reaching for her.

"I fucked up," Harper said, running trembling hands through her hair.

Thu's face turned to a mask of confusion as she craned her neck to look at Harper's screen.

"B minus? You're hysterical over a *B minus?*"

"I've never gotten a B before," Harper snapped, tugging at her hair. "Minus!" she added, throwing her hands in the air. She started pacing the room.

"Is the apocalypse upon us?" Indira teased, but shut her mouth at Thu's warning look.

"It isn't fucking funny, Indira," Harper said. "You all act like I'm some sort of fucking joke, like I'm an idiot for trying so hard. Do you think I want to be this way? Do you think I like feeling like this?" Harper gripped at her chest. "It *hurts*," she said through gritted teeth. "My body fucking hurts. All the time. And it's so easy for you guys to look around and think everything is fine and I'm overreacting because, yeah, technically everything is okay, but that doesn't stop my body from feeling like it's dying. Like the world is ending and adrenaline is eating me from the inside out."

Her hands were shaking as she pushed her bangs away from her face, feeling like she couldn't breathe. "And there's nothing

I can do about it. But instead of showing me a little patience, all you do is poke and tease me and tell me to fuck some guy because it makes a great punch line to your jokes."

She sucked in a rattling breath. "But I care," she said, jabbing a finger at her chest. "I care about my grades. And residencies care. And I care about getting into residency." She paused for a moment, her whole body shaking. "It's all I fucking have."

Walls were closing and air was in short supply. Her mind transformed into a highway, incoherent thoughts that she couldn't slow down racing from all directions. If they would just slow down . . . She was torn between the urge to sprint away or curl into a ball, but emotions rooted her body to the spot as hot, shameful tears slipped down her cheeks.

"Harper. Look at me. We need you to calm down." Thu stood in front of her, running soothing circles up and down Harper's arms. "We don't think you're a joke, we think you're amazing. But we also think you're human and too hard on yourself. Bs are nothing to be ashamed of. Residencies won't turn you down or revoke placement over one B. It's a great grade."

"Better than anything I could ever do," Lizzie said, eyes filled with worry.

"I don't— It's not—I—" Harper sucked in lungfuls of air. They didn't get it. No one really did. She didn't want to explain that the endless competition she felt was against some idyllic Harper that was always *just* out of reach—the spiraling feeling that she was never quite where she was supposed to be, never quite worthy enough. Of what, she wasn't sure.

"It isn't a comparison with you. Or other people. It's me. I have a standard." Harper rubbed sharply at the tears pouring down her cheeks. "I have to do my best. Be my best. I'm just . . . failing otherwise."

"No one doubts you constantly do your best—we all admire you so much for how hard you work—but some days your best can be a B and some days your best can even be a C or some days it could mean doing nothing at all but just breathing." Thu ducked to try to meet Harper's eyes. "And we'll still be proud of you. Your best isn't the same thing as your breaking, Harper. I think you confuse the two, but one of these days you need to learn the difference. You don't have to live with this pressure."

Harper let out a cold laugh. "Without the pressure, I don't perform. That's what this whole stupid Dan thing has proven. I don't focus and I don't perform. I'm just a normal, unimportant girl, doing normal, unimportant things."

"You are important! You're so important," Lizzie consoled, moving to stand closer to Harper.

"Harper." Indira stood too, choosing her words carefully. "Maybe you should think about going to therapy. I know you said you went as a kid after what happened with your mom, but maybe it could help. Your anxiety . . . You shouldn't have to live like this."

The monster clawed protectively at Harper's torso and she leaned into its embrace. Anxiety was terrifying to live with—but so was the idea of not knowing who she was without it. Thoughts looped and rushed and collided into this all-encompassing energy that fueled every step, heightened every emotion. It left Harper feeling out of control of her mind, but afraid of what would be left if it were gone.

"I'm fine."

"Therapy is nothing to be ashamed of."

"I'm not ashamed of therapy. I'm a therapy graduate. I learned what I needed to learn," Harper said. There was no way she wanted to confront the unhealed wounds that festered below the surface.

"I don't think therapy works like that, babe," Indira reasoned. Harper stared at her, cold numbness tingling down her limbs.

"Is it . . ." Thu cleared her throat and looked at the ground. "Is it because you don't want to talk about your mom?"

Harper jerked away, hunching her back and wrapping her arms around her middle.

"Thu, don't," Harper warned. The room started spinning.

"I know we don't talk about it, but you know your mom would be so proud of you, right? She'd love you no matter what and wouldn't want you to torture yourself like this. Killing yourself over school and residency won't bring her back, Harper. You know that, don't you?"

Silence descended on the room. Harper's blood pounded behind her eyes, making her see red.

"Get out," Harper whispered.

"We're only try—"

"Get out!" she screamed, thrusting a finger toward the door. Her friends hesitated for a moment before snatching up their things and making their exit. Thu stopped at the edge of the room and looked over her shoulder at Harper.

"I only said that because I love you."

Hot tears spilled from Harper's eyes as she stared at Thu. Wanting to scream. Wanting to lash out at her words. A humming filled her ears, and her body felt like it was about to fragment into a hundred pieces.

Thu met her eyes and continued. "If you want to go into tomorrow pretending this didn't happen, we can do that. If you need to call and scream at me, we can do that too."

Harper couldn't speak, her chest rising and falling against jagged breaths. She couldn't get enough air into her damn lungs.

"And if you do ever want to talk about it"—Thu shrugged—"let me know."

Harper waited until she heard the door click shut before crumpling to the floor and crying. Her body shook and her mind raced and her heart felt like it would punch out of her chest or stop working all together. She cried until her throat ached.

She cried like a child who needed her mother.

CHAPTER 24

HARPER

Harper spent the next two weeks avoiding Dan, using finals and the school's short winter break as excuses to gain some distance. She'd resolved to tamp down everything she felt for him. No more gushy heart-eyes at his smile. No more giddy squeals at his texts. She even turned down his offers for coffee.

It didn't do her much good.

A part of her mind was constantly circling around him, and it was exhausting to pretend to feel less than she did. But she created these boundaries and she needed to stick to them.

On Friday night, she holed up in a study room at school, determined to make serious progress in her *Clinical Results of Fixed Prosthodontics* textbook. Except it was boring as shit, and her mind kept turning to daydreams about a cute guy.

Her phone buzzed and her hand shot to it with embarrassing speed. She tried to hush the flood of excitement as Dan's name lit up her screen.

Are you at school?

Before she could stop and think too much, she shot off a response.

Yeah. Studying :/

The speed of his answering text made her smile.

I'm here too. Want some company?
Feel like I haven't seen you in a
while

She tapped out a reply, but her finger hovered over the Send button. She missed him. She missed Dan in a way she shouldn't. Her throat ached with it. She hit Send.

Would love some.
Study room 112 in
the basement

Balance, Harper reminded herself. *You are capable of balance. Probably. A little time together won't make the world crash down.* She thrummed her fingers on her textbook and made a valiant effort to pretend to read it. Her phone buzzed again. Thu.

You at school biatch? Alex asked
me to help him with their muscles
exam next week and I figured you
would already have a study room
locked down

True to her word, Thu, and the others, allowed the group to fall back into their normal rhythm, pretending Harper's meltdown hadn't happened. Harper was beyond grateful. She knew they wanted to return to the issue, but she trusted them to not push her on it further.

I'm in 112. Dan's coming

I bet he is ;)

you're disgusting

lawlz see you soon

The door to the study room opened quietly and Harper tossed her phone to the side. Dan walked in and her heart gave a squeeze in greeting. Damn, she'd *really* missed him.

She smiled and slid her backpack off the table, making room for him next to her. He grinned back, taking the seat.

"Hi," he said. He stared at her and Harper wanted to bottle the tenderness in his gaze and wear it like perfume. Indecision flickered in his eyes before he reached his arm around the back of her neck and leaned in, planting a soft kiss on the top of her head. Dan lingered for a moment, breathing against her hair. It was close and familiar and maddeningly intimate, making her body thrum with need.

She gave herself a half-hearted shake and pulled away. *You're moving. You're a mess. Stop.* The words repeated in her head like a sick mantra, but the cruel voice said them with weakened resolve.

"Hi," she finally said, her tongue thick and heavy. "Why are you wet?"

Dan ran a hand through his damp hair, making the gentle waves clump together.

"I had cadaver lab today. I went home and took a scalding hour-long shower and pretty much scrubbed my skin off."

An image of Dan washing his long, lean muscles under steamy water popped into her head and she resisted the urge to fan herself.

"How did that go?" she asked, shifting slightly away from him and subtly adjusting her thighs to alleviate some pressure. Cadaver dissection and horniness were not an acceptable combination.

"The shower was good, thanks." He shot her a cheeky grin and she batted his shoulder.

"How was *cadaver*?"

He shrugged, his teasing replaced with sheepishness. "It was kind of tough, to be honest—for me at least. I couldn't quite get past it being a person, you know? It's weird to be in a room with a dozen dead bodies and disassociate from the fact that they were once . . . *people*."

Harper nodded. Cadaver lab was a huge privilege for health professionals to learn from, but that didn't stop it from also turning her stomach.

"I had a hard time with it too."

Dan's eyes perked up. "Yeah? So I'm not a massive wimp?"

"Not because of cadaver at least. Other parts of you . . ." she teased, and he gave her earlobe a playful tug that set her heart racing.

Harper was starting to feel like her body was one giant pleasure nerve that only required Dan to take a deep enough breath before going off like a bomb, but her physiology textbook lacked a chapter called "Super Horny Girls Practicing Self-Denial," so she didn't have the science to back her up.

"But you felt weird about it too?" Dan asked earnestly.

"Oh, for sure. It's a really bizarre experience. You're there to learn and understand the body better, but it feels wrong to separate that from the actual human that was in there. You can't help but wonder who the person was . . . It reminded me of my mom's death, I think."

It felt like an anvil dropped in her gut and she scrambled to put a source to that admission. That was a thought she'd refused to even give form to in her own mind during cadaver—something that had lurked the whole time she dissected and analyzed the anonymous body on a table.

She waited for the sharp feelings and onslaught of pain that usually accompanied such clear thoughts of her mom, but they didn't hit her. The words had left her brain, traveled out of her mouth and into Dan's ears, and she didn't fall apart. She didn't break.

And she wasn't sure what to make of that.

She looked at Dan and saw the reflection of her surprise in his eyes. She also saw the moment he gingerly took her piece of honesty and cradled it in his mind. He nodded gently, telling her without words that he'd treat that piece of her delicately and with respect. No poking or prodding or nagging for it to be more. Just allowing it to be a small moment of her vulnerability that they now shared.

"The smell really freaked me out too," he said slowly, and Harper wanted to thank him on her knees for his willingness to move on.

"Ugh, yeah. It smelled like old sausage sandwiches left out in the sun. So gross," she said a little too loudly, but her shoulders relaxed a fraction.

"Right? Alex said he liked the smell. I think I need to move out after hearing that."

Harper made a gagging face. "So he's your class psychopath. Every year's got one."

Dan barked out a laugh. "Yeah? Who's yours?"

"Thu. She said the lymph nodes looked like berries and pretended to pop one in her mouth. I wanted to throttle her. Maybe we need new friends," Harper said with a laugh.

"At least we have each other."

Harper's smile fell and she shifted in her chair. *Too close. This is getting too close.*

She turned to her textbook and, after a moment, Dan did the same.

Harper lost herself in her notes for a while, slipping into that trance-like state where the various pieces start to click together into the bigger picture, when Dan's hand slammed on the table.

"Fuck!" His voice echoed sharply around the room and it made Harper jump. He fisted his hands in his hair, then scrubbed them over his face, hiding his eyes.

"I can't do this," he said, his voice harsh and raw. Harper instinctively moved her hands onto him, as if to absorb his pain so he wouldn't have to suffer.

"Hey, talk to me. What's going on?" she asked, tugging at his arm so she could see his face. He didn't budge. "Dan."

"I don't get any of this, Harps. I'm not an idiot, I swear I'm not, but I don't get it. None of it makes sense and it's so much detail and I can't do it," he said hoarsely, his voice drenched in embarrassment.

"What class is it? Let me help you."

He let out a humorless laugh. "It isn't just this class. It's all of them. It's cadaver. And pharmacology. Neurology. Metabolism. Osteology. I'm fucking it all up. I'm failing so fucking royally it's almost funny." He let out a shaky breath. "And it isn't even just school. I feel like I'm failing life. I feel like I'm doing it all completely wrong."

Harper wanted to grab him. Reach into him and stop the hurt. She didn't feel like she was doing life wrong, necessarily, but she could never shake the feeling that she was one step away from ruining it. She felt constantly out of control, her body always in a spiral of panic. It was like she only half lived in order to survive. Fully flinging herself into life would certainly be the death of her.

"Do you know why I'm even here?" Dan asked suddenly. "Pursuing this stupid degree?"

"No, I don't," Harper said, placing her hand on his thigh. "Tell me."

"I'm here because my mom asked me to be. Demanded I be.

She said it was my duty to help her run the practice after my dad died. And I just went with it. Isn't that pathetic?" he said, looking at her now. "I never wanted this. I resisted it for so long. I never wanted to be a doctor. I never had the drive. It just isn't me. But then my mom completely lost it, and here I am. Being dragged under by this sense of guilt and duty and bullshit."

He rubbed a hand over his forehead. "And what sucks the most is my dad was fucking right," he whispered. "I don't have what it takes, I'm a huge disappointment. In the end, I really didn't give a shit about disappointing him. But my mom? How am I supposed to answer her calls? Her texts? Tell her any of this? I don't know how you do it. I don't know how anyone does it. Even dumb-fuck Travis is able to stay afloat."

He took a deep, shaky breath and leaned back in his chair, head tilted to the ceiling and eyes clamped shut. "I can't even bring myself to care. I don't see the relevance. I don't have the passion for this like you do. I know how people talk shit about me. They judge me. They expect me to be this amazing prodigy and live up to my dad—and then they see I'm just an idiot with no clue what I'm doing and no desire to actually be here. I'm a joke." He sat motionless, the clock ticking on the wall the only sound in the room.

Harper moved slowly, perching herself on the table in front of him. She put her feet on the sides of his seat, bracketing his thighs.

"Dan. Look at me."

He didn't move.

"Please," she said softly.

Dan swallowed and she watched it travel down the column of his throat. His eyes blinked open and he moved his head to look at her. Stress and embarrassment creased his beautiful skin while pain and desperation rimmed his eyes. She held his gaze.

"Firstly, don't ever compare yourself to Travis Giles. He is a talentless asshole with the personality of a used tampon. I won't let you degrade yourself like that," she said, and smiled when he let out a tiny breath of laughter.

"Secondly, this place is the pits." Dan scoffed but she persisted. "I'm serious, it is. This school tries to break you. It pushes you to the ground and stands over your body, taunting you. It makes you wonder why you decided to do this because everything about it is an uphill battle. But you get up. Over and over. Just to take another punch, another hit." She reached for Dan's hand and held it to her chest.

"But when you get up, that one final time, battered and bloody and not sure you can take one more blow, it teaches you how to heal. And then you go out and heal others."

Dan looked away from her, lost somewhere she couldn't reach him.

She moved a hand to his chin and turned him to face her. "It isn't just you, Dan. No one can get it until they're going through it. We have final exams every week, eight hours of class every day. Clinical rotations, lab time, service hours, competencies—it's too much. Everyone finds it hard, they just aren't willing to be real about it." She stroked his cheek with her hand. "Your honesty about it makes you wonderful. It makes you real. And that's what'll matter when you're out practicing—that you're a real, live, human being who can relate to people, not that you can recite every enzyme and product in gluconeogenesis or lipid metabolism."

"I won't ever see a patient if I can't get a handle on these classes." He still wouldn't meet her eyes.

"Don't look at the big picture. What do you have this week?"

"Osteology and musculature of the skull. There are over three hundred structures to memorize. And then insertion and origin and—"

She brought a finger to cover his lips. "Hey. I'm going to help you. Okay?"

"You have your own stuff to learn."

She put her hands on his temples and forced him to look at her. "Let me help you. We'll give it half an hour and then I can go back to my stuff. But let's at least work through the first bit. Together."

He hesitated a moment longer, then nodded.

She beamed at him, studying his face. "This is as good a place to start as any," she said, squeezing gently where her hands rested on his temples. "This is your temporal bone. This front part, where my hands are, is the squamous portion of it. It's one of the most fragile spots on the skull."

Dan's green eyes were locked on her mouth, watching each word form.

"The muscle over it is called the *temporalis*. That's easy to remember, right? It's fan-shaped." She stretched her hands, fingers tangling in his silky hair. "Its origin is actually on the parietal bone"—she drummed the tips of her fingers where they extended toward the top of his head—"and travels all the way down to here." She dragged her hands down his skin to where his lower jaw met the upper. It felt so good to touch him, the heat of his skin warming her from the center of her body. Dan closed his eyes. "It allows you to open and close this smart mouth of yours." Harper gripped his chin and lifted it up and down. Dan smiled, his dimple peeking out.

"*I* have the smart mouth?" He laughed. "That's rich."

"Hush. I'm teaching."

He arched an eyebrow, his lips ticking up at the sides.

"*This*"—she traced hungry fingers over his teasing brow—"is raised by your frontalis. It also wrinkles your forehead." Harper scratched her fingers lightly against the golden skin, letting them wander back into his hair and rub his scalp. Dan's lips parted, soft puffs of air tickling her forearms, goose bumps rising along the path. She needed to touch every inch of him, learn and map him so she could trace him in her mind when miles and obligations separated them.

"I can't forget *this*," she said softly, dragging the pads of her fingers to his cheeks. Dan sucked in a shaky breath.

"You know one of my favorite things about you?" She began stroking lightly at the corners of his mouth.

Dan gave a small shake of his head. Harper felt the tension he held in every muscle, taut and ready to snap.

"Your dimple. It drives me wild." She rested the edge of one pinky where the devious indent usually made its mark, her other hand mirroring the position. He smiled and it popped to life below her touch. She smiled too.

"Yes. That. It's from having bifid zygomaticus major muscles. Quite the lovely anomaly if you ask me. It originates here." She moved her fingers to the far upper corners of his cheekbones. "Normally it continues as one straight line down." She traced her fingers along his cheeks, the prickles of stubble shooting feeling straight to her belly, where it pooled and dripped lower. "And it inserts at the corner of the mouth. But yours splits." Her index and middle fingers separated on their path, one coming to rest at the corner of his lips, the other resting an inch below.

She stared at her hands. She couldn't believe she could touch something so lovely. Her breathing stuttered, turning fast and shallow, her body unable to get enough air into her lungs. She saw the rapid rise and fall of his chest and knew he was drowning with her.

Her fingers started to wander, moving slowly, tracing over the silk of his lips.

His tongue peeked out, following her path, tasting her touch.

Her eyes made a languid journey up from his mouth, taking their time to absorb every beautiful inch of him, until they met his gaze. The desperate pull of their bodies had brought them closer, their noses almost touching.

Their panting breaths mingled in a cloud, fogging out the real world and leaving nothing but the raw feelings between them. Dan pulled back slightly, his eyes turning sharp and serious as he looked at Harper. He lifted an eyebrow, almost imperceptibly, in a heavy, silent question.

She knew what the answer should be. She should push away the fog, get off the desk, and pack up her things. She should go home and lay Dan to rest as the perfect fantasy.

In her imagination, he'd never hurt her; she'd always be enough just as she was, no more chasing her worth. In her wildest dreams, she wouldn't feel the weight of loss and fear and insecurities. In that golden fantasy bubble, she could step back from this endless pursuit of being perfect and instead choose to just *be*. Be with Dan. Be herself. Be in love.

Looking at Dan, petals of pleasure unfurled deep in her belly— some sharp and nearly painful, others soft and sweet. Her skin itched and ached for his touch, and an impatient desire hummed along her hands, desperate for the instant gratification of his body beneath them. She wanted to lose herself in him.

Staring back at his unspoken question, the tiniest movement of her head gave an equally subtle answer.

It was enough.

Dan was on her before she could even process what it meant.

His lips collided with hers—no finesse, no ability to exercise caution. Just pure, unfiltered passion crashing against her. She met him with equal force, an untamed need driving her to press closer and closer against him, wanting to be marked by him. Her hands weaved themselves into his hair, and the soft tickle of it against her raging skin unleashed her.

Dan let out a soft groan as she fisted it in handfuls. He swiped his tongue against her lips, and she opened to him, far beyond denying him anything he asked for. His tongue moved against hers, searching and feeling and loving every inch of her mouth as she lost herself in the sensation. Harper wanted to touch and grab and feel every part of him, but her arms were unable to do anything but cling around his neck.

His hands slid up her thighs, leaving scorched nerves in their path. He gripped handfuls of her hips and yanked her closer, bringing her flush against him as her legs straddled his chest. The contact made her whimper, and he dragged an opened-mouth kiss along her neck, his teeth grazing her skin. Harper's head fell back to give him more.

Her breath came in shallow gasps, and she decided she'd happily suffocate in the overwhelming sensations. His chest heaved against her with every ragged inhale, and the feel of it nearly drove her mad.

One hand still clutching her hip, he brought the other to her hair, gathering the short strands in a fist and using it to tilt her head to meet him more deeply with each kiss. Harper dug her hands into the collar of his shirt, desperate for any skin she could press her palms against.

With a grunt, Dan moved both hands to her ass, pushing out of his chair with such force it toppled behind him. He lifted Harper, gripping and kneading into her soft flesh before turning and pushing her back against the wall. All air left her, and she didn't miss it. She was drowning in the heady rush of need and want and all she cared about was his next kiss.

Lick.

Touch.

Teeth.

Caged against his chest, she could feel their hearts clanging wildly against each other, lost in their own battle to prove which of them was more desperate for the other. The kisses slowed in their fury, but not in intensity, each becoming long and drawn out, a silent conversation of how painful holding back so many feelings had been.

Dan pulled away, and Harper helplessly stared into the green depths of his eyes. Their gazes were tethered and locked, the intensity of it heating Harper even further. Dan licked his lips with a slow hunger. He took a deep breath.

"Harper, I—"

But he didn't get to finish his thought. The secret world they'd built around their pleasure was invaded. The door handle to the study room turned sharply, the metallic noise piercing their quiet peacefulness. Reality began slowly filling in at the edges. Instant panic filled Harper, and Dan's head whipped to the door.

It banged open and Thu's voice cracked through the last remaining layers of their shared fog. Thu's head was turned over her shoulder as she talked to Alex, who stood behind her. Alex's eyes bulged, and he let out a wet choking sound as he gawked at Harper and Dan's entangled form. Noticing his look, Thu's head snapped forward.

Her jaw dropped open. She was silent for a moment. But, because it was Thu, it was *only* a moment. "Fuck. Yes."

Her words broke Harper out of her shock. She pushed awkwardly against Dan's frozen arms, which gave out more easily than Harper anticipated. She toppled out of his grip, sliding down the wall in slow motion until she landed in a pile of contorted limbs. She didn't know if this could get worse.

"Holy shit, did you just drop her?" Thu's voice rang out with an incredulous laugh.

Dan's attention rocketed to Harper's rag doll slump and his eyes went even wider with fear. She worked to maneuver herself into a more dignified pose, but every joint felt leaden and uncooperative.

"Dude," Alex said with pure awe. He nodded slowly, a smile plastered on his face.

Something about their stupid grins allowed Harper to finally find her voice.

"Ohmygod, Thu, get out!"

"Get out? I feel like I should get a camera! I want to remember this for the rest of my life," Thu said.

"Thu! Get the fuck out!"

"Calm down, it's not like you were in full coitus . . . yet." She gave a snort of laughter.

Alex looked between Harper and Thu with a mix of fear and amusement before giving a small chuckle. Harper found her feet and moved toward her friend.

"Okay, okay! We'll give you a few minutes to—um—finish . . ." Thu grinned again, and Harper snarled at her. "Composing yourselves!" she added rapidly. "Finish *composing* yourselves. And then, Harper, you and I will teach these boys about bones." Thu said with a wink, turning to leave the room.

But before she was out the door, she said, over her shoulder, "Although, it seems like you were giving Harper quite the lesson there yourself, Dan."

Harper slammed the door shut and thumped her forehead against it.

Silence hovered in the room and Harper couldn't bring herself to turn and look at Dan. She felt mortified and ridiculous. But most of all, she felt mad at the interruption—the exact opposite of how she needed to feel.

"I should . . . go," she finally whispered to the wall.

"Can I come with you?" Dan's voice was hoarse and lost.

Harper squeezed her eyes shut until she saw little stars. She tried to count them as she swallowed past the lump in her throat. Harper steeled her nerve and turned to face him.

"I don't think that's a good idea. Nothing's changed. I'm still—"

"Leaving. In May. I know," he said, raking his hands through his hair.

"Yes. Leaving." Maybe if she said it enough times she could finally, *finally*, get that concept to sink into her own head.

He opened his mouth, looking like he was about to argue, but he slammed it shut.

She moved to the table and shoved her things into her bag, then walked back to the door. She opened it and paused, knowing what stepping out of the room would mean. She looked at him over her shoulder, meeting the hurt and confusion in his eyes.

"I'm sorry," she whispered. "I really am."

Then left.

CHAPTER 25

DAN

Dan stared at the door, frustration bubbling under his skin and threatening to explode from every pore.

Staying on brand for the world's most unwanted visitor, Alex tapped lightly at the door before poking his head in.

"All clear?" he asked, shooting Dan a wink.

"It's Friday night at a fucking school. Is there really no other room you could occupy right now?"

Alex stared at him blankly. "You okay, man?"

"Alex, get out."

"Oh, sorry." Alex whipped his head out of the door and slammed it shut.

Dan fisted his hands in his hair, pacing the small space and trying to adjust his aching cock to a more comfortable position. The walls felt close and suffocating, and he wanted to punch a hole through every inch of them.

He moved to the table, shoving his things into his bag and slamming the chair into place. One of the legs caught on something and he bent to pick it up. One of Harper's notebooks. Dan thumbed through it. Her small, curvy letters filled every inch of the pages, notes and diagrams scribbled into connections only her brilliant mind seemed able to decipher. He closed the book and tossed it into his backpack with the rest of his things.

He left the study room and plowed through the school, wanting to escape its stale air and taunting echoes. The cold night ripped at his skin as he stepped outside. He wanted more of the feeling. It was sharp and precise and worked to erase the softness of Harper's touch. He walked without direction, every step taking him somewhere farther from that room. It didn't really matter where.

It was a weird sensation, having the thing he wanted most also be what stood in the way. He'd left all the doors wide open for Harper, encouraging her to step inside. And she had. Repeatedly. She went in, wrecked the place, and left, only caring about her stake in the game, disregarding that Dan had something to lose too.

He'd kept his mouth shut and his head down, letting her take the lead, the constant bystander in his own life. It had done nothing but leave him a confused mess. Harper would expose herself just enough to screw with his head, but as soon as it felt too real, she ran scared and left him hanging out to dry, sitting like an idiot with his heart on his sleeve.

Hiding was no longer an option. If Dan was forced to face the reality of what he felt every fucking time she entered the room, she would too. She couldn't keep offering hints and clues that maybe she felt the same way, just to snatch hope from his grip.

His feet now had a purpose, and they weren't leaving their destination without answers. Dan would wait for Harper, but not with the games. Not with the confusion. He'd give her everything or wait with nothing, but this in-between had to end.

He punched her door buzzer and waited, tapping his foot against the pavement as the seconds ticked by.

"Hello?"

"You left your notebook." Dan's voice sounded coarse to his

own ears. Beats of silence marked the seconds, and he almost jammed his finger against the buzzer again before her voice crackled back through the intercom.

"I'll come down and get it."

"I'll come up."

"No, it's fine. I'll—"

"Let me up, Harper."

The silence stretched on, and Dan felt blood throbbing in his temples. He could wait all night. Harper must have sensed she was fighting a losing battle, and she buzzed him in. Dan ripped open the door and bounded up the stairs in an effort to tamp down the energy pulsing just under his skin.

He knocked on Harper's door, using his other hand to prop himself against the frame. She opened it just wide enough to expose half of her body. She wasn't inviting him in.

Dan instinctively leaned closer. She'd so thoroughly invaded his heart and commandeered his thoughts that the pretense of physical space felt superfluous. Harper held out her hand for the notebook, her eyes looking everywhere but at him. Dan tilted his head, forcing her to meet his gaze.

"I want to talk about what happened."

A small puff of air left her lips, and her hand fell limply at her side. She dropped her forehead against the edge of the door and scratched her thumbnail along the wood.

"There's nothing to talk about," she said at last.

The words were quiet, but their impact reverberated against Dan's chest. He stepped closer.

"Really? Because I think there is."

Energy poured off Harper, thrumming beneath her skin, electricity desperate to break free. Dan wanted to get close enough that it burned him.

"And I also don't think you get to decide for both of us anymore," he added. Her eyes shot to his face, and he leaned in closer.

"Everything with you is one step forward, thirty steps back. I can't play this game."

Dan put his palm against the door and gave it a push. Harper let it swing open and took a step back. She glared up at him, hands fisted at her sides. Dan stepped into the apartment and shut the door. She backed up against the wall, chin raised as their eyes locked.

"Don't give me that bullshit," she snapped. "I told you from the start I can't do anything more than friendship. You're the one who wants more. You're the one pushing this."

Dan let out a barking laugh. "That's rich, Harper. So rich. There's nothing you *can't* do. You *won't* and that's the difference. You're scared. You're scared as shit, so you pretend you don't feel this too. I've never been just a friend. Neither of us lasted a day with that."

Anger sparked in her eyes. "You don't get it. I have things to lose here. I'm graduating. I'm moving. I'm starting a career. I don't even know where I'll be living in a few months. Do you really think I could give you a relationship right now?"

"What if I don't care that you're moving? What if the miles don't matter to me? I'm willing to do what it takes to make this work."

Harper opened her mouth to deliver another blow, but he stopped her.

"You think I have nothing to lose?" Dan said, lifting his arms. "You have just as much power to hurt me as I do to hurt you. But I'm not scared of that. I'm willing to face it because being with you is worth more than the prospect of pain."

Silence pressed between them as Harper watched him, eyes sharp and wary. "Do you do this just to torture me?" she whispered. "Just to make me feel like an idiot?"

Dan jerked his head back in surprise. "What?"

"This!" she exploded, flinging her arms between them. "The

grand gestures and the smooth lines and the goddamn *prettiness* of you," she hissed, taking a step toward him. "You waltz in and out of my days and absolutely melt me. You back me up against a wall and say all the right things—it turns me into a fool!" She jabbed a finger against his chest. "You turn me into a fool. You make me all sweaty and nervous and tongue-tied. And you stand there—with your ridiculous *height*—and are completely articulate and composed like you aren't asking impossible things of me."

Dan tried to make sense of her words. "Are you telling me you're offended by my . . . height?"

Her eyes were angry saucers, and red blotches burned her cheeks.

"No. I'm telling you that I'm offended that you reduce me to some sort of infatuated teenager. You consume all my thoughts and fry my nerves every time you look at me. And you just get to stand there. Completely unaffected and immune to the ridiculous nightmare you're putting my system through. And on top of that, you're asking for something I'm not sure I can do."

Dan studied her. Challenge burned in the depths of her eyes, long lashes flicking up and down as she stared back at him. Her nostrils flared as she sucked in deep breaths, her chest rising sharply with the effort.

She was so beautiful.

"If you think I'm immune to you," he said slowly, "you aren't as bright as your reputation holds."

Her eyes shot wide with indignation. "Excuse me?"

He pressed his finger against her lips and watched a gentle tremble course through her body.

"If you can stand there—looking like a fucking dream with that perfect little mouth that tastes so sweet, and those big, round eyes that I want to see looking up at me while I'm over your body—and think you don't make my heart hammer and my palms sweat, make me half-hard every time you walk into the room, you don't have a clue."

Her pupils dilated and Dan watched the pulse beating in her throat. He wanted to run his teeth over the spot.

"You want to talk about consuming thoughts?" Dan's voice was a hoarse whisper. "You are the *only* thing I can think about. How to make you laugh. Smile. Blush. I don't think about anything without it being in the context of you. I lie in bed every night and think about your voice, the way your nose crinkles when you laugh, the way your eyes go wide every time I catch you looking at me when you think I'm not paying attention. I replay the feel of your kiss, wonder what every inch of your skin would feel like, naked, against my hands. If you think you aren't running through my mind on loop until I want to crawl out of my skin with wanting you, then you have no clue what the word 'unaffected' means."

He moved toward her.

Closer.

Closer still.

Both were fighting for air. Jagged breaths heaved their chests, just molecules and heat separating them from crashing together.

Every cell in Dan's body challenged her to contradict the energy between them, to deny that a spark so violent could exist, and Harper's wild eyes returned the dare.

Time constricted around them like a skin, moving too slowly for the speed of his heart and the immobility of his body. After an eternity in just a moment, Harper lifted her chin even higher, and her gaze pierced through him.

"If I don't know," she breathed, the words caressing his skin, punching at every nerve, "then teach me."

Dan crashed his mouth against her, not caring where it landed just as long as it was on her, and demanded more than words could give. His body caged her against the wall, and she pushed into him with her full force, arms locking around his neck.

There was no tenderness from either of them. It was the violent result of pent-up need—of tamping down the excruciating feelings they'd both been denying. It was messy and raw, the restrained heat and attraction pouring from their bodies.

Harper ripped his jacket open, clawing to get it off his arms, while Dan dragged his teeth against the curve of her neck, desperate for the taste of her, his mind feasting on her gasps.

"Is this happening?" The words tore from her throat in a ragged pant against his lips as his hands found the swell of her breasts.

Dan nodded, lips still pressed against her mouth. "Yes," he groaned against her skin. "Anything. Everything. Whatever you want. Nothing you don't." He dragged his tongue across her collarbone and lapped at the hollows. "But I can't keep my hands off you any longer."

He gripped at her hips and lifted her. Harper wrapped her legs around his waist, digging her heels into his back as she pushed closer against his mouth. He moved down the narrow hallway toward her bedroom, desperate to lay her down and worship her body.

Any hunger Dan felt, Harper returned. Her hands clawed at his shoulders and tangled in his hair. Kisses and bites bruised his lips.

More than once she pushed herself into him, trying to clutch him closer, making him lose balance and crash against the wall. He growled against her lips, and she wrapped herself even tighter.

He felt drugged by her abandon. Every sigh and gasp ripped his heart from his chest. He felt her walls crumbling to dust, left behind in the hall as they moved together.

He dropped her hips onto the edge of the bed, lavishing kisses against her temple.

Her jaw.

Her throat.

Anywhere his lips could reach.

Her shaky fingers fumbled with the buttons of his shirt, and he moved back just long enough to tear it over his head. His body jerked at the feel of her hands tracing over the planes of his stomach, and he wanted to press into her touch until they were fused.

Her clever fingers moved to his pants, undoing the button and pulling down the zipper, pushing them lower until he could kick out of them.

Dan grabbed fistfuls of her sweater and pulled it over her body, then unclasped her bra. He feasted on the sight of her. His heart pounded in an uneven intensity that made every inch of his skin feel more than he thought was possible.

They stopped their attack long enough to absorb the sight of each other's bodies. He'd never known a hunger like this. An absolute need to look and touch and lose himself in another person. His hands shook as he brought the tips of his fingers to caress the curves of her breasts. He splayed his fingers across her chest, laying his palm flat over her heart as it hammered against his touch.

He loved seeing his hand spread over her delicate body. The wildness in her eyes as she pushed closer against him, told him she loved it too.

A primal urge to reach into her chest and own her heart, the way she owned his, overwhelmed his senses. He pushed against her gently and watched her fall back against the mattress. Desire and tension pooled in her eyes as she stared up at him.

He trailed kisses down her stomach as his hands worked at the buttons on her jeans.

"Dan?" Her voice traveled to him on a whisper.

"Hmm?" he hummed against her hip bone, tugging her pants down her thighs.

"This isn't something I've done in a while and um . . ." She took a shaky breath.

A biting kiss silenced the rest of her thought. Dan's hands glided up her legs to grip the swell of her hips.

"Harper?"

"Hmm?" The noise finished in a sigh as he traced his fingers across her stomach and allowed them to linger at her panty line. He dragged a slow touch across the elastic before pushing it down.

"Don't think so much."

Their tongues tangled and moved in sensual exploration, hands discovering every inch of each other. The world dissolved around them, Dan's new reality centered on the feel of Harper's body. He felt overwhelmed by the need to breathe her in.

Harper twisted and squirmed beneath him in a delirious search for what she needed. She was trying to sprint, but Dan wanted to drag out every second, wring dry every sensation.

He lifted off her and flipped her onto her stomach, hungry fingers tracing the bumps of her vertebrae, sinking into the swell of her hips, touching every inch of her soft skin he could reach. He watched her body respond—noticing where she melted, when she jerked—cataloging the pressure that made her sigh and the touches that made her gasp.

He extended his body over hers, caging her writhing form in his heat and desire. Her hips pushed up against him and moved in desperate circles when he slid his fingers to where she wanted them. Pleading whimpers escaped her lips and her hands fisted into the sheets. Dan had to pause for a moment to collect himself.

He bit sharply at her ear and she let out a deep groan. "I want you. I fucking *need* you," he whispered against her skin. "And I'm going to devour you. But I'm going to do it slowly. We have all night, and I plan to use it."

"Please," she sobbed, her body fighting for more.

"Let go." Dan licked her skin and watched his next words dance over the spot, goose bumps rising in their wake. "Stop chasing it. Let go and let me give it to you."

He sat up and turned her onto her back, his eyes scouring up and down her body. Red blotches covered her chest and cheeks. Sweat glistened at her temples and her bangs curled across her forehead. His chest heaved and he felt like he couldn't get enough air.

Dan dragged his open mouth down her body to the juncture of her thighs. Their eyes locked over the slope of her stomach and Dan pushed her knees farther apart, settling between her legs.

Harper's eyes followed the movement of his mouth, moving slowly

      slowly

         slowly

until he touched her hot, swollen bud with the tip of his tongue. Her body shuddered beneath him, and he pressed his hands around her hips to hold her against the bed. Dan's lips locked around her and his eyes rolled back in his head.

He was an instant addict, wanting her taste to permeate his blood, to constantly circulate in his system so he'd never be without the pleasure of her body. He continued to swirl his tongue against her, sucking at her sweetness, and she moaned, clamping her thighs against his face. Harper's body arched against the bed, and Dan watched her head twist from side to side, corded muscles sticking out against her neck while her hands gripped and pulled at his hair.

"Not yet," she gasped, tugging at his head. "It's too much—I need— Not yet."

Dan pressed an open-mouthed kiss to her inner thigh, then her hip bone. "Fuck, Harper, you taste so good," he growled against her skin. She continued to squirm beneath him, her heels digging helplessly into the mattress.

Dan crawled up her body, placing bites and kisses along the

way, working to keep her anchored to the moment. They became a mess of tangled limbs and desperate kisses as he hovered over her.

"Do you have a condom?"

Harper nodded and pointed at the bedside table. "Lizzie keeps all our rooms stocked," she said, with something almost like a laugh.

"She's always been my favorite of your friends," Dan said, fishing into the back of the drawer before finding one. He turned back to her, tearing the foil packet open. Harper's eyes were heavy and glazed as she watched him roll it on with shaky hands.

Dan settled back between her legs, gripping her thighs and opening her wide to him, memorizing every inch of her. They watched Dan push slowly into her. Then moaned.

Dan felt lost in the sensation of her. He expected sex with Harper to dull the constant, sharp need for her, the raw aching. But it only heightened it, spearing through him and creating the singular focus of how their bodies felt together as he continued thrusting in and out of her.

He felt whole and consumed, nothing in the world but her.

Harper's nails scoured his back as he drove into her with long, hard movements, the tight buds of her nipples rubbing against his chest, driving him wild. Her legs quivered around him, her body taut with pleasure, while that overwhelming, electrifying pulse caressed his spine. Dan licked the light sheen of sweat at the hollow of her throat and she arched her head back with a cry.

"You taste so good. Fuck, you *feel* so good," he whispered into her ear, biting at the lobe.

She began thoroughly shaking and Dan didn't know how much longer he could withstand the blissful torture. His hand gripped tightly at her thigh, bordering on delicious roughness as he hitched her leg higher up around his waist. He felt her wrap her legs more tightly around him, drawing him deeper and deeper as they both let out another groan.

Harper's eyes snapped closed, and she writhed beneath him in a way that made his cock swell even harder. He moved a hand between them and stroked her in a matching rhythm.

"*Dan.*" His name was a hoarse cry, a battle raging behind her closed eyes. Even in their most intimate moment, she still tried to hide.

"Harper. Look at me." Dan slowed his pace, rolling his hips in a way that created maddeningly slow friction.

She pressed her cheek into the mattress, eyes squeezing tighter.

Dan stopped moving, pressing their hips flush with a deep push. Harper continued to twist beneath him, her body fighting for more while her mind tried to escape the overwhelming pleasure. He felt her pulse tightly around him, and it took all his control to not jerk forward again to match its rhythm.

"Look at me." His voice came out with jagged force. His hands gripped at her face and her eyes flew open, a wildness charging their depths.

Lust. Hunger. Fear.

Fear that the overwhelming feelings would last forever. Fear they would end too soon. He saw it all in her and felt the same.

He didn't understand how his heart could feel like it was simultaneously being ripped open and stitched together. He wanted to cherish her and wreck her. He wanted to give her everything and ask for nothing while another part of him wanted to demand she give her mind and body to him alone.

Her body continued to shake, the tremors nearing on frantic, and she threw her arms around his neck and buried her face at the base of his throat, lifting her torso so there wasn't an inch of their skin that wasn't touching. She clung to him with blinding force, making unintelligible whispers of distress while grinding her body against his in a way that was going to make him lose it.

"How is it possible to feel this much?" she whispered into his skin.

"I don't know," Dan answered honestly, moving against her. "But I feel it too."

She pulled back and her eyes sparked with vulnerability. She had never been so bare, and it took his breath away. Her nails raked down his back, digging into his skin as if she were anchoring her whole world on the connection of their bodies.

"Don't leave me. Please. Just . . . try not to leave me." Her lip quivered but fortified honesty filled her gaze.

His heart splintered into sharp fragments of tenderness. If she wanted him, he'd make sure she'd never be without him. Every doubt, triumph, misstep, and failure had been designed to bring him to this moment, where he could do nothing more than give Harper exactly what she asked.

"Never." His mouth crashed against hers with force, saying what words couldn't. He belonged to her in any way she wanted him.

As he felt her pulse around him, every part of her gripping him closer, he followed her over the edge, his body fracturing in the waves of pleasure.

As the sensation ebbed away, Dan hovered over Harper's body, her panting breath against his chest, and their eyes locked with a heavy intimacy.

She reached up a shaky hand and brushed his hair off his forehead, then rested it against his cheek. He turned and planted a kiss into her palm, watching the smile bloom on her mouth.

CHAPTER 26

HARPER

Harper stirred from a light sleep to the feeling of Dan's fingers tracing along her skin. She squinted one eye at the clock on her nightstand and realized she'd only been dozing for a few hours. The night had passed in short periods of sleep followed by bursts of kisses, touches, and sighs as they explored each other's bodies.

Harper turned her head and her gaze traveled up Dan's body. She ate up every piece—the long legs stretched under her comforter, his delicious bare chest propped against her headboard, the soft smile warming her from the inside out.

"Hi," she murmured, closing her eyes again to the soft tickling of his fingers.

"Hi." He slid down to lie next to her, faces level. "This is unexpected," he said, tracing a fingertip over her ribs. "I like it."

Harper stiffened. Her mind was so far removed from her sense of self—instead somersaulting about the future and what-ifs—that she often forgot about her tiny tattoo.

"It's kind of silly." Harper moved her arm from under her pillow to her side, covering it. Dan clucked his tongue and lifted her arm away.

"You seem to say that about the most interesting pieces of you." His dimple made a morning appearance and caused her pulse to beat so forcefully that her tattoo was probably dancing against her skin.

"So what's the story?" he asked, his finger returning to its tracing. "Why the canine?"

Harper arched an eyebrow at him. "Dental anatomy's going well, huh?"

Dan laughed but his eyes urged her on. She took a deep breath.

"It's a copy of the first anatomical drawing of a maxillary canine. I got it when I was accepted to dental school." She chewed on her lip, remembering the day. "I *never* planned on getting one. But when I got the call from Callowhill and it felt so huge and special and surreal, I needed to do something just as monumental to remember it."

She closed her eyes and a small smile tugged at the corners of her mouth as she remembered hanging up the phone and looking around her as if the world had just opened the door to its secrets. She'd felt the urge to dance and run—scream out with the overwhelming happiness that threatened to burst straight from her chest. The first coherent thought she'd had was that she wished she could tell her mom.

She'd indulged an impulse for the first time that day, celebrating the rewards of her careful planning with a poorly thought-out permanent reminder.

"I found the closest tattoo shop, walked in, and got it." She shrugged and opened her eyes. Dan stared at her intently. Moments from their night together popped through her mind: the hunger in the way he looked at her when they came together, his touch turning from gentle to greedy, the feel of his tongue, body, hands, against her skin. Heat flooded her cheeks.

"Why that tooth, though?" he asked gently, looking at Harper like she was the most fascinating person in the world. A foreign feeling danced in her chest from his attention, and she worked to place it.

Valued.

The way he looked at her made her feel valued. Interesting. Adored.

She wanted to wake up always feeling this way.

"I'm not sure," she said at last. "The canines have always been my favorite. There's something sharp and strong about them . . . I guess that's how I wanted to feel. What I wanted to be in this phase."

She blew out a breath, searching Dan's face, looking for a sign that would tell her how much more she should give. His green eyes were soaking her in, drawing out bits and pieces of her before she could even grasp that she was willingly handing them over.

"It also has the longest root," she continued. "I was kind of desperate to feel rooted too, I think. After my mom passed, my aunt and uncle took me in—they've always been so good to me— but being twelve and having them become my caretakers over- night left me feeling a little . . . disjointed. I felt like things could tip at any point and I'd have to start over again."

Dan observed her a moment longer, and she could almost see the questions he wanted to ask sitting on the tip of his tongue as he wet his lips, but she knew he wouldn't push. Harper couldn't pin- point the exact moment she'd started trusting Dan—whether it had been a specific smile, or one of the precious times he'd dropped his forehead to hers and laughed, or if he'd made a slow, steady invasion into her heart that now felt like it had an entire chamber dedicated to him—but she trusted him in a foreign, overwhelming way. It was the most comforting thing she'd found in a long time.

She pushed up to sitting, needing to break the intimacy of the moment before it broke her.

His flannel shirt was lying on the floor and she reached for it, sliding it over herself and enjoying the initial coolness of the fabric against her skin.

She reached for her phone and plopped back onto her pillows, aware of the drowsiness returning to Dan's breathing.

"What are you doing?" he mumbled against her shoulder.

"I'm looking for a song."

"A song for what?"

"To play," she said dryly.

He fixed her with a dull look, slow-blinking at her sarcasm to let her know he wasn't amused.

"It looked like you were about to fall back asleep, and I wanted to drown out your snoring." Harper's lips twitched but she otherwise kept a straight face.

Dan propped himself up on his elbow and hovered over her with a wolfish smile.

"I don't snore. And if you aren't careful, I'll have to force it out of you. What's the song for?"

"Yeah?" Harper cocked an eyebrow. "I'm terrified."

Dan's eyes held a predatory glint as he stared at her mouth. A nervous giggle bubbled from her throat, and the noise set off his attack.

He pounced on her, squeezing and tickling her sides. Squealing and flailing, she worked to move out from under him, but she was helpless against his big, teasing hands.

"You—asshole," she managed to choke out between gasps. She pounded her small fists against him, but Dan just laughed and nipped at her neck. He shifted his position and plucked the phone from her hand, switching up tactics.

"You're evil." Harper rolled from under him and lunged for her phone, but he snaked an arm around her waist and pulled her back with a laugh. "And annoying," she said, pushing herself back up.

Dan lay on his back laughing and holding her phone toward the ceiling. She scrambled over his body to reach for it, making sure to dig her knees into his ribs as hard as possible. Dan shifted again, pinning her to the bed.

"I'll ask you one more time." He scratched his stubble against her neck, making her squeal. "What's the song for?"

"You're making it a *thing* and it isn't a *thing*." She didn't want to give him the satisfaction of surrender.

He moved to start tickling her again and she caved.

"The moment!" she squeaked when he squeezed her side. "It's for the moment."

He stopped immediately, replacing his tickles with gentle touches against her skin.

"Good girl." Dan gave her a sweet kiss that warmed every inch of her.

"I hate you," she said against his mouth, her own breaking into a smile.

Dan laughed and pressed his lips to her tingling skin in a truce, making Harper sigh. She raked her fingers through his hair and gave it a gentle tug.

"What do you mean by 'the moment'?" he asked.

He nuzzled his face against her chest and held the phone so they both could see the screen. She swiped it open and scrolled to her music library.

"I don't know, it's probably silly," she said.

"There's that phrase again."

Harper chewed on her lip. She wanted to do this. She wanted to be open with him.

But wanting it didn't make *doing* it feel any less like pulling out her own teeth.

"I just like to play a song in a moment that's special or when I'm really happy. Something that always lets you go back to the memory when you hear the lyrics." She paused, feeling Dan's eyes burning into her as she continued to gaze at the phone in his hand.

"I told you it was silly." Harper moved to close out of the music app, but Dan stopped her, capturing her hand in his free one and kissing the fingers gently.

"I'm really happy too," he said quietly against her hand. "Like, stupidly happy. So let's find a song."

CHAPTER 27

DAN

Butter sizzled in the frying pan while Dan plucked eggshells out of the pancake batter. While Harper and Dan had enjoyed feasting on each other, their near thirty-six-hour sexfest had left them at a severe risk of starvation, and Dan took it upon himself to feed Harper something other than the gummy worms and noodles they'd scavenged from her cupboards. Dan heard Harper's feet dragging down the hall and he smiled as she rounded the corner, her hair sticking up in wild angles.

"What's this?" she asked, standing in the kitchen doorway with a bemused look. She wore his flannel, and Dan indulged the possessive thrill of seeing her in his clothes.

"Pancakes," Dan said, holding up his mixing spoon and letting some of the batter plop back into the bowl. Dan felt his heart skip a beat as her eyes went wide with excitement, a huge grin blooming across her lips.

"Are you even real?" she asked, shaking her head.

Harper shuffled over to a clear section of the counter next to the stove and hoisted herself up to sit on it. She reached over to a cabinet and grabbed a mug, moving to fill it from the fresh pot of coffee sitting next to her. "There's no way you're real."

Dan shrugged and placed a kiss on her forehead. She was the one who was too good to be true.

As he pulled back, Harper grabbed fistfuls of his T-shirt and brought him closer. He stood between her legs and bent to give her a soft kiss. She hummed against his lips and the vibrations echoed through his blood.

He could have her, and have her, and have her, and still be desperate for more. He set down the bowl and ran his hands through her tangled hair, tilting her head to different angles to deepen the kiss. Her fingers traveled up his throat to rest along his jaw, the soft pressure of her skin against his igniting small bursts of pleasure through him.

Harper's stomach made a low rumble and they both laughed into the kiss. He gripped her cheeks and placed rapid-fire pecks all over her face until she was laughing like a child. He'd never get over the thrill of touching her, being allowed to openly adore her. It was addicting.

"I guess we both have to choose between hunger and horniness," he said, picking up the mixing bowl and moving to spoon batter into the pan.

Harper grabbed a handful of chocolate chips from the bag sitting on the counter and popped them into her mouth. "Lucky for us, hunger and horniness are both pretty fun to alleviate."

Dan nodded and tilted open his mouth toward Harper, and she fed him some pieces of chocolate. He locked his lips around her fingers and she laughed again, pulling them out with a loud *pop*. He turned back to the pancakes, checking to see if they needed to be flipped.

"Did I really have all the ingredients?"

Dan turned to stare at her, his eyebrows shooting to his hairline. When he realized she was serious, a huge laugh erupted from him. He watched her earnest smile turn into a frowning pout and it made him laugh even harder.

"A simple 'no' would do," she mumbled, fisting her small hand around his chin. He wiped at his eyes and tried to take a steadying breath.

"*Hell* no. You didn't have *any* of the ingredients." Another laugh broke free as he remembered rummaging through the junk food closet that she tried to pass as a pantry. He was almost positive a tumbleweed of silly straws had blown across a shelf. "I ran to the store while you were sleeping. You did have three bottles of syrup though. How your teeth aren't rotted out of your mouth is a total mystery."

"I'm just a really good dentist," she said through a mouthful of chocolate.

Dan felt her eyes on him as he moved around in the kitchen, her attention making him feel light and warm. The simplicity with which he could be with her brought a sense of peace and domesticity he'd never realized he wanted.

"Where did you learn to make pancakes?" she asked, sipping her coffee.

"Culinary school in France."

Harper rolled her eyes and poked her foot into his thigh, making him laugh.

"My mom used to make them for me and my dad every weekend," he said. "I always liked helping her cook."

"Are you close to her?"

Dan shook his head, pressing his lips into a firm line. "We used to be. Things kind of . . . shifted though, when my dad died. I probably should call her . . ." he said more to himself than to Harper. "She keeps texting me that she needs to talk about something important regarding the practice. I just know I don't want to hear whatever it is."

He could sense Harper's trepidation, wondering if she could go there, ask the murky questions about his relationship with his dad, the obvious strain with his mom. He turned to her, placing his hands on either side of her legs, and leaned toward her.

"You can ask me. Nothing is off-limits when it comes to you." He kissed the tip of her nose and turned back to the stove.

"How did things shift?"

"We dealt with watching him die differently." Dan glanced at Harper, who stared at him intently, silently urging him on. "My parents met in dental school and got married before graduation. I do believe my dad loved my mom, as much as he was capable of loving her, but he also expected my mom to give up a lot. She originally wanted to go home to Lebanon after graduating, but he demanded they stay here. She was thinking about specializing, he wanted her to work at his practice. She wanted to bring her culture into her life here, he wanted her to assimilate fully into Americana. His career always came first. The practice always came first. So, growing up, she and I had an almost unspoken alliance that he was an asshole, and it ended up making us close. For the most part, she quietly supported me paving my own way, creating my own life, and it created distance between her and my dad, I think."

Dan scooped the pancakes onto a plate and added more batter to the pan. "But when he was diagnosed with cancer, we both reacted in opposite extremes, and it's created some tension between us."

" 'Extremes' in what way?"

Dan frowned down at the pancakes, using the edge of the spatula to check the bottoms. "My mom was consumed with guilt, I think—like she thought she should be the one dying instead of him, like his life was the important one. It made her reflect on things—their marriage, me, my career—in a not so flattering light." Dan reached behind Harper for his coffee cup, and she brushed her hand through his hair. The small gesture soothed the wound that was opening in his chest.

"I, on the other hand, felt anger. My dad was always obsessed with this ideal version of what my life should be, *who* I should be. I was supposed to follow his path, live up to his reputation, eventually go into practice with them, run it after they retired, repeat it all with my own family. But I was never interested. I swear he almost had a stroke when I told him I switched my major from biology to finance." Dan took a sip of his coffee.

"I still did all the prereqs and exams for dental school and was ready to start at Callowhill a few years ago, but I backed out at the last minute." He paused, staring at the pan for a minute. "He was so angry. It was like I was the scum of the earth. I never understood that. How could he care that much what I did? I loved math and business and found fulfillment in finance"—he shot her a teasing look—"much to your chagrin." Harper gave him a weak smile. "And yet it was like I was the biggest failure he could have conjured up. Not doing exactly what he wanted was the greatest sin I could commit." He played with the edges of one of the pancakes.

"I was actually pretty successful at it too," he continued. "Finance, I mean. I got a job at a decent firm up in New York after graduation, and I was primed to climb the ladder quickly. My dad pretty much stopped talking to me though. It was like I no longer existed once I deviated from his plan. My mom would come visit me without him, and when I went home, he'd look right through me—pretend I wasn't there."

Dan moved the pancakes off the heat and added the last of the batter to the pan. He couldn't bring himself to look straight at Harper, scared she'd see the lump sitting heavily in his throat.

"It didn't even bother me that much. I almost preferred his silence to him constantly telling me what a failure I was. But it never made sense to me. Like, how could I be doing as well as I was in a job I had busted my ass for, and it wasn't good enough? How could I be successful and happy on paper, but he hated me for that?" Dan shook his head to clear out the questions he'd never find answers to.

"But after he got sick, my mom fell apart. I came home to take care of her, do whatever she needed during that time."

Dan could still see his mom with blue-black circles below her eyes from countless hours at his father's hospital bed. Toward the end her back had taken on a permanent hunch, as if she could curl into herself and protect her body from the pain.

"I wanted to be there for her while she watched her husband die, no matter how I felt about him. But even in those last weeks, he still wanted to fight me, provoke me. It was like as long as he could find the breath to tell me how disappointing I was, he could keep living." Dan fiddled with the spatula, hearing his dad's harsh words echo over and over in his mind.

"Driving home after a particularly bad visit, my mom broke down sobbing and it ripped my heart out."

He shut his eyes at the memory. The anguish on her face. The way her hands fisted and knotted together as she'd cried.

"She kept asking me why I couldn't have just done what he wanted. Followed his footsteps. Continued the family name and reputation. She kept repeating how much easier everything would have been if only . . . Kept telling me how afraid she was. How everything was falling apart. Asking me how I could let them both down like this."

A weighted silence fell over the kitchen. Dan turned off the heat and moved the last batch of pancakes onto the plate. "It was just never something I wanted to do. It wasn't out of spite, I swear. I knew it wasn't for me. But I would do anything to take that pain away from my mom. And, eventually, she told me she needed me to come on and help her run the practice or she'd lose it and her livelihood along with it. She'd only worked part-time when he was alive, and now she's overwhelmed with the patients and money and bills and keeping everything above water. My dad had dictated everything. Told her where to be and when to be there. To suddenly have the weight of it all on her shoulders . . . She pretty much demanded I join the practice, saying it was my duty as a son."

Dan tried to swallow past the guilt that made his throat thick. "So I contacted Callowhill that night. I had missed the application deadline but since I'd already been accepted once before, and I had the name to back me up, they accepted me quickly. It felt gross how easy it was to get a spot, to use the leverage I resented so much."

Dan's eyes were fixed on the countertop, countless images from those last weeks flashing through his mind in an endless loop.

"I never even told him. He died a few days after I was accepted." Dan forced himself to look at Harper, to gauge her reaction.

Harper's head was bowed forward, her hair forming a protective curtain around her features while her fingers twisted in her lap. He moved to stand in front of her and she finally looked up. Red splotches dotted her skin. Her big brown eyes were shiny with tears, and wet tracks stained her cheeks.

He loved Harper in every form she came in, but he hated to see her cry.

"Hey, none of that, okay?" He cupped his hands over her cheeks, using his thumbs to brush away the tears. "There's no reason to cry."

He kissed up and down her cheeks then gave them a sloppy lick, and she let out a choked laugh. She pulled him closer, clutching her hands around his neck and wrapping her legs around his waist. She crushed him to her so tightly, his breath caught. He nuzzled into her neck, rubbing soothing circles up and down her back. She mumbled something into his chest that he couldn't make out.

"What was that?"

She pulled back just far enough to look at him, her eyes searching his face before she rested her forehead against his chin with a sigh.

"I said, 'I'm so sorry you're here.' I'm sorry he was awful, I'm sorry he made you feel less than you are. I'm sorry for the little boy that grew up with that kind of dad. I'm sorry you have this pain and I'm sorry you have to go through this because of him. And because of your mom. They shouldn't put this on you."

"Oh, Harps." He ran his lips over her hair, breathing in her scent. "I'm not sorry." She let out a disbelieving huff. "I'm serious. If not for all of that, I never would have met you."

Harper moved to look up at him. Different emotions passed behind her eyes before Dan could read them.

"That doesn't make up for doing something you hate. You should do something you love, something that you're excited about every day. Having to carry that baggage . . ."

Dan smiled and kissed the frowning corner of her mouth. "Knowing you makes up for it more than enough. I'll figure the career out, don't worry. I'll make it work."

They held on to each other, breathing in the other's scent, calming the other's storms. Dan took an unsteady breath. The urge to tell her the truth of how much he felt for her overwhelmed him. He pulled back, looking into her eyes.

He formed the words slowly, letting each one fall from his tongue. "Harper, I think I lo—"

A wild glint flashed in her eyes right before she crashed her mouth against his, kissing away the words with frantic energy. Dan blinked a few times before returning the kiss, loving on her mouth with calming strokes.

She wasn't ready to hear it; not sober at least.

And that was okay.

Dan could wait however long she needed. The words didn't

matter as long as he could be with her. He knew how he felt, and he'd show her every day until she was ready for the words.

Harper's hands moved to the elastic of his waistband, scrambling and searching. He smiled against her mouth. A hiss escaped his lips as she moved her hand up and down his length.

"Are you trying to give me a pity hand job?"

Harper pulled back and met his eyes, sadness and lust mixing in their depths. "Hand job, blow job, any job. Put me to work. Whatever makes you feel good."

Dan laughed and rubbed his nose against hers, circling her wrists with his hands and pulling her arms to rest on his shoulders.

"While I really, *really* appreciate the enthusiasm, I think I'd pass out from exertion if we did another round without some nourishment." Harper's stomach growled again as if to emphasize his point. "And you might too. Let's eat and then we can discuss your employment." They laughed and Dan moved to fix them both a plate.

Dan handed her a pile of chocolate chip pancakes, which she drowned in syrup.

"I could die, this is so good," Harper said through a giant mouthful, her eyes rolling back in her head as she chewed, making Dan bust out laughing.

"That's nice, but your sweet tooth doesn't seem particularly difficult to please," he teased, pressing a kiss to her hair, the dark memories pushed away for another day.

CHAPTER 28

HARPER

Harper glanced at the clock and groaned.

"It's five a.m. We have to get up in an *hour* for school. There isn't enough coffee in the world," she said, rubbing her eyes.

A messy to-do list whirled around in her head while her anxiety kicked up to a rate that would substantially contribute to the global energy crisis if she didn't get it under control. Turning her face to her pillow, Harper let out another loud groan. "Why did we stay up so late?"

The bed vibrated with laughter, and she felt Dan shift closer to burrow his face in her neck. A tickle of pleasure traveled down her spine, making her sigh.

"We were studying anatomy," Dan said against her skin.

"Oh yeah?" Harper giggled into the sheets. "That's what you call it?"

"Harper, it was extremely scientific." He nudged her onto her back and grinned at her. "Obviously some visual inspection. Physiological demonstrations. Experimentation. All in the name of academia."

Harper clapped a hand over her face as she snorted with laughter.

"Please tell me you aren't going to publish the data," she said, running the pad of her finger over his dimple.

Dan grabbed her hand and kissed it. "No, the world isn't ready for my findings. But I'm not even close to done with my research, so it doesn't really matter."

Dan propped himself on his elbow to stare down at her until her giggles subsided into a bubbly smile. His fingers traced along her jaw, igniting skin that had no right to be so sensitive.

"Do you have to go into the clinic today?" he asked.

"No, Mondays are all lectures."

He hummed approvingly. "I have an idea. You're not going to like it."

"What's that?"

"What if—and hear me out—we play hooky today."

A laugh burst from her lips. "We can't!"

"Why not?" Dan asked, nuzzling into her throat.

"Because . . ." Harper found it nearly impossible to come up with reasons while he pressed kisses along her jaw. "Because we shouldn't?"

Dan clucked his tongue. "You'll have to come up with something more compelling than that, Horowitz," he said, turning them both to their sides and fitting Harper against his chest, trailing his fingers softly up and down her arm.

All her possible arguments were shot to hell at that point. Despite the countless things she needed to get done, she didn't *want* to leave their happy little nest. It wasn't in her nature to find comfort in stillness, contentment in being.

But, for the first time, she found that with Dan.

The weight of that truth pressed against her heart. She scrambled for some way to show him how much it all meant. His affection, his humor, his body—they all filled a void in Harper's heart that she thought she'd patched up years ago but had really only taped over.

Harper didn't have words for all that she felt, and a trickle of anxiety moved down her spine at the confusing mess of it all. How could she be with Dan if she couldn't even tell him her feelings?

"Harper, I can *hear* you thinking. That's not how you play hooky. Rest that beautiful brain and sleep." He pressed a kiss to her neck and let his lips linger.

"Do you know what a honey mushroom is?" she blurted out, plucking at the hairs on his arm, which was wrapped around her.

He was silent for a moment before letting out a husky laugh. "No. Why?"

"It's the largest living thing on earth. Larger than trees, elephants, whales—this one living thing takes up over three square miles in Oregon."

She could almost feel him turning that random fact over in his brain. She was glad she wasn't facing him. This would be so much harder if she had to look into his eyes instead of at the wall.

"Like the mushroom cap is over three miles across?" he asked.

Harper shook her head. "No, no. That's the amazing part. When you look at it—the part you see aboveground—it's this tiny little mushroom head. It looks so insignificant. They just pop up here and there." She gestured with her fingertips as though she could draw them in the air. "But it creates this root-like system called *hyphae*. And the hyphae—it spreads and grows and, kind of . . . takes over underground. One living thing, every cell genetically identical, spreading below the surface to take up this enormous amount of space."

Dan was quiet for a moment. "Why are you telling me this?" he asked, placing a kiss into her neck.

Harper swallowed and fiddled with the edge of the sheet. "Because that's what my anxiety feels like—a honey mushroom."

She felt Dan tense behind her, but she pushed on. "A lot of

times, someone on the outside, like you, maybe, sees these clues to it—my fidgeting, my mind seeming a million miles away, panic attacks. But inside"—she tapped her chest—"it's this intricate network of sharp pain and fear that's constantly growing and pulsing through me. It's always there, right beneath my skin, huge and controlling, but no one can see it. I just feel it. And it hurts. So badly. It makes me want to curl up into a ball or sprint out of my skeleton. This huge, inescapable thing inside me that controls me."

She paused, picking aggressively at her nails. "It feels cruel to have your own body do that to you."

They were both quiet for a few minutes, Dan absorbing her words. She was scared of what he might be thinking, how he might be judging her. The constant beast of shame pressed on her psyche. But, in that vulnerable hour of the early morning, she found a bit more courage and pushed on.

"My anxiety became really bad after the accident," she said, switching gears. "After losing my mom."

Dan's arm tightened around her.

"I had always been an anxious kid—my mom used to run her hands through my hair when I'd start falling into an attack. She'd tell me I just felt things a little sharper than everyone else, but I'd be okay . . . But after she died I—" She stared at the wall, her nostrils flaring as she pulled in deep breaths. "It got really bad. I couldn't sleep, I couldn't eat, I couldn't function. I was always afraid another attack would come. Another panic attack would swallow me whole and there was no way I could survive it without my mom. My aunt and uncle took me to a psychiatrist and he diagnosed me with . . . what were his words?" She blinked a few times, searching her memory. "I think he called it 'Chronic Panic Disorder enhanced by post–traumatic stress.'" She sucked her bottom lip between her teeth and a tear slid down her cheek that she quickly brushed away.

While Dan had seen her at her anxiety-ridden worst, she still felt the urge to hide the extent of her disorder. She felt so uncomfortable saying the words out loud, shackling them to another person. Branding herself as broken.

She could still remember sitting in the drab doctor's office, the cold child psychiatrist rattling off descriptions straight from the *DSM-IV* while Aunt Rachel and Uncle Ben sent worried glances to each other over the top of Harper's head.

Recurrent and unexpected panic attacks
Palpitations
Depersonalization
Paresthesia
Derealization

The words had sounded shameful. Complicated. They still did. At the time, Harper hadn't known what most of them meant, but she knew the number of boxes she'd ticked in the doctor's thick, scary book seemed never-ending.

And no matter how close she was to the people in her life, there was a constant survival instinct to shield them from how out of control her anxiety made her feel. It was hard to believe that anyone could witness the irrationality of her jumbled mind and not run away.

"They sent me to therapy, wanting me to get better," she continued, her throat thick with pain and embarrassment. But something compelled her to keep being honest—for once in her life, to share with someone just how fucked up she was. "I hated it though. I hated talking about losing my mom and reliving it and having to process it. I started to refuse to go, and Aunt Rachel eventually gave up the fight. I fixated on every step that went wrong throughout that day. Everything that led to that moment. But it hurt so much to say it out loud. Share it with another person. A stranger. I couldn't look at them and admit that if I hadn't taken so long to find my boots, we could have driven through the intersection minutes earlier. If I hadn't finished off the milk that morning, it wouldn't have been so pressing we go to the grocery store. Even things as drastic as if I had only been born four years earlier, I could have been the one driving, not my mom . . ."

She squeezed her eyes shut. Dan ran his hands through her hair. He gave it the gentlest of tugs, mimicking what he must have seen her do a thousand times to center herself. The gesture nearly fractured her into a million pieces. His close watch on her, his careful observations. His relentless caring. It was terrifying to have someone know her like this, to flay herself open for another person. But Dan had her trust and her heart, and she didn't want to hide anymore.

"My mom didn't die on impact," she said, her eyes flashing open. "They found her alive, rushed her to the hospital in a separate ambulance." She paused, trying to steady her breathing.

"They took her into surgery. Her worst injuries were to her head and neck. She hit the steering wheel before the airbag deployed. Oral and maxillofacial surgeons are often called in for car accidents, restructuring jaw bones and eye sockets, operating on the cranial nerves and jugular arteries and veins." She said the last part with a detached, clinical voice.

"She died on the table," Harper said simply, turning to look into Dan's eyes. "I was never told it was a surgical mistake, or anyone's fault. But I always assumed it was. I always assumed it was the hands of someone else that took my mom from me. And I've always thought, maybe if I'd been that oral surgeon, I could have saved her." Tears streamed down her cheeks, but she continued to hold his gaze. "Maybe it's ridiculous. Maybe it's true. I don't think it really matters."

Dan stared back at her, anchoring her. He brushed his fingers over her cheeks, wiping away the tears.

"All my life, I've been working toward this *one thing* I'm supposed to do. It's almost like if I fail, she'll have died for nothing." Harper's lips twitched and she lost the ability to form words. She started crying then. Truly crying.

Ugly, raw sobs ripped from her body, threatening to break her apart. Pain so intense it felt powerful enough to kill her.

And through it all, Dan held her. He pulled her close to his chest and didn't let her go, placing soothing kisses to her hair, running his strong arms over her back.

When she'd finally cried herself to exhaustion, exposed herself to her messiest core, her body relaxed. She felt afraid of what he thought, ashamed at her weaknesses, her shortcomings. But she also felt nurtured. Protected.

Neither of them said anything. Harper doubted they would. She'd propelled all that tangled emotion into the world, onto someone else, and she didn't want to unravel it.

So instead, she gently drifted off to sleep in the comforting nest of his arms.

CHAPTER 29

HARPER

"Dr. Horowitz!"

Harper catapulted out of her Dan-drenched daydream and landed firmly in the middle of the surgery she was assisting Dr. Ren and a resident on. Harper absorbed Dr. Ren's disapproving look and panicked, moving to suction the patient's socket with gusto.

"What are you doing?" Dr. Ren said calmly, grabbing the tip of the suction and moving it away in the universal dental school signal that said, *You really fucked up your one job, huh?*

Harper looked down. She'd accidently suctioned up half the bone graft Dr. Ren had placed.

"I'm so sorry," Harper said, taking a step back. Dr. Ren gave her a sharp, warning glance to not act alarmed in front of the patient, who's wide eyes had swiveled to look at Harper with fear.

"I'll get more," Harper said, scrambling toward the cupboard.

"Not with your gloves!" Dr. Ren scolded as Harper almost compromised the sterile cupboard environment.

Harper wrestled the tight rubber off her sweaty hands, panic humming in her chest as she grabbed more grafting material and handed it to the resident.

Dr. Ren eyed her for a moment before quickly repacking the

material. She turned to the resident. "Dr. Wiles, I'm going to have you suture up the patient. I'll meet you both in post-op." The woman nodded and moved to replace them.

"Come with me."

Harper and Dr. Ren stripped off their isolation gowns, then exited the operatory. Harper followed Dr. Ren into the hall, a steady thrum of dread beating in her ears. How could she be so stupid? How could she take her surgical privileges for granted, daydreaming like a lovesick teenager?

A cold sweat pricked at her skin, and Harper pulled at the neck of her scrub top as she followed Dr. Ren to her office, trying to anticipate what her reprimand would be.

"Please shut the door."

Harper did as she was told and turned slowly to face her mentor. Dr. Ren gave Harper an appraising glance, her eyes softening at what must have been unfettered fear on Harper's face.

"Harper, take a deep breath. You look like you're meeting your executioner."

Harper let out a nervous laugh and her fingers plucked restlessly at her scrub pants. "That's kind of what it feels like."

"Not today. Please take a seat." Harper collapsed into the chair opposite Dr. Ren's desk and waited.

"I know the last semester of school makes it incredibly hard to focus." Harper opened her mouth to protest, but Dr. Ren held up a hand to silence her. "If anyone deserves a little slack, it's you. All I ask is that you keep focused during procedures. Vigilance is key. You know that."

"I'm sorry, Dr. Ren, it won't happen again. I'm ashamed of myself."

Dr. Ren let out a quiet laugh. "There's no need to be dramatic. It happens."

Harper's pulse hammered in her palms.

It doesn't happen to you. It's never supposed to happen to you.

How could you drop your focus? Cruel words continued to hum through her mind, making her want to run.

"Harper?"

"Sorry, what?" She realized she'd missed something in the conversation.

Dr. Ren's eyes bore into Harper, making her fidget. "I mean it. Let it go."

Harper nodded, wishing it were that simple. She knew what was coming. The shame and anxiety would build and build and build until it felt like it would swallow her whole. It would ricochet around in her body until she felt empty. Useless. Spent.

"Thank you, Dr. Ren."

Dr. Ren smiled and excused Harper with a wave of her hand. Harper left the office and made her way out of the building, trying to shake off the feelings clawing at her stomach.

Dan was waiting for her at the street corner, ready to walk her home. He beamed at her, but the anxiety must still have lined her face because his expression quickly turned into a frown.

"What's wrong?" He pulled her in for a tight hug, one hand cradling the back of her head while she burrowed her face into his chest, breathing him in.

He was like a charging port she could plug into. The fist in her chest eased a bit, calmness permeating from him into her. She let out a sigh and pulled away.

"Nothing, just a long day." Despite her moment of honesty in those early morning hours, she still felt anything but comfortable describing just how much her anxiety ate her up. It felt too real, too abnormal to say in the light of day.

Dan laced his fingers through hers and placed their hands in his coat pocket, shielding their skin from the cold.

They started walking, and he pressed their joined hands closer to his body and rubbed teasing circles against her palm with his thumb. They kept up a steady stream of chitchat—her day, his, another week of shitty weather—and the rumble of his voice smoothed over her frazzled nerves, the worries evaporating from her skin. Harper still didn't know the language of her feelings, but she was learning not to fight them.

He kissed her at every intersection, each one hungrier than the last. When they finally got inside her apartment, they were a blur of clumsy fingers and rough hands, stripping and clawing at layers until they could finally press skin to skin.

Harper had never been particularly needy for sex, never craved it like her friends seemed to, but Dan's touch unearthed some hidden sex drive that couldn't be satiated—an overwhelming and consuming want to be as close to Dan as possible. When her heart pressed against his, it was like she could let go of the years of pain so deeply coiled in every single muscle with a sigh of relief.

They collapsed into a giggling tangle of limbs in her entryway, scaring Judy in the process.

After fumbling with a condom, Harper straddled him, sinking into the connection that was starting to feel as necessary as breathing. She moved over him, watching his face. His lips were parted and brows furrowed in concentration. She watched a swallow travel down the column of his neck and felt his large hands gripping her hips.

"Can I be honest with you?" she asked, planting her hands on his chest for support.

"Hmm?" Dan's eyes were locked on her breasts and Harper couldn't help but giggle. She lowered her mouth to his ear and nipped at it.

"This is really hurting my knees," she whispered as seductively as possible. Dan's eyes traveled down her body to where her knees were digging into the hardwood floor. After a beat, he threw back his head and laughed. Harper wanted to capture the sound of it in a painting—see its deep reds and rich blues decorate her walls.

"If this is honesty hour," he said, looking up at her, "I don't love the cold floor on my ass."

He sat up suddenly and Harper squeaked in surprise. He wrapped her legs around his waist and used one hand to push to standing, the other gripping tightly around her butt. He moved them toward the bedroom, feasting on her mouth as they went.

"So are we officially bed people?" Harper asked into the kiss.

Dan gave a gravelly laugh before flinging her onto the bed. He crawled toward her with a dark heat that she felt in her stomach, its warmth spreading like a droplet of ink onto paper. He ran his hands up her body before pushing back into her with a deep thrust, causing her to throw her head back with a groan.

"We're bed people." He pushed into her with an exaggerated thrust. "And couch people. And bend-you-over-your-desk people."

He bent his head to suck her nipple into his mouth, causing her to cry out. "And I'm going to buy you knee pads and then we can be floor people. And later tonight I'd like to make us shower people. Because there isn't one spot in this apartment I don't want to take you."

The tension built in every cell of her body as he continued to move in and out of her, touching and stroking her in a rhythm that drove her wild.

"How can it always feel this good?" Dan whispered, more to himself than her.

He fisted his fingers in her hair and bent down to kiss her. It was all she needed. Her muscles snapped, her body arching with the delicious pleasure of it as she flew over the edge.

With a loud groan, he followed her, his hard movements slowing to a stillness as they both worked to catch their breath. He kissed her again, then moved off her to deal with the condom. She lay there, a shimmering pool of pleasure and satisfaction, and wouldn't have been surprised if Dan could see the waves of golden happiness dancing off her skin.

CHAPTER 30

DAN

"I really need to study."

Dan released a deep breath through his nose before turning his head to face Harper.

"*That's* what you think about after sex? I need to reassess my technique."

Harper giggled and clapped a hand over her eyes. "I'm sorry! That was awful timing—stupid brain. I have no complaints about your technique."

Dan leaned over and kissed her cheek before sitting up in bed and reaching for his clothes scattered across her bedroom floor. He'd been spending so many nights here, he had more than a few outfit choices.

"I need to study too. Word on the street is we have a pop quiz in perio tomorrow."

Harper's brow wrinkled. "No, you don't."

"I don't?"

"It's a furlough day tomorrow and Friday. We have off."

"No . . . that's next week."

Harper stared at him for a beat before jolting up so fast it made Dan jump. She clutched at his arm. "What? Are you sure?"

"Yeah, we—"

She didn't wait for him to get the words out. She scrambled off the bed and fumbled for clothes as she moved into the hall. Dan felt waves of nervous energy radiating off her body as he followed her.

Harper kneeled on the floor, ripping through her backpack. She pulled out her laptop and agenda, then tore through the pages. Dan's stomach sank at the look of wide-eyed horror plastered on her face.

"Fuck!"

Dan moved toward her, but she lurched to her feet and moved around the apartment with ridiculous speed, grabbing a notebook here, a textbook there. Dan's post-sex brain was having trouble keeping up.

"Fuck, fuck, fuck!" Her voice was shrill and frantic as she dropped her things on the table, ripping open textbooks and scouring over them with manic eyes.

A sense of helplessness filled Dan as he tried to figure out what was happening. What he needed to do. Angry blotches were spreading along her neck, and her hands clawed at the collar of her T-shirt. He moved to her and placed a hand on her back, hoping to soothe her. She flinched away.

"God, what? What do you want?"

Dan's head jerked back at the venom in her voice.

"Harper, what's going on?"

"I fucked up. That's what's going on." Her chest was heaving and her voice sounded tight. Dan moved to touch her again but thought better of it, his hand hovering in no-man's-land between them. She stared at his limb like she wanted to rip it off.

"I've been so fucking distracted by you, I didn't even know what week it was," she said, jabbing a finger toward him. "I have a huge exam tomorrow and I thought I had another week to prepare." She snatched her things off the table and moved to her room. "I'm so fucking stupid!" The words were emphasized by her slamming the door.

Dan froze with indecision. He could hear sobbing gasps coming from behind the door. His gut told him to give her space, but his chest ached to fix things. He couldn't leave knowing how upset she was. If she decided she wanted him, he needed to be there, ready to take care of her.

Her words buzzed in his ears, poking at his insecurities.

Was this his fault? Was he holding her back? Did he fuck this up too?

Dan wasn't sure how long he stood rooted to the spot, torn between the desire to barge into her room and demand a way to fix it, and common sense that told him to leave the apartment altogether. He eventually grabbed his own backpack and settled onto the couch, flipping through his notes and trying to study for tomorrow.

～

Dan jolted awake to a heavy pressing on his groin. He blinked rapidly as Judy came into focus, kneading happily at his junk. He pushed her away, and she curled her toddler-sized body next to him on the couch, purring happily. Judy loved him in the most aggressive way a cat could.

Dan scrubbed his hands over his face and tried to get his bearings. He didn't know at what point he'd fallen asleep while he waited for Harper to emerge from her room. He'd tried to coax her out with promises of food and coffee, but she'd gone from snapping at him to leave her alone to total radio silence. He'd never felt quite as useless as this, sensing the anxiety raging in her and being helpless to bring her out of it.

Looking around, the sunshine streaming in through the window made his heart stutter to a stop, then pick up at a punishing pace. Morning was not a good thing.

Checking his watch, Dan scrambled to his feet. He knocked on Harper's bedroom door, but when she didn't respond, he pushed in.

Harper sat at her desk, her torso draped over textbooks and a mountain of scattered papers. His stomach sank even deeper as he tried to think of the best way to handle this.

"Harper?" He moved his hand up and down her back, then gave her a gentle shake. She shot upright.

Anxiety rimmed her puffy eyes, and red blotches still clung to her cheeks. She shot him a wild look, and the situation must have shown on his face because she bolted from her chair before he could say anything.

"Shit. Please tell me it isn't morning. Please."

"Harper, you need to calm down. Everything will be okay."

"What. Time. Is. It," she gritted out through her teeth, rushing around the room.

Dan swallowed. "It's 8:27."

For a moment, Harper stopped. All the vibrating energy came to a crashing halt as she froze on the spot. Her back was to him and he'd have given anything to see her face—to understand what was happening in her mind. The stillness scared him. She slowly turned to look at him, a sickly sheen of sweat glistening across her forehead and upper lip, the deep blue circles under her eyes making her look almost haunted, pain cracking her features.

Something in her broke, her body trembling as she fisted her hands, biting into the knuckles.

"Fuck!" The word tore from her throat as she turned and ran from the apartment, leaving Dan staring uselessly after her.

CHAPTER 31

HARPER

Anxiety shackled its hands around Harper's ankles, forcing her to pull its dead weight as she sprinted toward Callowhill. It felt like the harder she pumped her legs, the slower she went. Her scrub pants were on backward, her shoelaces whipping at her calves as she moved. She'd even left home without a coat, but her body felt on fire despite the cold. She was sure she looked like she was fleeing an asylum, but none of it mattered. She was late for her exam.

Harper burst into the lecture hall, not caring about the turned heads and whispers as she barreled toward Dr. Ren at the front of the room. Dr. Ren's eyes went wide with recognition as Harper stopped in front of her, panting and sweaty.

"I'm sorry. I'm so sorry." Harper brought shaking hands to her hair, trying to smooth it down. "Please let me take the exam. I'm so sorry."

Dr. Ren looked around the classroom, Harper's classmates watching the train wreck unfold with rapt attention.

"Back to work," she snapped. Her tone gentled as she turned back to Harper.

"Harper, there's protocol. I'm sorry, I can't let you take the exam right now."

A sob escaped Harper's lips, and she clutched a hand to her chest as anxiety tried to claw it open.

"Please. I'll do anything. Please just let me take the exam."

"Harper, honey, you aren't listening," Dr. Ren whispered, eyes softening. She looked around the room one more time before pulling Harper into the hall.

Harper shook as she scrubbed at the hot tears streaming down her face. She saw everything she'd worked for dissolving in this single moment. A rational part of her brain whispered that one mistake wouldn't be the end of her, but the louder, angrier part repeated over and over what a fuckup she was.

Harper felt the anxiety permeating her body like a toxic gas, embedding itself into all her cells until they were a shriveled mess of raw pain and adrenaline. Her breathing was shallow and she gulped at air.

Dr. Ren placed her hands on Harper's shoulders and bent down to meet her eyes.

"Listen to me, Harper. You need to get a grip. I'm worried about you and I need you to breathe." Harper attempted a shaky breath. Dr. Ren didn't look pleased with the result. "I promise you we'll work something out. I *promise*." She gave Harper a mild shake. "Believe it or not, this happens frequently."

Words were locked in Harper's throat, and she stared at her mentor, a rapid fire of emotions battling inside her chest.

"I'm going to send you home while they finish the exam. We'll meet next week to organize an alternative assignment."

Dr. Ren's sharp eyes pierced into Harper. Guilt hummed through her body. She'd failed the woman she admired most.

"This is me telling you that this incident will not cause you to fail. I need you to indicate that you understand that before I let you leave."

Harper nodded numbly. Her brain let out a tiny sigh of relief at the words, but the sick part of her mind yelled at her that it couldn't be trusted. Something would go wrong. The worst-case scenario was the one bound to happen.

"Email me, and we'll schedule something. But you need to get yourself under control. Mistakes happen, Harper, it will be okay."

Harper's head was swimming, the words coming to her like murky echoes. Mistakes like this didn't happen to her. Mistakes led to accidents and failure.

Self-reliant, successful, safe—that's what she needed to be. Not this unfocused, disappointing mess.

No more distractions.

"Please go home and calm yourself. I'm excusing you from the clinic this afternoon."

An unintelligible protest burst from Harper's lips, but Dr. Ren held up her hand.

"That isn't a punishment. You need to take care of yourself before you care for patients."

Harper had to look away, heat coursing up her neck, threatening to burn her down. How embarrassing. How shameful.

She couldn't keep it together. Couldn't do the one thing she was supposed to accomplish.

Dr. Ren gave Harper another wary look before pulling her into a stiff but kind hug. She let Harper go quickly and moved back into the lecture hall.

Harper moved through the school with a thrumming numbness, her hands shaking and her steps clumsy. How many exams had she taken during school? Thirty a year? Forty? How many quizzes and practicals and competencies had she conquered, always prepared?

But not anymore. She didn't know this person. This distracted, humiliating person who thought she could actually pull off this career without giving it every ounce of herself.

Her pulse pounded at her temples as wave after wave of shame and panic threatened to drown her. She was letting all that pain of her past be for nothing. She was supposed to do one thing, and she was fucking it up.

She somehow made it to the school's atrium, her breaths coming in ragged bursts. She couldn't get her heart to slow, couldn't get her body under control.

Then her eyes landed on Dan, her biggest distraction, sitting on the bench in front of the building's exit, forearms resting on his knees, head hanging in tiredness or resignation—Harper couldn't tell which. She wasn't sure she cared.

Harper didn't want to deal with what was coming. She didn't want to say what needed to be said. She wanted to run, but her body had her cemented to the floor. It felt like she couldn't get enough air, like she'd choke on the words she needed to say.

Dan's head lifted, and, seeing her, he stood and walked to her, cutting off her exit path.

"Hey. What happened? What did the professor say?" He reached out a hand to her, but she flinched away. She'd crack if he touched her. Cold sweat prickled across her skin like sharp needles while a high-pitched humming filled her ears.

Say it. Say goodbye. Say the words, you stupid failure.

She squeezed her eyes shut then opened them, little black stars floating in her vision.

"Harper? Talk to me."

I don't want to talk. I don't want to explain. I don't want to need you like this. I just want to breathe. Why can't I breathe?

"I don't want to see you anymore." Harper felt the recoil of her words reverberate through her body. Hurt and confusion flooded Dan's features, but Harper couldn't focus on them, her vision swimming in and out, darkness creeping in at the edges, while that incessant humming grew louder and louder.

"What?" Dan said, the word pushing through Harper, disrupting her center of gravity until her stomach flipped, and the world started to sway.

"I have to get out of here" was all she managed to say through her closing throat and the tingling of her lips, her vision tunneling to the point that she felt blind. Lost.

She tried to take a step, then another. But the floor was on the ceiling, and the walls were closing in.

Then everything went black.

CHAPTER 32

HARPER

Harper didn't know that pain could come in the form of noise. But a rhythmic beeping hammered a stake through the right side of her brain, dragging her out of the darkness and into a piercing light that pressed through her closed eyelids.

Slowly, she opened her eyes. She felt violently disoriented as she stared up at a white-tiled ceiling she didn't recognize, the murmur of unknown voices starting to carry over that annoying beeping. She looked down, seeing her body wrapped in a paper gown and a thin, blue blanket, a pulse oximeter pinched on her forefinger.

Harper jolted to sitting, looking around wildly to try to figure out where she was.

"Hey, easy. You're okay." A warm hand curved around her shoulder, and she followed the arm to Dan sitting in a chair next to her, his face lined with worry. Her eyes locked with his for a moment, and their last interaction slammed into her chest.

She looked away, trying to get her bearings. A pale pink curtain circled around her bed, and an EKG machine sat on her left, wires snaking from it and diving below her hospital gown to attach to her chest.

"What the hell is happening?" she managed to ask, still not

looking at Dan. A wave of mortification swept through her as she guessed the answer.

"You . . . well, you passed out. And when you fell, you hit your head. They brought you next door to the hospital to make sure you were okay." Dan reached for her hand, closing his long, cool fingers around hers. "Are you? Are you okay?"

Harper was not okay. She was filled with such an acute sense of shame that she felt like her bones would crack from it. She pulled her hand away, looking down at the old, blue blanket across her lap.

"I think you should go," she whispered. She needed to be alone, needed to drown in the embarrassment of her own instability in private. Silence pressed heavily around them, and Harper snuck a glance at Dan out of the corner of her eye. He stared at her like she'd just slapped him.

"What?" he finally asked. "I'm not going to leave you. Not when—" Dan's words were cut off as the curtain surrounding them was flung open and a young doctor stepped inside.

"Ah, Harper. Glad you're awake. I'm Dr. Ross. How are we feeling?"

"Fine," Harper lied as her head pounded behind her eyes. "Totally fine."

"Mmm," Dr. Ross hummed, leaning toward her as he flashed a penlight in her eyes. "Follow my finger," he dictated, tracing a letter *H* in the air in front of her. He started moving his finger rapidly from side to side. "Any headache with that?" he asked.

"No," Harper lied again, blinking rapidly.

Dr. Ross gave her a skeptical glance as he reached out and palpated a tender spot near Harper's right temple, causing her to hiss in a breath. "Some pain there?" he asked with disinterest, grabbing up a clipboard and making notes. Harper didn't even bother answering.

"All right," Dr. Ross said, clapping his palm against the back of the clipboard with a loud *smack* that made Harper wince. "It seems you have a concussion, nothing a few days' rest can't fix. No bright lights, no exercise, no mentally strenuous activities. Give that brain a rest."

It took every ounce of her willpower not to roll her eyes. *Right, no strenuous mental activities. Not like I'm trying to become a doctor or anything.* But she just smiled and nodded. "Of course."

Dan shot her a look that told her he knew exactly what she was thinking. She chose to ignore it.

"Will I be discharged soon?" she asked, trying to infuse calm into every word when her hands were itching with the anxiety to get back to her textbooks, disappear into the pages, work away the all-consuming shame that was drowning her. She needed to get away from this hospital bed. Away from Dan. Away from everything.

"Fairly soon," Dr. Ross said with a casual nod. "We're just waiting on the hospital psychiatrist to make a stop and ask you a few questions."

Harper's head jerked back, and she tried not to wince. "A psychiatrist? Why?"

"Your elevated blood pressure and the events preceding the fall indicate it wasn't caused by syncope. And with your history of mental illness, it's more indicative of a psychogenic blackout. The psychiatrist will want to make sure you're getting the help you need."

Harper was stunned. Her stomach turned itself inside out, a queasy, pulsing dread coursing through her. The words sounded so dirty and pathetic. "I don't need help," Harper spat out. "I'm not crazy. I'm not sick."

"No one's calling you crazy, Harper. We just want to make sure—"

"Where did you even get this 'history,'" she said, cutting him off and giving him a piercing look.

Dr. Ross shot a nervous glance at Dan, who sat in the corner, his face ashen and drawn.

"From *him*?" Harper said, her voice rising. "He doesn't know my medical history. He's in no position to be reporting on me."

"He simply indicated you have a history of anxiety attacks and we—"

"Well, *I'm* telling you I'm not mentally ill. *I'm* saying I do not want, nor will I participate in, a useless conversation with a psychiatrist. I don't have time to be here and play these stupid games."

"Harper." Dan's voice was soft, barely even a whisper, but it drew her attention like an alarm bell. He looked at her with tenderness, with worry. But all Harper saw was pity. The disgusting pity of a normal person looking at some sort of untamed, unwell creature, wary of its next move.

She wanted to lash out; she wanted to scream. How could he share that with someone else? That tiny piece she'd been so afraid to admit to anyone—how could he expose that to the world? It was like the more people who knew about her diagnosis, the more power the disorder would hold over her. The firmer it would attach itself to her, panic and shame gluing the label of mentally ill to her chest like a scarlet letter.

"What?" she spat out. "I don't. I don't need to be here." Her heart pounded, each beat like a sledgehammer to her sternum. The traitorous monitors revealed its frantic rhythm.

127 bpm

129 bpm

133 bpm

The numbers kept ticking up and up, revealing the chaos in her chest.

Harper took a deep, calming breath, trying to grapple her pounding heart into submission. She used all her effort to give the doctor a kind smile.

"I'm sorry. It's been a long day. It was an accident, and all I want is to go home and rest like you said." She met Dr. Ross's eyes, trying to hold them with a steady serenity that she didn't feel. He stared back at her for a moment before glancing back to Dan, searching for an answer.

And there it was. Damn him. And damn men. Damn the labels and the stigma that she'd been running from her whole life. This was what she hated. That label, that shameful fucking label. Mental *illness*. As soon as that was attached to a person, they lost validity in society's eyes.

"Don't look at him," Harper snapped. "Look at me. I don't want or need to speak with a psychiatrist. As you said, it's a concussion from a freak accident, and I want to be discharged. Do you understand me?"

Dr. Ross stared at her, weighing his options. He could keep going back and forth, wasting minutes that were so precious to every doctor, or he could wash his hands of it. With a sigh, he nodded. "I'll have the nurses gather your discharge papers," he said, making one last note on his clipboard before clicking his pen shut and swooping from the room.

Silence pressed around Harper and Dan like an amorphous weight threatening to crush them. Harper wanted to scream. She wanted to cry. She hated being such an embarrassing mess. And she hated that Dan looked at her like that, with a stare she could *feel*.

A look that whispered, *It's okay to be a mess, you can be a mess with me.*

Because a part of her so desperately wanted to believe that. She wanted to let out her ugly and trust that he'd still be there. But if she did that, she'd be weak. If she softened even a fraction, she'd crumble. She instinctively knew it. Her survival depended on control.

If she broke now, it would all be a waste. Her mother's death, the pain of losing her, the years of loneliness and fear—it would all be for nothing.

"There's no shame in getting help. In going to therapy. I think it could be really good for you," Dan said, breaking their silence.

Harper wanted to laugh. No shame? There was nothing but shame.

Shame saturated her so profoundly, permeated her so acutely, that she could drown in it. She was supposed to be strong. Smart. Independent. But she wasn't any of those things if she accepted that sometimes her mind was outside her realm of control, her emotions these unwrangleable creatures that chewed her up and spit her out. There was no greater shame than admitting that.

"Can I ask you a question?" she whispered, all her countless feelings globbing together into anger.

"Of course," Dan said, leaning toward her, reaching out for her. She avoided his touch.

"Who the fuck do you think you are?" she asked evenly, fixing him with a cold stare.

"W-what?"

"Who. The. Fuck. Do you think you are? Telling someone I'm mentally ill? Telling me I need therapy? I'm just curious where you get off."

"Excuse me?" Dan said, his head reeling back, his temper rising to the surface. "Are you fucking kidding me right now, Harper? If you didn't notice, you've been having a full-blown meltdown for the past twenty-four hours that resulted in you being *hospitalized*. And you're mad that I told a *doctor* about it?"

"I didn't have a meltdown!" Harper nearly shouted, her blood pounding at her temples. She knew she was a dirty little liar. But lying was better than admitting the truth, better than submitting to the reality of how much anxiety controlled her life. "And none of that information was yours to tell. I don't go broadcasting your bullshit around."

"My bullshit?"

"Yeah, Dan. Your bullshit." She couldn't stop herself. All that shame, all that embarrassment, swelled inside her, lashing out in a rage. Striking at the closest thing. "*You're* the one who needs help. You're the one walking around like some precious martyr for your dead dad. 'Oh, woe is me. I had a meanie father, and now my mom wants me to come work with her after school. My life is so hard *whaaa whaaa whaaa.*'" Harper was being cruel. Absolutely awful. And she hated how good it felt. Anything to remove the attention from her own fucked-up mind.

Dan stared at her, the anger draining from his face, leaving nothing but fractured sadness across his features. She wanted to cry. She wanted to snatch the words out of the air and cram them back down her throat. She wanted to choke on them.

"I shouldn't have said that," she whispered, her fingers knotting together in her lap.

"You aren't wrong," Dan said, running his hands through his hair. He wouldn't look at her. "I am fucked up. I carry around so much guilt, I sometimes think my spine will snap from the weight of it. I'll suffocate under it. But I'm also willing to work on it. Are you willing to work on yours?" he said, fixing her with a raw stare. "Because, I'm not sure it's good for us to be together if you're not."

"What are you saying?" Harper's throat seemed to close around every syllable as she forced the words out.

"I'm saying I want to be with you, but not in an unhealthy way. I've had enough damaged relationships in my life. I don't want this to be another."

Harper shook her head, tears streaming down her face. "I can't do this. I've told you from the start—I don't want this."

"Bullshit. You're scared. You're scared because this feels more real than the safe little life you imagined for yourself."

He stood, pacing the small length of floor along her hospital bed, before turning on her.

"Being together wasn't part of your precious plan. So what? The world won't end just because your plan changes. We could make a new plan. Together. You don't have to be perfect, Harper." He grabbed her hand, rubbing his thumb over her knuckles as he spoke. "But you deserve to be happy. You deserve to live without this pain pressing on you."

Sharp tears pricked at Harper's eyes. It would be so nice if her mind would let her trust that—let her break out of this constant cycle of doubt. But she couldn't. She felt betrayed. She felt humiliated. She felt so many awful things at once, she thought she'd be ripped in half by the strength of them.

"I think you should go," she said, pulling her hand away, tugging at her hair.

"Let me take you home," he said quietly. "We can talk this out."

Harper shook her head, staring fixedly at the peaks and valleys on the EKG next to her. "I can't have you take me home."

"Why?"

She took a shuddering breath, tears brimming over her eyes. "Because if you do, I'll invite you up."

"Would that be the worst thing in the world?" Dan asked softly.

"Yes."

"Why?"

"Because then I would have to let you in."

The hurt radiating from Dan's body was almost palpable, her skin absorbing every wave of it like a punch to the gut.

All was silent for a few minutes before she spoke again. "You need to leave."

"Harper, I—"

"Go! Fucking go!" she yelled, looking at him with rage and hurt and confusion. "I don't want you here. You're the last thing I need."

"Trust me," Dan said, staring at her for a moment longer, raw and vulnerable, before fixing his features into an emotionless mask. "I'm done." He turned on his heel and left the room.

Harper waited a full minute, kept everything under control for sixty whole seconds, before she broke.

She balled her hands in her hair, sobs ripping from her throat. She grabbed a pillow, biting into it as she cried.

She allowed herself

One

    Two

        Three

            Four

                Five

seconds of tears

  Six

    Seven

        Eight

moments of rocking back and forth to the pulsing pain in her head. In her chest.

Nine

    Ten

        Eleven

            Twelve

instances of wanting to be held, of wanting to let go of control.

Then she gritted her teeth, wiped her eyes, and waited calmly for her discharge papers.

It wasn't until she got home, sitting on the edge of her lonely bed, that she noticed the list of psychiatrists attached to the forms.

CHAPTER 33

DAN

Dan walked around the city aimlessly. He didn't know where to go, what to do. The words *"You're the last thing I need"* propelled each step forward until hours had passed.

His phone buzzed in his pocket, causing his heart to jolt in his chest, pathetically hoping it was Harper. He accepted the call so quickly, he didn't read the caller ID until it was too late.

And he was officially on a call with his mom.

Cursing under his breath, he brought the phone up to his ear. "Hi, Mom."

There was a pause on the line, and Dan knew it was for dramatic effect.

"Daniyal?" his mom said. "You're alive, habibi?" While the endearment was a nice touch, there was no masking the sharpness in her words.

Dan let out a sigh, pinching the bridge of his nose. "For the most part," he said.

"And your phone? It works?"

"It seems to."

She clucked her tongue. "Then I must need to take *my* phone in for a repair."

Dan decided to humor her. "Why's that?"

"Because, Daniyal, I call, and I call, and I call some more. I leave messages. I even *text* you, and rarely get a response. My phone must be the problem."

"Did you need something, Mom?" he asked brusquely. He was done with this shit. Wasn't it enough that he was acting as her little guilt-ridden puppet? Did he have to play the games too?

"I actually do. Are you free this week? For lunch, perhaps? I need to talk to you. I can come to the city."

"Talk about what?" Dan said, a dull sense of dread sliding through him.

"About the practice. Nothing bad, don't worry."

Dan choked back a bitter laugh. Of course it was about the practice. It was always about the practice.

"Are you all right, Daniyal?"

Dan was silent, trying to swallow past the emotions clogging his throat. He wasn't okay. He felt alone. He felt stuck. He felt stupid. He felt heartbroken.

"Talk to me."

Dan sighed. He let all the air out of his chest as though he could rid his cells of the pain they carried.

"Can I come see you?" Dan said suddenly without thinking. "Tonight?" he added. He didn't know where the impulse came from, but suddenly, he needed nothing more than to see her. To look for the mom she'd once been before grief had morphed her into this different person. Maybe if he hugged his mom, everything would be okay.

Farrah was silent for a few moments before her voice cut through the line, her words tinged with heavy emotion. "Of course, hobi, I'll see you soon."

Not allowing himself time to think better of the idea, Dan jogged to Thirtieth Street Station, buying a ticket for the next train to Haverford. He regretted his decision every second of the forty-five-minute ride, yet his feet still carried him off the train and the few blocks to his childhood home.

Standing outside the door, he hesitated. He wasn't sure why he was there. He didn't want to hear whatever she had to say about the practice. He didn't want her to ask about school. He didn't want to see his father's degrees and awards littering every wall of their house.

Despite all those things, he knocked on the door.

Farrah opened it almost immediately, as though she'd been sitting on the staircase off the entryway, waiting for him.

Dan stepped in and stripped off his coat, avoiding looking at her. It felt painful to look at her and miss the person she used to be to him.

When he finally steeled his nerves and met her gaze, she was staring at him like it was the first time she'd seen him in over a year.

She looked aged, sadness and grief scoring lines across her face. But the softness in her eyes, the sense of knowing that she really saw him, made it feel like his mom was back. She was back, and she'd make things okay in the way only moms seemed able to do.

Farrah reached out a hand, gently tracing the dark circles beneath Dan's eyes with her thumb. "I'm glad you're here. Are you tired? You look tired."

All Dan could do was nod. He was exhausted. From the pressure to save her, from pretending to be someone he wasn't. It all culminated in a bone-deep tiredness that threatened to lay him out on the floor.

"You aren't happy." It wasn't a question.

The lump in Dan's throat swelled. He wanted to admit it, tell her how none of this made sense for him, but the guilt of failing her, leaving her stranded, clawed at his chest. He loved her too much to let her down.

Minutes stretched as she stared at him, countless emotions flickering behind her eyes. Finally, she nodded, reaching out with strong, sure arms and pulling him into a hug.

That small gesture almost fractured him into a hundred pieces. The lavender scent of her skin, the strength of her arms around him, the softness of the comforting circles she drew on his back—all felt like coming home for the first time in years.

Eventually she pulled away, moving them to the kitchen and motioning for him to sit, sliding a plate of maamoul in front of him while she prepared tea.

When Dan finally felt like he could trust his voice, he asked, "How are *you*, Mom?"

Farrah let out a sigh before answering, walking two mugs to the table and taking her seat. "I'm okay," she said at last. "I made a new friend."

"Yeah?" Dan felt a twinge of guilt that this news surprised him—a painful reminder of how alone she was.

"Yes. I met her at my grief support group." There was a brief pause as she took a bite of a cookie. "Her husband was an asshole too," she said, offering the tiniest hint of a smile before she covered her mouth with her mug.

Dan choked on a sip of tea, coughing and spluttering until Farrah smacked him on the back.

"Holy shit, Mom. Is this what a therapist would call a break-through?" Farrah had all but petitioned for his dad's sainthood the past year.

She let out a rusty chuckle and shot him a mock chiding glance. "What? He was. Don't pretend you forgot."

"I'm definitely not the one who forgot."

She blinked at Dan before looking away, taking a few sips of tea while her mind lingered somewhere else.

"I know," she finally said, resting her mug on the table as she watched the steam rise from it. "I loved him, though—I still do. I love the man he was beneath that."

"Yeah?" Dan frowned. "Who was that?"

"A man who wanted to heal. To serve. He was always so

passionate about it. I fell in love with how much he loved his work. It felt special to be part of his world."

Dan didn't know what to say. He'd been detached from his father's career, his research, his practice—it was a thing Dan was jealous of as a child and resentful of as an adult.

But he understood what his mom meant. He thought of Harper. Her ability and passion. It was impossible not to love the healing she held in her hands.

"When he was dying," his mother continued, pushing through the wall that separated them, "I felt like the world was losing that man. Not the one we endured—not the bully at home—but the doctor who helped people. The one who traveled the world with his tools, who lectured at universities, who won humanitarian awards—that's who I mourn, Daniyal."

She looked at him with such intensity in her green eyes, Dan had to look away.

"Well, I'm glad the world got the best of him," he said at last, taking a sip of his tea.

"I'm not."

Dan's eyes snapped back to her.

She took a shaky breath. "You deserved the best of him. We, his family, deserved the best of him, no?"

Dan wasn't sure what to say, and they stayed silent for a few minutes.

"I've been putting my needs before yours," she said, breaking the silence. Dan made a noise of protest, but she held up her hand to silence him.

"I have. I don't know if I can forgive myself for it. Growing up, I was always told exactly what to do, who to be. I hated it. But before I knew it, I found myself married to a man who told me the same things. He told me not to specialize. He told me the hours to work. He told me where to be, what to do. I convinced myself that it was his way of caring for me. Caring for *us* as a family. And

I certainly wasn't the first woman to accept that her husband's career should come first. I won't be the last either."

She blinked, turning her head to look out the window as she gathered her words. "I always promised myself that if I were to be a mother, my children would decide life for themselves. But after a lifetime of someone else dictating your actions, you lose faith in your ability to do anything on your own. When he died, it was the first time I was the only person in charge of myself, and it terrified me. I thought I would lose everything he'd worked for if I didn't have someone to lead me. So I placed that burden on you."

She wiped a stray tear from her cheek, then turned back to look at him. "Grief does scary things to people," she said in a whisper. "It's so powerful, it can change you, rewire everything you thought you knew. And I had so much grief. So much. I looked at the things that had been broken when your father died. Our family was a mess; he and I resented each other for so many things. I looked at these fractured pieces and some voice in my head told me, if I had listened better, been the wife he had expected, the type of mother he had told me to be, we wouldn't be so broken."

Dan was left speechless by the weight of everything she was unpacking.

After a few moments, she spoke again. "Daniyal, I want you to listen to me. I will never be able to tell you he was proud of you. I will never be able to make you believe he loved you, even though I think he did. Something in you—your spirit, your joy, I don't know—it threatened him. It scared him to see those things in you because they were things he couldn't find in himself."

Farrah sniffled as she cried, and a few tears rolled down Dan's cheeks. She took a steadying breath before continuing.

"His inability to know what an amazing son he had will always be his tragedy. But not mine. I love you. All I ask is you find happiness. You deserve it. Everyone does."

Dan wiped a hand down his face.

"I've thought about it, and I'm selling the practice."

Dan's head jerked back. He'd have been less surprised if she'd just told him that every night she sprouts wings from her back and flies around as the tooth fairy.

"You are?" he finally asked, still in a state of shock. "But what about money? What about . . . everything?"

"I've talked with an accountant. I even hired a consultant. Everyone assures me the practice will sell well." She was silent for a moment, lost in distant memories. "That had just never been an option before."

"But what about the name? And Dad? That practice was everything to you two."

Farrah stared at him. "That practice being everything is exactly why I need to let it go. Somewhere along the line, I got lost in his dreams, not my own. Work like this was never what I wanted. I never intended to have this kind of devotion to a building. To a man's ambitions that weren't my own. That was never supposed to be me." She took a sip of tea. "I don't want that to be you either."

Farrah took his hands, hers aged and soft as she held on to his, stroking her thumbs across his knuckles. "It was wrong of me to do this to you, habibi. My grief was never your burden to bear. Your father's visions were never yours to fulfill, and I'm sorry those things were placed on you. That's never meant for a child to endure."

"Mom, I—"

"Let me finish. Whether you want to be a dentist or work in finance or wait tables, I want you to do it for *you*. And only for you."

Dan sat there absorbing her words, a lightness slowly flooding his chest until he thought he might float. For the first time, he faced freedom, absolution from the crushing sense of duty that had plagued him for so long.

He knew what he needed to do.

CHAPTER 34

HARPER

"You look like shit."

Harper started so violently at the unexpected voice that she bit down on her tongue and cracked her knees on the underside of her disaster of a desk. She clutched a hand to her chest and turned to see Thu leaning in the doorway.

"You scared the hell out of me! How did you get in here?"

Thu dangled Harper's spare key from an extended finger.

"Jesus, Harps, when was the last time you slept?" Thu narrowed her gaze. "Or showered?"

Harper ran a hand through her greasy hair. She'd been so lost in studying, it had been longer than she cared to admit. More than a week had passed, and Harper had isolated herself as much as she could through it. To her dismay, her concussion had forced her to take a few days off from clinic, which felt like dumping gasoline on the already roaring fire of anxiety in her chest. When she'd finally gone back, she'd taken great measures to avoid everyone, picking up extra night rotations to catch up, sprinting home to study into the early hours of the morning. Detaching as much as she could.

If she continued to drown herself in work, she wouldn't have to think about what happened with Dan.

"Your desk is atrocious," Thu noted.

Harper could only nod. She used to keep it so clean and orderly, but lately it had dissolved into chaos, herds of coffee mugs and stacks of papers making it difficult for her to find anything.

Thu continued to study Harper. Something she saw made her face soften in sadness.

"Come on," Thu said, nodding her head toward the living room.

"What are you doing here?"

Thu didn't bother answering, already making her way down the hall. Harper sighed and saved the work on her laptop before following her friend.

Thu was laying carryout containers on the kitchen table when Harper entered. A six-pack of beer sat next to the food, and Judy jumped onto the table to investigate.

"What are you doing here?" Harper asked again. She wanted Thu to leave.

She wasn't mad or annoyed at her friend's invasion. She didn't have the energy for such complicated feelings. She just wanted Thu gone so she could go back to work, back to reading word after word until her body was numb and her mental image of Dan's pain-stricken face was blurred.

Thu turned, anger flashing in her eyes.

"What am I doing here? Oh, I don't know, Harper. Maybe it has something to do with you having a massive meltdown? Or maybe it has something to do with you avoiding me at school? Or ignoring my texts and calls for over a week? Or maybe it's the fact that I *knew* if I broke into your apartment, I'd find you greasy-haired and tearstained, hunched over a textbook, looking like Gollum?"

The words floated through Harper. She could understand their meaning, but she couldn't feel them. She couldn't feel much. Just pain. And if she tried hard enough, she could pretend she didn't feel that either.

Thu moved suddenly, wrapping Harper in a strong hug, squeezing her tightly. Harper wasn't sure what to do; her arms didn't seem to be working. A sudden sense of exhaustion flooded her, and she felt her body soften under Thu's embrace.

"I'm here to figure out what the fuck is going on. And then to help you fix it."

"Thu, I—"

"Shut up. We aren't talking right now."

Thu dropped her arms and returned to the food. She picked up a container, grabbed two beers, and settled onto the couch. When Harper didn't immediately follow, Thu fixed her with a no-nonsense glare. Harper reluctantly grabbed a carton of Thai food and sat next to Thu.

The food was from her favorite spot, the same place Dan always picked up takeout for her. The familiar smell of it made her stomach knot.

"Eat."

"Thu, I appreciate all of this, but I've got to get back to—" Harper pointed toward her bedroom, but Thu cut her off before she could finish.

"Eat the goddamn food, or I'll hurt you."

Harper didn't have the energy to fight.

She wrapped a small rice noodle around her fork and brought it to her lips. Glancing back at Thu, who still gave her the evil eye, Harper ate the noodle. It was delicious. She tried to remember the last time she ate, and when she came up blank, she began shoving bigger bites into her mouth.

"Now, drink." Thu twisted off the caps of the bottles and thrust one at Harper. Harper opened her mouth to protest, but one look at Thu's cocked head and challenging eyes forced her to accept it. She took a tiny sip and set it down, digging back into her food.

Seemingly satisfied with Harper's steady consumption, Thu turned on the TV. And flipped to football.

Intentionally.

Thu intentionally put on sports.

Something was terribly wrong.

Harper waited for Thu to crack a joke or turn it into a 'gotcha' moment, but after several minutes without Thu's eyes leaving the screen and even a loud "*Oh!*" at a tackle, Harper's curiosity won out.

"So . . . what's this?"

Thu took a swig of her beer. "It's called football. Very popular with kids these days."

"Huh . . ." Harper said, tapping her nail against her beer bottle. "Why are we watching it?"

"No reason we shouldn't engage in America's pastime like everyone else."

"Baseball is America's pastime, and we don't like sports."

"Semantics," Thu said with a wave of her hand.

Harper gave it a few more minutes, periodically looking between her friend and the TV, trying to get the joke.

"But why *football*?"

Thu shrugged. "Alex likes football."

"So?"

Thu turned to face Harper. "*So*, I like Alex. And that means I'm trying to like football. Because that's what you do for the people you like—you accommodate them into your life." She gave Harper a pointed look before turning back to the TV.

Harper blinked at her.

"You officially like Alex?"

Thu huffed out a laugh and rolled her eyes. "Yeah, I think so. But that's not the point."

"I know," Harper whispered, picking at the sticker on her beer bottle.

"The point is," Thu said, turning to Harper again, "you can't keep doing this to yourself. Living like this."

Harper gave her a weak smile. "I know that too. And I'm trying."

"But what are you *actually* doing to work on it, Harper?"

Harper didn't have an answer for that, not one that would satisfy Thu anyway. Harper wasn't sure how to explain that slowly she was rebuilding every wall she'd let crumble. Getting back to protecting herself in fortified isolation.

Harper could see the concern behind Thu's eyes. Tendrils of warmth spread from Harper's heart, but they magnified the pain, and she rubbed at her aching chest. Thu put her arm around Harper's shoulders and gave a brief squeeze before turning back to the game.

"Is Dr. Ren letting you make up the exam?" Thu asked a few minutes later.

Harper nodded. A pulsing mix of sadness and anxiety was starting to move through her system. "She gave me an alternative assignment. Fifteen-page systematic review on invasive intervention in oral cancer."

"Oh, so just some light reading."

Harper gave a half-hearted laugh and took a swig of her beer, hoping Thu would bring up Dan.

Harper missed him in the sharpest way possible. It felt like her skin had been flayed open. Like she was exposed and bleeding out. She was angry at him for telling her secrets, for taking that ugly thing inside her and judging it, deciding she needed treatment for it.

But what made it worse was that, on a rational level, she knew she'd brought it on herself. She'd pushed him until he couldn't come back. She'd broken her own damn heart so Dan couldn't do it for her.

Because that's what hearts did. They filled and swelled and pushed at their confines until they inevitably fractured into pieces with sharp, jagged edges that cut your fingers when you tried to put them back together. She'd worked too hard to allow one moment to set her off course like that.

Or so she thought.

She felt so directionless—so impossibly lost, it was hard to do anything but breathe.

"Aren't you going to ask me what happened with Dan?" Harper eventually said.

She craved and dreaded the question. Part of her wanted to be forced to face what she'd done—have the words pulled from her so she could be free of them.

But Thu shook her head. "You'd tell me if you were ready to talk about it."

Harper stared at Thu for a moment before nodding and snuggling into her side. Thu switched the channel and shifted to a comfortable position.

After a few minutes, Thu spoke again, her voice tinged with uncharacteristic caution. "You know what's happening, though, right?"

Harper shifted to look at her friend. "Happening with what?"

Thu let out a long sigh, chewing on her bottom lip. "You haven't heard from him at all?"

"He called me once but I didn't answer. Why? What aren't you telling me?"

Thu looked down at her hands, seeming to search endlessly for words. A trickle of dread snaked down Harper's spine. Thu was *never* at a loss for words.

Thu finally looked up, meeting Harper's eyes. "I just really think you need to go talk to Dan."

CHAPTER 35

HARPER

The next morning, Harper made her way to Dan's apartment. She hadn't been able to get any more information from Thu, who just repeatedly told her it wasn't her information to share, whatever the hell that meant.

Harper knew she should have called first, but she had a feeling that whatever it was, it wasn't something she wanted to learn about over the phone. And, for some reason, the idea of dialing his number, taking the chance of the call ringing into the abyss unanswered, felt way more daunting.

But, as she mounted the stairs to his apartment, the queasy jostle of nerves in her stomach had her second-guessing that decision.

As Harper stood outside his door, trying to find the courage to knock, she realized how weird it was that she'd never been to his place before. He had so easily melded into her space, into her life, never forcing her to take a step out of her own little bubble.

She was pathetic.

Taking a deep breath, she lifted her fist to knock, but the door swung open before she could make contact. It took Harper a few moments to process what she saw.

Dan blinked at her in surprise, and she returned the look. Two cardboard moving boxes were stacked in his arms, leaning against his chest. She stared at those boxes until her vision blurred into nothing but that jarring brown.

"Is . . . Is Alex moving?" Harper heard herself ask, her brain functioning in slow motion.

"What are you doing here?" Dan said, his voice flat.

Harper blinked up at him. That was the question, wasn't it? She didn't even have an answer. Harper still felt a sharp and keen sense of shame at his suggestion that she needed help. She felt betrayed by him for turning it around on her. But Thu's words had burrowed into her brain. *You accommodate the people you like into your life.*

And she liked Dan. He was her best friend. And she'd said nasty, terrible things to him. She felt too much shame and other messy emotions to even think about going back to where they'd been, but she didn't want to lose him entirely.

"Thu told me I should probably come see you," Harper said, still unable to process what was happening.

"Oh. Thu." Dan nodded once, looking away from Harper. After a moment, he blew out a breath and set the boxes down. He leaned against the doorframe, crossing his arms. He wasn't going to let her in.

"Is your head okay?" he asked.

No. I think my head is about to explode from confusion because what the fuck is happening here?

"Yeah, it's fine," Harper said, staring down at those boxes. "What's going on?"

"I'm moving," Dan said with a bored wave toward the evidence. She'd never seen him be this cold before. His stiff posture, the stern line of his mouth, the disinterested way he looked at her—all of it pierced through her skin like a thousand blunted needles.

"Where?" she managed to get out, looking up at him. He didn't quite meet her gaze.

"New York, actually," he said, dragging a hand through his hair then down his face. He looked tired.

"New York? But what about . . ." *What about everything? What about school? What about your mom? What about me? What about us?*

"Yeah, well, I . . ." He paused, sucking in a deep breath then fixing her with a hard stare. "You were right, it's time for me to stop with the bullshit."

Harper blinked at him, the sharp prick of tears starting behind her eyes, pressure building in her throat.

"What about your mom and the practice?" she managed to ask with an even voice.

"It's really none of your business," he said.

She deserved that. But it still hurt like hell.

Dan looked away from her, shaking his head. "I talked with my mom," he said, staring down at the boxes. "We've . . . I don't know, come to an understanding, I guess."

"An understanding of what?"

"That there's nothing here for me," he said, his green eyes flashing up to pierce into hers.

Harper didn't know what to say. She wanted to cry. She wanted to take back every cruel word she'd said to him, all the ugly parts of herself she'd exposed him to. She suddenly realized how much she wanted to be his reason to stay.

"Nothing?" she pressed out.

"My mom has decided to sell the practice. With everything . . ." *With you . . .* The unspoken words hung between them. "I realized it's time for me to stop pretending. To stop walking around in a life that isn't meant for me."

"But—but . . ." Harper wasn't sure what she even wanted to say. He stared at her the entire time she searched for words, his cool gaze trapping every protest in her throat. It felt like nothing short of rejection. He was leaving. She was being left. It was exactly what she'd asked for.

"What are you going to do in New York?" she heard herself ask.

"I begged for my old job back," he said.

"And you got it?" she asked incredulously.

Dan let out a humorless laugh. "No. But I was always on good terms with my boss. He was surprisingly understanding. He gave me a position that's about ten steps down from the level I'd been at, but a job is a job, and it's something I actually want to do."

Harper nodded weakly, every muscle in her body going numb. She didn't know how to process any of this. "And you have a place to live?"

"I'm renting a room for a bit and then moving into an apartment at the start of the month."

"When do you leave?"

"As soon as I finish loading up the truck," Dan said, scrubbing his knuckles along his jaw. "Which is taking longer than I thought. Alex is supposed to be helping but he keeps stopping, saying he needs to 'process his feelings.'"

"Wow," Harper managed to say, sucking in her lips and nodding quickly. She felt the urge to flee.

At the same time, she wanted to tell him.

Holy shit, did she want to tell him. Tell him she knew she'd fucked up. She knew she *was* fucked up.

But fear gripped her, the inevitability of rejection paralyzing her. Because, really, who could love someone like her?

"Well, I guess this is goodbye, then," she managed to say, blinking back tears she didn't want to burden him with.

And then, like an *idiot*, she stuck out her hand to shake his.

A *handshake?* she screamed at herself. *Really?*

Dan stared down at her outstretched hand, and something in his cool demeanor broke. His eyes lifted to hers, vulnerable and honest.

"Harper," he whispered.

There was too much in the way he said it. It seemed impossible that so much could saturate the whispered sound of her name. Those two syllables threatened to break her apart. She wanted to fling herself at him, tell him not to leave her. Tell him she was wrong. Tell him how sorry she was.

But, just as she was about to lose all control and do that, his words from earlier rang through her ears.

There's nothing here for me.

Grasping at one last shred of dignity, Harper dropped her hand, gave him a weak smile, and left.

CHAPTER 36

DAN

MARCH

It took about six weeks, but Dan eventually found a rhythm to surviving with his heart beating outside his chest. He became somewhat of an expert on pain: its nuances, its complexities.

He discovered how pain ebbs and flows—some moments, it felt like it had the power to kill him. To flay him open and destroy him. Other moments, it was a dull ache, consuming him before he'd even been able to acknowledge it.

Sometimes the pain surfaced as a thousand cuts of residual guilt, the feeling of failure and shame slow to abandon him, no matter how his mom's words had set him free. Other times, the pain erupted in anger at all the time he'd wasted being someone he wasn't.

But most of the time, the pain came from missing Harper.

At the end of January, Dan had learned from Instagram that Harper got into residency. Lizzie had posted a photo of the four friends, drinks in hand, smiles huge, with the caption OUR GIRL IS GOING TO BE A SURGEON! typed beneath it.

Harper had looked so happy. And Dan had felt so proud of her, amazed by her. But he'd also felt bitterness. Hurt.

He had poured himself a drink in his lonely apartment that day, and sat staring at her smile. He'd traced his thumb over her image, desperate to feel the softness of her skin one more time.

He'd almost texted her. He'd written out one hundred drafts and deleted them all. He'd wanted to tell her how special she was. How angry she made him. How much he cared for her. How much he hated her. How, despite everything she'd said, he forgave her. How he hoped she could forgive him too.

But every time he'd gone to hit Send, her voice cut through his mind. *You're the last thing I need.*

He'd turned off his phone and poured another drink.

Slowly, Dan started having more days of the dull, aching pain than the days that threatened to kill him.

He leaned into his new job, reacquainting himself with all the things he loved about numbers and patterns. He learned how to paste a convincing smile on his face with his coworkers and clients, carving out a space for himself in the office.

He laughed with his new buddy Tom at work. He ate lunch in the break room and accepted happy hour invitations from co-workers.

At the bar one night, he'd even tried to flirt with a woman.

She was pretty and blonde and seemed genuinely nice.

And it had hurt. It had felt physically painful to look at that lovely woman. To want so desperately to make a connection. But the only thing he could think was that this new, beautiful woman wasn't her. It wasn't Harper.

So, when she'd passed him her number on a napkin at the end of the night, he'd thanked her, waited for her to leave, and threw it away.

He'd then ordered another drink. And another. And another.

And a night out with the coworkers had turned into New Buddy Tom dragging Dan back to his lonely apartment, staring at him with a look of pure alarm as Dan cried like a fucking idiot, describing the girl with short, black hair and the most beautiful hands in the world.

Tom invited him out less after that.

CHAPTER 37

HARPER

APRIL

Harper hefted her suitcase up her stoop, barely noticing as it smacked against her ankle with each step. She didn't notice much anymore. A dull, pulsing sadness originated in the center of her bones, perfusing further out each day until she was encased in it. The only things that interrupted the sadness were consistent jolts of abandonment, regret, and panic.

At the door, she fumbled with her keys, then lugged her suitcase into the elevator, exhaustion from the past few days hitting her all at once. She'd attended orientation at her future hospital, meeting her co-residents and attending physicians. For the first time in months, she'd felt a swell of true excitement break through her sadness as she toured the OR and dingy on-call bunk beds. She'd finally made it. And she couldn't wait to start.

But the trip home had left her too much time to think. She always had too much time to think. Even now—as she pressed the back of her head against the elevator wall, staring up at the ceiling while trying not to notice the happy phantom memories that lingered in the space—she thought.

It always came back to Dan. The months hadn't dulled the hurt of it, just changed it, leaving her with an empty ache that she feared would never fully leave her. Guilt over what she'd said wrestled endlessly with feelings of rejection and abandonment.

She sighed as the elevator doors dinged open. There was no point in reliving it. No point in constantly pressing her fingers into that open wound. She knew she was too broken for another person to want her.

Focusing on making it to her cat and bed, she trudged the final steps and pushed open her door.

Then she almost peed her pants as she let out a piercing scream.

"Surprise!" Lizzie cheered, standing about six inches from the door, a cake in her hands and a huge smile on her face.

"Holy FUCK, Elizabeth. You scared the hell out of me," Harper said, pressing her hand to her chest.

"Hence the 'surprise,' grumpy goose," Lizzie said, unfazed by the likely permanent damage she'd just done to Harper's heart.

"What are you doing here?" Harper asked, stepping fully into her apartment and toeing off her shoes.

"I made you a birthday cake!" Lizzie said, leading Harper toward the kitchen.

"My birthday was in September and you made me pie," Harper said, dragging a hand down her face. She loved her friend, but she desperately, *desperately* wanted her to leave so she could shower and cry in private. Like a lady.

"Well, it's not a *birthday* birthday cake," Lizzie explained, setting it on the counter. "It's like a . . . I don't know. New-life cake. A happy-residency-visit cake."

Harper stared at Lizzie.

"It's hard to be sad when you're eating cake," Lizzie said at last, giving Harper a soft smile. "And you've been exceptionally sad, so you need an exceptional cake."

Harper blinked away a few sudden tears. The cake *was* exceptional. It looked like a work of art: swirls of pastel frosting, ac-
cented with opalescent sprinkles.

"Thank you. It's beautiful," Harper said, ducking her head as
she searched for a knife and plates so Lizzie wouldn't see the
emotion in her eyes. She handed the knife to Lizzie, who cut a
generous slice and slid it onto Harper's plate.

Harper groaned at the first bite, the perfect, fluffy cake seeming to warm a corner of her chest. "It's incredible."

They ate in silence for a few moments, both enjoying the masterpiece.

Harper cleared her throat. "How was your—"

"Did you know I was heavily medicated as a child?" Lizzie
interrupted.

Harper blinked at Lizzie, confused by the curveball.

"Don't look so upset, sweets. This isn't a sad story," Lizzie said,
taking her own bite of cake straight from the platter.

"I . . . I didn't know that," Harper said.

Lizzie nodded. "It's not something I talk about a lot because . . .
well, the past is the past and there's no use living there. But I was.
My mom would shop me around to psychiatrists, demanding
higher and higher dosages to control my ADHD, complaining
how I was this unmanageable creature." Lizzie pulled her chin
back to make a goofy face, but Harper didn't laugh.

Lizzie pressed on. "I hated it. I grew up thinking that psychiatrists were evil. Therapy was a trap. That I was broken. Yada yada
yada."

Lizzie licked frosting off her fingertip. "When I turned eighteen, I stopped all meds. Broke up with my therapists. Peaced the
fuck out," Lizzie said, taking another bite of cake. "And it was a
mess, Harper. I can't even begin to tell you what a walking tor-
nado I was," she said with a loud laugh, a grin breaking out across
her freckled cheeks. "I was moody and shaky and *wrecked*. But I

was gripping at this defiance, this belief that with sheer willpower I could break free of medications and my diagnosis and everything else."

Lizzie scooped up a bite of cake and nudged it toward Harper, feeding her the bite. "But, even after the withdrawals passed, I still wasn't . . . *well*. I couldn't shake the feeling that I wasn't treating my brain the way it needed to be treated. So, I did the thing I always swore I'd never do. I went to a psychiatrist. And it was hard. It took time, and coaxing, and work, and tears, but I eventually realized that the way my mom had handled my brain was to cage it. But that isn't the point of getting help. The real purpose is to unshackle your brain from the weight of overworking, liberate it with the neurotransmitters it's been missing. Let it do what it's supposed to do."

Lizzie took one more bite of cake, then dropped the fork with a *clang*, brushing her frosting-covered fingers over her jeans. She grabbed Harper by the shoulders, pulling her into a tight hug. Harper's stiff muscles slowly softened at the touch, molding closer to her friend's embrace.

"I'm sorry you went through that, Lizzie."

"Oh, stop it. It made me who I am," Lizzie said, pulling back and smiling down at Harper. "But here's the catch of me telling you. I'm going to leave a slip of paper on your counter. It will have the name and number of the woman that helped me. *Still* helps me. You don't have to call the number. You don't have to go see her. But I want you to know there's a safe space in this city where you can lay your soul bare and maybe rebuild the pieces along the way."

"Lizzie, I—"

"Or," Lizzie said, putting up a palm, "you can toss it away. It's none of my business what you do with it." Lizzie fished in her pocket and pulled out a slip of paper, slapping it on the counter. "And we won't say another word about it tonight. Instead, I'm gonna grab this cake, and we're gonna lie on your couch and find a Henry Cavill movie to mentally masturbate to while pretending to watch it for the plot."

Lizzie popped two forks into her mouth, then scooped up the cake tray and took a step toward the living room.

"Lizzie," Harper said, reaching out and putting a hand on her friend's elbow.

Lizzie raised her eyebrows.

"Thank you," Harper said, meaning it more than her friend could know.

Lizzie smiled against the forks and leaned in, pressing their foreheads together before leaving the kitchen.

Harper stared at the paper on the counter, Lizzie's words humming through her. Without leaving enough time to talk herself out of it, she snatched it up, pulled out her phone, and dialed the number.

CHAPTER 38

HARPER

MAY

Slowly, life started to feel a little better for Harper. While months of compounded pain and longing still held permanent residence in her heart, the hurt turned a little duller with the combination of Prozac and sunshine.

By the time graduation rolled around at the end of May, Harper truly believed she'd be okay. Therapy was helping her find a balance of medications and mental exercises to get her to a better place. She was slowly shedding the layers of shame and grief and internalized ableism that held her captive. It wasn't easy. It took backbreaking work to rewrite the narrative of her mind, to learn to be gentle with herself. But if Harper was anything, she was a hard worker.

Gradually, she was learning to let go of her mother, realizing that freeing herself from the pain of it allowed her to feel closer to her memory than ever before. Which is why, on the morning of her graduation, as she sipped coffee and scratched Judy's head, thinking about everything that had happened, every step that had led to this milestone, she was able to smile, knowing her mom was with her.

The one person that wouldn't be with her, though, was Dan. And she felt his absence like a phantom limb—she'd learned to function without it, but that didn't mean she didn't long for it.

"I miss him, Judy," Harper whispered as she gently rubbed the cat's chin. "So much. How can it still hurt this much?"

Judy blinked at Harper.

"I can't call him," Harper said, moving to stroke down Judy's long body. "What would I even say? I was so awful . . . I pushed him too far to ever hope he'd forgive me."

Judy nuzzled against Harper's knee, purring lightly. "Oh, Judy, you dirty flatterer. You only think he would because you love me." Harper placed a kiss on her cat's giant head, then looked out the window with a sigh.

She no longer blamed Dan for trying to help her, trying to free her from the shame she kept herself shackled with, but she felt so much remorse for how she'd treated him, she didn't think he'd want to hear from her.

And she still held on to a little bit of that hurt, a little bit of that feeling that he'd left her. That she was unwanted. No matter how hard she tried, she couldn't let that sharp fragment of feeling go.

She pressed her forehead against the windowpane, her stomach sinking lower and lower, back into that gentle rhythm of sadness, when a knock sounded at the door.

In a swirl of giggles and hair spray, Thu, Indira, and Lizzie burst into her apartment, Lizzie's arms overflowing with containers of cupcakes and bottles of champagne.

"What do you think of my new dress?" Lizzie asked, strutting across the tiny living room a few minutes later with a coffee mug of champagne held in one hand. Although Lizzie wasn't a student, she'd been gushing with so much excitement for her friends that they all joked she should be getting an honorary degree.

"It's so short, I can almost see your vagina," Thu said, carefully swiping on her mascara in front of a pocket mirror.

"I know!" Lizzie beamed, doing a twirl. "Isn't it perfect?"

Indira, whose commencement had been the week prior, let out a whooping laugh, spanking Lizzie on the butt as she passed by her to get more champagne.

Their smiles and love didn't leave much room for Harper's sadness after that.

The rest of the morning passed in a blur. Three curling iron burns, twelve mimosas, one broken dress strap, and two outbreaks of group tears later, they were headed to the school for the last time.

The ceremony was long and boring, the humid Philadelphia spring making it drag even more. But as Harper stood at the edge of the stage, waiting for her name to be called, she floated above the ground. She looked out at the audience and indulged the immense swell of pride at what she'd accomplished. The pride was tinged with the slightest bite of pain as she kept catching herself searching for the one face she knew wouldn't be there.

At last, her name was announced, and she strode across the stage, doing what had so often felt impossible: becoming a doctor.

The afternoon was filled with endless pictures, congratulatory hugs, and a late lunch, ending with goodbyes and grumbles of traffic. When all the family members had finally left, Harper and her friends looked at each other, breaking out into huge grins as the real fun began.

The girls and Alex made their way to Center City, Thu having reserved a corner of a patio at a trendy spot. It was the ideal compromise: Harper had plenty of room to breathe and relax in the open air while her friends dipped in and out of the pulsing dance floor.

The night felt almost perfect. Little vignettes of joy and

laughter filled the happy centers of Harper's brain: All of them clinking glasses and cheering out a toast. Thu and Alex slow dancing. Lizzie making out with some hot stranger in the corner. Indira putting on bright red lipstick and marking each friend with a kiss.

It was wonderful.

Except for when it wasn't. Harper probably had one drink too many as she sat at the table, zoning out of whatever wild story Lizzie was telling to make everyone laugh.

She missed Dan.

She missed him so fucking much.

As if her longing had spanned the miles that separated them, her phone buzzed, a text with his name on it lighting up her screen.

She blinked, not believing it was actually there.

With shaking fingers, she slid her thumb across the screen and opened the message. It took her a minute to read it, going temporarily blind from a few unshed tears that threatened to fall.

> Happy graduation! I'm so proud of
> you.

The tears started slipping then. He was thinking of her. He was proud of her. It was as though he'd reached through her phone and caressed her cheek. She wasn't sure what to say, her fingers hovering over the keys for so long her phone screen went black. Finally, she sent a simple:

> Thank you! I can't believe it finally
> happened.

But it had been so long since she'd heard from him. So many days of desperately wanting to talk to him. And she'd had just enough alcohol that she typed out a second, dangerous message:

I miss you.

And then, to seal her fate of *going there*, she sent one more.

I wish I hadn't pushed you to leave.
I never wanted you to leave.

Harper watched the read receipt pop up under the message and the little texting bubble bounce in and out of the screen, holding her breath the entire time. It disappeared for a full minute and Harper let out a breath. He wasn't going to respond.

A call popped up on her phone, Dan's smiling picture taunting her to answer. Her eyes went wide with panic and she let out a little yelp of surprise. She declined the call so fast she almost broke her thumb, then tossed her phone between Thu and Lizzie. She'd been drinking, yes, but she hadn't been drinking enough for *that*.

"What the hell was that for?" Lizzie asked with a laugh, taking a minute to dig the phone out of the crack between the seats. She looked down at the screen, and whatever she saw made her eyes bulge out of her head. She turned the phone so Indira and Thu could see it. They all looked at each other for a long moment, then whipped their faces to Harper.

"What's this?" Thu said, snatching up the phone and holding it in front of Harper's face like it was a murder weapon.

"What's what?" Harper said, taking a long pull from her drink.

"Harper Hannah Horowitz, DMD, don't you dare play dumb with us," Indira said. "Why do you have a voice mail from Dan?"

Harper's stomach dropped. Of course, he left a message. She

was so scared of what he'd say. She didn't want to hear him admit she'd drove him away. She didn't want confirmation that she was too much to handle. That she couldn't send texts like that.

"I don't know what you're talking about," Harper said, looking over the balcony at the city lights.

"Have you and Dan been in contact?" Indira said, grabbing Harper's cheeks and forcing their eyes to meet.

"He texted me congratulations," Harper admitted through her squished cheeks. "And I may have said I missed him. A lot. But then he called and I panicked."

"Jesus Christ, Harper, could you be more annoying?" Thu said.

"What?"

"No, seriously. Can you? Because you've been walking around with your heart outside of your chest over this boy for months, and he finally reaches out and you don't pick up the damn phone?"

"He's probably calling to say how he's still mad at me! Or he's glad he left me," Harper said, pulling her face from Indira's hands. "I'd deserve it if he did. And maybe I'm still mad at him for everything that happened. I don't want to listen to that message."

"No," Thu said, fixing Harper with a hard stare.

"What?"

"No, you don't get to be a scared little chicken anymore. You're going to listen to this message right now or so help me God, I will tie you to that chair and *make* you listen to it."

"Why are you so violent?" Harper said. Thu gave her a bored look.

Defeat and curiosity getting the better of her, Harper took her phone, clicking open the voice mail. She chewed at her nails as she waited for it to start.

"Hi, Harper. It's Dan." She wanted to melt at the sound of his voice, drown in it. She closed her eyes, tears already slipping down her cheeks.

"I know—well, obviously you don't want to hear from me, and I get that, I guess. But I want to tell you something. Actually, there are a million things I want to tell you. An hour doesn't go by without something reminding me of you, making me reach for the phone to call you." He took a deep breath. "I know you don't want a relationship with me. I won't try to change your mind."

Was that what she still wanted? Because the past three months had been so unbearably painful, she kicked herself daily for being an idiot.

"But I hope you know," Dan continued as Harper's thoughts swirled and the emotions built in her chest. "I didn't leave because of you. I've never wanted to leave *you*. I left because I had to. I was playing pretend at someone I was never meant to be. But what you need to know . . ." Harper sucked in a breath, nearly choking on a sob. She heard Dan take a deep breath too, and she wanted to lean her ear against his chest, hear the air filling his lungs.

"Just because I left doesn't mean I stopped loving you." There was a brief pause. "I don't think I'll ever stop loving you."

Another moment of silence filled the line, and Harper wanted to hear his voice again more than anything. She wanted to dissolve in the music of it, claw the words from her phone.

"But I'll leave you alone. Bye, Harper. I'm so proud of you."

And the line went dead.

Harper sucked in a shaky gasp of air, her whole world fracturing around her.

He still loved her.

He. Still. Loved. Her.

He loved her.

She dropped the phone to her lap, scrubbing at her tears. She had to do something. Anything. She didn't want him to leave her alone. She didn't want to hear goodbye.

Because their friend group lacked anything that even remotely resembled boundaries or privacy, Lizzie snatched up Harper's phone. Indira and Thu crushed their faces close to Lizzie's as they strained to listen to the message.

By the time it was finished, they all had tears pricking at their eyes as they stared at Harper—all except Alex, who was blissed out in his own drunken stupor.

"What do I do?" Harper cried, lost in how to navigate the complex map of everything she felt. All the love pulsing through her body.

"Isn't it obvious?" Thu said, running a brisk hand across her cheeks to wipe away the tears. "We go to New York."

CHAPTER 39

HARPER

Harper blinked at Thu. "What? No. I . . . When?"

"Now," Thu said, standing from her seat and gathering her things. She tapped away at her phone for a few seconds before turning the screen to Harper. "A Megabus leaves in fifteen minutes. We can make it if we run."

"What!" Harper said, gripping the edges of her chair like it would anchor her in the swell of the confusion. "Tonight? You think I should go tonight?"

"*We* are going tonight," Thu corrected, helping Lizzie organize herself. "I just bought us five tickets. Now hurry up."

"Why would you come?" Harper asked. Everything was happening too fast. She needed a day. Or five. Maybe a week. Just a little bit of time to process everything that was being said. Dan loved her. He was actively *in love* with her. And she loved him. Holy shit, did she love him.

"We're coming because you can't be trusted to follow through on something you absolutely need to do. I'm not sure if you're aware of this, Harper, but you tend to overthink things and talk yourself out of stuff," Thu said, shooting her a wink.

"I don't even know where he lives," Harper said weakly, taking Indira's proffered hand as she pulled her up to standing.

Thu shot Harper a smug look. "Don't worry about that," she said, swooping her gaze to Alex, who was smiling and bobbing his head to the music, completely oblivious.

"Alex, honey?" Thu said sweetly, walking up to him.

His mood instantly changed, a look of pure fear flashing across his features. "What did I do?" Alex said, staring at Thu.

Her head jerked back. "What? Nothing."

"You only use that nice voice if you're about to yell at me," Alex said. Lizzie let out a booming laugh and burrowed her face in Indira's shoulder.

"That's not . . ." Thu considered this. "Well, that's not true *right now.*"

"It's not?" Alex said, a skeptical look in his eyes as he took another sip of his drink.

"No. Right now, I need a big favor."

"What favor?"

"I need Dan's address."

"Why?"

Harper wanted to ring his neck for not paying attention, and she opened her mouth to say something, but Thu held up a finger to silence her.

"We're going to go see Dan," Thu explained, gently slipping Alex's phone from his pocket.

"Who is?" Alex said, his head darting around the group.

"We all are, kitten," Thu said, picking up his hand and using his thumb to unlock his phone.

"Even . . ." Alex shot a wide-eyed glance at Harper then back to Thu. "Even Harper?" he whispered loudly.

"Especially Harper, you dimwit. Listen, I'm gonna need you to keep up here, buddy," she said, scrolling through his phone for a moment before smiling.

Alex beamed at her. "Ah, there's my Thu," he said, dragging his hands over his face.

"No time to waste," Thu said, making a beeline for the door. "We have a bus to catch."

And they followed her, Indira and Lizzie both dragging one of Harper's hands behind them, somehow making her feet move.

On the street, the cool spring air and the alcohol in Harper's blood mixed perfectly to propel her forward as they ran the five blocks to the Megabus stop.

They got there just in time, the last person boarding as Lizzie screamed for the bus to wait.

Panting and slick with sweat, the friends hopped onto the bus, nervous laughter pouring out of Harper as they took their seats. A moment later, the doors *swoosh*ed shut and the lights dimmed as the bus pulled away from the curb, making a few turns before merging onto the freeway and heading toward New York.

A bus was objectively the worst possible form of transportation for a romantic gesture. It was also an awful place to sober up. The air was stale, the seats sticky, and the jostling of the vehicle did nothing to help Harper's rattling nerves. For two and a half hours, while her friends joked and laughed, all Harper could think was *Oh shit. What am I doing?*

By the time they descended the bus steps and set foot on the sticky New York pavement, Harper was convinced this was the worst idea she'd ever had.

"Hey," Thu snapped. "Look at me," she said, bending to catch Harper's eyes and flicking a finger between them. "What are you thinking right now?"

"That I'm going to throw up," Harper answered honestly.

"Oh, for fuck's sake, Harper. Do you love Dan?"

Harper's spine straightened. "Yes."

"Good. This is your moment. Don't fuck it up."

Harper stared at her friend for a second before nodding, a smile cracking across her face. This *was* her moment. It was scary and terrifying and almost awful to love someone this much. She couldn't wait to tell him.

"Come on," Thu said, pulling up directions on Alex's phone. "It's only a mile away."

"A *mile*?" Indira said, looking down at her heels and dress before shooting a glance at everyone else's. "Should we get a cab?"

"Where's the fun in that?" Thu said over her shoulder, already trotting up the block. Harper was in step with her, a swirling sense of nervousness and excitement creating a kaleidoscope of happy emotions in her chest.

None of them was dressed for a run through the city, least of all Lizzie, whose six-inch heels only allowed her to cover about four inches with every step. But it didn't matter; they tore through the streets, an invisible tether pulling Harper closer to some exhilarating pinnacle she didn't quite understand but couldn't wait to reach.

They weaved through crowds and piles of trash, the energy of the city pulsing around them. Harper was lost in her thoughts on what she'd say to Dan when a shriek from Lizzie cut through her mind.

"Oh fuck!" Lizzie's scream came from behind them, followed by the sound of flesh smacking the pavement. Thu and Harper stopped short, Indira and Alex almost crashing into them as they all turned to look at Lizzie lying facedown and spread-eagle across the pavement, one of her sharp stilettos broken off and lying next to her like a murder weapon.

"Lizzie?" Harper said, taking a few steps toward her friend. Lizzie lifted her head, her hair a wild, red mess around her. They all locked eyes for a moment before Lizzie broke out into giggles.

"Go on without me!" she cried melodramatically, waving them on.

Harper's face broke out in a huge grin and she started running, Thu close on her heels.

"Oh my God, not you, Indira," they heard Lizzie yell after them. "Help me up, you beautiful bitch."

Harper, Thu, and Alex started to wheeze with laughter as they moved through the city.

They continued running for what felt like forever, sweat trailing down Harper's back and heels rubbing her feet raw, but she didn't care.

Turning onto a quieter street, Thu came to an abrupt halt, Harper zooming past her.

"What's wrong?" Harper asked, circling back to where Thu and Alex stood.

Thu grinned at her, her eyes misty and filled with encouragement.

"It's right there," Thu said, pointing at a brick building two down from them, an awning for a deli at its base. Harper's heart pounded against her chest in excitement. *Home*, it whispered with each beat. *We're finally going home.*

Thu stepped to Harper's side, Alex hanging back. Harper grabbed her, pulling her into a huge hug.

"Thank you, Thu-Thu," she whispered. "For everything."

"Oh my God," Thu said, pulling back and furiously scrubbing at her eyes. "Stop being so dramatic."

Harper laughed, running her hands down her dress. "How do I look?"

Thu looked her up and down before giving her a smile and a shrug. "Like a girl in love." Harper smiled. "And also super sweaty, but I'm sure he won't care."

"Thu!"

"You asked!" Thu said with innocence. "Unit 3B," she added, pointing her chin toward the building. "Go."

Harper nodded and turned, sucking in one last deep breath before marching toward the building. Her body thrummed with energy, every cell feeling electric, as she stared at the row of intercom buttons. A few tears slipped out of the corners of her eyes as she lifted her finger to the button for 3B.

She felt afraid and exposed and vulnerable and overwhelmed, and she embraced it. She let herself feel every emotion that flooded her as she pushed the buzzer.

After a few seconds, a familiar, beautiful voice came through the intercom.

"Hello?" Dan said.

Harper licked her lips, her body trembling and a smile threatening to split her open as she pressed the button to talk.

"Hey," she said, her voice cracking on a happy sob. "It's me."

CHAPTER 40

DAN

With shaking fingers, Dan buzzed her in. He absolutely did not trust his mind.

He paced the small length of his studio apartment, dragging his hands through his hair. No way. There was no way she was here.

But, sure enough, a minute later, a light tap reverberated against his door, shooting into his apartment and directly into his chest, knocking his heart against his ribs.

He crossed the room, his hands clenched in fists as he stared at the doorknob. It felt like he was moving underwater. He turned the knob, swinging the door open, almost afraid to look.

But there she was.

Harper.

Standing in his doorway.

She was out of breath and sweaty, her hair a riot of waves and her eye makeup slightly smeared at the edges.

She'd never been so beautiful.

His eyes scoured over her, trying to absorb every detail, unable to take all of her in at once.

He re-memorized the angle of her collarbones. The delicate curve of her ears. Every knob in her kneecaps. He devoured every inch of her because he didn't believe this was real. But if it was a dream, he wouldn't let it slip away.

And she stared back, her chest rising and falling with rapid breaths as she looked over him.

Eventually, their eyes met and held, everything else blurring at the edges.

"Hi," she said at last, a tear slipping down her cheek. "Can I come in?"

Dan nodded, not trusting his voice. He stepped aside, letting her in and shutting the door behind her.

"I like your place," she said, another tear trailing down her cheek. She tilted her head back and laughed. "Your ceiling is so low even *I* could touch it. Almost."

A smile tugged at the corner of Dan's mouth, but he didn't let it grow.

There was a heavy, awkward silence, and Harper patted her hands against her thighs. "I got into residency," she said at last.

Dan nodded. "I saw Lizzie's post. Which program?"

"Dwyer's Hospital," she said, her teeth sawing into her bottom lip. "Here," she added.

The statement pressed like a heavy weight against his lungs. He wasn't sure what to do with that, what to make of it. And he was terrified of the flicker of happiness it ignited in his heart.

"What are you doing here?" he finally managed to ask, his voice hoarse.

Harper stared at him before taking a deep breath, one that seemed to suck all the air from his own lungs.

"I got your voice mail," she said.

Dan nodded. The voice mail. He wanted to regret it. He wished he could be mad at himself for putting it out there. But he couldn't. Harper was loved. He wanted her to know that.

"And there are a few things *you* need to know," she said, stepping forward. Her hands reached for him, but she hesitated, her fingers hovering an inch away from his. Dan closed the distance, engulfing her hands in his palms. Harper let out a sigh, and Dan couldn't ignore the soothing feel of her skin against his. He was hungry for it.

Harper closed her eyes for a minute, chewing on her bottom lip, before her eyes flashed open, connecting with his, more present than he'd ever seen them.

"I'm sorry," she said, licking her lips. "There aren't enough words in the world for me to explain how sorry I am. I need you to know that, first and foremost."

"I'm sorry too, Harper," Dan said, needing to get the words out. "I'm sorry for everything I said. For telling your secrets. I didn't mean—"

She pressed a finger to his lips, silencing him. "I know," she said. "I know."

She took another deep breath before starting again. "I've spent my entire life afraid of pain," she said, tears streaming freely down her cheeks. "Losing my mom . . . It felt like something broke in me after that. My body felt in constant danger. I cling to routine and order and perfection because I think I can control those things. If I can control my life, things can't hurt me."

She blinked, tilting her head back as tears traced down her cheeks. "I'm terrified of letting people in and losing them. So scared of experiencing that pain again," she continued, looking at him. "And losing someone I loved so much has made me unsure how to love without losing."

She closed her eyes for a moment, and Dan reached out, cupping her cheek in his hand. She nuzzled into the touch.

"I've always believed if I could avoid pain," she continued, "I would be okay. And I was good at it. I built walls around me and walked through life like any misstep would detonate a land mine. And then you came along." She was laughing and smiling through her tears as she reached up and placed both her palms on his cheeks. "And my feelings for you . . . they crumbled every careful wall I've ever built. You seeped into every crack, every fragment. My best friend. My lover. And I was so scared to feel everything I felt for you. It was easier to be angry. It was easier to throw blame around than admit the truth."

"What's the truth?" he asked through a hoarse throat.

Harper smiled. A big, luminous smile that shattered his heart in his chest. "The truth is, falling in love with you was the most inevitable, uncontrollable thing to ever hit me. I couldn't stop it even if I wanted to. And it scared the shit out of me. I thought it would hurt me. But now I realize that being apart from you hurts so much more. I miss you so much, my bones ache with it."

"I miss you too," Dan said. It was simple and honest and the sum of his feelings.

"I'm sorry," Harper whispered, the words passing lightly over his skin. "I'm so damn sorry. You shouldn't forgive me for what I said. How I acted. But if you can forgive me, I promise I will spend every day making it up to you."

"Of course I forgive you," Dan said, placing his hands over hers where she still touched him.

"I know I'm a mess. I know . . . I know I'm not easy to love . . ."

"Harper, loving you is the easiest thing I'll ever do."

Dan couldn't say who moved first after that.

Maybe Harper leaned fully into him.

Maybe he grabbed her.

It didn't matter.

They sank to the floor, gripping each other like life rafts in a storm. They held and squeezed and cried together, months and years of pain released to the world with each tear that fell. The pain couldn't be held by the other, the suffering wasn't the opposite's to endure, but they could hold each other through it, root the other to a safe spot. Be the other's home.

Days passed in minutes as they sat, wrapped in each other's

arms, words tumbling from lips, and sobs eventually turning back into breaths.

Dan smoothed his hands over Harper's hair, her back, her arms. Anywhere he could reach, he wanted to touch.

"I'm going to therapy," she whispered against his heart.

"I am too," he said, pressing a kiss to her forehead, dragging his lips across her temple and down to her cheek. "I'm sorry I hurt you. I'm sorry I left the way I did. I felt like if I didn't get out, I would drown."

"I love you for leaving," she said, leaning in to kiss along his jaw.

"You do?"

"Yes. I love you for chasing what you love. I love you for doing what you needed to do for you." She kissed across his eyelids, his nose. "But, most of all, I love you for showing me that love doesn't have to end in loss."

Harper pulled her head back to look up at him. There was nothing he could do but kiss her.

It wasn't frantic. It wasn't wild.

It was the calm in the eye of the storm.

It was everything they needed.

Mind.

Body.

World.

All centered on that singular point of pleasure where their lips met. They were a million shattered pieces kissed back into place.

EPILOGUE

6 MONTHS LATER

"Get. Off. Me."

Harper pushed against Dan's deadweight stretched along her body. His laugh pressed her further into the mattress.

"Let me sleep in peace, you monster," she said. She'd just finished a brutal on-call rotation at the hospital, and had dragged herself to Dan's apartment, only to sleep for sixteen hours straight.

"I've made coffee," he purred into her ear. "Will you get out of bed for coffee?"

Harper smiled against his chest but shook her head. "I don't want to get up."

Dan pushed up onto his hands and looked down at her. His eyes narrowed and she giggled in anticipation. He dove back down, rubbing his day-old scruff against her neck without mercy.

She shrieked and laughed, thumping her fists on his back.

"I know what will wake you up," he whispered against her skin, pulling back to fix her with a lazy grin before dropping a kiss against her neck.

He moved down her body slowly, lovingly, placing kisses along every inch of her. Her fingers, the backs of her knees, the soles of her feet—nothing was spared from his devoted onslaught.

And then the asshole started tickling her. Mercilessly. Torturing her until she shrieked and giggled and swore on Judy's life that she'd get out of bed, dear God, just stop! She loved every second of it.

Pleased with his work, Dan planted a kiss on her lips then got out of bed.

"Up, lazy bug. It's our day off."

With her on-call rotations, and Dan's own work demands, their schedules didn't align as much as either would like, but they always sucked up every second of their days off together, laughing and running around the city like two maniacs in love, and today would be no different.

Dan stood in the square of light pouring in through the window and stretched while Harper admired her usual morning view. She'd never get tired of looking at him. Lean limbs reaching toward the ceiling, a hand running through mussed hair, his radiant energy brightening the room.

Even though they didn't officially live together, they spent most nights at one person's place or the other, creating little happy nests in both small apartments.

Harper loved his patterns and quirks. Her heart swelled in tenderness when he'd fumble his long legs into sweatpants, at the way he stripped off his socks at the end of the day. The pad of his steps through the apartment was the soundtrack to her happiest moments.

"I love you," she said.

He turned and grinned, dimple and all. "Say it again."

"I love you," Harper repeated.

"One more time."

"I love you!"

And she did. Saying the words for the first time opened the door to a new form of freedom, a giddy high that only increased with time. She couldn't stop saying it.

Good morning—I love you.

Do we need coffee from the store?—I love you.

Why can't you ever remember to put the toilet seat down, you gross boy?—I love you.

"Love ya back, Dr. Horowitz," Dan said with a grin, turning and moving across the studio to the kitchen. His intercom buzzed and he answered it while he was passing.

"Delivery from—"

"I'll be right down." Dan cut the person off. He trotted back toward the bed, throwing on a T-shirt and hopping into a pair of discarded pants.

"What's the delivery?" Harper asked, still wrapped in the covers.

"A construction crane to get you out of bed," Dan said, trying to bite back a smile. Harper grabbed a pillow and chucked it at him. He easily dodged it with a laugh.

"Tell me!"

"I'll be right back," Dan said, slipping on his shoes and *whoosh*-ing out of the apartment. Harper stared after him, wondering why he was being so weird.

Giving her limbs one final stretch, she rolled out of bed and padded to the kitchen, pouring a large cup of coffee for them both. A few minutes later, Dan reentered the apartment.

And he was holding a bouquet of purple flowers.

And a huge box of donuts from her favorite place.

Harper thought her heart might explode.

"What's all this?" she said, her eyes going wide and a smile splitting across her face as she walked toward him, giving him a kiss.

"A surprise," he said, going to hand her the flowers while she reached for the cinnamon rolls instead.

"And they're warm," Harper nearly cried, opening the box and taking a huge inhale, her eyes rolling back in her head. "A surprise for what?"

Dan didn't say anything, looking at her nervously for a moment before plastering on a smile and moving around her to put the flowers in water.

Something was off, and a little rattle of anxiety twisted in Harper's tummy. But she let it pass through her. She was learning how to do that: acknowledge her anxiety, but allow it to move along, letting it slip away without gaining purchase. Therapy was still a priority in her life, and it was helping tremendously with the stress of residency. Dan also continued seeing a counselor, coming to terms with his own issues of guilt and grief.

"Why are you being so weird?" Harper said through a mouthful of gooey cinnamon roll, sitting down at the tiny table off the kitchen.

Dan moved to sit next to her, his forearms leaning on his bouncing knees, making his whole body shake.

"What's up with you?" Harper said, real concern furrowing her brow. She even set her cinnamon roll down to grab his hands in hers.

"I'm a little nervous," Dan admitted, hanging his head with a laugh.

"About what?"

"Well . . ." He waved a hand toward the cinnamon rolls and flowers, letting out another nervous chuckle. "I guess I might as well go for it," Dan said with a sheepish smile that morphed into his crooked, lazy grin. She loved him so much it hurt.

Then he reached into his pocket.

And pulled out a little velvet box.

Harper's heart bounced into her throat. She hadn't been expecting that.

"Holy shit." Her voice was hoarse.

"Harper Horowitz," Dan said.

"This seems a bit fast—"

"Will you do me the honor . . ."

"Is this not fast? I want to marry you but we haven't even hit a year, I—"

"Of moving in with me?"

"Of course it's a *yes* but—wait, what?"

Dan opened the box. A tarnished gold key sat where a ring normally would.

Her eyes shot to his and she saw him trying to bite back a laugh.

"You ass!" She punched him on the shoulder. "You made me think you were proposing!"

"What would make you think that? I'm not even on one knee."

"I hate you!" Harper said, flinging her arms around him and placing rapid-fire kisses all along his cheek and neck. Her heart felt like it would take flight and leave her chest.

"Is that a *no*?" Dan asked, wrapping his arms around her and laughing.

"Of course it's a *yes*. I—" She pulled back, a crucial thought popping into her head. "Judy can move in too, right?"

Dan shot her a look that said *duh*, and Harper beamed at him, happiness radiating from her as she hugged him again.

"Are you sure?" she asked, because it all felt too good to be true. Granted, it wouldn't change much of how they'd been living, but it still felt monumental to take that next step with him.

"Of course I am. I want to fall asleep next to you every night. Wake up to your smile every day. Have *both* our names on the utility bills. I'm not sure there's anything more romantic."

"I'm not sure there is either," she said with a laugh, a few tears forming at the corners of her eyes.

She kissed him, savoring the moment fully. His smell, his warmth, his energy. Him.

"Ask me who my favorite person is," she said, pressing her hands to his cheeks, every cell in her body vibrating in radiant happiness.

"I thought questions like that make your brain melt," he teased, running his hands up and down her rib cage.

"Ask me."

"Who's your favorite person, Harper?"

Harper leaned in, pressing a smiling, happy kiss to his lips before answering.

"You."

ACKNOWLEDGMENTS

In so many ways, writing this book saved me. It was my space to pour emotions onto a page and discover that vulnerability is a superpower. It was written in the backs of lecture halls and during stolen moments between patients, words filling the pages at three a.m. when I was supposed to be studying. It was my brightest spot in a dark season of my life. But this book wouldn't exist without the support of countless people, and I'm humbled to have so many to thank.

Ben. My dime piece. My bae-goals with the bagels. Thank you for loving me exactly as I am. Your endless belief in me makes writing romance possible. I remember being on the subway to Dim Sum Garden that cold January night when you waved your hand in front of my eyes and asked where my brain had wandered off to. I looked up and told you I had an idea for a character. Three years later, you've let me disappear into my mind more times than I can count, and you're always there, cat and pizza in hand, to welcome me home. It's life's greatest gift to be in love with my best friend.

An endless, screeching thank-you to my editor, Eileen Rothschild. Thank you for taking a chance on me and helping make this dream come true. You challenge and push me to become the best writer I can, and I'm a better person for it. Thank you for embracing my voice, for your keen eye, and for championing my characters. Working with you is a humbling privilege and I still pinch myself regularly that this is my real life. Lisa Bonvissuto, my fellow Clevelander! Thank you for being so kind and helpful and answering my endless questions. You've made this process such a joy.

Kelli Martin. I could fill an entire book with gratitude for you. Thank you for believing in my book. Believing in Harper and Dan. Believing that this is a story that needs to be told. My heart lives in these pages and so much of that is thanks to you. Thank you to the superstar team at Wendy Sherman Associates for cheering me on in the background; I feel so lucky to be represented by such an agency.

Hamda. Having you as a friend is better than winning the lottery (although, if I did win the lottery, we could finally escape this cruel life and live on a beach with nothing but romance novels and cats). Quite simply, this book wouldn't exist without your tireless support and encouragement. I love you.

Helen Hoang, thank you for welcoming me into the world of authorhood with open arms and a shoulder to worry on. Your work never ceases to inspire me and to call you a friend is an honor.

Chloe Liese. My angel. My neurodivine partner in crime. You get me in a way few ever have. There aren't words for what you mean to me, but my world is a brighter place for having you in it. I hold you close to my heart always.

Megan Stillwell, I've never met someone as fiercely loyal as you. You make me laugh till I pee, pick me up when I'm low, and cheer me on so loudly I can hear it across the country. I'm so lucky to know someone as wonderful as you.

Mama, thank you for our Friday night dates at Borders and for my love of reading. Thank you for seeing my struggles with anxiety and getting me help, instilling in me that doing so is a radical act of bravery.

Dad, thanks for giving me just enough trauma to make me funny.

Kristen, Katie, Ash, Mien, and Tara, thank you from the bottom of my heart for being early readers of this book. I will never be able to convey what your gorgeous, screaming kindness and love means to me. Hannah, thank you for being an invaluable sensitivity reader and an all-around wonderful soul. Gigi, thank you for giving me so many excuses to laugh and sip wine. (Sebastian St. Vincent sends his sincerest regards. From my couch where he's cuddling me. Because he's desperately in love with me. Katie and Mien, that goes for Rhys Winterborne too. It's published, so it's official.) Thank you to Eliza for reading the first pages I ever wrote of this book. You truly are my writing fairy godmother.

To my Bookstagram fam that has screamed with me about books for years, thank you for your friendship; it's one of the most special things in my life.

Sarah Hogle, Rosie Danan, and Rachel Lynn Solomon, thank you for embracing me as I awkwardly slid into your DMs and asked if you wanted to be friends. Thank you for reading this story early and sending me reaction memes that had me screaming into my pillow like a preteen with a gut-punch crush. You all inspire me beyond compare. (This isn't a line; I truly can't get over the pure *talent* you all have. Hot damn.)

To my team at St. Martin's Griffin, how do I even begin to express my gratitude to you? So many of you had to say yes for this dream to happen, and I'm forever grateful for each and every one of those. Thank you, Jennifer Enderlin, for the oh-so-small thing of *naming my book* and coming up with a title I literally want to put on everything. Thank you, Kerri Resnick, for designing the cover of my dreams and screaming in DMs about it with me. You are a creative genius. Thank you to Monique Aimee, for capturing Harper and Dan so perfectly. Thank you to Brant Janeway, Marissa Sangiacomo, Alexis Neuville, Maria Vitale, and DJ DeSmyter for all the work you've done to help this book reach readers and for putting up with my super-hyper, less-than-professional, excessively exclamation-point-filled emails and responding with matched enthusiasm. Not sure how I got so lucky.

And, to my readers with a mental illness: I see you. I believe in you. You are worthy of love just as you are. Hold strong in your faith of the happily ever after, whatever that may look like. It isn't a fantasy but a reality you deserve.